THE WILDE WOMEN

Meet Pearl Wilde, one of the unpredictable daughters in the unforgettable family of Wildes. When Pearl discovers her sister, Kat, dressed up in her favourite pair of shoes — and in a compromising position with Pearl's fiancé — she catches the very first express train out of town. Three years later, Pearl returns home to Five Points. This time, her claws are razor sharp and her new demeanour is so cool, the citizens of her home village begin to doubt she even has sweat glands . . .

PAULA WALL

THE
WILDE WOMEN

Complete and Unabridged

CHARNWOOD
Leicester

First published in Great Britain in 2007 by
Black Swan
an imprint of
Transworld Publishers
London

First Charnwood Edition
published 2008
by arrangement with
Transworld Publishers
A Random House Group Company
London

British Library CIP Data

Wall, P. S. (Paula S.), 1954 –
The Wilde women.—Large print ed.—
Charnwood library series
1. Sisters—Fiction 2. Revenge—Fiction
3. Large type books
I. Title
813.6 [F]

ISBN 978–1–84782–314–4

Published by
F. A. Thorpe (Publishing)
Anstey, Leicestershire
Set by Words & Graphics Ltd.
Anstey, Leicestershire
Printed and bound in Great Britain by
T. J. International Ltd., Padstow, Cornwall

This book is printed on acid-free paper

For and forever, Bill.

Acknowledgements

Every year my girlfriend and I watch the Academy Awards together. We stuff our faces, talk trash about the actors like we know them, and spit popcorn at the screen when the award for best movie is some maudlin message epistle that will fade in Hollywood history like a political bumper sticker. During the acceptance speeches, we usually moan and mute it. Who wants to listen to some grovelling actress speed-reading a bunch of industry mogul names in the hopes that next year she won't be doing dinner theatre in Boca Raton?

That being said, I would like to thank the following people:

Francesca Liversidge, you are a rock star. Thank you for your patience and support. Emily Bestler, you are more important to your writers than you can imagine. Michael Meller, your e-mails make me write another day. Sheila Marie Blevins, friend and sister, thank you for giving me 'Erin'. Aaron Priest, I can't think of anything sweet to say, but I like that in an agent.

The Lord giveth and most women piss it away. Perhaps this is why they lack the equipment to aim. Some women piddle their life away in a slow incontinent dribble while squatting in the shadow of a man. Others are so busy trying to overshadow men they miss the mark. Most manage to cover up their little messes like a cat scratching in a litter box, but a few always get caught with their pants down. For this reason, Lorna Wilde bestowed upon her daughters the wisdom her mother bestowed upon her, 'Never wear holey underwear.' Being enterprising young women, the Wilde sisters never wore underwear at all.

The sisters dove headfirst into this world on fire with life and expectation. When the doctor spanked their baby butts for it, they squealed with delight. Hair black as midnight, eyes blazing blue, they were so bright white hot they hissed when you touched them.

In school they knew the answer before the question was given, broke the hearts of boys they never noticed, were the envy of rich girls who had it all. Could have had any man they wanted. Could have been anything they set their mind to. But like their mother and their mother's mother before them, the Wilde sisters took the path of most resistance. At every crossroad in life, there is always one right choice. Inevitably, Wilde women go left.

They trace their poor sense of direction to the day their great-grandmother left Cyril Rudolph waiting at the altar. As the organist played the Wedding March, Fidela stared at her reflection in the beveled bride's mirror and saw her future — a pampered life of luxury with a man who worshipped her — and promptly jumped out the window.

Fidela fell from grace into the arms of Bodine Wilde, a part-time riverboat musician and a full-time scoundrel. Leaning out the church window, Cyril caught one last glimpse of his beloved running toward the river as if the Devil were after her, rose petals scattering from her bouquet and wearing nothing but bloomers and a whalebone corset.

Cyril Rudolph was a decent man who deserved better. Decent men have the farthest to fall. After all the guests had offered their condolences, he stood alone at the church altar, humiliated and in such pain he did not think he could bear it. Tears running down his face and fists clenched so tight his nails drew blood, he turned his head to heaven and threw open his arms. 'Let her suffer as I suffer,' he charged through gritted teeth, 'in this life and the next!'

The only difference between a prayer and a curse is the one who stands to profit.

Cyril's words hissed like steam in the hallowed air and rose to the rafters. They echoed off the arched oak beams and whispered back to him from the balcony where his beautiful young slave rocked back and forth in the shadows, her

2

slender black fingers braiding a pale strand of Cyril's hair pulled from his horsehair brush as she chanted the words that would set her free.

A cloud passed over the sun and the azure eyes of Cyril's stained-glass Savior seemed to close. The eternal flame flickered in its red globe and the stone church grew dark as the end of days. Cyril knew what he had done, but he didn't care. If Fidela did not love him and him alone, it was only right that she be damned. Love turns to hate like wine to vinegar.

Fidela spent her days dragging Bodine Wilde out of bars and the arms of other women. When she wasn't nursing a squalling baby, she was expecting one. When she wasn't swollen like a tick, she was working like a dog. But an odd thing happened. Instead of Fidela breaking, she grew stronger. Her back ached and her fingers cracked and bled, but her constitution hardened like cast iron. Cyril's words had tangled with the black woman's whispered spell in the church rafters. While Fidela would always be possessed by love, she would never be any man's slave.

One woman's crumb is another woman's cake. Cooing, preening, and parasols twirling, women flocked to Cyril. But he would have none of it. Cyril Rudolph was wed to revenge. Hate burrowed into his core like a worm into an apple, rotting his soul from the inside out. His hair turned white, his eyes faded to ice blue and spite surged through his veins like venom. Every night he stood alone at the church altar and renewed his vow. 'She will never share her bed with a man who loves her like I do,' he prayed through gritted teeth. 'Bring her back to me. Bring her home.' And every day Cyril paced back and forth at the dock waiting for his prayer to be answered.

To prove his faith and to pass the time, Cyril set out to build Fidela a home to come home to. It was a mansion the likes of which none had ever seen in these parts, an antebellum castle of sorts with marble mantels shipped from France and mosaic tiles from Italy. It took two years for the glass dome to arrive from Europe and twenty-six men with mules and pulleys to lower it into place.

A house possesses the personality of its owner. Despite all the expense and attention to detail, the chapel of Cyril's devotion was as inviting as the snap of a whip. The heavy doors had locks on the outside as well as in. Every tree, shrub and patch of tall grass dense enough to crouch behind was sheared to the ground. And the wrought-iron mullions on the windows were scarcely wide enough to pass a tin plate through. His beloved's Bastille perched on the highest hill in the county, glaring down at the river. Every night Cyril lit a lantern in his bedroom window, a dark star to guide Fidela home. It seared a red spot in the black sky and the locals took to calling it the Devil's Eye.

Eventually a business dispute involving five queens and a pair of Colt revolvers left Bodine Wilde floating face down in the Tennessee River. Fidela didn't have the money to bury her husband. And so she filled his pockets with stones, kissed his cold lips and watched his

4

handsome face fade to the muddy bottom.

Cyril was eagerly waiting at the dock the day Fidela came home. But when she stepped off the riverboat every jaw dropped. Fidela Wilde was hanging on the arm of an even worse rascal than the one she'd run off with in the first place.

Despite living fast and hard, Fidela had scarcely aged a day since she left. Nothing stuck to Fidela long, not even time. She was laughing as she walked by Cyril, gay as a drunk on a sinking ship. Their eyes met and she smiled. What was meant to be kindness, Cyril took for pity. But the truth was Fidela did not recognize the withered old man standing on the dock. Nothing remained of the Cyril she once knew.

In the end, Fidela took four good-looking, good-for-nothing husbands to her bed. How many she interviewed for the position is anyone's guess. But she never gave Cyril so much as the time of day. Fidela would never share her bed with a man who loved her as he did. In cursing Fidela, Cyril had cursed himself.

The sins of the mother are visited upon the daughter. From that day forward, every Wilde woman has been born with a sliver of the Devil's mirror in her eye. A gentle boy with love in his heart sends her running for the hills. A clean-living, hard-working, church-going man turns her frigid as an icicle hanging off the eave.

Wilde women are drawn to wild men, men who would sooner chew their arm off as slip a ring around their finger. Dangerous men with trouble in their eyes make a Wilde woman's lips part. A man who answers to no law but his own

5

makes her legs fall open like a nutcracker.

When a woman looks into her mother's eyes she sees her future. When she looks into her daughter's eyes she sees her past. But when she looks into the eyes of the man she shares her bed with, she sees the life she has chosen. Love lifts a woman up or drags her down. When a Wilde woman dies, they don't have to dig a hole.

1

The stock market crash in 1929 was not the only event that darkened that black Friday in Five Points, Tennessee. That was the day Pearl Wilde found her little sister moaning in the springhouse next to the butter molds. It was cool and dark, but Pearl had no doubt it was her only sibling. Along with her favorite pair of shoes, Kat was wearing Pearl's fiancé.

Naturally, Pearl put all the blame on her sister. A man is like a water well. He has absolutely no control over who primes his pump.

'This is all your fault!' Pearl screamed, stabbing her finger at Kat's legs sticking straight up in the air.

Slowly, Bourne Cavanagh looked back over his broad bare shoulder, his handsome face blurred with whiskey and desire. Pearl sank into those watery blue eyes like an unholy baptism and her resolve began to dissolve. Bourne knew all he had to do was say the right thing and Pearl would be begging *him* for forgiveness.

'Please, darlin',' he slurred. 'Give me just one more minute.'

It just shows how low a woman is willing to go that, for a full thirty seconds, Pearl considered it. But then something rose up inside her, something so deep she didn't know she had it in her. Grabbing the empty whiskey bottle that rolled on the floor, she threw it with all she had.

Bourne's hand flew to his face as the bottle smashed against the wall, but not fast enough to stop the shard of glass from slicing him from brow to cheek. He touched his fingers to his face and stared at his blood. Then his cold blue eyes slowly rose to Pearl's. The look that passed between them said it all. But then body language had always been their preferred form of communication.

Ripping her shoes off Kat's dirty feet, Pearl caught the first train out of town.

The next three years of Pearl Wilde's life are somewhat murky. Frank Merrill, the pharmacist, thought he spotted her getting into a shiny black limousine in Chicago, but the man with her roughly assured Frank he was mistaken. How Pearl ascended from Five Points into a Chicago limousine was a mystery, but everyone knew she had been born to climb.

Then halfway through *Grand Hotel*, Eddie McCowan jumped up and stabbed his finger at the flickering screen. 'That's Pearl Wilde!' he cried out in the dark theater. Dickie Deason, who worked the camera booth on weekends at the Roxy, rewound the projector and played the scene over and over until the film finally snagged and hung. They watched quietly as Pearl's face melted away, but the vision of her covered in shimmering rhinestones and sipping champagne from a long-stemmed glass was forever burned into their minds.

The only other hint of Pearl's whereabouts was the postcards that arrived every month postmarked New Orleans, Chicago, New York,

Paris, Rome, Berlin and some place in the Orient nobody at the post office had ever heard of. Regardless of the card's origin, the message was always the same.

'Kat Wilde, I still hope you burn in Hell!'

'Pearl always did have beautiful penmanship,' Miss Mabel Hilliard said, running her finger over the exotic stamp with a touch of longing. 'And she was a persistent child. Once she sank her teeth in, there was no letting go.'

Miss Mabel had been enlightening the bright and the dull alike in the one-room schoolhouse on the Ridge for over forty years. She knew every child in Five Points who had made it to adulthood, and every fall she planted chrysanthemums on the neglected graves of those who hadn't.

'That Pearl Wilde was a looker.' The Postmaster put in his two cents' worth as he stamped an inkpad and then a stack of envelopes with a rhythmic thud.

'Her sister Kathryn is just as pretty,' Miss Mabel said resolutely.

Being a progressive teacher, Miss Mabel treated all her students equally, even when they weren't. She'd had both Wilde girls in her class and knew what they were made of. Born less than a year apart, the sisters were as different as the sun and the moon and just as reluctant to be outshone.

The Lord dealt each Wilde girl a winning hand — looks, luck, brains and each other. But like most gamblers they were determined to play the man, not the cards. Pearl slipped from the womb offering her hand to the doctor, while Kat shoved the old bonesetter out of the way and crawled out of her own accord.

Pearl entertained herself with her mother's make-up and jewelry. Kat tossed her dolls aside in favor of the rusty toolbox her mother's latest lover left outside the bedroom door. In school, Kat knew the answer before the question was given. Pearl knew anything taught in a one-room schoolhouse would be of little use to her. Kat could beat any boy at any contest with one hand tied behind her back. Boys surrendered to Pearl just as easily, but it was usually *their* hands that were tied. Kat was a hellcat, Pearl as pampered and sultry as a Persian with a rhinestone collar.

'Everyone always overestimated Pearl and underestimated Kathryn,' Miss Mabel said absently, as she turned the postcard over to study the painting of a winding red dragon on the front. 'The serious are always taken more seriously than the light-hearted, the assumption being that happy people are too dim to know they are unhappy.'

Pearl had a diamond-shaped beauty mark at the corner of her mouth and that set her tone. There was no doubt in anyone's mind she would make something of herself. Just as there was no doubt that Kat, being the spitting image of her mother, would fritter her life away. But Miss Mabel did not judge a book by its cover, or a child by the mother who bore her.

'Kathryn was a smart child. She could do math better than any of my boys.'

Miss Annabelle, the town telephone operator,

huffed. 'Kat Wilde dropped out of the womb a little smart Alec all right.'

'She was a gay child,' Miss Mabel corrected.

'Kat gets her *gayness* from her mother,' Annabelle declared to the postmaster, as if he didn't already know. 'Lorna Wilde would have tap-danced on the *Titanic*. My barn cat is a better mother than Lorna Wilde was to those girls.'

At that, Miss Mabel was silenced. She could not defend Lorna Wilde's mothering or lack thereof. Lorna Wilde had always been a wing-walker. She didn't let go of one man until she had a firm grip on the next. It was a preoccupation that didn't leave much time for motherhood. The sisters reared each other and did their best to raise Lorna up as well. Despite their efforts, nothing elevated Lorna's mind much higher than a mattress.

'Lorna Wilde,' Mayor Hardin Wallace sighed the name as he tacked a city council meeting notice onto the post office bulletin board. 'Now there was the real looker in the family. Had legs from here to eternity.'

Hardin was immediately sorry that he'd said it. It was not something a politician should say in mixed company, especially when his wife is standing in the mix.

June Wallace sucked in a quick ragged breath and a stricken look came over her perpetually furled face. Hardin braced himself for the scene that was sure to follow. The only thing worse than being married to a jealous woman, was being married to a crazy jealous woman. Crazy

11

June Bug Wallace was well established on both counts. Not the best situation for a man with one eye on the governor's mansion and the other eye on the legs of every woman in town.

Clutching her pocketbook to her breast, June ran out of the post office, Hardin right behind her.

'Now, June Bug,' he pleaded on his way out the door, 'you know you are the love of my life.'

Everyone in the post office watched through the front window without much interest. The Wallace's marital strife was, after all, old news. Then Miss Mabel passed the postcard to Annabelle and the two old maids continued their debate about the Wilde women. Since the government had yet to start taxing gossip, it still traded freely in Five Points. By the end of the day everyone in town had examined the latest postcard and presented it as evidence to support their pre-existing position. The optimists insisted Pearl had married a rich man, maybe some kind of royalty, and was living a life of leisure. The pessimists, whose standing in life was only improved by the failure of others, insisted no woman except a missionary's wife would dirty the soles of her shoes in the heathen Orient. If there was one thing everyone did agree on, it was that while Pearl Wilde was no doubt spreading something, it sure as hell wasn't the word of God. Needless to say, by the time Kat picked up her mail, the picture of the exotic red dragon had been all but rubbed away.

★　★　★

In December of 1932, no postcard came. That and the depression caused a gray gloom to settle over the already depressed little town. There were no jobs, no money and no hope. To add to their despair, an ice storm moved in on Christmas Eve. The temperature dropped so fast the mercury could not keep up. Every surface glazed with sooty ice and the town square seemed made of black glass. Along with the economy, Mother Nature had also turned against them.

While the women stuffed old newspapers into the whistling cracks around the windows to keep out the biting cold, the men sat slumped at the kitchen table. They stared into their coffee cups, trying to build up the courage to leave home and travel north to the steel mills. Of course, no man wanted a life living like a red-eyed rat in a mill town, sweltering six days a week on swing shift, sucking soot, and having holes branded into his skin from the molten metal spitting out of the giant crucibles. He might as well skip life and go straight to Hell. But it paid thirty-six cents an hour. So the question became, At what price was he willing to sell his soul?

Outside, electric lines bowed and ice-glazed trees snapped like swizzle sticks. The wine at St Jerome's church turned to a blood red slush in the communion cup and icicles hung from the slated eaves like crystal cat teeth. When the buzzards roosting in the tangled old oak tree in the church cemetery tried to take flight, their frozen wings were so heavy with ice they flopped to the ground and froze there.

A cold, gray silence fell over Five Points. Layers of ice frosted the wooden Nativity scene until the features blurred and Midnight Mass was cancelled. Those who didn't want to waste precious money on lighting, and those who didn't have any money to waste, crawled into bed at dusk.

And so the town was asleep when Pearl Wilde stepped off the train at the Five Points Depot.

'Pearl Wilde?' the porter asked, as though seeing a ghost. 'Is that really you?'

She had always been a fast girl. Now, from the looks of her, she traveled at the speed of light — blue-black hair bobbed, lips blood-red, eyes smudged in charcoal liner. She wore a white cashmere dress under a full-length white chinchilla coat. Even Pewitt knew a woman wasn't supposed to wear white after Labor Day. From the looks of her, Pearl Wilde shouldn't wear white at all.

'Folks have been wondering about you,' he said, as though it were an accusation.

The decisions a woman makes make the woman, which at least partially explains why when a man looked at Pearl his thoughts immediately turned to an unmade bed, eyes half drawn like bedroom shades and an attitude cool as cotton sheets. Pewitt did the math and figured she must be around twenty-seven now. Twenty-seven was getting up there for a woman by Five Points' standards. But while Pearl had hardened during her absence, she had not aged. The ice in her veins had preserved her.

She was still as aloof as a cat. Pewitt always

thought she had a big head, the way she stood back and watched the world without expression. He'd never found the courage to talk to her when they were young. But he was a man now, married, two kids, and an employee for the L&N Railroad. And it was just the two of them standing on that platform in the dark.

'Lord,' he said, in a husky voice his wife would not have recognized, 'you sure are looking good.'

While he stomped his feet and beat his gloved hands together to keep from freezing, Pearl seemed oblivious to the cold. Her coat hung open and the slit up her dress flapped in the wind. Pewitt's eyes fixed on her leg, praying for a glimpse of more.

Taking a long slow draw off her cigarette, Pearl took a detached look around. As a rule, Pewitt never got involved, not even in his own life. But that night he followed her stare to the crumpled newspapers blowing on the street, the faded paint peeling off the train station, and the boarded-up storefront windows grimy with soot and apathy. Then her eyes landed on him. Pewitt pulled his arms up in his coat sleeves to hide his ragged cuffs.

'Times have been hard here since you left,' he said as if to apologize for the state of affairs.

An apology is not an admission of guilt. Pewitt was, after all, just a porter at the train station. What can one man do? There was no expression on Pearl's face one way or the other.

'Are you home for good,' he asked to fill the silence, 'or just passing through?'

Taking one last drag off her cigarette, she

dropped the spent butt onto the gritty platform and ground it into memory with the toe of her high-heeled shoe. A wisp of white smoke lingered at her parted lips as she gazed past him. The look on her face was so cold, Porter felt sure a man's mouth would freeze to her lips if he tried to kiss her.

'I've decided to open a whorehouse.'

2

Most budding madams start out small, a cracker-box house with a couple of girls whose only marketable skill is the ability to chew gum and moan at the same time. But there was nothing small in Pearl's way of thinking. No one knew where she got all that money, but they had a good time guessing.

The house on Dog Leg Hill was exactly the sort of place Pearl was looking for, a seven-bedroom Victorian on the wrong side of the tracks with a scandalous reputation. Close enough to town to walk, but far enough away for discretion.

The old place had been built by Mr C. W. McCauley, a railroad man who divided his time between Louisville, Kentucky and the switching station at Five Points. C. W. was a hard-driving man. He kept a watch in each pocket, a house in each town, and a wife in each house. Life is short for a man who burns his butt at both ends. C.W. died in his own bed — at least one of them — if not peacefully, then fully spent. The Lord took him quick, but not quick enough to keep C.W. from calling out his Tennessee wife's name as his Choo Choo made its last trip into the Louisville tunnel.

'LuLa, I'm coming!' he cried, right before his engine sputtered to a stall.

Being the first woman down the aisle, the

17

Louisville wife had dibs on his estate. And so, as the barbershop quartet sang 'I've Been Workin' on the Railroad' and the pallbearers carried C.W. to the end of his line, the first Mrs McCauley was having her husband's 'affair' put in order. The second Mrs McCauley and her six children arrived home from the funeral to find the doors padlocked, a FOR SALE sign in the yard, and their personal belongings in a pile outside the front gate.

The house sat empty for two years. When prospective buyers heard the story, the husband always seemed a little too interested in the details. 'Two wives,' he'd muse. 'How on earth does a man manage to pull that off?' To which his wife would bristle, 'This is not the sort of place a decent woman would rear her children!' Neither financial reasoning nor a rock-solid foundation could change her mind.

The old Victorian's reputation was ruined and no amount of Old English furniture polish could bring back the virgin shine. Pearl felt immediately at home there. She made an insultingly low offer and the realtor indignantly balked. 'Tell the owner, I'm opening a whorehouse,' Pearl ordered. And to the realtor's surprise, the first Mrs McCauley from Louisville sold her the place for a song.

It's hard enough to get a husband to keep one house up, much less two. After sitting empty for years, the house on Dog Leg Hill had gone from looking neglected when C.W. owned it, to looking abandoned. The dusty rose paint had weathered to gray, the tongue and groove slats on the wrap-around porch had rotted and fallen through, and the swing dangled by one rusty chain. Cooing pigeons had taken over the cupola, flying in and out of a missing pane, plastering the floor with down feathers and bird droppings. Wild cats, subsisting on mice and pigeon eggs, occupied the bedrooms, while garter snakes slithered in and out of the cool cellar through gaps in the stone foundation mortar. Ivy crept though broken windows into the living room and grew up the peeling wallpaper as if part of the garden-gate pattern. Outside, gray slate shingles littered the lawn like fallen tombstones.

One hand on her hip while the other twirled her new keys, Pearl stood in front of the wreck of a house, sizing up the place. The old Victorian's windows, dark and hooded, seemed to look away, ashamed of what had become of her.

'Don't worry, old girl,' Pearl said quietly, 'we'll have you roaring again in no time.'

⋆　⋆　⋆

Along with being the town telephone operator, Annabelle Boyd was the town crier. If a woman didn't have a telephone, Annabelle was more than happy to deliver the news in person — whether the news was any of their business or not. By week's end, the only person in Five Points Annabelle hadn't told that Pearl Wilde was opening a whorehouse was Pearl Wilde.

There was a lot to be done to the old place before Pearl could open for business. A go-getter would have knocked on Pearl's front door and asked for work. Since all the go-getters in Five Points had long ago got up and gone, Pearl had to go hunting for handymen.

A man without work to occupy his time tends to gravitate toward his natural state, which in Five Points was a state of lethargy. In summer, the boys could be found lounging lazily on the front porch of the Widow Green's General Store, whittling a stick of hickory and watching the grass grow. At first frost, they migrated into Bud Mangrum's Hardware store, where they hibernated cozily in front of the pot-belly stove until spring.

Bud Mangrum hated summer. In summer, he spent most of his days digging wax out of his ears with a Phillips screwdriver and watching cockroaches scamper across the dirty wood floor. When his daddy ran the store, there were six full-time employees. Bud and the economy had managed to whittle that down a bit. Other than selling a box of nails and a couple of two by fours every now and then, his only real business came from Colonel Cavanagh's illegal distillery. As most of those transactions were conducted after hours, Bud spent most days alone in his store, lonely as an old maid. If he needed help loading lumber, he yelled across the street and one of the boys rocking on the porch of the general store would meander over to help him. The paycheck he offered for work rendered usually consisted of his tearing up a few IOUs. Since Bud had no other way of collecting the money they owed him, from the boys' point of view, this wasn't much incentive.

All day Bud leaned against his counter watching the boys play checkers and spit tobacco. Bud knew they were discussing something he would never know because he wasn't there to hear it. A story can never be told the same way twice. Details are forgotten, enthusiasm lost. Once a tale is told, it's gone for ever. Bud stared out the window of his father's hardware store watching the boys shoot the shit, and his heart ached.

He tried every way in the world to lure the boys into the hardware store in the summer. He turned the radio up real loud and hung calendars on the back wall with pictures of women with hourglass figures wearing shorts, hip cocked, shirts tied above the waist and kissing an open-end wrench. He bought cushions for the ladder-back chairs, and left empty nail barrels around for them to kick their feet up on. He put in a ceiling fan, stocked up on Royal Crown Colas and mounted a snack rack of salted peanuts and Moon Pies on the wall. But Bud could never lure them in during the summer for any other reason than to use his john and pick up supplies.

'So what you boys talking about today?' Bud would ask eager and hasty.

'Same old shit,' Woody would say, as he sauntered out of the bathroom zipping his zipper and shaking his leg to get his boys back in line.

'*Farmer's Almanac* is calling for an early frost this year.' Bud always tried to get the

21

conversation going without sounding too desperate.

'You don't say,' Woody would say, as he pulled six Royal Crowns out of the washtub of ice.

Taking Moon Pies and peanuts off the shelf, Woody stuffed them into his pockets. Then he'd drop an IOU in the can and stroll back over to the general store.

The harder Bud tried to woo them during the summer, the more the boys blew him off.

But come first frost, when Bud fired up his wood stove, he could see their heads turn his way. There was a coal furnace in the basement that heated the hardware store just fine, but nothing draws a man like a crackling fire. The day the thermometer hung at forty, the boys began to meander into the store. Bud held himself in until they were settled into their chairs and fixated on the fire. Then he let loose. After six months of solitary confinement, Bud had a lot to say.

'Had to raise the snack rack off the floor,' he said, exuberant as a puppy, 'mice was getting the saltine crackers on the bottom rack. Used concrete nails to drive it into the brick. 'Course that old brick around the furnace flue is soft as a biscuit. But if I'd put her there it woulda dried up the crackers. Here,' he said, sliding a barrel under Roy Lester's boots, 'put your feet up.'

The more Bud rattled on, the quieter the boys got. The quieter they got, the harder Bud tried.

'Been thinking about gittin' a Frigidaire and keepin' baloney and cheese. But we're talking real money there. Maybe get a jar of pickled franks. How d'yu boys feel 'bout pickled eggs — '

'Je-sus Christ!' Roy Lester finally bellowed. 'If I wanted this kind of racket, I'd sit in my own living room and listen to my wife prattle!'

Of course, everyone knew Roy Lester couldn't sit in his own living room even if he wanted to. His wife, Joy, who was anything but, never let anyone set foot in her living room except for Christmas and funerals. But they caught Roy's meaning.

Bud would pout for a while, stick his lip out and pretend to be busy at the cash register. But when the boys were in his store nothing could keep him down for long.

'You boys in the mood for beans and cornbread?' he said after awhile. 'Thought I'd put a pot a pintos on the stove for dinner. Got some hot pepper chow-chow and I could slice up an onion . . . '

Bud had to restock the snack rack and Royal Crowns twice as often in winter, and every so often one of the boys borrowed a screwdriver or a pair of pliers on a permanent basis. But it was a small price to pay for companionship. From the boys' point of view, who else would put up with Bud for peanuts?

★   ★   ★

The boys knew Pearl Wilde would come looking for them and for two weeks they waited. They were starting to get insulted when Bud finally spotted Pearl walking down the sidewalk.

23

'Here she comes!' he called, hurrying to take his chair in front of the potbellied stove with the others.

Word was Pearl Wilde was still as hot as a fire-cracker. But since their opinion was pretty much the only thing they hadn't hocked at Mendelson's pawn shop, the boys would make up their own minds.

When more time passed than should have, Bud turned in his chair and stretched up off the seat to see what the hold-up was. Pearl was standing in front of his store window. With the sun behind her, all he could make out was her silhouette, but he still would have known her anywhere. It was the way she held herself — hand on her hip, weight shifted to one side. She'd had that air about her since they were in school together, as if she were unaware that the world was watching her. Or maybe she just didn't give a shit. All Pearl Wilde ever had to do to get a man's undivided attention was show up.

As Bud strained to make out Pearl's face, he suddenly grew lightheaded and a wave of nausea moved over him like seasickness. He'd never actually seen the ocean, but he was pretty sure this was what it felt like. The room rolled, his stomach turned, and he flushed with fever. At first he thought it was the flu coming on. But as he watched Pearl study his dusty storefront window with the two pairs of faded Levi™ overalls draped limply on the stand, he realized what was wrong with him. He was ashamed.

Bud's eyes moved slowly around the hardware store and his stomach turned. He saw his

24

father's business as Pearl would see it, piles of half-empty cardboard boxes burst open, merchandise spilled on the floor, a rusty bucket of stagnant rainwater catching a drip in the roof, a layer of grit on every surface, the counter-top stacked with unrecorded receipts so old they were starting to curl and yellow.

When something fell off a shelf, Bud left it there. When something was stocked in the wrong place, he left it there. His daddy had spent his life building the business and Bud had worked there since he was big enough to push a broom. He looked around and wondered when he had stopped trying.

The bell on the front door finally jangled and a bolt of electricity ran through the boys. Pearl strolled in and lingered at the counter for a minute taking a casual look around. She always hesitated when she entered a room, like a stripper taking a brief pause as she slipped off her glove, as though she hadn't quite made up her mind whether she would — or she wouldn't. Most women have no sense of timing. They are either all stop or all go. For Pearl, every breath was an invitation and every movement a tease. She was not unaware of her allure. She was just so damn good, she didn't have to think about it.

Finally, they heard her walking down the dark aisle between the bins of washers and screws. You can tell a lot about a woman by the way she walks. Some women's heels hit the floor as if they're hammering nails. Some skitter like apologetic mice. Pearl's walk was smooth and easy. The boys got the impression she had all the time in the world, but that her time did not come cheap.

All the boys except Eddie McCowan, who was the baby of the bunch in more ways than the obvious, had known Pearl all their lives. But there's knowing a woman — and then there is *knowing* a woman. While they'd all gone to Miss Mabel's one-room schoolhouse with Pearl, and devoted far more time at St Jerome's church worshipping her profile instead of the cross hanging in front of them, Pearl was as mysterious as the moon. And just as impossible to land on. Bourne Cavanagh had staked his claim on Pearl shortly after she hit puberty. And everyone knew better than to trespass on Cavanagh property.

Halfway across the store, the sound of Pearl's high heels tapping on the dirty floor stopped. The boys grew impatient. Cautiously lifting their heads, they squinted toward the front to see what on earth was causing her delay. Pearl stood with her back to them in front of the fancy brass doorknocker display. Naturally, they stole a free look. Most women in town drew a black ink line up the back of their calves to make it look as if they were wearing silk stockings. Pearl was wearing the real thing. Eyes lingering on her ankle, the boys traced the seam from her heel to the hem of her white chinchilla coat. From there, their imaginations took over. They pictured the silk stocking hooking to her lace garter and that soft bit of pale perfumed skin in between. Roy Lester blew a silent whistle. And the room suddenly grew very warm.

Turning from the display, Pearl started toward them again. They immediately fell back in their chairs. By the time she reached the stove, the boys were wearing their best 'don't-give-a-shit' attitude, arms crossed, legs stretched out in front of them and wads of chew stuffed in their cheeks.

Standing in front of the stove, Pearl held her hands out to warm them, but mostly to give the boys a chance to warm to her. Half the light bulbs in the back of the store were burned out. Bud was too cheap and too lazy to replace them. Between the quick glimpses and the squinting, the boys figured they were missing a lot of the details. Roy Lester shot a look up at the dead light above Pearl's head, then glared at Bud. Bud hung his head. He knew he'd let them down.

'Hello, boys.'

Pearl had a smoky southern whisper that a man didn't so much hear as inhale. Her voice hung at the belt buckle, causing a man to lean forward, holding his breath for fear of missing a word or an opportunity.

'I don't know if you all heard or not, but I bought the old McCauley place up on Dog Leg Hill.'

Of course she knew they knew, and they knew she knew. But a man never likes to be told what he does or does not know. And if there was one thing Pearl knew, it was men.

'She's in real sad shape.' Pearl sighed sadly.

Slumped in their chairs, the boys stared at their worn out work boots. Inky Mott rolled a toothpick from one side of his mouth to the other and Dicky Deason pretended to read a week-old newspaper.

'Buck Darnell,' Pearl said, as though the thought had just come to her, 'your daddy used to build the finest cabinets I've ever seen. You know, I'll be needing a lot of cabinets and closets. And I'm going to need a space cleared in the back for parking. Roy Lester, I hope you still know how to plumb. I'm going to need a slew of indoor bathrooms.'

Roy Lester spit a long brown stream of tobacco into the rusty coffee can next to his chair.

Sensing she'd given them enough foreplay, Pearl got down to it. Turning to face them, she looked at each in turn, holding their eyes just long enough to spark their dead wood. Hope rose in the room, or perhaps it was testosterone. For most men, they're one and the same. A crooked smile formed on Dickie's face and Inky Mott twirled the toothpick in his grinning mouth like a baton. They felt cocky and sure as if they were back in school and the world was ahead of them. For the first time in a long time, they felt like men. But the muscles were weak from disuse. Almost immediately their confidence began to go soft. Their eyes dropped and their shoulders slumped. Pearl's heart would have ached for them if she wasn't so disgusted. They had given up on life so easily. There wasn't enough starch left in the boys to hold up her stare.

'I pay fifty cents an hour, plus noon dinner and all the coffee you can drink,' she said flatly.

Well, that put them in the mood. Fifty cents an hour was more money than they were paying in Nashville to build the new post office. The boys still stared at their shoes, but they were breathing hard.

When no one spoke up, Pearl's patience began to wear thin. But no one knew better than Pearl that if you rush a man you can destroy the mood altogether.

'Well,' she said after awhile, 'if you hear of anyone looking for work . . . '

Glancing from side to side, Eddie McCowan slowly pushed himself up from the chair. The Great War had taken the brave, and the Depression had taken the ambitious. The men left in Five Points were the kind of men who get left behind. But of all the discards, Eddie McCowan was the last man Pearl would have chosen to come work for her. Eddie was a beautiful young man, bright eyes and a head of golden curls. Put a little bow and arrow in his hand and he could pass for Cupid. Many a girl had tried to steer him down the aisle. But it is virtually impossible to maneuver a man when he's curled in the fetal position. Eddie was a mama's boy, nineteen years old with the umbilical cord still attached.

Opening her silver cigarette case, Pearl slipped a cigarette out and tapped it thoughtfully on top of her engraved initials. She stared at Eddie so intensely a normal man would have withered. Having spent his life being stared at, Eddie didn't blink.

Flipping her silver lighter open, Pearl lit her

cigarette. 'How's your mama doing, Eddie?' she asked, taking a long drag.

'Doing real well, ma'am. Appreciate your asking.'

Judging by the way Pearl forced smoke from the corner of her mouth this was not the answer she'd been hoping for.

'Eddie, do you know how to plumb a bathroom?'

'Miss Pearl, my Mama says I can do anything I set my mind to,' Eddie assured her.

The boys had their eyes on Pearl now like dogs watching to see which way the rabbit was going to run. Pearl might be brazen enough to open a whorehouse in her own hometown, but it took a death wish to contradict a boy's mother. They knew Pearl knew Eddie was a mama's boy, and she knew they knew. And Eddie didn't have just any mama. Maysie McCowan was a brutal force of Mother Nature.

If Pearl hired Eddie, Maysie would nail her to the cross for corrupting her boy. If Pearl didn't hire him, Maysie would take it as an insult and make sure no other mother's son in Five Points worked for her either.

Pearl was caught between a son-of-a-bitch and a hard place. And everyone in the room knew it. Taking a drag off her cigarette that left an inch of ash, Pearl stared at Eddie so hard the boys held their breath.

'Miss Pearl,' Eddie said, 'I swear I'll shovel shit, if that's what you need done.'

He said it with more sincerity than any man should ever admit. Sighing white smoke, Pearl turned on her heels.

'Do your job right,' she said dryly, 'and hopefully we won't have to.'

★   ★   ★

Eddie went to work that day, if you call work sitting at Pearl's kitchen table drinking coffee and telling her all the gossip in town. Pearl sat across from Eddie, smoking cigarettes and watching him eat his pie.

'Tell me about my sister,' Pearl finally said.

Eddie looked up at her, still chewing.

'Kat? What about her?'

Pearl took a long draw and held it.

'Everything,' she said on the exhale.

3

At five o'clock, Pearl sent Eddie home with four hours' pay and a handwritten note on white linen stationery with a fancy 'W' embossed at the top. While Eddie took a nap on the couch to rest up from his hard half-day of coffee drinking, Maysie McCowan stood at her kitchen sink and read Pearl's note twice.

> Dear Maysie McCowan,
>   Enclosed you will find Eddie's pay for the excellent work he did today.
>   You must be proud beyond words of your Eddie. You have reared a fine son with a fine work ethic.
>   Most Sincerely,
>   Pearl Wilde

Maysie looked up from the letter and grunted. Her 'fine' son had never had a real job in his life. Eddie didn't climb out of bed before breakfast was on the table and, if he didn't get his afternoon nap, he'd fall asleep standing up. The only chore she'd ever made him do around the house was rinse his water glass and turn it upside down on the sink next to hers. Maysie had ruined Eddie and she knew it. But she couldn't help herself. He was the most beautiful baby she or anyone else in town had ever seen. Maysie had rocked him for hours just to stare at him.

Kicking his little feet and waving his arms, he'd laugh and smile and coo at her until her heart melted. But then, he did the same for every woman who held him.

Wolves are less ferocious guarding their young than Maysie McCowan had been with Eddie. She babied and sheltered him right into manhood, fussing over him and protecting him with teeth bared. No boy dared pick a fight with Eddie. No adult dared correct him at church. And no girl held his attention for long. Eddie had spent his life hermetically sealed in mother's love. Now he was as useless as wet toilet paper.

Maysie stared out her kitchen window. A blue-black crow perched on her clothes line, iridescent feathers ruffled, head drawn low and bead-black eyes glaring at her. Maysie tapped the pane with her chapped knuckle but the crow continued to stare at her. It was a sign. Death or change was in the air. For some, they are one and the same.

Maysie knew Eddie couldn't find a hammer in a toolbox, and she knew Pearl Wilde knew it. She sincerely doubted the boy knew what a toolbox looked like. But working for Pearl Wilde was the first thing Eddie had ever shown any enthusiasm for in his life. Maysie McCowan was torn. On the one hand, if she put her foot down and told Eddie he couldn't work for Pearl Wilde, who knows if he'd ever get off his dead ass again. On the other hand, if Eddie made a mess of things, it would reflect badly on her mothering. Maysie was caught between a hussy and a hard place. Opening the envelope, she re-counted the crisp dollar bills. Then, of course, there was the money.

Slipping her dead husband's jacket off the hanger in the hall closet, Maysie pulled it on over her overalls. Opening the door just a crack, she peeked in on Eddie in the living room. He was curled on the couch, hands folded under his beautiful face and smiling in his sleep. Since the day Eddie could walk, Maysie had prayed for one thing — a wealthy woman who would take him off her hands. She should have been more specific. Working at a cathouse was not what she had in mind for her only son, but you have to work with what God gives you.

Quietly pulling the front door closed behind her, Maysie stood for a moment on her front porch. Dark came early in winter in Five Points. The gas street-lights cast a hazy amber halo over the other houses on the street. She could see her neighbors going about their lives through their windows like actors on a stage. Buck Darnell, red-faced and mad because dinner was so poor, his wife Luella yelling at him and the three boys about one thing or another. Pewitt, the porter, and his wife, Addie, sitting silently in their living room like two strangers on a train. Annabelle, the town telephone operator, bent over her Bible, fingers underlining the words as she read. The curtains were always closed at Roy and Joy Lester's house, but that did not conceal the discontent. Life turns out, one way or the other.

Pulling her cap low on her head, Maysie turned the coat collar up and stuffed her hands deep into the worn pockets. Then she set her jaw and started walking toward Dog Leg Hill.

34

* ★ ★

Eddie was back at the hardware store the next day, same as usual. But when he stepped inside the door, he stopped short. For a second, he thought he was in the wrong place. Inky Mott was pushing a broom, Woody was standing on top of a ladder screwing in new light bulbs, Dickie Deason was knocking cobwebs down in the front window and Buck was hammering on a busted shelf.

'What's up?' Eddie asked.

'Same ol' shit,' Bud said, not looking up as he polished the counter.

Sunlight poured into the store like glory. The front window was so clean it was as if someone had kicked the glass out. No boxes piled in the corners, no dusty cobwebs spanned the shelves, no grit on the floor. The room smelled like Borax and furniture oil. There was a brand new brass spittoon by the boys' chairs where the rusty Maxwell House coffee can used to sit, and the old bent fireplace poker usually leaning by the stove had been replaced with a brass fireplace set.

Normally, Roy Lester would have been bursting with questions for Eddie about Pearl and the whorehouse. Instead, he stared at the stove, drinking coffee out of a brand new enamel mug in dazed silence. Some men are like catfish. Sudden changes to their environment send them into shock.

Being on Pearl's clock, Eddie got down to business.

'I'm going to need to order a few things,' he said, pulling a piece of Pearl's fancy white stationery out of his shirt pocket, unfolding it and smoothing it on the counter.

It'd been so long since Bud wrote down an order he had to dig through his cigar box for a pencil. 'O.K.' he finally said, touching the pencil lead to the tip of his tongue, 'what ya need?'

'Eight sinks, eight bathtubs and eight toilets,' Eddie read from the list.

Bud's hand hovered above the invoice as though he'd forgotten how to work a pencil.

'Eight?' he finally said.

'Eight,' Eddie said firmly. 'And Miss Pearl wants the tubs with claw feet.'

Roy Lester's head popped up. 'Claw feet? That's a mighty old-fashioned way to take a bath.'

'That's what I told her,' Eddie agreed. 'But Miss Pearl said a man who thinks a tub is just for bathing has never explored the bath's full potential.'

All progress paused while the boys considered this. Inky leaned against his broom, Bud's pencil rested on the paper and Buck's hammer hung in midair. Nothing gets in the way of a man's performance like thinking.

'Filled the bathtub with ice one time,' Buck finally said from the front window. 'Pulled so many catfish off my trot line, worried they'd go bad 'fore Luella got home to clean 'um.'

This turned their thoughts to fishing. And life as they knew it went on.

'What color she want?' Bud asked.

36

'White,' Eddie said. 'Miss Pearl's mighty fond of white.'

Roy Lester huffed from his chair at this bit of information, more out of habit than anything else. Having no original opinions of his own, he always huffed at the opinions of others.

'What's that supposed to mean?' Eddie demanded.

Truthfully, it hadn't meant all that much. But once Eddie challenged him, Roy had no choice but to defend his position.

'Just think white's a funny favorite color for a woman like Pearl Wilde,' Roy shrugged.

Eddie McCowan, who'd never shown a bit of aggression in his life, clenched his soft young fists.

'What exactly are you trying to imply, Roy?'

Roy rolled his eyes toward the boys. He naturally assumed they'd jump on his side of the argument. But the boys were lost in deep deliberation. They did not take sides lightly. Buck stroked the stubble on his chin with his thumb, Dickie sent a stream of tobacco into the spittoon, and Inky rolled his toothpick from one side of his mouth to the other. While technically Roy was right, Pearl favoring white did strike them as a fashion blunder, defending a woman's honor was the obvious side of valor. And if a man doesn't have chivalry, what the hell has he got?

'Pearl Wilde is one classy lady,' Inky Mott decided.

'From that head to toe,' Buck nodded in agreement.

Mouth gaping at their betrayal, Roy turned to Bud. Bud always jumped on Roy's side in things. But in this instance, Bud took time to reflect. He thought about the eight bath tubs, then he glanced at the rest of the items on the long list in Eddie's hand. He also gave a passing thought to the fact that this was the first time the word 'imply' had ever passed through Eddie's lips. Pearl Wilde's worldly ways were already rubbing off.

'White never goes out of style,' Bud said firmly, casting the deciding vote, 'hard to keep clean, but always fashionable.'

Roy pouted and Eddie's fists unclenched.

'Miss Pearl is the finest lady I ever met,' Eddie said, leaving no doubt as to exactly where he stood.

If any other man had said it, the boys would have assumed he was milking that cow. Of course, that wasn't the case with Eddie. Roy suspected Eddie still hadn't been weaned from his mama's tit. Still, there was something more in his feelings for Pearl that they couldn't quite put their finger on. And that made them doubly curious.

Woody helped fill the rest of Eddie's order, packing a box with the small stuff and calling out the items while Bud rang them up at the register. Meanwhile, the boys put in their two cents' worth for free.

'Since Pearl's pockets are so deep, I'd go with cedar under the tubs,' Buck said.

'Scrimp on the brass faucets and you'll be paying for it forever after,' Dickie Deason threw in.

By the time Eddie got to the end of Pearl's list, it was more business than Bud had done in six months. When he hit total on the cash register, it caught his breath. For a second, the boys thought he was going to cry. They watched in humble silence as Eddie counted out the money. It had been a long time since they'd seen that much cold cash.

'How about a Royal Crown,' Bud said, feeling generous as he tucked the money in the register. 'On the house.'

'Don't mind if I do,' Eddie said, leaning back against the counter.

Inky pulled an RC out of the ice, knocked the top off on the counter and handed it to Eddie.

'Moon Pie?' Bud asked.

'Moon Pie sounds pretty good.'

'The man's going to need some peanuts in that bottle,' Bud ordered, and Buck tossed Eddie a bag of salted nuts.

'So,' Bud said, after Eddie was contentedly chewing, 'Pearl happy to be home?'

'Seems happy enough.'

'She ever get lonely up there in that big house?'

Eddie shook his head. 'She likes her own company.'

'There's a quality you don't find in many women,' Bud said, and the boys nodded.

'She ever ask about Bourne?'

Eddie turned the bottle up. They could tell he was dying to talk about it.

'Can't think of anything worse on a woman than catching her fiancé with her sister,' Bud said, laying on the sympathy to grease the way.

'She asked if Bourne had settled down,' Eddie admitted.

'You don't say.'

'I told her Bourne was still running through women like a hound through high grass.'

'And how'd she take that?'

'She said, 'Let him run. He'll never catch the tail he's really after.''

Bud raised his eyebrows at the boys. This struck them as a fascinating bit of news.

'She was real interested in her sister, Kat, too,' Eddie went on.

'What'd you tell her?'

'Warned her about that dog of Kat's. You know, in case she decides to go visit.'

At the mention of Kat's dog, Inky Mott rubbed his leg.

'Things still pretty raw between the sisters, then?'

Glancing behind him, Eddie leaned close and the boys met him halfway.

'If you ask me,' he said quietly, 'Miss Pearl's gonna skin Kat alive and nail her pretty hide to the wall.'

★ ★ ★

After Eddie finished making arrangements for Inky to deliver the rest of Pearl's order he hurried back to Dog Leg Hill. It was almost time for his morning coffee and pie.

All that work inspired the boys to take a break. They were just getting settled at the stove when the door jangled open again.

On a good day, Maysie McCowan looked like something you'd kill with a hoe. Hair slicked back so tight in a knot it drew the corners of her eyes to a slant and skin dry as parchment. She was a hair over five foot, a hundred pounds soaking wet, and had the disposition of a hornet. Her attire never varied, be it for church or a funeral, a pair of Eddie's hand-me-down Duckhead overalls, scuffed work boots and a green John Deere tractor cap pulled low over her jaded eyes. Rumor was she had a fine figure once. To look at her now, a man would never believe it. Any evidence of Maysie McCowan's womanhood was kept hidden like a lie.

Stomping to the stove, she swung around to face the boys. Maysie was like a .22 pistol, not much caliber but still commanding respect. Without a word, she had their immediate attention. The boys sat quiet as rabbits and Maysie cut straight to the chase.

'Roy Lester, you forget how to plumb?'

Roy huffed. 'Shoot, I could plumb in my sleep.'

'Roy, here, is a surgeon with solder.' Bud jumped to Roy's defense and the others nodded in agreement.

'Then why in God's name are you sitting here when there's plumbing work to be had?'

Roy splattered a stream of spit into the new spittoon.

'Well?' Maysie demanded impatiently.

'If I help build that whorehouse,' Roy finally

41

admitted, 'the little missus will see to it I have to squat to pee.'

Maysie straightened herself to her full five feet.

'There isn't any sin in an honest day's work. Now, you get yourself over to Dog Leg Hill and do something other than sit on your hands for a change.'

Roy rubbed his knees as if to suggest he had any say in the matter, then pushed himself to a stand. Truth was he was itching to see inside Pearl's house, as was every other man in town. Then, of course, there was the money.

'I'll go,' he finally said, 'but Joy cain't know.'

A shine came into Maysie's black eyes and the corners of her thin chapped lips turned up into a haunting smile. The boys shivered as if a ghost had stepped on their grave.

'You let me handle Joy Meachum,' she said, so cold you could see her breath.

The boys cut sideways glances at each other. The feud between Maysie McCowan and Joy Lester was well known. They would pay to see that cat fight, if they could put it on credit.

At the front door, Roy lifted his hat off the coat rack. He could see the hangdog look on the boys' faces that he was getting to go to Pearl's and they weren't.

'I'm guessin',' Roy said, resting his hat lightly on his head with a slight tilt, 'Miss Pearl will be wanting some walls around them toilets. I don't know the first thing about carpentry.'

'Well?' Maysie's voice pricked them like a pin. 'The rest of you going to wallow here like hogs at the trough waiting for the President's New Deal to throw you some slop? Or you gonna go do an honest day's work?'

One by one, they trudged behind Roy out the door and down the sidewalk. As soon as they passed the hardware store window, they ran all the way up Dog Leg Hill.

4

Maysie was smoothing Eddie's chenille bed-spread when she felt the magazine. Sliding her hand between the sheets, she pulled out a year-old *Vanity Fair* with Greta Garbo on the front. Eddie had never once shown any interest in a local girl. In her efforts to instill confidence in her son, Maysie feared she may have set his sights a little high.

Her eyes drifted around the small bedroom. The smell of the aftershave just about suffocated her. Eddie had Gladys Green at the general store special order it. There was an ashtray and lighter on the nightstand, even though Eddie had never smoked a cigarette in his life, and a cut-crystal whiskey decanter on the dresser. Maysie didn't allow hard liquor in the house, so he kept the decanter filled with tea. The wallpaper was pinned with slick photos of movie stars he'd mailed off for and a white silk ascot lay folded on top of the dresser. The one and only time Eddie had worn it, Maysie made him take it off. 'Have you lost your mind?' she'd said flatly. 'Go prancing around town with a dandy's scarf around your neck and the LaRue boys will pinch your head off like a tick!'

Picking up the gold pocket watch on the dresser, she ran her finger over the engraved inscription. *To my beloved son on his eighteenth birthday.* Eddie never carried it. He preferred a cheap, flashy wrist watch that didn't half keep time, like John Barrymore wore in *Grand Hotel*. Setting the pocket watch down, Maysie stared at the foreign trinkets her son had gathered and felt a sting of jealousy. There was no doubt Eddie was her child. She'd been fully alert the day he'd made his entrance. But she had no idea where he came from. Maysie felt like a chicken who'd laid a peacock egg.

Maysie was not the kind of woman who expected gratitude. She chose to have Eddie. She chose to devote nearly twenty years of her life to him. But if only he had found some part of her worthy to take with him through life, some proof she'd been there. But there was no evidence of Maysie in her son.

Lifting the bedspread, she tucked Greta back under the covers.

'Ungrateful little shit,' Maysie muttered, as she pulled the door closed behind her.

* ★ ★ ★

Eddie had been a miracle baby. Maysie had been a widow ten months and eleven days the night he was born. Partially because of his late delivery, but mostly because of the unresolved circumstances of Maysie's husband's death, the midwife had refused to deliver him.

'He's a dead man's spawn!' the midwife shouted over Maysie's screams from the bedroom door. 'Ain't no good tuh come of it!'

Maysie realized she was alone in the world. But then most women are; they just don't know it. Snarling and hissing like a woman possessed, Maysie reached down between her knees and pulled Eddie from her womb all by herself. Lifting him into the air like a bloody trophy, she laughed like a crazy woman. The midwife swore Maysie bit the umbilical cord in two with her teeth and tied it all by herself. But then she also swore Crazy June Bug Wallace was born sucking on a tiny silver spoon.

Regardless, Eddie was the most beautiful baby anyone had ever seen. With bright sky blue eyes and smudged rose cheeks, he looked like a china doll. People were always touching him to see if he was real. And Maysie would slap their hands as if they were dipping their fingers into her cake batter. Eddie was so unearthly pretty he made the other babies in town look plain. The young mothers couldn't help but feel envious. They had suffered nine months for a baby that took honorable mention at the fair.

No one resented Maysie's motherly good fortune more than Joy Lester. But then Joy willed the worst on everyone. She fed on the misfortunes of others like a buzzard feeds on road kill. It wasn't personal. It was her biology.

Before Joy married Roy Lester, she was a Meachum. The Meachums were a morbid clan who mined their enthusiasm from the suffering of others. What they tried to pass for concern always seemed a little closer to wishful thinking. The Meachums were filled with foreboding, and the only thing that titillated them more than an unidentified body floating bleached, bloated, and half-chewed in the river was the scandal of a neighbor. Naming a Meachum child 'Joy' would have been taken as a joke, if the Meachums had possessed a sense of humor. Through heredity and diligence, Joy had descended to a level of malevolence previously unattained by any Meachum who crawled before her. And she was proud of it.

'A child this pretty never lives long,' Joy Lester said that day, so lightly the thought seemed to slip into the other young mothers' minds all on its own.

They circled Eddie's crib in the church nursery, staring down at him as he slept innocently. They could smell the lavender on his baby quilt that Maysie put in the rinse water and it raised their envy to a frenzy. Their breath quickened, their hearts raced and their fingernails itched to draw blood. They knew the malice they wished on the child, but didn't care. When two or more catty women are gathered, there is no limit to the harm that can be done.

'This one belongs to the angels.' June Bug Wallace divined the words breathily.

'Or the Devil,' Joy Lester said, her lips barely moving.

When the young mothers looked up and saw Maysie darkening the nursery door, they quickly stepped back, and dropped their blushing faces in shame. All except Joy Lester, whose chin rose and eyes shone.

Joy Lester always wore a serene smile. She had soft sable eyes, creamy skin and a voice that purred. Even folks who had known her all her life forgot her true nature until it was their turn to be stabbed in the back.

'We're just trying to prepare you, Maysie,' she whispered, as if Eddie already lay cold in a child's coffin.

Hands shaking, Maysie reached down and gathered her baby up. She held him so tight to her pounding heart his little pink tongue poked out. Maysie was twenty-nine years old, nearly ten years older than the other mothers in the church. In some people's minds, that put her at a disadvantage.

'Every word and every thought you have for my baby,' Maysie swore, voice shaking and eyes burning a brand of shame into each woman's heart, 'will hold true for yours!'

Her threat brought them back like a slap. June quickly made the sign of the cross over the unborn baby she carried, and Addie rocked her child back and forth on her shoulder urgently whispering the only Psalm she knew by heart, ' . . . deliver us from evil . . . '

But Joy simply stood there, titillated by the hate burning in Maysie's eyes.

Word traveled fast in Five Points. From that day on, every mother in town prayed for Eddie McCowan as if he were her own. And Eddie never had a cold. Never broke a bone. When he got the measles and mumps, they were so easy on him it was little more than a holiday from Miss Mabel's classroom. The chickenpox completely passed him by. When Eddie was twelve, he would have been named the healthiest child in the state, except for a girl from Bottleneck whose uncle was one of the judges.

Meanwhile, Joy fumed and festered. The only thing she despised more than another person's good fortune was her inability to change it. Every Sunday, while the rest of the congregation kneeled at their pews, fingers laced and heads bowed, Joy had her eyes fixed on Eddie from the choir loft. She studied the color of his skin for yellow jaundice and monitored his breathing for any hint of tuberculosis. Her hopes soared every time he coughed or sneezed. She willed every scratch to scar and longed for a permanent tooth to be knocked bleeding out of his mouth. When she saw him heading toward Yellow Creek with a towel tossed over his shoulder or riding his bicycle too fast down Dog Leg Hill, she grew so excited her nipples perked. When he returned home unscathed, her spirit sank like a stone.

Some say it was pure coincidence that Joy Lester never took a baby to term. Some say losing four babies is what turned her mean. Most knew it was the other way around.

Regardless, there was no doubt in anyone's mind that the battle between Joy Lester and Maysie McCowan would rage until death declared the winner.

5

The South is haunted by the ghosts of grandeur past. Stately homes stripped of their conceit line the streets, gaiety and leisure supplanted on the wrap-around porches by rusty wringer washers and rotting wicker rockers. But unlike the once proud and prosperous towns that surrounded her, it was not Union soldiers or carpetbaggers who brought Five Points to her knees. It was politics.

The day Tennessee Prohibition padlocked the doors on the town's largest employer, Cavanagh's Whiskey Distillery, Five Points began a fast decline. No jobs meant no money. No money meant no commerce. And no commerce meant no jobs. It was simple economics, but a concept Mayor Hardin Wallace, a second generation lawyer who married money and, half-heartedly, the wife who came with it, failed to consider the first time he ran for office on the temperance platform.

When the distilleries in Tennessee closed, their suppliers began to fall like dominoes. Corn, barley and rye rotted in the fields. The crops would have cost more to harvest than the farmer could sell them for. Discarded barrels filled with rainwater. Sawmills that supplied the oak for charcoal sat rusting. Bottle-making plants closed down and the printers who printed the labels locked their doors. After all was said and signed at the legislature, as many men were unemployed in the state as employed.

Stripped of their spirit, the town turned mean. Five Pointers were suspicious of strangers, critical of neighbors and flat out nasty to everyone in between. They subsisted on pessimism seasoned with bitterness and then washed it all down with religion.

Every evening Hardin stood at his office window in the courthouse looking down at the dry and dried-up town square. Merchants dared customers to buy anything. The storefront windows that weren't boarded up were so black with grime Hardin had to press his face to the pane to see the dusty display. It was hardly worth the effort. Frank Merrill hadn't bothered to change the bleached boxes of Epsom Salts, codeine cough syrup or faded red enema bags in the drugstore window since the stock market crash. The mannequins at the Five and Dime wore the same cobweb draped Levi overalls and faded flannel shirts all year round. Even the fancy gold filigree lettering on the First National Bank window had tarnished and was flaking off the glass.

Five Points was as hospitable as rusty barbed wire. When the train ground to a stop at the station, passengers glanced out the windows then quickly looked away. No one ever got off, not even to stretch their legs. Gladys Green, the widowed owner of Green's General Store, had to sell her sandwiches, candy bars and soft drinks through the train windows, which added considerable overhead costs, what with having to wrap the sandwiches and pickles in wax paper and all.

Twenty miles up the road, their sister city, Bingham, had barely heard there was a depression going on. Barges lined the riverbank waiting their turn to pick up dark-fired tobacco or unload sand for the concrete plant, and the sound of construction went on from daylight to dark. Meanwhile, in Five Points, the only legal business doing well was Mendelson's pawn shop.

The old clung to their memories of how the town used to be as desperately as they clung to the few heirlooms they had not yet pawned. They sat on their porches exhausting the young with stories of the town's glory days — days when neighbors visited on Sunday and a man could not sleep if the whitewash on his picket fence was fading.

Meanwhile, the only ambition on a young man's mind was getting out of town. The young felt no responsibility for the town's situation and so took no action to improve it. In their minds, it was God and the government's doing, and so they left it to God and the government to fix it. Those who stayed in Five Points guardedly eyed each other. They were resigned to live hand to mouth as long as everyone else in town was gnawing on their knuckles as well.

Like a two dollar hooker, Five Points could not afford to be choosy who pinched her behind. And so when word got back to the town council that Pearl Wilde intended to open a whorehouse, the councilmen were torn. On the one hand, whoring was illegal. On the other hand, it was the first business to locate in Five Points in nearly ten years.

The Mayor called the meeting of the town council for the usual time and the usual place — after sunset and behind closed doors.

'Can you tax whores?'

'Don't see why not.'

'Well, it *is* against the law.'

'All the more reason to tax it.'

'It'll promote drunkenness and disorder.'

'Just as likely to contain it.'

'What about the wives and the preachers?'

'What about 'em?'

'They aren't going to sit quiet while we let a whorehouse move to town.'

'Whorehouse?'

All heads turned toward the head of the table.

'What whorehouse?' Mayor Hardin Wallace demanded, looking shocked at the notion. 'Why, I haven't heard anything about a whorehouse.'

The mayor slowly looked each councilman in the eye.

'Any of you boys heard anything about a whorehouse?'

Rubbing their chins and tapping their fingers on the table, the twelve men contemplated this moral loophole and could think of nothing that would hang them with it. Sensing no dissension, the Mayor called for the vote.

'All in favor of turning a blind eye . . . say 'aye'.'

Glancing from side to side to make sure no one was thinking independently, the councilmen voted unanimously to turn the other cheek. Then Mayor Hardin Wallace poured them each a shot of the good stuff to seal the deal. He had no trouble getting the council to toe the line, as long as the taxpayer was footing the whiskey bill.

★　★　★

In the middle of the courthouse lawn was a round flat rock wide as a wagon wheel and at least a yard thick. It was an unusual hunk of red-veined granite not found in these parts. No one in town knew where it came from, how it got there, or who made it, but they revered the rock like a redneck icon. Five arrows had been chiseled deep into the face. The north arrow clearly pointed the way to Louisville, the east to Nashville, the west to Memphis, and the south to New Orleans. But the aim of the fifth arrow was the subject of much debate. The true destination had long been edited from history, if it had ever been recorded.

The mysterious arrow floated in geographical limbo. Tom Deeter, in an effort to stake a claim as one of the county's founding families, insisted it pointed to a piece of train track that wound its way through his cornfield and dead-ended at his corn silo. But no one bought it. The rock was there long before the first Deeter, a traveling snake-oil salesman, slithered down from Virginia, drank his entire inventory, and was forced to marry an old maid to keep from starving. Another theory came from Hoochie Booth, the town drunk, who swore an angel told him the arrow pointed the way to heaven, which would have situated the pearly gates somewhere between the towns of Bucksnort and Fly. While no one doubted they resided in God's country, they couldn't quite put their faith in a man who sat on the courthouse steps talking to angels.

Regardless, not knowing where the fifth arrow pointed didn't seem to bother anyone in Five Points. Without it, they reasoned, they'd have to call themselves Four Points. And they weren't about to concede a point, even if they didn't know what it was.

6

'She wears nothing but Chanel No. 5. Orders it all the way from Par-ee.' Gladys Green waved a bottle of the perfume in the air for the ladies to take a sniff. 'Even dabs it on her Irish linen pillowcases.'

To hear the widow tell it, Pearl was a regular customer at the general store. But the truth was, since her trip to Bud's hardware store, no one in town had actually seen Pearl outside the house on Dog Leg Hill. Eddie ran her errands, Maysie did the grocery shopping, and the rest of her needs were delivered to her front door by delivery truck or the postmaster himself. Occasionally, someone spotted her casually strolling along the wrap-around porch of the old house or passing in front of a window. But after the boys installed the wrought iron fence around the grounds and the gate at the drive, even those sightings began to dry up.

Other than brief glimpses of her tucked in the back-seat of Inky Mott's cab on her way out of town, Pearl's activities were left to pure speculation. Where she went, what she did, and who she did it with was a mystery. Inky's lips were sealed. What they did know was Pearl was always dressed to the nines and she sometimes stayed gone for days. And when she returned, Eddie would always make a deposit at the bank that made the president jump in the air and click

56

his heels together. It didn't take a calculator to add two and two together.

Maysie tucked a dried red cayenne pepper in every window sill and above the doors of the old house to ward off jealousy, but gossip raged and rancor escalated.

'We have to nip this whore in the bud,' Joy Lester said, and Addie Pewitt, Luella Darnell and Crazy June Bug Wallace nodded solemnly.

The career opportunities for a woman in Five Points were somewhat limited. She could be a wife, a widow, or an old maid. The number one choice, by far, was widowhood. The benefits greatly outweighed the other career paths. After cooking, cleaning and waiting on a man for forty years, half the funerals in town were little more than a retirement dinner interrupted by a burying.

In the minds of the women of Five Points, marriage was the oldest trade union in the world. The job description was clearly defined in the contract and, regardless of her performance, a woman was pretty much guaranteed lifelong social security. But once she popped out three or four babies and was vested, she sometimes felt the need to strike. As far as she was concerned, she'd fulfilled her part of the contract. If her husband wanted anything extra, it was going to cost him.

And so, when word got around that Pearl Wilde was opening a non-union shop, the wives immediately perceived it as a threat to their job security. The last thing they wanted was competition. There would be no scabby whores crossing their picket fences.

Bound by moral indignation, the four mismatched women marched down the middle of Gracie Avenue. It was an unlikely alliance. Under normal circumstances June Bug Wallace, being the mayor's wife, did not socialize below Main Street. But nothing unites people like a common enemy. And Pearl Wilde was as common as you get.

If the city council wouldn't stop Pearl from opening her den of sin, the good women could at least make her life hell on earth until the good Lord got around to transferring her there on a permanent basis.

Addie Pewitt, the train porter's wife, led the mob. Her fleshy arms pumped back and forth like pistons and her tiny hat perched on top of her head like a doily on a honeydew melon. Addie had been a lovely bride. Now she was so fat her ruddy cheeks looked like two cinnamon candy apples and her brown eyes like two Hershey's chocolate kisses lost on a dinner plate.

Addie, June, and Joy Lester managed to sidestep the muddy pothole in the middle of the street. But Luella Darnell, whose eyesight was fading faster than she and Buck could afford eyeglasses, stepped smack dab in the middle of it. Luella's appearance was as blurred as her vision. Near blindness gave her translucent blue eyes a heavenly vagueness, while her pale home-permed hair billowed around her face like a cloud. When the cold muddy water filled her shoes, she let out a string of profanity, as she was prone to do. The counterpoint between her angelic face and her devil's tongue never failed to shock.

'Is that kind of language really necessary?' June Bug winced.

'You're damn right, it is!' Luella snapped, as she squished along behind them.

Women too long without love grow cold and bitter. Luella had passed the sour stage and was starting to curdle. If Buck looked at her wrong she'd bite his head off. Even though it wasn't his fault that the only carpentry work within fifty miles was at the whorehouse, Luella still punished him by depriving him of her wifely affection. The irony was Buck was taking it much better than she was.

Some might think it illogical that a wife who wouldn't let her husband touch her should object to his seeking services elsewhere. After all, if a wife has a leak under the kitchen sink and her husband can't plumb, he wouldn't complain if she called Roy Lester to fix it. But that's not how it works. Adultery is a deadly sin, and not just because someone usually gets stabbed, shot, or strangled as a result of it.

If Gladys Green tipped her vegetable scale a little heavy at the General Store so that a customer got one less tomato than she paid for, or Mayor Hardin Wallace never quite got around to paving Gracie Avenue as he promised every election, or four envious wives stood over a baby's crib and wished him harm — well, nobody's perfect.

But there can be no tolerance for conjugating without the conjugal. In the hierarchy of sins, sex topped the charts. Lying, stealing and coveting took a back seat to adultery. The trespass that people are most fond of blockading is the one they are most tempted to travel.

The ladies stormed single file up Maysie McCowan's front steps. After a little post-walk grooming on the porch, they looked at each other and nodded. Addie lifted her fleshy fist to knock but the door swung open before her knuckles made contact.

'Well,' Maysie said, stepping aside to let them pass, 'isn't this a pleasant surprise.'

Despite living within peeping Tom distance of each other, none of them had ever set foot in Maysie's house. As they stood awkwardly clutching their pocketbooks in the rose-papered vestibule, they took in their surroundings and tried to make out the peculiar aura of the place. Slowly, they realized it was . . . tranquility. A grandfather clock serenely ticktocked. A canary contentedly sang in its cage. A hymnal lay open on the upright piano, the spine broken at 'Just As I Am'. Purple violets lined the sunny window sill. Sunlight passed through the sheer curtains casting a warm lace shadow on Maysie's winged-back reading chair, an afghan draped the back, and a marked book rested on the arm. Maysie's slippers sat neatly beside the footstool and a crocheted doily lay on the endtable within mindless reach of her cup.

It was a widow's lair and a wave of envy burned through the wives.

'I hope you don't mind if we visit at the kitchen table,' Maysie said, leading them down the dim hall. 'I have Eddie's supper on the stove.'

'The kitchen?' June Bug mouthed, arching her eyebrows at the other women.

June Bug Wallace longed for her old life, when a lady would never entertain at the kitchen table. If she must, in this new time, form alliances with the likes of porters', plumbers', and carpenters' wives, she would treat them, if not as equals, as brief visitors to her honorable world, a world to which she felt sure the others would never be invited for a permanent stay — at least, not by her.

As the women followed Maysie down the hall, Luella dragged behind. The hall wall was lined with photographs of Eddie. He was even more beautiful in a frame than in the flesh. The camera loved him. Luella lingered at each shot of Eddie, but hung on one in particular. Stopping in front of it, she leaned close. Bud Mangrum must have taken it. Only Bud would have deemed the scene worthy of a photograph. While the other men posed stiff and unsmiling on the courthouse steps, Eddie leaned back on his elbows, shirt open, sleeves rolled up, flirting with the camera. Something about the smooth texture of his skin and the hollow of his cheeks caused the lens to add a depth to Eddie that he did not possess in real life. All the others in the photograph, including Luella's husband Buck, disappeared. Only Eddie held the eye. A warm flush ran over Luella that she hadn't felt in a very long time. Eddie McCowan might be good-for-nothing, but no one could say he wasn't good to look at.

While Maysie filled the percolator with water, the wives sat with their arms crossed, smirking at her overalls and scuffed work boots. They felt smugly superior to the widow for dressing like a man. But as they sat bound in bras, squeezed breathless in girdles, and wiggling their numb toes in stiff pumps that blistered their heels, Maysie effortlessly tossed kindling into the stove firebox, and a crack of doubt began to form.

'I'm right in the middle of fixing a little celebration supper for Eddie,' Maysie said. 'He's gone and got a job working for Pearl Wilde, you know.'

The wives rolled their eyes at each other.

'Eddie's working for Pearl Wilde is what we came to talk to you about,' June Bug began, with the authority vested in her by her husband's being mayor.

'Really?'

Maysie cracked the oven door to check on her pie and the ladies lifted up out of their chairs to catch the scent.

'Is that a coconut pie you got baking?' Luella asked.

'Grated the coconut fresh this morning,' Maysie said, stepping aside so Luella could get a good squint at the coconut toasting on top of the golden-brown meringue.

For a split second the women forgot the reason for their visit. Such is the way of temptation. One lust leads to another.

Closing the oven door, Maysie lifted the lid on her cast iron skillet and poked the pork chops with a fork. Luella's stomach growled so loud it hurt. Luella and her family always had a cabbagey smell. It clung to their clothes like dye. She'd fed Buck and her three boys nothing but boiled backbone, hot-water cornbread and cabbage since the crash. If she didn't meet quota at the shirt factory, they went without the backbone. Luella could not remember the last time she fixed a meal like the one boiling, baking, and frying on Maysie McCowan's stove.

Joy Lester, on the other hand, would sooner stir trouble than gravy.

'Pearl Wilde is opening a *whore*house.' Joy enunciated the word, as if Maysie were hard of hearing along with being hard-headed. 'Have you thought about that, Maysie?'

'She's paying fifty cents an hour,' Maysie said flatly. 'Have you thought about *that*?'

That much money gave the women pause.

'It's easy for you,' Joy said, sharp as a shard of glass. 'You're a widow. You don't have a husband to keep in your bed.'

'From what I hear, Joy,' Maysie said calmly, 'neither do you.'

June Bug, Luella and Addie developed a sudden fascination with the blue willow pattern on Maysie's cups. But the impassive look on Joy's face never faltered. Only her pupils drawing to black pinpoints gave her away. Any other woman would have made the sign of the cross to protect herself from the cold vicious look Joy gave Maysie. But Maysie stared Joy straight in her evil eyes.

'Now, you all listen to me,' Maysie said, resting both hands flat on her kitchen table and leaning toward them. 'A satisfied husband has no desire to go elsewhere. Do your job right and your husbands won't have the energy to shop around.'

Face furled, Luella looked doubtful. Whether she doubted a man ever stopped shopping or whether she doubted her ability to do her job right was uncertain. Regardless, keeping Buck satisfied sounded like a whole lot of charity work to her.

'Besides,' Maysie added, 'none of your boys could afford to set foot in Pearl's. It's a private club. She's charging just to walk through her door.'

Addie blurted a huff. 'What man is going to pay big money for a whore from around these parts?'

'Pearl isn't hiring from around here,' Maysie said simply.

It took a while for them to comprehend what Maysie had just implied. When it finally sunk in that Pearl planned to import her labor, they were livid.

'Well, of all the nerve!' Addie hissed.

'What?' June Bug huffed indignantly. 'Local whores aren't good enough for Miss Pearl Wilde?'

Since the crash, many an amateur had turned pro. But the closest house of ill repute to Five Points was Miss May's in Bingham. Since most Five Points men didn't have the money or the initiative to travel that far, Miss May's girls only served to whet their appetite. If Miss May could have figured a way to charge for whetting, she would have been a millionaire.

'Where the hell does Pearl intend to bring them in from?' Luella asked, forehead creased.

'New Orleans,' Maysie stated matter-of-factly.

A stunned and fearful hush fell over the table. Everyone knew about those French Quarter girls. They were weaned on absinthe and dropped out of their mothers' wanton wombs licking their lips and rubbing their legs together like crickets. French women knew the magic of the flesh that turned a man into their slave. For a wife who had to neuter her husband to keep him from running off during the night, nothing was more threatening.

As the wives' minds raced over this revelation, Maysie pulled on her quilted oven mitt.

'Half the women south of the Mason-Dixon Line have watched their men go north for work in the mines and the mills and either come back maimed, in a pine box, or not at all,' she said, as she opened the oven door.

The wives shifted guiltily. These did not sound like bad options to a woman in a bad marriage. But then a woman in a good marriage would not have been sitting at Maysie's table.

'A man who can't find work always finds trouble. At least working for Pearl Wilde, you can keep an eye on them.'

Maysie slid the hot bubbling pie out of the oven and placed it on the trivet in front of them.

'Then, of course,' Maysie said, 'there's the money.'

7

Kat Wilde was sewing sleeves on shirts at the Rudolph & Hughes shirt factory the first time Mason Hughes laid eyes on her.

'Who is that?'

The plant manager didn't have to ask which of the girls working on the floor the owner's son was enquiring about.

'Kat Wilde,' Mason repeated slowly. 'She seems like a very . . . faithful employee.'

Of all the words Crockett would use to describe Kathryn Wilde, 'faithful' was not one that came to mind.

The two men stood at Crockett's office window looking down at the factory floor. From that angle the room looked like the bottom of a well. Little light made it through the dirty windows. The deafening clack of sewing machines bounced off the brick walls and cotton-fiber dust hazed the stagnant air. Two dozen women, mouths set and heads bowed over their machines, deftly guided flannel shirt pieces under the driving needles at an inhuman speed.

Crockett glanced down at Mason and tried to figure out what on earth he was doing there. The plant manager was a full head taller than the owner's son but was still wary of him, and not just because his daddy signed the paychecks. Mason Hughes had a suave, laid-back way about him that bordered on shifty. Crockett knew the kind. He'd dealt with them all his life. And he knew it was a mistake to assume that men who have it all don't want more.

It was the first time Mason had ever set foot in the factory and Crockett knew no good could come from it. The last thing he needed was a bored college boy looking for a hobby and telling him how to do the job he'd been doing for fifteen years. Of course, this did not mean Crockett wasn't fully prepared to kiss Mason's butt.

Mason could not have cared less about Crockett or what he was thinking. His attention was fully fixed on Kat Wilde.

Kat's hair was tied back with a ragged scrap of flannel to keep it from getting tangled in the sewing machine, her dress was hiked up and tucked between her knees as if the material might cause drag on her aerodynamics. While the other girls on the floor trudged through their work, suffering and despising every second of it, Kat was an exercise in emotionless efficiency. In a seamless flow her left hand reached for an unfinished piece to be sewn while her right guided the working pieces under the driving needle. Just before the shirt fell from the back of the machine, she reached around, caught it, and tossed it onto her stack. All the while the speed of her machine never slowed.

As if sensing someone was staring at her, Kat's eyes turned straight up into the eyes of Mason Hughes. The look she gave him sent a surprised surge through him. No woman had ever looked at him with such utter blasé indifference.

There are those who hold that a meeting of minds is far superior to the instant, uncontrollable urge to rip a stranger's clothes off. They espouse that it is the union built on mutual respect and aligned thinking that separates man from beast. Mindless physical attraction is a vulgar flaw that must be cut from the human fabric.

God wasted flesh and blood on these people.

Kat's head dropped back to her work, but the damage had been done. The combination of indifference, beauty and nimble productivity trapped Mason Hughes like a fly in amber.

Kat was the only one whose eyes were not fixed on Mason Hughes. Without exception every girl on the floor had taken him in, slowly, from head to toe. Their intent was to dislike him, the rich boy who owned them. But once they got a good look at him, they had a change of heart. He had that way with women.

But the only woman Mason saw was Kat Wilde.

'What time is her next break?' he asked quietly, his voice husky.

Mason Hughes did not ask if Kat was married or any other particulars. None of that mattered. In Mason's world everything was for sale. And with his kind of money anything could be bought.

★ ★ ★

The Rudolph & Hughes shirt factory came into Mason's family via his mother. Olivia Rudolph

68

Hughes inherited the factory in Five Points, along with eleven hundred acres and an antebellum house, from an eccentric great-uncle who had never married. It was but a drop in the Rudolph reservoir.

The factory was a three-story red-brick monolith two streets off the town square. In the summer it was so hot you could bake biscuits on the floor. In winter, the girls' fingers got so cold they couldn't feel the buttons on the shirts. Kat sewed her thumb to the machine once but didn't notice until she tried to clip the bloody thread. Crockett had to take the sewing machine apart to pull the needle out. Kat wrapped a rag around her thumb then went right back on the line. Crockett still docked her pay twice, first for missing quota and second for bleeding on the product. He figured if he didn't, all the girls would be sewing their fingers to the machines to get out of work.

'Just be glad I don't put you back down in cutting,' he said, as he handed Kat her paltry paycheck. That was all he had to say to keep the girls in line. Half the cutters were missing at least half a digit. The image of Sue Ellen Post wearing her wedding ring on her thumb kept even the most rebellious girls in line.

Factory girls were forbidden to wear pants, smoke, chew or use profanity. No fraternizing with the men on the loading dock was tolerated, on or off the job. Except for having to wear a skirt, Kat got away with breaking most of the rules for one simple reason. Crockett could not meet production without her.

The train track ran behind the factory where heavy bolts of fabric brought up from the Hughes cotton mill in Mississippi were unloaded and the finished shirts bound for the Hughes warehouse in Chicago shipped out. Men yelling and the trains grinding up and down the track made the dock a sooty deafening place, but it was out of the wind in winter and out of the sun in summer. This was where Kat took her breaks.

Leaning against the brick wall, she took a drag off her cigarette and stared down the tracks. It was the pose of a woman comfortable in her body, if not her current position in life. When she heard footsteps approaching, she knew without looking who it was, Mason Hughes had the walk of a man who wore his cock on the outside of his perfectly fitted custom-made suit. The second time he cleared his throat, she rolled her eyes his way.

Mason had expected Kat to flaunt her beauty, as beautiful women tended to do, to toss her hair or pout her lips. But Kat made no effort. Beauty was not a card Kat had to play.

'My name is — '

'I know who you are.'

Under normal circumstances all Mason Hughes had to do to get a girl's attention was mention that half the roads, buildings, and bridges in the state were named after a relative of his family. If a woman wasn't impressed by his pedigree, he had absolutely no idea what to do with her.

'Tell me, Miss Wilde,' he said, casually straightening his cuff links, 'are you happy working for Rudolph & Hughes?'

It was a question designed to remind Kat of her status in the situation, which was that she had none. Some games are best played dirty.

'I'm so happy,' Kat said, dragging the 's' like a match against his skin, 'I've been thinking about telling them to keep my paycheck.'

Mason smiled and his eyes shone. He had a live one.

Word spread fast through the factory that Mason Hughes had Kat cornered on the loading dock. The girls in sewing rubbed a clean spot on the windows with their sleeves and pressed their faces to the glass. Those on break hurried outside and huddled near the double doors, whispering behind their hands. They could only imagine the negotiations going on between Kat Wilde and the owner's son.

'Look,' Kat said, glancing toward her co-workers, 'why don't you just cut to the chase.'

Leaning close, Mason rested his hand on the brick wall next to her to keep from running it down her blouse. His eyes were on her mouth, but not because he was particularly interested in what she had to say. She could feel his breath moist and hot on her neck.

'I'm just here for the day,' he said quietly. 'I thought maybe you'd like to take a ride.'

Kat's eyes rolled up to his. He had her attention. Kat liked a man who was up front about his intent and the length of the engagement. She followed his nod to the convertible roadster parked next to the building in the spot reserved for the owner.

'Is that a Mercedes SSK?' she asked.

'One of the first in this country.'

Another man might wonder about a small town factory girl knowing the make and model of an expensive foreign car. But Mason's mind was on his destination, not the mode of travel.

'I like to take her fast as she can go,' he said, pressing the warm key into her palm.

Kat's territory was small. The biggest city she had ever been to was Memphis. She depended on instinct, not experience, to get by. And she instinctively knew that Mason Hughes had the personality of a piggy bank. Take away the money and he was a hollow pig. But she didn't hold that against him.

Kat slowly scanned Mason Hughes from wingtips to lifted aristocratic nose. He was smooth as cream. Which was too bad, she preferred her men rough. She glanced at the car again. When she turned back quicker than he expected, catching him off guard, Kat caught a brief glimpse of his true nature before he could conceal it with a smile. Underneath the pomp and polish was pure wolf — hungry and dangerous. And it thrilled her.

It is the smallest of decisions that sends a life spiraling off course. Mason thought her hesitation meant she was wavering. In fact, Kat was merely working out the logistics. She couldn't simply walk out of the plant and climb into the owner's son's car. If Mason had shown his true colors, things might have worked out differently. But he was in a tremendous hurry to get things going. And so he blurted out what a man like him thinks a woman like her wants to hear.

'A man could get used to taking care of a little woman like you,' he whispered into her hair.

A switch seemed to flip off in Kat. Shrugging away from him, she ground her cigarette out on the wall between them. Mason didn't have a clue what he'd done wrong, but knew instantly the deal was going sour.

'Look, I'm not normally so forward,' he lied, which showed how little he understood the qualities Kat looked for in a man.

'This isn't going to happen,' she said, dropping the spent butt in her apron pocket.

'What makes you so sure about that?'

Kat pressed the car key into his hand.

'I just don't think I could get used to taking care of a little man like you.'

Pushing off the wall, Kat left him standing there. Of course, Mason didn't buy this for a second. Kat had a way about her that no matter what came out of her mouth, the rest of her seemed to be whispering, 'Yes.' He watched her walk down the loading dock, shoulders rolling and hips round and fluid as if buoyed in water. It was a walk that called, 'Come to me.' Mason watched mesmerized. He had no doubt the invitation was intended for him and him alone.

As she passed the dockworkers, a long resonating wolf-whistle pierced the air. Kat stopped mid-stride. Slowly turning, she faced the pack of men frisky with collective courage and drunk on testosterone. But the lethal look in her eyes sobered them instantly. There was no doubt which one did it. He was new, a big brawny country boy with a full-lipped grin that made his mouth look as if it were sliding off his face. Sleeves rolled up, thumbs hooked in his belt loops, and built like a stacked rock fence.

A heat ran through the factory girls watching. Their fingers curled toward the pad of their palms and they panted hot breath. They were sure Kat was going to scratch the boy's eyes out and their mouths watered. These women had been caged too long to fight as a pride, but they still relished watching the kill.

Kat took a step toward the boy and his fellow workers parted. Hands on her hips, she fixed a hard look on him. Heat rose on his smooth young cheeks like the red hot eye of a stove. He grinned like the good-natured fool that he was and Kat knew the boys had set him up. It is the nature of males to toughen the young.

'What's your name?'

'Sam Meeks, ma'am.'

'Sam Meeks, do I look like a coon dog to you?'

'No, ma'am.'

'Then why did you whistle at me?'

Sam Meeks furled his forehead in painful thought, the brain being his only undeveloped muscle.

'Ma'am,' he said slowly, 'I reckon I wanted you to come.'

The men exploded with snickers and the factory girls' backs arched. Kat suppressed a grin.

'Trust me, Mr Meeks,' she said, her eyes pinning him willingly to the wall, 'you couldn't handle this kitty.'

Kat had pulled in her claws. Only the girls knew it and they felt betrayed. They wanted blood. But it was not in Kat's nature to bite a man's balls off. It was just one of the traits that would always make her at home with men and treated with suspicion by her own kind.

While the boys believed it to be a full-fledged put-down, it still came out as if Kat was slowly running her tongue up Sam Meeks like he was a lollipop. Even her rejections gave a man hope. As she sashayed away, the boy patted his heart and blew as if he was on fire and trying to blow himself out. The dock howled with laughter. The men dug their elbows into his ribs and cuffed him on the chin. Sam Meeks could not have been happier. When he caught sight of Mason Hughes glaring at him, he beamed, lifting his chin as if they were the best of buddies. The one thing a poor man has in common with a rich man is an appreciation for a fine-looking woman.

Mason did not coil before he struck. Storming into the office, he pulled Crockett straight to the outside window.

'See that man,' Mason said, pointing down to Sam Meeks. 'Fire him.'

'He doesn't work for you,' Crockett said, hands in his pockets. 'He's with the L&N railroad.'

Mason was at a loss. If he couldn't fire a man, he had absolutely no idea what to do with him.

'I want a sign put on that wall that says, 'No

whistling at the women,' ' Mason ordered. 'And I want to see it there today.'

'Yes, sir, Mr Hughes,' Crockett said, scribbling himself a note on a pad. 'That's a real good idea. Treat a woman like a lady, my mama always says, even if she ain't one.'

8

'Sugar, shit, and shinola!' Luella slammed her hand against the side of her sewing machine. 'My damn machine's tore up again!'

In assembly work, time is money. It was not Kat's job to fix the sewing machines when they broke. But by the time the mechanic got there, smoked a cigarette or two, shot the shit with the foreman, and hopefully figured out what was wrong, Kat would have Luella's machine up and running.

'I swear you could tear up a steel ball,' Kat said, pushing Luella aside.

Along with her vision impairment, Luella lacked all coordination. She had been known to miss her mouth completely when drinking coffee and regularly tripped on flat ground. Despite working through morning break and eating her noon meal at her work station, Luella still missed quota half the time. If she hadn't been Crockett's niece by marriage, she would have been long gone.

'I never had any trouble with my damn pedal Singer,' Luella said.

'No problems except your knee stayed swollen twice its size from pumping the pedal all week.'

Sliding into Luella's chair, Kat studied the ragged seam on the shirt while Luella squinted over her shoulder. Even if Luella hadn't been half blind, she still would have had trouble seeing. On cloudy days the factory floor was so dim and full of shadows the girls had to feel what they were doing. Whenever one of them said something about it, Crockett told them the best seamstress he ever had couldn't see the nose on her face.

'Never complained,' he said, this being his definition of an outstanding employee.

Digging a small screwdriver out of her apron, Kat made a slight adjustment to the tension knob. Running a scrap of material through, she held it up, checked the stitch, then made another adjustment.

'Hey, Kat!' one of the girls called over the rattle of the machines. 'What'd the owner's boy want?'

Since all of the seamstresses except Luella could do their job with their eyes closed, they passed the day minding and mending the business of others. When two or more women gather, there is sure to be gossip. Crockett didn't care what they did as long as they met quota. It had been his experience that a woman's performance has absolutely nothing to do with where her mind is.

'He wanted to know if she was happy working here,' Betty called back over her shoulder. Betty had swept up at the saw mill until it shut down. As a result, she could read lips better than most women could hear.

'He wanted a quickie down at the river, is what he wanted,' Joy Lester said darkly.

'At least Kat would get a half-day off,' Luella threw back at her.

'I'd give anything for a couple of hours of doing nothing,' Addie said, cracking her spine with a groan. Addie's belly stuck out so far in front of her she had to stretch her arms out straight to reach the machine. It was hard on the back.

Quickies down by the river turned their thoughts to loose women, which naturally turned their thoughts to Pearl Wilde.

'Kat, you seen Pearl yet?' Betty asked.

The girls cocked an ear while Betty focused on Kat's lips. Ignoring them, Kat pumped a drop of machine oil into Luella's machine and turned the wheel.

The girls depended on the lives of others to spice up their own bland existence. And any gossip about the Wilde women was like a splash of Tabasco. Even before Pearl caught Kat in the springhouse with Bourne Cavanagh, their mother, Lorna Wilde, had been the favorite subject whispered behind every hand.

'Pewitt said Pearl was wearing a full-length white chinchilla coat when she got off the train,' Addie said, dropping a finished shirt in the box to her left and grabbing another shirt to be sewn from the box on her right.

'I guess you heard Pearl bought the old McCauley place on Dog Leg Hill.'

'They say she plans to open a whorehouse.'

'A whorehouse in Five Points. Heaven forbid!'

'If you girls got paid by the word instead of by the hour,' Kat said, as she turned the machine back over to Luella, 'you'd all be rich by now.'

'Miss May charges ten dollars an hour for her

girls,' Betty blurted out.

Every head swiveled Betty's way.

Miss May's den of sin had prospered in Bingham since before most of them were born. The stately house sat at 1116 College Street, just past the two-year college, and was fondly referred to by the professors as Miss May's School of Epicurean Knowledge. Many a young woman had discreetly put herself through secretarial school working for Miss May, just as many a young man had graduated from the bordello with honors.

Betty's intimate knowledge of the establishment could only be surmised. There were five daughters in her family, all surviving on potlick and cornbread except one. Somehow, Betty's middle sister, Diane — the only sibling without an overbite that could pop the cap off a Royal Crown Cola bottle — managed to graduate from secretarial school. It didn't take a two-year college degree to put two and two together. Now, Diane had a job in Nashville working for none other than Mr Hubert Hughes himself, owner of the Rudolph & Hughes shirt factory. Diane only came home to Five Points for holidays and funerals, and wiped the red dirt off her patent leather pumps on her way out of town.

The factory girls often daydreamed about Diane, kicked back in Mr Hughes's plush air-conditioned office filing her fingernails. The only justice they could derive from this situation was that, while they would spend forty years sweating in the shirt factory, Diane would spend eternity roasting in hell.

'Ten dollars an hour?' someone echoed in disbelief.

'What man could go an hour?' Addie snorted.

'Maybe she starts the clock at the foot of the stairs,' Luella suggested.

'Miss May charges twenty-five dollars to take a man 'round the world',' Betty told them eagerly.

There was a long silent pause until Luella finally asked, 'How do you take a man 'around the world'?' which allowed the others to admit they didn't have a clue either. They all turned to Betty. She shrugged her ignorance which irritated them to death. Betty never asked the pertinent questions.

In lieu of any reliable secondhand knowledge, they turned to Addie. You would never know it to look at her, but before Addie married and tripled her dress size, she'd been quite the girl about town. She once went parking with two men on the same day with barely enough time in between to brush her teeth.

'How the hell should I know how to take a man around the world?' Addie puffed her apple cheeks indignantly. 'I've never been east of Chattanooga!'

A decent woman would never sell herself by the hour. It was a lifetime contract or nothing at all. But as the realization slowly sank in that a woman at Miss May's made more per hour lying flat on her back than they made in a week, a heavy gloom fell over the room. Nothing lowers the spirits like realizing you've sold yourself short. Gradually, every sewing machine slowed

81

to a stop. They sat in mourning until their silence forced Crockett to get up from his desk, walk out of his office onto the mezzanine and lean over the rail.

'What's the problem down there?' he shouted down. 'Need I remind you girls, if you don't meet quota, you're all working Saturday!'

One by one, the machines started up. Satisfied, Crockett walked back to his office.

'Twenty-five dollars for a trip around the world,' Luella muttered, as she stomped her sewing machine peddle to the floor. 'For that much damn money, I'd be willing to travel.'

★　★　★

Five minutes after the whistle blew, the front doors on the factory burst open and the girls started pouring out. Most of the seamstresses stockpiled a few extra shirts during the week to give themselves a little cushion on Fridays. By the time the whistle blew, they had their hats and coats on and held their lunch pails in their laps.

Head bowed over her machine and eyebrows knitted, Luella continued to work furiously. When the room was empty and they were alone, Kat walked over and dropped a pile of finished shirts onto Luella's short stack.

Luella couldn't bring herself to look up. 'I wish this damn place would burn to the ground,' she said under her breath.

There were two types of girls at the factory — those who hated working there, and those who hated working period. Punching the factory clock either meant your husband couldn't support the family, or you didn't have a husband. Either way, it was not something to be proud of.

'Luella, I keep telling you, your work station is set up all wrong,' Kat said, studying the situation. 'You have your unfinished pieces on your right side and the finished pieces on the left.'

'What difference does that make?' Luella jerked her arm into her coat.

'You're left-handed. Your work station is set up for someone right-handed.'

Luella blinked at her blankly.

'When you cross your left arm over to pick up an unfinished piece, you can't see the needle. So you take your foot off the pedal. That slows you down and makes your seams crooked.'

Luella sighed with bitter exhaustion. She didn't have the energy to care. Even if she did, she wouldn't waste it on her job. Making a shirt that would be worn by someone she didn't know or would never meet and who didn't give a damn about her or her efforts — what was the point? What did it matter if a seam wasn't straight or a button didn't line up with the hole? Luella would never see the man who wore it. She worked for one reason and one reason only. Money. They all did — all except Kat. And no one knew what Kat's motivations were — about anything.

'I'll set you up right on Monday,' Kat said, as they walked through the empty factory. 'You'll see.'

'I'll be sewing sleeves on shirts until I can't see

to thread the needle,' Luella said bitterly. 'Hell, I can barely see the damn thing now. Tell me how you can always be so hopeful. I mean it, Kat, tell me.'

Kat would have explained if she could. She was that kind of girl. She was not the kind to leave an ingredient out of a recipe so that other women would fail. But the question made no sense to her. One person looks at a rose and sees the petals, another sees thorns. And some only see the manure it is planted in.

'I figure I have two choices in life,' Kat said, lifting her timecard from the rack and dropping it into the punch clock. 'I can be happy or I can stick my head in the oven.'

Luella cooked on a wood stove. The only way a woman could kill herself with a wood oven was to bake herself to death. This reminded Luella she had to chop wood before she could start supper. She had no doubt Buck had forgotten to sharpen the ax. And the wood box was most likely empty and she'd have to empty the ashes . . .

Grabbing Kat's arm, Luella spun her around.

'Kat, look in the mirror! You don't have to be here. God gave you a way out. You can have any man you want. Nobody could blame you for taking up with a man who could get you out of this place. Nobody could blame you for taking a ride with Mason Hughes. Hell, I'd go for a ride with the Devil if his heater worked.'

'Trust me,' Kat said, looping arms with Luella and dragging her along, 'the only thing in Mason Hughes's pants worth having is his billfold.'

'Trust *me*.' Luella sighed wearily. 'The only thing in *any* man's pants worth having is his billfold.'

★   ★   ★

'Dinner's on the table!' Luella shouted from the kitchen.

After yelling over the sewing machines all day, Luella's volume was still set on high when she got home.

'Did you bake fresh biscuits?' Buck asked, as he pulled his chair back from the table.

'Did *you* bake fresh biscuits?' Luella fired back so hard and harsh the baby started to squall.

After a day bent over a sewing machine at the factory, then coming home to chop wood, cook dinner, wash the dirty dishes and care for the children, Luella's tension was still set on high as well. Her neck ached and she had no feeling in her fingers from pushing shirts through the machine all day. Her wrist hurt so bad she had to use both hands to pick up the skillet. Later, her thumbs would start to swell. But she wouldn't be able to soak them until after she put the baby down.

Luella was the first woman in her family to work outside the home. She had no reference as to how to handle it. She went to bed tired and awakened exhausted. She didn't have the energy to smile. Even though Buck hadn't found carpentry work in going on two years before the whorehouse came along, it never occurred to him to give Luella a hand. Taking care of the house and the boys was woman's work. His helping her would have insulted them both.

'As if I don't have enough to do, there wasn't a stick of kindling in the wood box,' Luella fussed, as she lifted the crying baby off the floor and slammed him into the highchair. 'It was so dark I nearly cut my foot off chopping it!'

Collapsing in her seat across from Buck, she fired a look at the two boys. Lacing their fingers, they dropped their heads.

'For what we are about to receive . . . Bucky spit that damn gum out! . . . may the Lord make us truly grateful,' Luella said fast and furious. 'And if you could send a little more of it our way,' she grumbled, 'we'd be grateful for that too. A-men.'

'A-men,' Buck and the boys sang as they dived into a bowl of boiled cabbage.

'The least you could do is sharpen the ax,' Luella said, picking up right where she'd left off.

Mashing a boiled potato, she touched some to her lip to check the temperature then held up a spoonful. Accustomed to Luella's poor aim, the baby's begging mouth bobbed to catch the spoon.

Luella always fed her family before she ate. The boys assumed she did this to leave her mouth free to complain through dinner. They never paid much mind that she stood at the stove and scraped the pot with her finger before she dropped it into the dishpan. They never noticed that she ate the leftovers off their plates. The boys ate without slowing down to taste it, thinking only of getting away from the table and their mother's constant carping.

Catching a glob of potato off the baby's chin, she shoved it back into his gaping mouth.

'Blasted wood cook stove!' Luella grumbled. 'I couldn't even stick my head in the oven if I wanted to!'

★ ★ ★

Friday night in Five Points was like Friday night in any other town. A single girl stared across the front car seat at her date and dreamed about being married. A married woman stared at her husband snoring on the couch and dreamed about being single.

Up on Dog Leg Hill, Pearl was dressed for company. A white satin dress poured over her body like cream, the bare back dropping to a rhinestone brooch that glittered in the firelight. Carrying a silver tray from the kitchen into her private parlor, she set it down on the bar.

Pearl's personal apartment was the first part of the house the boys finished. Double pocket doors in the front foyer opened into her parlor, which had originally been C. W. McCauley's office. The room was paneled in dark cherry, the fireplace outlined in black granite. It was minimally furnished, a large velvet sofa, a couple of winged-back chairs, and a poker table. Pearl had the boys add a bedroom, bath, walk-in closet and private entrance. The boys did an outstanding job, if Roy did say so himself. No one would ever guess Pearl's rooms were not part of the original floor plan.

Pearl lit the tapered candles on the mantel and stared at a photograph of her mother in a silver frame as she blew the match out. Lorna was a looker. Pearl had seen few who could top her. She'd caught Eddie staring at the photograph more than once. When a man walked into a room, Lorna was the first thing he saw. Pearl ran her finger around the frame, then turned Lorna face down on the mantel.

Dipping a silver knife into a mound of beluga caviar, Pearl spread a thick layer on a point of toast. Pausing to study the firm black orbs, she parted her lips and took a slow deliberate bite. Closing her eyes, she hummed as she chewed and sighed as she swallowed. She licked her lips lightly so as not to disturb her dark red lipstick.

A Russian diplomat from Saint Petersburg had introduced Pearl to the delicacy. He said watching her eat caviar was better than making love to his wife.

'Why did you marry her?' Pearl asked.

'A man marries the mother of his children,' he said casually, as he scraped caviar from Pearl's bare stomach and licked both sides of the knife. 'It is the sacrifice all responsible men make.'

Pearl flipped through her phonograph records and found the one she was looking for. Slipping the album from the cardboard sleeve, she slowly blew around the record, her breath fogging the vinyl. Placing the record on the spinning turntable, she carefully lowered the needle. The speaker crackled and popped before catching.

'*I ain't gonna play no second fiddle,*' Bessie

Smith sang, so angry and sure Pearl could taste the grit.

Finding Bessie's pulse, Pearl danced, shoulders rolling, hips swaying, slow and dirty. It had taken three years and ten thousand miles to learn to dance alone. Now, Pearl Wilde was a woman who didn't need a man to party.

9

Mason Hughes was a blue chip off his old man's block. His father, Hubert Hughes, had chiseled good looks, an inflexible backbone and the crisp air of a man with a mission. That mission was making money. The talent was built into his biology and required no conscious effort on his part. Hubert Hughes made money like a bee makes honey. If you had stripped him of everything, he still would have ended up rich. Hubert Hughes was all about making money, even when it came to his marriage.

It was inevitable that the Rudolphs, whose money came from manufacturing, and the Hughes, whose money came from money, would someday merge through matrimony. The fact that Olivia Rudolph worshipped Hubert made the arrangement all the more attractive.

While their families lived within skeet-shooting distance of each other, Hubert didn't get around to noticing Olivia until the Cotillion Ball in the autumn of '06. He would not have noticed her then if another man had not noticed her first. Hubert was not unaware of Olivia's assets. He simply preferred proven acquisitions.

'Tonight is the night,' Lawson Mitchell said, fortifying their punch with a flask from his inside pocket.

Lawson was Hubert's former classmate, friend by proximity and personal lawyer. Hubert had never been particularly interested in what Lawson had to say, but he had an instinctual need to better Lawson, which required he stay informed.

'The night for what?' Hubert asked absently.

'Olivia Rudolph.'

'Olivia Rudolph?'

At this, Hubert scanned the ballroom to take a fresh look. When his eyes finally landed on Olivia, she was already looking back at him.

Olivia was not Hubert's type. She was too eager. Her flirtation had all the subtlety of a cattle prod and she was old-money attractive — praying-mantis thin and neutered.

'What about her?' Hubert said into his glass.

'I'm going to ask her to marry me,' Lawson said, fingering the ring box in his pocket.

'Whatever for?'

'With Olivia on his side,' Lawson said, 'a man could do anything.'

It was Lawson's tone that caught Hubert. Lawson was utterly besotted with Olivia Rudolph. And Hubert knew he had to have her.

It did not take much for Hubert to lure Olivia out to the parking lot for a ride in his new roadster. 'I like to take her fast as she can go,' he'd said, pressing the warm key into her hand as Lawson waved his blessing.

They never came back. Lawson sat on the front steps of the country club in his tuxedo until sunrise. Then he walked out to the fourth hole, took Olivia's engagement ring out of his pocket, gritted his teeth and pitched it into the lake. Fortunately, the box floated long enough for him to take his shoes and socks off, roll up his trousers, and wade out to get it. Opening the box, he lifted his mother's engagement ring out and stared at it. For four years, he had imagined sliding the ring onto Olivia's finger. For four years, he had imagined the life they would make together. Lawson wept, not only for his loss, but for Olivia's. Hubert would never love her as he did. Wiping his face on the sleeve of his tux, he tucked the dripping box back into his breast pocket and slowly waded back to shore.

Lawson never spoke of the ordeal again.

Hubert was not the kind of man to waste time courting a woman. They eloped the same week he proposed, depriving Olivia of the wedding she had dreamed of planning all her life. She was too much in love to care.

With so much inbreeding among the rich, one would think they would be sterile as mules. But Olivia's ovaries held true to the rule that money makes money. She returned home from the honeymoon expectant and expecting and immediately threw herself into the art of homemaking. Olivia handled everything. All Hubert had to do was show up. And if he didn't show up, well, that was OK too.

Olivia was everything an ambitious man could want in a wife. She was attractive if not beautiful, impeccably proper, a tactful conversationalist, and a team player. She could entertain at the drop of a starched napkin. She served on every committee in town, could organize any event and was suitable for any occasion. Furthermore, while all the other men in Hubert's circle

92

constantly complained about their wives' constant complaining (nerves and female problems led their ailments), Olivia serviced all her own needs. She was, by any measure, maintenance-free. Hubert was the envy of his club.

Hubert was satisfied with Olivia, if not in love with her. Olivia was in love with Hubert, if not satisfied. It was a better marriage than most.

From Hubert's point of view, Olivia had only one intolerable habit. She regularly consulted with a clairvoyant.

Lady Laetitia was born in Martinique and refined in New Orleans. She was the product of a French rum trader and an island woman who marked her baby with chicken's blood before slipping the white lace christening gown over her head. The Lady's eyes were smoky topaz and her skin the color of rum. She wore caftans that dragged the floor and she covered her nappy red hair with silk turbans. In response to her clients' needs, her accent grew thicker by the day while her English diminished by the hour. Fortunately, the spirits she channeled had no problem understanding her.

Despite her affectations, the Lady was the real deal as clairvoyants go. Whenever her annoying neighbor developed a migraine headache that felt as if a nail were being driven into his temple, it usually was. The Lady's religion was a hodgepodge of Santería, voodoo and orthodox Catholicism. One group sacrificed saints, the other chickens. It was not that great a leap of faith for her.

Hubert could not fathom why a woman as

grounded and level-headed as Olivia would waste time and money on such irrational rubbish. 'Why,' he demanded, 'can't you just go to church on Easter and Christmas like the rest of your friends?'

But Lady Laetitia had been right too many times for Olivia to ignore. The spiritualist told Olivia she would marry Hubert. And she told her she would return from her honeymoon pregnant. She had also warned Olivia, in so many obscure words, that the stock market was going to crash. And so, while Hubert lost almost everything except his conceit on Black Friday, Olivia's fortune never faltered.

Despite all the evidence, Hubert refused to believe Lady Laetitia was anything but a sham — even as Olivia wrote out the check that allowed him to rebuild his fortune.

Olivia had a standing appointment with Lady Laetitia on Fridays. She was never late. Most weeks she arrived early. Olivia had an urgent need to know what was ahead of her — even though, by the time her future arrived, she was already bored with it. Lady Laetitia's apartment building was an uneasy place for a woman like Olivia. Colored men, needle thin musicians who played the clubs, their collars open and eyes half-moons on dark faces, grinned at Olivia as she passed them in the foyer. They looked at her in a way no man in her part of the world would feel free to do. When the maid, who did not speak English but understood it perfectly, finally opened the door, Olivia's face was always flushed, but not always from embarrassment.

'I'm early,' Olivia said, as the maid led her down the dark hall to the parlor, where her tea was already waiting for her.

Lady Laetitia's apartment was just the sort of place a spiritualist should dwell, small, dark and exotically cluttered. But then spirits take up very little space. The furnishings were too large for the room, couches like beds and plush wool rugs stained with spilled drinks and other unidentifiable fluids. The paintings and sculptures were expensively avant-garde, and Olivia suspected obscene. But she was too naïve to be sure and too insecure to ask. The curtains were always pulled, holding the room in perpetual midnight. Olivia lost all sense of time and place in the room. Her heart always sank when she stepped outside onto the sidewalk and found the sun shining and the world just as she had left it.

Olivia sat perfectly still on the couch as the maid lit candles around the room and the Lady readied herself. Eyes closed, Lady Laetitia swayed hypnotically back and forth, a deep drone vibrating in her throat. Olivia never failed to effervesce at that moment, every cell sparking with expectation. She sank small and boneless into the deep overstuffed couch as a sense of euphoria slipped warmly and lightly over her like a scarf. She gave into this as if falling into the arms of a dangerous lover. It was the only daring in Olivia's life of secure sameness. The risk she took being there gave her absolution. That and the drop of laudanum Lady Laetitia put on her sugar cubes.

The parlor air was sweet and heavy with the

smell of Lady Laetitia's perfume and the underlying hint of opium left over from the night before. Along with the otherworld, Lady Laetitia was well acquainted with the underworld. In her mind, they were not so different.

Opening the carved wooden box on the coffee table, Lady Laetitia carefully lifted the fertile chicken's egg and held it flat in her palm.

'Dear God,' Olivia sighed, as she reached to touch the shell, 'I wish *something* would happen.'

Lady Laetitia jerked the egg back, but it was too late. Olivia's fingertips had grazed the brown shell. The Lady could already feel the future shifting. The spiritualist's eyes grew dark at all the foolish rich women who came to her, with no color in their lives and no common sense.

'*For the bird to fly,*' the spiritualist said, tapping the egg on the side of the shallow copper bowl, '*the egg must crack.*'

She spilled the bloody embryo into the bowl and stirred it with her long brown finger.

'What do you see?' Olivia demanded, staring down into the bowl with pupils drawn to pinpoints.

'You will take a journey soon . . . short in distance . . . remote in every other way.'

'Really!' Olivia's face lit up at the prospect of change, her blurred mind already planning what she would pack.

Lady Laetitia continued to lean over the bowl memorizing the quickly fading images of

Olivia's future, most of which she would never tell her. Olivia preferred her fortunes bullish. Women like Olivia seldom got what they wanted in life, but they always got what they asked for.

10

When Mason announced that he intended to move to Five Points, his father's whiskey tumbler paused in midair.

'Move to Five Points?' Hubert stared at his son expressionless. 'What on earth for?'

Lighting a cigarette, Mason fell back in his chair.

'I've decided to take a more active role in managing the shirt factory.'

'But you've never even set foot in the place,' Olivia said incredulously from the couch.

'I was there just yesterday.'

'But the factory has managed itself for years,' Olivia insisted to Hubert.

'And it's beginning to show,' Mason cut her short.

Pulling the stopper from a crystal decanter, Hubert poured another whiskey. Alcohol was illegal in the state. But there was no threat of police bursting into the Hughes mansion. Hubert's money helped put the mayor and the governor into office. Men who make the laws, or pay to have them made, always live above them.

'You were at the factory yesterday?' Hubert asked casually.

'Stopped by on my way back from Lexington,' Mason answered just as incidentally.

Hubert hid his satisfaction at this news. Getting Mason's attention had always been the problem.

'What did you have in mind?'

'Nothing definite, just yet,' Mason said, in a way that implied just the opposite.

Hubert stared at the whiskey swirling in his glass. He was intrigued. He knew his son. Whatever Mason had in mind for the old factory would be entertaining and profitable. Like himself, Mason was all about making money. Hubert rolled the proposal around and could find nothing wrong with it. The shirt factory was a drop in the Hughes's fortune. If Mason spilled it, their net worth would never miss it.

Since the factory was Olivia's inheritance, common courtesy would have suggested Hubert allow her some input into the decision-making. But Olivia held the same position in the Hughes boardroom as the Hughes bedroom — silent partner.

'The factory is yours,' Hubert said, into his glass. 'Do whatever you want.'

'Then it's settled,' Mason said, grinding his cigarette out.

Pushing out of the chair, Mason left the room. Olivia watched him take the stairs two at a time through the double living-room doors, something he hadn't done since he was a boy. She was intrigued. Olivia knew her son. She knew that whatever Mason had in mind, his moving to Five Points was not entirely about business.

★   ★   ★

'May I come in?' Olivia asked, pushing her son's door open with her fingertips.

A hyperactive dust mop followed Olivia into Mason's room, yapping and hopping, his painted toenails clicking on the wood floor like castanets. Mason rolled an annoyed glare at the Pomeranian as Olivia lovingly shooed the barking ball of belly-button lint out of the bedroom.

'There, there, darling,' she cooed, as she closed the door between them, 'Mother will be right out.'

She turned to find Mason staring at her.

'Mother?' he said, only half amused.

'I hate for the title to go to waste,' Olivia replied dryly.

Dropping a folded shirt into his suitcase, Mason returned to packing. He neatly tucked and stacked with the concentration and precision of a surgeon. His friends would have been surprised to see this side of him. Mason had the deserved reputation of a bored and impassive playboy. But the truth was that he had always been intense, even as a child. When Olivia was nursing him, he had stared up at her, his tiny forehead creased as though he had serious doubts she knew what the hell she was doing.

Grabbing his horsehair brush from the dresser, he dropped it into his shaving kit. He was packing just enough to get by until the rest of his things could be delivered. Olivia doubted he would take anything personal. There was barely anything personal in the bedroom he'd occupied for twenty-six years. Mason kept an apartment in town, where she suspected her real son lived, and where she had never been invited.

Olivia wandered around the room, lifting a

100

book off the nightstand, fluffing a pillow on the bed, in lieu of doing what she really wanted to do, which was to hold her only child, kiss his face and smooth his hair. Mason had denied her a child's affection, just like his father had denied her a man's. Deprived of any warmth from the men in her life, Olivia had switched species. And, for the most part, she found dogs and mink coats to be a surprisingly adequate substitute for men.

'Is it a woman?' Olivia asked, as she rolled a pair of his socks.

Mason blurted out a laugh. And Olivia knew she'd hit the nail on the head.

Taking the socks from her, Mason shoved them into his suitcase. On those rare occasions when his mother showed some insight into him, it threw him completely off balance. Like his father, Mason believed Olivia was mostly ornamental.

'She must be very special,' she said.

'Not really.'

'Then, she must be very unattainable.'

'So much so, I fear she is a figment of my imagination.'

Here's the way it was with her son. If Mason were the hunter and females the game, women would have tied themselves to the hood of his car, thrown themselves on the floor for him to walk on, or gladly mounted themselves on the wall in order to be his trophy. But the easier the conquest, the quicker he grew bored. There wasn't enough wall space in Olivia's house to accommodate all the heads that had been lost over her son.

'Where will you be staying?'

'The old house, of course.'

'It's haunted, you know.'

'Haunted. For chrissake.'

Like his father, Mason found his mother's attraction to the ethereal annoying as hell.

'What's her name?' Olivia said to change the subject.

'Kat,' he said. 'Kathryn Wilde.'

Olivia lifted her eyebrows. She was surprised he answered. As a rule, he never mentioned a woman except in past tense.

'Wilde,' she said slowly, trying to trace the heritage.

'She works at the factory.'

He waited for Olivia's reaction. Her passive expression never changed, but he had no doubt her mind was racing. Like most of the women in her circle, Olivia was a social idealist. She fully supported the right of workers to unionize, just not in her gene pool.

From Olivia's point of view the math of mating was simple. When two people of equal social status marry, their stock goes up. When a woman marries beneath herself, her stock falls while the man's rises, but usually less than he had counted on. But when a man marries beneath himself, the outcome is unpredictable. One simply cannot foresee if the woman will rise to the occasion or fall flat. The only sure thing is that a great many people will try to trip her up.

Mason never slummed. Olivia suspected this factory worker was little more than a dalliance. But there is a window of opportunity in every man's life when just about anything with two legs and a cleavage can climb through. Mason was skirting thirty. Most of his friends were engaged or married. Many had children. A few already divorced. Mason didn't seem to mind living outside his social pack, but he could only buck the system for so long. It was a mother's job to be the voice of reason when her son's hormones raged. Still, Olivia knew the worst thing she could do was try to dissuade him.

'Oh, darling,' Olivia said light as froth, 'it's your father's reaction you should worry about. As far as I'm concerned, you can marry the maid.'

Mason laughed lewdly at her unknowing insight. He had no doubt what Hubert's reaction would be to Kat Wilde. The last thing he needed was competition.

Her son had never looked more like his father than at that moment. Olivia couldn't help but touch his face. And Mason couldn't help but shrug away. He searched his room to see if he had forgotten anything. Lowering the lid on the case, he snapped the clasps closed.

'I'm going to miss you,' she admitted.

'Oh, Livvy, it's less than an hour away.'

Short in distance, Olivia thought. Remote in every other way.

11

Mason Hughes shifted the roadster into fly and left civilization, as he knew it, behind. For a poor boy hitching a ride, Five Points was just a hop, skip, and a jump from Nashville. For a rich society boy, it was a long evolutionary tumble down the wrong family tree.

The highway snaked alongside the roaring Cumberland River, brick red from March rains and bleeding into the bottoms. Wet-weather waterfalls spilled from the bluffs and redbuds and dogwoods blurred by like a smeared watercolor painting. The midday sky had been clear when he left Nashville. But up ahead, dark clouds churned over the hills like ominous smoke. Mason saw none of it. Jaw set and leather driving gloves gripping the steering wheel, he forced the pedal to the floor. Another man might have been stirred by the day and the drive, and the possibility of what lay ahead. The only thing on Mason Hughes's mind was Kat Wilde.

Mason's hair blew straight back from his determined face. His ears were numb and his fingers stiff. It was too early in the year to ride with the top down, but he had it down anyway — not for hope of better weather, but more as a test. He had played football in college instead of tennis, which he preferred, for the same reason. Unlike his teammates, getting the wind knocked out of him and his face rubbed in the dirt was his motive for the game. Having a life free of discomfort, he felt the need to self-impose a little punishment from time to time, as if a wind-burned face and a bruise here and there compensated for his feather-bed existence.

The roadster cut through a cold patch of fog, briefly outrunning the whine of the motor and blinding Mason. He never slowed. A mile outside of Five Points, he was finally forced to downshift to a crawl behind an old farm truck, smoke choking from the corroded tailpipe and rust eating through the fenders. The ten-year-old boy sitting on a milk crate in the bed was scrubbed clean for his Saturday trip to town. His shirt was ironed and his overalls mended neat as a doctor's stitches. He carried a fresh brown hen egg in his front overall pocket that he intended to trade for a pack of chewing gum. It was a glorious day for Bucky Darnell, Jr and the sight of Mason's fancy roadster sent his hopes over the top.

Mason was too busy checking his watch to see the boy smiling and waving. He was timing the trip, and efficiency took precedence over niceties. Hammering the horn, he slammed his foot on the gas pedal and didn't let up as he passed. Bucky's granddaddy wasn't used to fast men in fast cars and the situation spooked him like a horse. Cutting sharp to the shoulder, the old truck dipped toward the ditch, slinging Bucky against the side of the bed. He looked up just as the crate was coming down. It smashed into his face, busting his lip and the fresh brown egg. Mason flew past, engine whining, oblivious to the cold damp spot the boy now carried over his heart.

Something happens to people when they migrate to the city. Something is lost. A man who hunts for food at a grocery store and reads the next day's weather forecast in the newspaper instead of studying the moon grows docile and dependent as a lapdog. His natural instincts fade and become dull.

Hill people, on the other hand, remain somewhat wild. They can sense the nature of a man like a wolf catches the scent of a rabbit. Even before Mason Hughes climbed out of his fancy car, the boys loitering on the front porch of Green's General Store picked up his scent, and their mouths began to water. They knew they had a live one.

'Mighty fine car you got there,' Inky Mott said, wiping his hands on a rag as he admired the roadster.

Inky minded the gas pumps at the General Store on Saturdays. In exchange, he got a pound of bologna, a box of saltines, a tank of gas and — every time he rang up a customer — the best view in town up the widow's skirt. Gladys Green had some fine-looking legs on her. And she knew it. She spent a large part of her day halfway up the grocery ladder, straightening, organizing and stretching for canned goods, one long, lean gam held out behind her, toe pointed like a ballerina. The position had served her well. It was how she snagged her deceased husband and most likely what killed him. She'd practiced the position so long she could crack walnuts with those legs.

Widowhood was a role Gladys had been born to play. She wore a gold filigree locket around her neck, the tiny faded photograph of her late husband swinging like a pendulum between her dewy breasts. Within five minutes of meeting a man, she confessed with sorrowful candor that she was all alone in that big white paid-for free-and-clear house behind the store but — sigh — she would not be marrying again. It drew suitors like honey.

Inky's part-time job was the envy of every man in Five Points and he had to guard his turf like a junkyard dog.

'Just fill her up,' Mason said, as he climbed out of the roadster.

And that was all he said, which in the minds of the boys hanging out on the porch was worse than saying nothing at all. It was an insult, plain and simple. A man of few words is thoughtful. An abrupt man is an asshole.

Mason tried to hide any sign of being half frozen as he stiffly climbed the steps in his long white driving coat. Pulling off his driving gloves a frozen finger at a time, he surveyed the weathered chairs and decided to stand.

'Morning,' he said.

Woody and Dickie Deason lifted their chins. They had wandered across the square to watch Inky work for the day. Lately, Bud had been working them to death at the hardware store and they needed a breather.

Hands clasped behind him, Mason took in his surroundings, such as they were. A coon dog, sprawled on the porch like a speckled mud puddle, eyed him without affection, the fur on his back twitching from time to time to discourage a horsefly. A red Coca-Cola clock ticked away the day on the weathered silver, gray board-and-batten wall, and a mustard yellow Shell gasoline sign, laced with bullet holes like a slice of Swiss cheese, swayed in the wind on a rusty pole. Through the sooty store window, Mason could see Gladys Green dusting shelves on the rolling ladder, one leg extended in a perfect arabesque. When Mason's eyes landed on the Christian Temperance meeting poster tacked to the wall, he read it out loud.

'That's Miss Annabelle Boyd's doin',' Woody informed him, the brim of his hat tipped down and his feet kicked up. 'Founding chairwoman of the Five Points Christian Women's Temperance Society.'

Mason sensed by Woody's tone that Miss Annabelle Boyd was not the most popular woman on the porch.

'Seems ironic that the most fervent disciple of abstinence is a woman so ugly a man would have to be three sheets in the wind to kiss her,' Dickie said.

'Prohibition put the nails in that old maid's coffin,' Woody agreed.

'Some folks can't stand to see other folks happy. Next thing you know they'll be outlawing . . . tobacco!'

'It's damned un-American,' Woody said, taking a drag off his cigarette like it might be his last.

There was a pause in the conversation and

Mason decided to cut in.

'Prohibition,' he said casually. 'A man's either for it or against it.'

Dickie leaned over and neatly spit a squirt of chew over the rail into a dying yellow yew.

'Or too weak willied to vote his mind.'

'Hope them state legislators drown facedown in their holier-than-thou-piss,' Woody added, exhaling a white plume then inhaling her back in.

Having established he was among — if not friends — men of like minds, Mason got to the point.

'My name is — '

'Know who you are.'

'I'm moving into — '

'Already heard.'

Mason shifted his weight.

'Should a man be in the mood to quench his thirst with something stronger than spring water, who would you suggest he talk to?'

If Mason Hughes had been on fire, the boys would not have pissed on him to put him out. But just because you oppose one man's temperament doesn't mean you should impede another man's commerce. Especially Cavanagh Whiskey commerce.

'Gladys Green's the woman you should talk to.' Woody threw a thumb back over his shoulder toward the door of the general store.

'I sincerely appreciate the information,' Mason said, backing off the porch.

Woody and Dickie rolled their eyes at each other. They *sincerely* doubted Mason Hughes had a *sincere* bone in his body.

Mason was paying Inky for his gas when the Darnell truck rattled up. Bucky Jr jumped out of the bed before it rolled to a stop and stormed up to Mason, scrubbed face burning and hands balled into tiny fists.

'You broke my egg,' Bucky yelled, lip bloody and swollen, 'and, by God, you're gonna pay for it!'

Mason scowled down at the little piss ant. He didn't know what in the hell the boy was talking about.

'You and that fancy car of yours drove my granddaddy off the road!'

Mason followed the boy's pointing finger to the old farm truck and vaguely remembered the old truck's dragging muffler. Then he looked down at the boy. His thin arms were covered with chigger bites and his hair looked as if it'd been cut with pinking shears by a half-blind barber — which it had. Under normal circumstances he would have swatted the kid like a gnat, but Mason had a soft spot for spunk.

'If a cow ran you off the road, would the cow have to pay for your egg?'

'If a cow ran me off the road, I'd shoot the durn cow!'

Mason struggled to keep a straight face.

'Well then,' he said, reaching into his pocket, 'I guess I'm getting off easy.'

He dropped a handful of change into the boy's blistered palm. Staring down at all that money, Bucky bit his lip, wrestling with his most difficult moral dilemma to date.

110

'I only want what's coming to me,' he finally said, picking a dime and a nickel out and handing the rest back. 'I ain't askin' for charity.'

'It wasn't charity.' Mason dropped the change back in his pocket. 'I just didn't know what the going price for an egg was around these parts.'

It was a nickel. Bucky took the dime for damages.

'Are we straight?' Mason asked, holding out his hand.

The boy's fists were still bunched and his eyes still blazed. There is nothing in the world harder to give up than a good strong hate. It gets the blood boiling and gives a man purpose and direction. Bucky's head had been spinning with the payback he planned for Mr Mason Hughes all the way to the store — letting the air out of his tires, putting a cow patty on the radiator of his fancy car, soaping his windows. Of course, he and his pals probably would have done these things even if Mason hadn't broken his egg, but vandalism was far more satisfying when revenge was involved.

'Yeah,' Bucky grumbled, slapping his hand in Mason's. 'We're straight.'

As much as he would have enjoyed a good long-term feud with Mason, Bucky figured he'd better forgive him, seeing as how he'd stolen the egg from Joy Lester's henhouse in the first place.

A truce having been made, Bucky went inside the general store to buy his chewing gum.

Slipping a piece of paper out of the inside pocket of his coat, Mason handed it to Inky.

'How do I get here?'

'Wild Lane,' Inky read, squinting down at the address Crockett had scrawled on the paper. 'You sure you got the right address?'

Inky naturally assumed a man like Mason would be looking for Pearl's place.

'Positive,' Mason said.

'Well, sir, you're gonna go all the way round the square.' Inky pointed the way with a greasy finger. 'Then you're gonna take the second right at Bud Mangrum's Hardware. That'll be Gracie Avenue. Ride her to the end and down the hill. Right 'fore you drive off the bank and drop into the river, there's a dirt road cuts to the left. Not much more than a cow path. Wouldn't take her down it though,' he said, nodding at the roadster. 'Road goes right through Lick Creek. Water's high and mighty this time of year.'

Mason was swinging open the car door when Inky added, 'Kat Wilde's house is the little log cabin at the end. You can't miss it.'

'I never said I was looking for Kat Wilde's house.'

'Only house on Wild Lane.'

'The address is Two Wild Lane,' Mason said, checking the slip of paper.

'Number 1 was Kat's mama's place, Lorna Wilde. Washed away in the big flood.'

'Good Lord. What happened to her?'

'Ran off with Annabelle Boyd's fiancé.'

'And how did Annabelle Boyd feel about that?' Mason asked, swinging open the car door.

'Still sharpening the ax,' Inky said, backing away from the car.

Mason dropped into his seat only to arch his

back up. Reaching underneath his white riding coat, he scooped up a handful of dripping egg shell. Woody and Dickie grinned as he slung it to the ground and wiped his hands and coat tail with the clean shop cloth Inky handed him. Spreading a newspaper over the wet spot on the leather seat, Mason slid in and started the car. Shifting it into gear, he pulled toward the street.

'Watch out for Kat's dog! He'll take yer durn leg off!' Inky called out, rubbing his leg as he said it.

★ ★ ★

Wild Lane was appropriately named. Mason would have driven right past if he hadn't spotted the NO TRESSPASSING sign nailed to a tree at the entrance. Pulling his car off the road, he climbed out and started walking.

Jumping over ruts and rivulets, he followed the muddy path down toward the sound of roaring water. Tree branches laced overhead creating a dark natural tunnel. The air was fresh and crisp. Mason's stride lengthened, his riding coat flapping open and his arms swinging freely. In the city his breath was always checked by the possibility of noxious odors, car exhaust, sewage, and industrial fumes, the toxic smells of man at his worst. But here in the woods, Mason's breathing was deep, liberated and hungry.

The path ran into the creek, roaring, foaming and chewing away at the bank. He spotted the old cabin on the opposite bank tucked in the trees as if it were growing there. The logs were

113

black as charred whiskey barrels and Virginia Creeper grew up the stone chimney. A springhouse had been carved in the hillside behind the cabin. Ice-cold spring water gushed out of a hollow wooden pipe and spilled into a stone trough beside the ancient door. Except for glass wind chimes clinking softly on the porch, the place looked more like a fox's den than a house.

Seeing the cabin put the situation in perspective. Mason had no illusions that he and Kat would have anything in common. How could they? But then he wasn't there for intellectual pillaging. This foray was purely carnal.

The only way across the creek was a precarious old wooden footbridge. Water sprayed and splashed over the rotting mossy slats, keeping them slick as slime. Several of the boards had burst through, the rest hung on rusty nails. Mason studied the distance between the bridge and the creek, assessing the situation. It was a fall that would do some damage. And the pay-off waiting on the other side was uncertain. If this had been a business venture, Mason would have backed away. He never bet his kidneys.

The snap of a twig caused his head to jerk toward the woods. Searching, he saw no one. And so he returned to the problem at hand.

Raking his fingers through his hair, he grabbed the rusty metal cable, set his jaw, and took a cautious step. The old bridge groaned and swayed under his weight. Eyes straight ahead, he

114

inched tensely across. Halfway, he suddenly stopped. Mason looked down at the icy water. Spray misted his face and wilted his starched shirt. The rocks below had been polished smooth by the rushing water. Mason took a deep breath. His expression calmed, his posture straightened and his hand loosened on the cable. He walked the rest of the bridge without looking down.

Jumping to safety on the opposite bank, Mason let out a breath only to suck it back in. Glaring at him was a red-eyed hound from hell, one ear chewed off, most of the hair missing from his back and the scruff of his neck laced with white jagged scars.

'His name is Satan.'

Kat leaned against a tree watching him. He had no doubt she'd been there all along. Her cheeks were flushed from the crisp holler air and her dark unruly hair whipped around her face. She wore rolled jeans and a shirt tied at her waist. Mason had arrogantly assumed she'd be embarrassed by her humble circumstances. That showing up unannounced might even put him at an advantage. He was wrong. Kat watched him with cool confidence. He was on her territory now.

'What happened to him?' Mason asked, eyes fixed on the huge mangled beast.

'They used to fight him. He was half dead when they dumped him at the end of the road.'

'I'd like to see the animal that did that to him.'

'You'd have to beat the buzzards off to do it.'

Kat patted her leg and the old fighter trotted to her side. Digging her fingers into his musky fur, she scratched him behind his one good ear. Satan leaned against her leg possessively, giving Mason a dead glare. Mason looked from the dog to Kat. He wasn't sure which of them posed the greater threat.

'I just happened to be in the neighborhood,' he said, hands shoved deep in his pockets. 'Thought I'd drop by for a visit.'

He waited for her to invite him to sit on the porch. Country people would extend that much courtesy to a mortal enemy. Kat simply stared at him.

'Is this a bad time?' he finally asked.

'Yes.'

'Then why didn't you stop me before I crossed the damn bridge?'

'We never thought you'd make it.'

Mason weighed his next move like a trout fisherman deliberating which fly to tie on his line. He was a civilized man who had never hunted anything but civilized women. Most of the society girls he reeled in tended to lie there like dead fish. It wasn't so much an act of catching them, as resuscitating them once they'd fallen into the sack. Mason had absolutely no idea what to do with a woman with a little fight in her.

'I'm moving to my great-uncle's old house,' he finally said. 'It could use a woman's touch.'

Most women would have swallowed this bait hook, line, and custom-made sofa. Not having a domesticated bone in her body, Kat crossed her arms. She wasn't biting.

116

Annoyed, Mason tapped his foot unconsciously. He knew women. He knew Kat was not playing hard to get. Something was killing the deal. He just didn't have a clue what it was.

'Is someone here?' he demanded, throwing a look toward her house.

'No.'

'Then why can't I come in?'

'I have to work.'

'It's Saturday.'

'Only to those who don't have rent to pay.'

'I can help,' he said with complete authority.

All men have some percentage of bullshit in them. They stretch what they know, what they've done and what they can do like adding soda to whiskey. How much a woman can stomach depends on her taste and her level of desperation. Kat was not desperate. She took her men straight up, although during moments of weakness she had been known to partake at any angle.

But Mason was not exaggerating. When it came to business, he knew what he was doing. It was built into his biology. And something about that drove straight to Kat's core. Mason was staring at her, honestly intrigued by what she was working on. For the first time, she dropped her eyes from his. It was the first spark of interest Mason had seen in Kat and he quickly fanned it.

'Show me what you're working on,' he said, taking a step toward her. 'Two heads are always better than one.'

For a second, she seemed to consider his offer. Biting her lip, she studied the ground.

'No,' she finally said, shaking her head. 'This isn't going to happen. For the sake of efficiency, just go away.'

Mason's eyes widened. 'For the sake of efficiency?' Hearing the word 'efficiency' coming out of a woman's mouth shocked the devil out of him. In his vocabulary 'efficiency' was the greatest reward for the least amount of effort. It had been his experience that a woman was anything but. He assumed her use of the word was either a fluke or an attempt to impress him. And he took the advantage.

'You're afraid I'll break your heart,' he half teased, half challenged.

Kat's eyes rose to meet his and held. 'Trust me. I'm not the one in danger of that.'

Bending down, she whispered into the dog's ear. Eyes fixed on Mason, Satan listened with grave intensity. Without so much as a goodbye or a good riddance, Kat turned and headed toward her cabin. When Mason tried to follow, Satan lunged for him, teeth bared and froth foaming from his mouth.

Jumping back, Mason took off. Snarling and snapping at his heels, Satan did not stop charging until they reached the creek. This time Mason did not hesitate as he jumped onto the bridge.

Kat slowed her pace as she strode toward the cabin. At the foot of the porch, she paused. When she took a quick glance back over her shoulder to make sure Mason made it safely across the bridge, a glowing red cigarette butt in the woods dropped to the ground. The look on

118

Kat's face as her eyes followed Mason up the path said it all. Kat always flirted with the man she didn't give a flip about and cold-shouldered the man she really wanted. She had treated Bourne Cavanagh as if she were going to spit on him. Right up to the day she licked him from head to toe.

Pushing off the tree, Pearl headed back to Dog Leg Hill. She had the information she'd come looking for.

12

Mason followed the stacked stone fence that bordered the road for nearly two miles before turning the roadster into the main entrance of the old plantation. It was another half mile up a tree-lined drive to the big house. Most visitors felt a chill run over their skin when Devil's Eye came into view, as if a ghost had stepped over their grave. Some thought it was the way the cut-stone lintels hooded the sunken windows, or the way shadows seemed to lash the limestone walls like whip marks. Regardless, one couldn't shake the notion that the dark iron-clad front door opened straight into hell.

Legend had it that when Yankee soldiers marched up the drive, they found the place deserted — not a man, woman or child. Even the stalls in the barns and the chicken coop were empty. The air was deathly quiet. No birds or insects made a sound.

The young lieutenant in charge took one look at Devil's Eye and ordered his men to burn it to the ground. His soldiers did not have to be coaxed into destruction. They stacked furniture and books head-high in the foyer and doused the pile with kerosene. But every time a match was struck, it went out. Cursing the private's incompetence, Lieutenant O'Malley grabbed a kerosene lamp himself and smashed it on the oak floor. Wood that is soaked in kerosene will burn floating on water, but this flame flickered and snuffed itself out.

A slave appeared at the top of the stairs, a beautiful child-woman, her black face powdered ghostly white. She was dressed in an old wedding gown that hung off her bare shoulder, the silk yellowed and the lace hoop skirt tattered like a torn spider's web.

'What's your name?' O'Malley called up.

She looked down at him, chin high and haughty.

'I be the Black Fidela,' she told him.

The soldiers snickered. Then they licked their lips. During their time in the south, a few of O'Malley's men had developed a taste for dark women. The soldiers took their time climbing the stairs. Where was she going to run? But the slave made no attempt to escape.

'The Devil's blowin' it out, the Devil's blowin' it out,' she singsonged, the words crawling up their skin like spiders. It was the way her black eyes fixed on them that made the soldiers hesitate. *'The Devil's blowin' it out,'* she whispered, in a voice that would haunt them to the grave.

The soldiers stopped. Hands on their sabers, they backed down the stairs. But it wasn't flesh and blood they feared. They abandoned the wagon of loot they'd scavenged and mounted their horses. O'Malley said a frantic prayer as they galloped full-speed down the tree-lined drive. 'God protect us,' he prayed.

Hubert's inclination was still to burn Devil's Eye to the ground. But Olivia wouldn't hear of it. She had spent her summers there as a child and still used it as a getaway several times a year. Otherwise, the housekeeper governed. Hubert refused to set foot in the architectural miscreation and Mason had never found a reason to spend more than a weekend in the place. But as his car whined along the drive, he slowly took possession.

The grounds were surprisingly well-maintained. The pastures were groomed, the fences cleared and the barns freshly painted. With cattle and tobacco, the place was still self-supporting and even turned a small profit.

Mason envisioned Tennessee Walking Horses grazing in the pasture, a swimming pool off the back of the house and a tennis court beside the garage. As he swung the car around the circular drive in front of the main house, he imagined children, two maybe three, running down the steps to meet him and a wife waving from the doorway. Mason tried the dream on as if slipping into a jacket to see how it fit. And it fit comfortably. On a lark, he slipped Kat Wilde into the picture and the dream immediately stalled.

Climbing out of the car, Mason reached his arms up and stretched. He was leaning into the trunk for his bags when the shadow passed over the car. Looking up, he ducked just as the black blur skimmed his face. Hissing and cawing, the crow glided in for a landing on the front-door transom. Pacing back and forth, the creature screamed at him as though cursing.

'A damn black bird nearly took my eye out!'

Mason was still brushing the feel of the crow

122

out of his hair when the housekeeper stepped aside to let him pass.

'Crow means change or death is in the air.'

'Change it is,' Mason said, handing her his coat.

Mrs Sadie LaRue's voice was a slow dirge played on a musical saw. She was small and dark with walnut stained skin, fierce eyes and oil-black hair braided and coiled like a chicken snake at the nape of her neck. She had never read a book in her life, including the one she lived by. Her apocalyptic gloom was buoyed only by her inconceivable air of superiority. She had no doubt her way was the only way. Hanging on her sinewy neck was a wooden cross large enough to crucify a small child.

'Is it always so cold in here?' he asked. 'I can practically see my breath.'

'You plan to complain all the time?' she snapped, eyes flashing.

Her belligerence caught him off guard. Mason simply stared at her. He was so taken aback, it left him speechless. No one had ever used that tone with him, certainly not an employee.

'I'd like my breakfast at nine,' he said firmly.

It was best to establish right off who was boss.

''Morrow's the Lord's day. Don't cook on the Lord's day.'

Picking up his suitcase, the old woman started up the curving staircase. Mason half expected her to caw, flap her arms and fly to the second floor. As soon as she was out of sight, he went straight to the study and found a phone.

'This is Operator Annabelle Boyd,' Annabelle answered.

Mason hesitated when he heard the name. Prohibition may have put nails in the old maid's coffin, but it obviously had not buried her.

'Devil got your tongue?' Annabelle finally asked.

'This is — '

'Know who you are.'

'Yes, well, I'd like to place a call to Lawson Mitchell in Nashville. The number is . . . '

Mason barely finished saying the last number before he heard ringing.

'Lawson,' Mason said into the phone, 'I'm calling from Devil's Eye.'

'Mason.' Lawson Mitchell was accustomed to his clients not identifying themselves. 'What can I do for you?'

Glancing up the stairs, Mason pulled the sliding doors to the study closed.

'The housekeeper here . . . '

'Mrs LaRue.'

'Fire her.'

'I can't.'

'What do you mean, you can't?'

'She doesn't work for you.'

'What do you mean she doesn't work for us?'

'It's clearly specified in your great-uncle's will that she has the job for as long as she wants it.'

'That's the craziest thing I've ever heard of,' Mason huffed indignantly.

'Mrs LaRue is paid out of a trust fund that was left on her behalf. Her grandmother and mother . . . ' Lawson cleared his throat, ' . . . worked for your uncle.'

This was a polite way of saying Sadie's mother

124

and grandmother had been Cyril's slaves. Lawson knew this because his father had written the will. There was a long pause on Mason's end while he absorbed this. Lawson took the opportunity to pour cream in his coffee.

'Is someone knocking on your door?' Lawson finally asked.

Mason forced his foot to stop tapping.

'Continue to pay her, if we have to,' Mason decided. 'But I want her out.'

'I wouldn't be so hasty. She runs the place and does a damn good job of it. It would take three employees to replace her. Besides, it's almost impossible to get help to stay at Devil's Eye.'

'For God's sake, there's a depression going on! A hundred women would kill for the job. Find a replacement and send the old bat packing.'

'I'll see what I can do.'

It didn't bother Lawson a bit that rich men paid him for advice they refused to take. Of course, he had no intention of wasting his time looking for a new housekeeper. He had no doubt Mason would quickly find he could not live without Mrs LaRue. At which point, Lawson would politely forget this conversation ever took place.

Hand fidgeting with the car keys in his pocket, Mason stared out the window. The lawn was so perfectly groomed it looked like a painting.

'By the way,' Mason finally said, 'I want you to find out who owns the land off Gracie Avenue near the river on Wild Lane.'

Mason was a wealthy man. When he wanted a car, he went shopping. He saw no reason why he should not do the same with women.

'And once I find out?'

'Buy it.'

'Whatever for?'

'No reason.'

It had been Lawson's experience that there was always a reason, but he let it pass.

'How's Devil's Eye, otherwise?' Lawson asked, taking a sip of coffee.

'Just got here.' Mason glanced around the study. He could see Olivia's touches, a vase here, a throw pillow there. Otherwise, the place looked much the same as the day Cyril Rudolph walked the halls. Reaching up, Mason ran his finger along the walnut bookshelf and checked it for dust. There wasn't a speck.

'How's your mother?' Lawson asked so vaguely, Mason's head cocked.

'Fine. Why do you ask?'

'No reason.'

It had been Mason's experience that there was always a reason, but he let it pass.

'Well, then . . . '

Business conducted, Mason said an abrupt goodbye. He didn't bother to hang up the phone. Tapping the receiver several times, he got Annabelle Boyd back on the line and asked her to place another call.

'Mason?' Olivia said, shocked to be getting a call from her son. 'Are you alright?'

'Of course I'm alright. How could I call you if I weren't?'

'Then obviously you must need something,' she said.

126

Hearing her kissing her Pomeranian's nose, Mason rolled his eyes.

'Well,' Olivia said dryly, with a mother's sixth sense.

'I'm freezing to death up here. Call the furnace man and have him come take a look at the place.'

'They have repairmen in Five Points.'

'I want it done right.'

'How did you get to be such a horrible snob?'

'By example would be my guess.'

'Well, don't put on airs with Sadie.'

'Sadie?'

'Mrs LaRue. The housekeeper. She's a dear friend. We played together as children. If you do anything to insult her . . . '

Mason was amused to hear Sadie LaRue had ever been a child. He assumed she'd gone straight from ovum to full-grown shrew. He wasn't surprised his mother counted her as a friend. Olivia collected eccentrics like normal women collected china eggs.

'She's morbid,' Mason said darkly.

He said it as though morbidity was a distasteful disease, like leprosy or poverty. He preferred his employees bullish. Olivia couldn't say anything. Mason had inherited this by example as well.

'Darling,' Olivia suddenly grew serious, 'do you know what you're doing?'

She sounded genuinely concerned. Mason was both touched and annoyed.

'Have the repairman here Monday morning.'

Mason ended the phone call before his mother

127

was ready for it to end. When he turned away from the window, Sadie was standing in the middle of the room with her hands folded.

'Lord!' He flinched, startled. 'You scared me to death!'

'If it was tuh death,' Sadie said flatly, 'you wouldn't still be yammerin'.'

Mason wondered how long the old hag had been standing there, how much she'd heard, and how the devil she'd got in. The sliding door was still closed tight. As far as he could tell it was the only way into the room.

'Supper's on the table,' Sadie said.

'Supper?' Mason checked his watch. 'It's only five o'clock.'

'A man goes tuh bed on a heavy stomach or a heavy heart won't make old bones.'

'But I always take my evening meal at eight.'

'I feed at five,' Sadie said, turning on her heels, 'or I don't feed.'

The truth was he was starving after the drive. Consoling himself with the fact that he wouldn't have to put up with her much longer, Mason dropped the receiver back in the cradle and followed. He assumed he would be eating in the formal dining room. He was more than a little taken aback when Sadie led him through the dining room to the kitchen.

He was surprised to find that Olivia had completely renovated the kitchen. As far as he knew, his mother never cooked a meal at their home. Sadie, in her starched black dress and wooden crucifix, looked out of her time period in the modern room. The original kitchen, a squat

128

brick cube formerly connected to the house by a dog trot, had been turned into Olivia's studio. The same watercolor she had started when she took the art class was still mounted on the easel. The slave shacks, which once stood beyond the old kitchen under the trees, had mysteriously burned to the ground.

As the situation was temporary, the food was on the table, and there was virtually no hope of changing the old woman's mind, Mason pulled out a ladder-back chair and sat down. He had never eaten a meal at the kitchen table in his entire life. And he had never seen food quite like the parade of pots Sadie was setting before him.

'What is *that*?' he asked frowning down into a bowl of something so green it seemed to writhe.

'Polk salad.'

Mason looked skeptical. He didn't like the sound of it. He did not like to try new things and he was certain a polk had never crossed his lips. Mason stared at the earthenware platter and an ominous feeling came over him. Something didn't smell right, and it wasn't just the mystery meat.

'What is it?' he asked, as she slapped a hunk on his plate.

'Deer meat.'

Of course Mason had eaten venison before, but it had been thinly carved by a chef and garnished with parsley and rose radishes.

'You won't find a cow more tender,' Sadie assured him. 'Soaked it in buttermilk.'

She saw no need to mention that the front end

129

of her son's pickup truck had done most of the tenderizing.

'That there's spoon bread,' she said, pointing to bowls, 'home-churned butter, mashed taters, crowder peas, fried corn, chow-chow and pickled peaches.'

'I can't possibly eat this,' he said.

Sadie assumed he was referring to the quantity of the meal.

'Folks is goin' hungry in this country,' she said, drowning his plate with a ladleful of milk gravy. 'You'll down eve' bite.'

Picking up his napkin, which turned out to be a dishcloth, Mason spread it on his lap. When Sadie had her back turned, he held his fork up to the light. It was spotless.

Standing by the table, Sadie waited. Hesitantly, he aimed the fork at the plate.

'You plannin' on sayin' grace?' she said abruptly.

He wasn't. Shaking her head, she clasped her hands on top of her apron and squeezed her eyes shut. Slowly setting his fork down, Mason closed his eyes and strained to remember a prayer, any prayer at all.

'Devil got yer tongue?' Sadie finally asked after the awkward stretch of silence.

Mason looked at her blankly.

'Lord,' Sadie called out, as if the Almighty were hard of hearing, 'thank ye fer this here food on this here table. A-men.'

Annoyed by the whole situation, Mason stabbed his fork into the hunk of deer and held his breath as he shoved it in his mouth. He chewed critically until his brow slowly smoothed.

'I never would have guessed this could taste good,' he said, with his mouth full.

'Such is life,' Sadie said. 'Ya never know till ya take a bite out of it.'

Except for the polk salad, Mason was visibly and verbally impressed by the whole meal, humming his approval.

'Our cook at home puts chives in her mashed potatoes,' Mason said, as he helped himself to a second helping.

'Boy, when yer kissin' a girl, do you run your mouth 'bout 'nuther girl's kisses? When yer eatin' my cookin', I don't want tuh be hearin 'bout 'nuther woman's recipes.'

When he was sure he could not eat another bite, she opened the oven door and pulled out a cobbler. Somehow he managed to have two bowls.

'I could eat this every day,' he sighed, falling back in the chair.

'Well, ya won't be,' she said flatly, as she poured him a cup of coffee from the percolator.

Every cook has her Achilles heel. Some women can't bake a moist cake on a rainy day. Others could dry beef out in soup. Sadie's downfall was beverages. The woman couldn't make a decent pitcher of tea if Mr Lipton were talking her through it. It was commonly believed that a stout drink of Sadie LaRue's lemonade right before death would save the family the cost of embalming. Even her mother's milk had tasted like wild onions. The men in the LaRue family turned to moonshine at an early age for survival.

There was no telling how long the percolator had been simmering on the stove, or how many times the grounds had been reused. The dark goo oozing into Mason's cup did not resemble a liquid in any way. But having been pleasantly surprised by the meal, Mason took a leap of faith. Downing a scalding mouthful, he sat straight up in his chair as the molten black sludge paved his tongue like road tar.

'That stuff would take the silver off a spoon!' he choked.

'It'll make a man outta ya.'

'I'm already a man,' he sputtered.

'That,' Sadie said, as she topped off his cup, 'remains tuh be seen.'

★　★　★

Mason made his way back to the study after supper and eased himself onto the worn leather sofa in a satiated daze. He had planned to tour the house before dark and inventory what needed to be done to make the old place livable. Now, sitting and staring at the fire seemed the better plan.

It was a little past six by the clock on the mantel, but it seemed much later. Shadows slipped into the room like a smoke-gray scarf being pulled across the floor, and the dark wrapped around him. A warm satisfaction slowly moved over Mason. He stretched luxuriously and sighed with satisfaction. Then he quickly caught himself. Mason did not allow himself the luxury of contentment. A contented man never amounted to anything.

He promptly reviewed the list of his ambitions and his mood was properly adjusted. Not having Kat Wilde straddling him on the couch at that moment topped the list.

He thought of her leaning against the wall, his face so close he could smell her, and he felt charged with adrenaline. The anticipation of having Kat, which he knew he would, was like champagne fizzing through the veins. Mason never felt more alive than during the acquisition of a woman. But as much as he enjoyed the thrill of wanting Kat, he never allowed himself to entirely give in to desire. Desire distorts reason like light passing through a prism. A vacant stare is easily mistaken for cool aloofness when a man's hand is inching up a woman's thigh. A grating cackle transforms into a trilling laugh after the third whiskey. Men who forget this wake up one morning stuck with a piece of overpriced property they can't easily unload.

Mason was not a man set adrift by passion. His eye was always on the bottom line, even while the rest of his body was otherwise engaged. His mother need not worry about him. When he did wed, it would be a compatible and profitable merger. He fully expected to fall in love and he fully expected to marry — just not to the same woman.

Mason had no delusions about Kat Wilde. His thoughts of her were neither tender nor loving. She was a factory worker who had caught his eye. Theirs would not be a long term partnering. He felt no remorse about this. He fully intended to leave her better off than he'd found her. Her time with him could only increase her worth when he turned her over to her next investor.

This was what he told himself as he stared at the fire and imagined ripping Kat's dress open and taking her warm full breasts in both hands.

He was so deep in carnal thought he didn't notice the draft at first. It wasn't until he actually shivered that he sat up on the couch. The air had suddenly turned frigid. He swung around and Sadie stood staring at him so quiet he wondered if she was holding her breath.

'There's a draft in this room,' he said, going to stand by the fire.

Sadie stood perfectly still, hand clutching her cross. The fire flickered on her face and her head was slightly cocked.

'Old houses are always drafty,' he muttered as he turned his back to the fire.

The cold air that pressed against him was so dense it seemed solid. All the warmth felt drawn from his body. Rubbing his arms, he frowned questioningly at Sadie. It seemed less like a cold draft, than something seeking heat.

'It's him.'

Sadie lifted her chin to the portrait of Cyril Rudolph above the mantel and Mason blurted an involuntary laugh. The look on her face quickly sobered him.

'I kin see the resemblance,' Sadie said.

Mason studied the portrait of his great uncle. White hair draped the old man's shoulders and

134

ice-blue eyes stared directly at the viewer. The hollow cheeks were smooth as bone. The hands, calcified into arthritic claws, gripped a Bible in his lap.

'We don't look a thing alike,' Mason insisted indignantly.

Her eyes narrowed and her mouth hardened.

'Weren't talkin' 'bout looks.'

A rush of cold air passed through the room. A less grounded mind might have called it a sigh. Mason told himself it was just a breeze blowing under the window sill or down the chimney. The reasoning did not stop his skin from crawling. Sadie was oblivious to him and the cold. Her bead-black eyes were fixed on the portrait of Cyril Rudolph.

'A man's actions linger in the air long after the deed is done,' she said darkly.

Mason took this as an accusation and the hostility in her tone made him seethe. He would not be held responsible for the sins of his ancestors. His great-uncle had, after all, given the old woman a job for life. What more did she want? Mason was on the verge of giving her a good tongue-lashing when he realized Sadie had her coat on and her pocketbook draped on her arm.

'Where are you going?' he demanded.

'Home.'

'Home?'

'I jest work fer ya,' Sadie said, tying a wool scarf tight under her chin. 'I ain't yer slave.'

Mason followed on her heels to the front door, rubbing his arms to warm them.

'But what if I need something?'

She cut him a sharp look and he said no more. Sadie liked her men independent. Mason was independent, as long as he had employees he could depend on.

'There's smoked ham and biscuits on the stove for yer breakfast and a plate of fried chickin' in the icebox for your dinner,' she said, pulling the front door open. Glancing back, she lifted her chin at the yellow light coming from the library door. 'Leave a snort a whiskey on the pee-anner. He'll settle down after a bit.'

Irritated and speechless, Mason followed her through the door. It struck him that the air outside the house, while chilly, was warmer than inside. Sadie stood perfectly still on the porch staring at the sky. The red sunset bled onto the horizon as dusk consumed the day.

'It's the gloam,' she said. 'God'll be walkin' his hills tuh-night.'

Eyes sharp and ears cocked she searched the landscape. She lifted her nose as if sniffing the air, as she descended warily down the front steps. Her bundled body seemed to hobble across the yard, but when she reached the pasture she found her natural stride. Sadie moved through the tall grass as if her feet were a foot above ground. Mason followed her black silhouette until she disappeared into the fog rolling in from the river. He wasn't sure if Sadie LaRue worked at Devil's Eye or haunted it.

It is never as dark in the city as in the hills. Night crept imminently toward Devil's Eye. Trees became black bony hands reaching out of

136

the dirt and rustling shrubs whispered. Mason stood alone on the porch, legs apart and body unconsciously steeled. He found himself staring down at the river, for what he wasn't sure. His heart grew inexplicably heavy. He felt filled with longing, but for what he wasn't sure. Shaking it off, he boldly walked the length of the porch, his footsteps heavy on the wood flooring as if drumming a warning. His narrowed eyes searched the woods beyond the yard, threatening anything that might be looking back.

Having marked his territory, he returned to the entry. He closed the heavy door behind him, locked it, and shook the handle to make sure it was tight. He refused to consider the possibility that the very thing he was trying to lock out might be on the inside.

The temperature had returned to normal in the study. Mason walked around the room running his hands along the window frames, the baseboards and the mantle searching for the source of the draft. He suspected it was drifting up from the cellar. It had a musty smell to it. In the morning, he would go down and check the furnace. He had no doubt the sound he had heard was the wind whistling up one of the chimneys or a radiator pipe hissing. Throwing two more logs on the fire, he poked it until it was roaring. He gave some thought to driving back to his apartment in Nashville. Sitting all alone in the empty old house was a hell of a way to spend a Saturday night. But by then the fog was so thick he could barely see past the porch from the study window. Scanning the shelves, he pulled down a book, poured himself a whiskey and settled onto the couch. His mind drifted on the first page. He decided to make a call.

'Hello,' Kat answered.

'Hello, this is — '

'I know who it is.'

Mason took a stout sip of whiskey.

'I've settled into Devil's Eye. It's lonely as hell.'

If he couldn't seduce her with money, good looks and charm, he was not above seeking pity. When Kat didn't say anything, he moved straight to concern for his well-being.

'My housekeeper thinks the old place is haunted.' He laughed.

He took her silence as a positive thing. She hadn't hung up on him.

'No, I mean it,' he went on, looking around the room. 'She honestly thinks my great-uncle walks the halls.'

'Of course Devil's Eye is haunted,' she said flatly. 'Why do you think no one will work there?'

Draining his glass, Mason poured himself another. All women are crazy. A man's willingness to put up with a woman is directly proportional to his desire to sleep with her.

'I don't think it's safe for me to stay here all alone,' he said, making his voice childish.

'Then go home.'

He made a mental note to rule out boyish behavior in the future.

'You know that isn't going to happen,' he said firmly.

'Then you might want to get yourself a big dog.'

Mason heard the dial tone. He held the receiver in his hand and just stared at it. He contemplated calling her back, but he'd already made three calls since he arrived. He didn't want Annabelle Boyd spreading the word that he was a man who talked on the telephone all day.

Hanging up the phone, Mason stuffed his hands in his pockets and wondered what to do with the night. He spent very little time alone. When he didn't have a woman to entertain him, he filled the void with chums from school or the country club, men he'd known all his life but did not necessarily like. For an only child, Mason was oddly uncomfortable with solitude. Or perhaps he just didn't like his own company.

Standing in front of the fire, he looked up at the portrait of his great-uncle. Except for the eyes, there was a flat falseness about the painting. The artist's attempt to give his subject nobility had failed. Mason could not decide if the artist had captured sadness or cruelty in the eyes. Regardless, Cyril was the only company he had. Holding the decanter of whiskey, he started to pour his uncle a shot. Holding the bottle up to the light, he realized there were only a half a dozen drinks left. Barely enough to get him through the weekend. He certainly didn't want to waste it on the dead. Scavenging through the liquor cabinet, he found a dusty bottle of moonshine, poured a glass, and set it on the grand piano.

'To saints and sinners,' he said, tapping the

glass of moonshine with his whiskey.

If the Devil buys the first round, a man spends eternity paying for the next. Mason fell asleep before finishing his third drink. He awakened the next morning, stiff, still in his clothes and face down on the couch. The fireplace was cold and the study smelled charred and bitter. Remembering where he was, he pushed himself to a sitting position and immediately wished he hadn't. Cheap whiskey, he thought. His head throbbed and his mouth tasted rancid. He sat for a while rubbing his temples, trying to clear the cotton out of his brain and reviewing the events of the night before. He cringed when he remembered his telephone call to Kat. As strategies go, that had been a bad move.

Shaking it off, he glanced around the study to get his bearings. Sunlight revealed the room to be spartan but spirit free. His eyes passed over the shot glass on the piano, then back. The glass was still full. Smiling to himself, he shook his head.

He was about to push off the couch when the decanter of whiskey caught his eye. Going to the liquor cabinet, he picked it up and held it to the light.

It had been drained dry. And Mason was absolutely certain not by him.

★   ★   ★

Sunday morning at St Jerome's, no one heard a word of the sermon. The news that Mason Hughes had moved into Devil's Eye was the

140

message of the day. The old church buzzed with speculation on why he was in town, how long he planned to stay and what he planned to do while he was there. Gladys Green let it be known he was 'a looker'. Many a young woman's heart sank when Annabelle Boyd let it slip that Mason Hughes had placed a call to Kat Wilde the night before, and that she might have overheard his mentioning he was lonely. All eyes rolled to Kat's empty pew. 'Like mother, like daughter,' they said.

Out in the cemetery, Hoochie Booth was digging a grave. It would be a small one. A baby's grave. Premature and stillborn. The death was a blessing to everyone but the mourning mother. The shovel cut easily into the earth. The ground was soft from the rain. It wouldn't take long. He was supposed to have dug the grave the day before, but he'd laid one on and didn't get around to it.

Hoochie worked a little harder when he saw the doors swing open. No one noticed. Everyone was still discussing Mason Hughes as they poured out of the church, down the church stairs and across the lawn.

It came as no surprise to Hoochie to hear Cyril's kin had moved to town. The night before, he'd seen the light burning up on the hill, a searing molten red scar in the black sky like the Devil cracking open his eye.

13

Roy Lester had been working for Pearl for two months before Joy got wind of it.

'Buck says we'll have enough money to pay off the grocery bill just as soon as Roy sets the tubs,' Luella let casually slip during their ten o'clock break.

The minute the words left her lips, Luella knew she'd made a critical error. The man who said you have nothing to fear but fear itself had never rubbed Joy Lester the wrong way.

'*Roy* sets the tubs?'

The faint smile on Joy's face never faltered. But all the blood drained out of Luella as if someone had pulled her plug.

'I wasn't supposed to tell!' Luella whispered frantically. 'Promise you won't tell Roy you heard it from me.'

'How long have you known about this?' Joy asked quietly.

'Oh, not long.' Luella's mind raced while her mouth stuttered and stalled. 'Not long at all.'

The air between them had grown cold. Fortunately, Addie Pewitt hurried up at that moment.

'You're never going to guess who has gone to work for Pearl Wilde!' Addie said breathless. 'Maysie McCowan!'

The look that came over Joy's face made both women take a step back.

★　★　★

That night, Annabelle Boyd heard a racket coming from the Lester house that made her put down her Bible and go to her dining-room window. Peeking between her lace sheers, she traced the ruckus to the Lesters' kitchen window. Swinging a skillet with both hands, Joy chased Roy around her kitchen table. He dipped and dodged, and shoved chairs in her path.

In a moment of desperate self-preservation, Roy grabbed Joy's great-grandmother's Irish cake plate from the china cabinet and held it in front of him.

'You put that down,' Joy said, with ghostly calm.

'You put that skillet down,' Roy countered, as he backed toward the door.

Raising the black iron skillet over her head, Joy brought it down with such a force it flattened a quart Mason jar of bread-and-butter pickles on the table.

'Put it down,' she said through clenched teeth, as sweet vinegar and slivers of glass dripped to the floor.

Reaching behind him, Roy twisted the doorknob on the kitchen door, backed through, and ran for his life, taking the cake plate hostage. Shrieking, Joy flew out of the door like a banshee and took off across the yard after him. Diving into the chicken coop, Roy barricaded himself from the inside. Joy proceeded to beat on the door with the skillet until the nails started pulling out of the hinges. The chickens were

143

going crazy, squawking, running in every direction and flapping against the tin roof of the coop. Feathers flew out the mesh window like a busted-down pillow. Every dog in the neighborhood started howling.

It was about this time that Joy caught sight of Annabelle Boyd standing at her dining-room window watching. Growing perfectly calm, Joy lowered the skillet behind her back.

'If I find one chip in that plate,' she hissed through the chicken-coop door, 'you're a dead man.'

Lifting her chin, Joy marched back to the house, skillet hanging at her side.

That night a cold rain set in. Joy's first concern was for her chickens.

There was only one soft spot in Joy's cast-iron heart and that was for her Rhode Island Reds. Nothing brought Joy more joy than throwing out cracked corn and watching her chickens scratch and peck, their little heads bobbing up and down, their dainty feet dancing. Joy could stare at them all day. She knew each chick by name and, when no one was looking, she'd gather Miss Ruby into her lap, stroke her soft shiny red feathers and softly sing 'A Frog Went a Courtin'. Joy's chickens were the first thing she thought of in the morning and the last thing she thought of when she turned the light off at night. They were the only thing on this earth that she truly loved.

The day Roy drop-kicked Miss Ruby off the back porch for getting shit on his boot was most likely the beginning of the end of her marriage.

Joy stood in the yellow glow of her bedroom

window staring down at the chicken coop. She'd been after Roy for two years to fix the tin roof. 'It don't leak when it ain't rainin',' he'd say.

Well, it was raining now. There wouldn't be a dry spot of chicken shit for him to rest his head on. He'd be soaked to the bone by morning. She imagined Roy curled on wet, nasty straw, shivering, fever setting in, throat starting to swell. Probably get chicken fever. Maybe it would go into pneumonia.

Swinging open her cedar wardrobe, Joy flipped through her dresses. Pulling out her black funeral dress, she hung it on the back of the door to air. Neatly turning back the covers, Joy climbed into bed. Reaching up, she turned off the light and pulled the quilt up to her chin. A rare little shiver of joy caught her breath. Few things brought her greater happiness than anticipating her own widowhood.

The next morning, Joy stood at her kitchen sink and stared out the window. In the middle of the muddy yard, Roy was leaning on his ax. His hair was matted with wet straw and feathers, and his clothes were speckled white. The ax blade was as dull as a butter knife. She'd been after him since last fall to sharpen it. 'Ain't dull unless you use it,' he'd say.

When Roy spotted her standing in the kitchen window, he centered her grandmother's Irish cake plate on the chopping block. Raising the ax over his head, he took a slow glimpse back over his shoulder to make sure she was still watching, then brought it down. Over and over, Roy slammed the ax into the chopping block until the cake plate was ground to its original Irish clay. When it was reduced to dust, Roy jumped up on the block, stomped his feet, flapped his elbows and danced a jig.

Joy watched, expressionless, eyes dry as talcum.

14

'Don't get me wrong,' Buck said, as he pulled a Royal Crown out of the box and actually paid for it. 'Luella is a fine cook and keeps a good house. But seems to me Colonel Cavanagh's got the right idea. If a man was to put pencil to paper, it'd be a whole lot cheaper to hire a housekeeper and a hussy than to marry.'

'Be even better if you could hire a hussy that kept house,' Bud Mangrum reasoned from the counter.

'Hell,' Woody huffed, 'if I could find a good lookin' hussy that kept house, I'd marry her.'

It was Saturday morning and the boys sat around the hardware store in comfortable congregation. Bud had started opening until noon on Saturdays to accommodate all the poor husbands whose wives had been motivated by the hammering, sawing and painting going on at Pearl's house up on Dog Leg Hill. Saturday had become his second most profitable day of the week. Customers stopped by to pick up supplies, have a Moon Pie and Royal Crown with the boys and add their two cents to the topic of debate. Bud could not have been more contented. Despite an occasional drift in the conversation to politics and religion, the subject always gravitated back to the men's center of gravity — sex and the lack thereof. When a man's thoughts are not on sex, his mind is wandering. God created

147

cleavage so a man wouldn't spend all his time talking behind a woman's back.

'A woman takes a commodity product and charges a premium,' Bud said, as he thoughtfully twisted a screwdriver in his ear. 'There's something wrong with making a man sign a lifelong contract for a once a week service that the wife usually stops supplying about halfway through the deal.'

The boys looked at Bud in stunned admiration. Right before their eyes he was turning into a respectable businessman. And it had made him far better company. It was already March and they still hadn't migrated to the general store. If Bud air-conditioned the store, they might never leave.

'Now, if said service was readily available at a reasonable cost, the price would naturally go down,' Bud reasoned. 'The only thing better than a woman who charges by the hour would be a woman who gave it away for free. Of course, that ain't never gonna happen.'

'Never.' The boys all agreed. All except Eddie McCowan, who was still young, hopeful and horny.

Grunting, Roy Lester spit bitterly into the new brass spittoon at the foot of his chair. 'Hell! Who in this here room is gettin' any at all?' he demanded.

It was a harsh question to ask, but the boys didn't hold it against Roy. Living in the chicken coop for going on two weeks had put him in a foul mood.

'If you don't marry you die lonely. If you do

marry, you wish you were dead,' Roy grumbled. 'God's got a man comin' and goin'!'

'Roy,' Eddie mused, 'if you could have got the milk for free would you have married Joy?'

'Hell,' Roy huffed, 'I was gettin' the milk for free and I still married the heifer.'

'Must have been real good milk,' Woody said, arms crossed on his chest and staring at his boots.

'She was a starting to curdle even then,' Roy admitted.

'Then why'd you marry her, Roy?' Eddie asked.

Leaning sideways, Roy scrunched his face and spit.

'When a man's dying of thirst, he'll drink warm piss.'

The boys got a bad taste in their mouths. None of them had ever been that thirsty.

'But what's wrong with her, Roy?' Eddie pressed.

'She's a Meachum,' Roy said plain and simple.

It was all that need be said. Everyone knew about Meachum women. Meachum women were like Venus Flytraps. When they were young, they were physically alluring. But as soon as they trapped a man, they started eating him whole. Roy was a mere shadow of the man he once was. It was just a matter of time before all that was left of him was a wad of chewing tobacco dripping on the rocker.

'Boy, you listen to me,' Roy warned direly. 'Never let yourself fall in love with a girl until you get a good look at her mama. Look hard into that old woman's eyes and you'll see exactly what you're marrying.'

At the mention of Joy Meachum's mama, the boys' testicles drew up for safety. Miz Meachum was the stuff of nightmares. She dyed her hair boot-heel black and smeared blood red lipstick around her drawn mouth to give the impression she had lips. Eleven children had sucked her dry — body, mind and soul. She hated all men in general and the one she was married to in particular. It didn't matter the time of day or the season of the year, Mr Meachum sat in his rocker on the front porch staring straight ahead with a stunned and terrified look on his face, his manhood chewed completely off.

'Maybe someday Joy will come around,' Eddie offered kindly.

Roy shook his head. 'A black widow spider don't lay chicken eggs.'

Roy's melancholy bled through the room like blue ink in water. The boys stared at the potbellied stove in silence.

'Well, I reckon I better . . .'

When no excuse came to mind, Roy pushed out of his chair and headed toward the door. He lifted his hat off the hook, but didn't seem to have the will to put it on. They watched him walk slumped and listless past the storefront window. Roy didn't even notice Bud's new display of RCA radios.

'Cain't be easy on a man sleepin' in a chicken coop.'

'Cold, dark and damp.'

'Chickens can be right noisy when they're restless.'

'It's better than living under a bridge,' Bud reasoned. 'Least he's got walls.'

'Those walls are cedar board and batten with steel railroad rails for support,' Buck pointed out. 'I built her tight as chicken coops go.'

And that's what gave Eddie McCowan the idea.

★   ★   ★

After walking home from work at the shirt factory, Joy Meachum Lester went to her kitchen sink to fix herself a little supper. When she turned on the faucet to wash her hands, she caught sight of it. Joy didn't bother to grab her sweater off the hook by the back door on her way out. The screen door banged twice off the frame behind her. Driving a path through her squawking chickens that were scavenging in the unmowed grass, she came to a stop in front of the chicken coop and just stared. The weathered gray board and batten had been painted white and there was a brand new red tin roof. A small window had been cut in the side, just large enough to let light pass. It was hung with red shutters. The door was locked with a shiny new Yale padlock.

Cupping her hands around her eyes, Joy pressed her face against the small window. Inside was as sweet as a honeymoon cottage, wrought-iron bed with an Irish knot quilt on it, braided rug on the new pine floor and a rocking chair in front of a little potbellied cook stove. There was no sign of chicken manure anywhere.

When Joy caught sight of the part in Annabelle Boyd's dining-room curtains, she calmly turned away from the chicken coop and walked back to her kitchen. As soon as the screen door slammed, she grabbed her butcher knife and drove it into the kitchen table so deep she broke the tip when she pulled it out.

For the next two weeks, Joy stood arms crossed and expressionless at her kitchen window while Roy carried cardboard boxes of supplies from his truck to his chicken coop like a rat lining its nest — a *Farmer's Almanac* calendar for the wall, an old mirror he'd picked up at Mendelson's pawn shop, a kettle and a cast iron skillet. When he pulled into the driveway with a commode in the back of his truck, Joy knew she was never going to get rid of him.

That was when she decided to kill him.

For some wives hate grows slowly, one hurt feeling at a time. For others, it is instant combustion. For Joy, it was her nature. Joy hated Roy. She hated the look of him. She hated his smell. Watching him eat made her lose her appetite. The sound of his voice made her dig her fingernails into her palms until the flesh bruised. Only Joy's need to breed had brought them together. Once that possibility passed, the biological switch that had temporarily rendered her harmless shut off like flipping the safety switch on a gun. Like a queen bee shoving the drone out of the hive in winter or a praying mantis biting the head off her mate during coitus, Joy had to be rid of Roy.

There are a hundred ways for a wife to kill her husband. Joy gravitated toward slow poison. A mysterious lingering decline in health is always well received.

Joy was not a stupid woman. If she'd bought the poison at the General Store, Gladys Green would never have said a word. Widows stick together. But Joy was too mean to kill Roy without the satisfaction of his figuring out who did it before he croaked.

'What d'yu need rat poison for?' Roy asked skeptically from his chair by the stove at the hardware store.

Bud and the boys' eyes volleyed from Roy to Joy.

'Got a rat I can't get rid of,' Joy said matter-of-factly, as she studied the label with an artist's rendering of a rat lying flat on his back holding lilies.

'Since when?'

'Since he started sniffing around my place.'

'Your place?' Roy huffed. 'Hell, my people was livin' on that place 'fore your people stowed away on the boat.'

'Tell me,' Joy said, looking at Bud, 'does the rat suffer?'

'I'd guess it ain't no picnic,' Bud said.

Joy snapped open her coin purse and counted out the money.

It was relatively easy to kill a husband and get away with it in Five Points. All it took was a few carefully chosen comments at the right time and the right place.

'Roy grabbed his heart the other day and turned pale as a ghost,' Joy told the girls during morning break. 'Scared me to death.'

'Why you poor thing,' Addie said, patting Joy's hand.

'You know his daddy's heart stopped before he was forty,' Joy said.

All the girls looked at each other and nodded. No one could deny it. Roy's daddy's heart did indeed stop before he was forty. Right after that tree fell on him.

Joy made the cornbread just the way Roy liked it. But as she held the spoonful of rat poison over the bowl, she weakened. It's one thing to be in favor of the death penalty. It's another thing to be the one who pulls the switch. In the end, Joy could not bring herself to add enough poison to kill Roy. And so she tapped only enough into the batter to get his attention. Maybe put him into a mild coma.

The cornbread was still crispy and hot when she carried the plate across the yard. Holding the hot plate with her potholder, she lifted her free hand and knocked on the freshly painted chicken-coop door.

'What's this?' Roy asked, sniffing the plate.

'What's it look like?' she said, lifting the dishcloth covering it.

'It smells a little funny.'

'This from a man living in a chicken coop.'

'Why?' he demanded.

'Why what?'

'Woman, you haven't given a bee's butt 'bout me since the weddin'.'

154

'I made extra and didn't want it to waste,' she shrugged.

Roy studied her skeptically. He knew she was up to no good, but he wanted her anyway. If liking a woman was a prerequisite for wanting her, the human race would teeter precariously on the brink of extinction.

'Come inside,' he said gruffly, grabbing her around the waist.

'Eat your cornbread while it's hot,' Joy insisted, prying his fingers off her waist.

'Only if you come inside,' he said, pulling her to him.

'If I do, will you eat your cornbread?'

'I'll lick the plate,' he swore.

An hour later, Joy tumbled out of the chicken coop looking like she'd been rolled down a hill in a barrel. Hair every which way and clothes a jumble. Pulling her blouse together, she staggered across the lawn like a drunk. All the while, Annabelle Boyd was taking it in from behind her curtain. When Joy got to the porch, she glanced back at the chicken coop. Roy was leaning against the door, grinning and chewing.

Joy went inside and fixed a glass of spirits of peppermint for her nausea.

The next morning, Joy woke up thinking about funeral music. She was humming 'In the Garden' as she parted her bedroom curtains. Glancing out the window, her breath caught. The yard was covered with dead chickens, eyes glassy, stiff little feet straight up in the air, and cornbread crumbs on their parted beaks.

Roy whistled 'Happy Days are Here Again' on

155

his way across the yard to his truck. Looking up at the window, he blew her a kiss.

After Roy left, Joy sat crumpled in the wet grass. Gathering the limp body of Miss Ruby into her lap, she smoothed the soft red feathers as she rocked her back and forth. Tears running down her cheeks, Joy sang, '*A frog went a-courtin', he did ride* . . . ' Then wiping her red eyes with the sleeve of her nightgown, she turned her thoughts to accidental death.

15

In 1911 the honorable Jack Daniel died. They said it was blood poisoning that got him. Truth was it was Tennessee Prohibition that sent Gentleman Jack to the grave. Ten years before the rest of the country lost its spirit, a statewide Prohibition bill passed over the governor's veto making illegal the manufacture, sale, transport or possession of intoxicating beverages — except for medicinal purposes. Needless to say, the health of the state's citizens went into an overnight decline. Every law-abiding adult who didn't wave the temperance flag developed a sudden death-rattle cough that could only be subdued by a fifty-proof tonic — a far cry from the eighty-proof they were accustomed to.

Whiskey distillers were given one year to dismantle their operations. Most Tennessee distillers were compliant. They simply moved their operation across the state line and transported the finished product back when the law wasn't looking.

Colonel Corbett Cavanagh, owner of the Cavanagh Whiskey Distillery, took a slightly different approach.

It took eleven months and thirty days to disassemble the Cavanagh Whiskey Distillery — and exactly one month to reassemble it across the river in Steamer Holler. The illicit distillery was half the size and employed half as many men, but it made five times the net profit. Overnight, the Cavanaghs went from being one of the most prominent and well-respected families in the state to being outlaws. Fortunately, lawlessness looked good on Cavanagh boys.

The division of labor in the Cavanagh bootleg business was neatly drawn. The Colonel kept the right palms greased to keep the law off their backs, Devin, the Colonel's youngest son, kept an eye on the books, while Bourne, the Colonel's oldest, broke the arms of anyone who tried to double-cross them.

Selling illegal whiskey did not require marketing. On the contrary, every effort was made to keep word of their product well contained. When a prospective client came calling, it was the client who had to do the selling.

'What can I get yuh?' Gladys Green asked.

'Just keep the cup full,' Bourne said, sliding onto a stool at the counter at the General Store.

A prospective client sat by the window sipping coffee and playing with a piece of pie. Bourne studied the man's reflection in the mirror across from the counter. A bootlegger has three problems to contend with, revenuers, other bootleggers and a client who goes bad. For the most part, revenuers turned a blind eye on the Cavanaghs. The Colonel had friends in high places. It was much easier to bust some poor hick squeezing a living out one jug of moonshine at a time and call it a day. Bourne could spot a revenuer the minute he got out of his car. He either had the air of a man who thought he was bullet proof, or the air of a man fully aware of his mortality and not getting paid enough to take the chance. And competitive bootleggers were polite enough to announce their arrival in juiced-up Fords fitted with Cadillac engines and rear ends jacked up like a cat's butt.

Clients were the tricky ones. Maybe a man gets a little behind on his tab and decides it would be cheaper to turn you in for the two-dollar reward than pay his bill. Or maybe another bootlegger gets to him and encourages him, in one way or another, to rat you out. Or maybe his wife gets sick of his drinking and sick of no money. Or maybe he just gets greedy and starts thinking he deserves a piece of the action for keeping his mouth shut. There were a dozen ways for a buyer to go bad. The best way to avoid trouble was to avoid the man who might be.

The prospective client sitting by the window was giving Bourne a little trouble. There was no doubt he could pay his tab. He had money written all over him. But there was something not quite right about him. He wasn't a revenuer or a competitor and he was too well dressed to be on the government's payroll. And so Bourne was feeling cautious when Eddie McCowan walked up to the counter and stood next to him.

'Miss Pearl needs ten cases of your best,' Eddie announced for the whole world to hear.

Eddie was too naïve to know the look on Bourne's face meant he would soon be sipping his meals through a straw. Grabbing Eddie by the front of his shirt, Bourne welded his butt onto the stool next to him.

'Why don't you say it a little louder? I don't think the sheriff in the next county heard you.'

Eddie sat quiet while Gladys, smirking, poured him a cup of coffee. Then she watched as the boy dumped a quarter cup of sugar into the cup, followed by so much milk the coffee spilled over and filled the saucer. Eddie blew on the syrup until it was tepid, took a cautious sip, then dumped more sugar in. When he was at last satisfied, he mirrored Bourne's posture, elbows on the counter, hunched over the cup and a lethal glint in his eyes. Gladys rolled her green eyes. The boy was a mockingbird.

The two sat side by side drinking their coffee in silence, a truly unnatural state for Eddie. Bourne was staring into his cup when he noticed the ripples in his black coffee. He rolled his eyes up to the mirror and saw that the prospective client's knee was bouncing like a wringer washer.

When Eddie caught Bourne studying the reflection of the man sitting by the window, he jumped at the opportunity.

'That's Mason Hughes.'

Bourne cocked his head Eddie's way.

'Can I have a piece of pie?'

'Give him a piece of pie,' Bourne ordered.

'With ice-cream,' Eddie called out, as Gladys took the cover off the pie.

When his pie was in front of him, Eddie continued.

'Mason Hughes of the Rudolph & Hughes shirt factory,' he said with his mouth full.

'What's he doing in town?'

160

'Moved into Devil's Eye.'

'What the hell for?'

'Word has it he's after Kat Wilde.'

Bourne shifted uncomfortably on the stool.

'He's rich as Midas,' Eddie rambled on, 'but they say Kat won't give him the time of day. Women are a wonder, aren't they?'

Draining his cup, Bourne slid off the stool and pulled his money clip out of his back pocket.

'You tell your Miss Pearl if she wants something from me, she can ask for it herself,' he said, tossing three one-dollar bills on the counter for a fifty cent tab.

As Bourne headed across the restaurant, Gladys slid the money off the counter and counted it under Eddie's wishful gaze.

'What are you lookin' at?' she snarled. Actually, Eddie was thinking three dollars should rightfully buy him another piece of pie. But, under the circumstances, he let it pass.

Mason Hughes did not hear Bourne walk up to his table. When he looked up and saw him standing there, he involuntarily clenched his fists.

'You looking for me?' Bourne asked.

'Mr Cavanagh?'

Bourne straddled the chair across from him. Mason had never directly dealt with a bootlegger. His father had a man in Nashville who handled all that. He had expected someone very different. That Bourne didn't look as if he'd crawled out of a dirt floor shack surprised him. Mason naturally assumed that a man engaged in lowbrow activities would look lowbrow. He and

Bourne were about the same age. Had political circumstances allowed, they would have sat at the table as equals.

'How do we handle this?' Mason asked.

'Handle what?'

'The transaction.'

'That depends on how much you want to transact.'

'Of course,' Mason nodded. 'May I start with a case of whiskey?'

The corner of Bourne's mouth turned up slightly and Mason's eyes flashed. He did not appreciate being the source of amusement.

'Yes, you *may*. But you *may* want to taste what you're buying first.'

'Yes, of course.'

Picking up Mason's cup, Bourne poured the remains of the coffee in a pot of mother-in-law's tongues on the window sill and dried the cup with his handkerchief.

'The word 'whiskey' is Irish for 'the water of life,'' Bourne said, as he slipped a silver flask from inside his coat and poured Mason a shot. 'Whether a man finds courage in it or drowns face down in it is his own doing. Either way, don't blame the creator.'

Mason lifted the cup under his nose, took a slow deep breath and held it. Swirling the cup, his eyes followed the liquid amber whorl as if it were Communion wine. Finally taking a sip he let the elixir rest on his tongue before allowing it to slide down his throat. When he finally swallowed with a sigh, a faraway look came into Mason's eyes. There was whiskey and then there was Cavanagh whiskey.

Bourne smiled.

'Make it two cases,' Mason said, his voice mellow.

'You're not buying rot-gut. It'll cost you.'

Mason gave him a grin that assured Bourne money was no problem.

Turning to the window, Bourne gazed toward the courthouse lawn. He was combing his fingers through his hair, when suddenly Mason noticed his jaw tense. Mason's heart lunged and his head swiveled. He had no doubt revenuers were headed their way. Instead, his eyes landed on Kat Wilde and her hellacious dog walking toward them on the sidewalk. When Kat spotted Bourne and Mason sitting together, she stopped. Turning around, she patted her leg for Satan to follow.

Slowly, Mason turned back to Bourne. His mood had instantly gone black.

'I take it you're acquainted,' Mason said quietly.

'Everyone in Five Points is acquainted.'

The two men's eyes met and held. Bourne was a bull next to Mason. While Hubert was showing Mason how to putt a golf ball across the green, the Colonel had his boys loading trucks. All the men at the distillery would see was a couple of fifty-pound burlap sacks of corn dragging across the yard and they knew the Cavanagh brothers were underneath. Bourne had been rolling barrels of whiskey up a loading dock since he was tall enough to reach the rim. In a fair fight, he could whip Mason with one hand tied behind his back. But he could see now that Mason was

163

not the kind of man who let fairness get in the way of winning. Bourne's opinion of Mason Hughes ticked up a point.

'I was more *acquainted* with her sister.'

'Kat has a sister?'

'Pearl,' Bourne said, as his thumb slid down the scar on his cheek.

A look of recognition slowly came over Mason. Crockett had told him all about Pearl's upcoming business venture. But somehow he had not put Pearl and Kat together. He didn't know how he'd missed it.

'It's hard to believe God made two of them.'

'He made three,' Bourne said. 'You should see their mother.'

Mason was fascinated and wanted to hear more, but Bourne cut him short.

'When the bill comes,' Bourne said, 'pay it.'

'But when do I receive my merchandise?'

'You already have.'

Turning in his chair, Mason followed Bourne's nod to his roadster parked down the street. One man stood watch on the sidewalk while another loaded cases into the car.

'That's service,' Mason said, as he turned back around.

But Bourne was already gone.

'More coffee?' Gladys asked pot in hand.

'Just the check,' Mason said, slipping his wallet out of his inside coat pocket.

As Gladys figured his tab in her head, Mason leaned in his chair to look down the street. Gladys knew exactly who he was looking for and why he was looking.

'Kat Wilde is a pretty little thing,' she said, cutting her eyes to his billfold.

Mason pulled out a crisp bill and held it in the air for her to continue.

'She comes in here every Monday to pick up ham bones for that dog of hers,' Gladys said, plucking the bill from his fingers. 'Kat Wilde may go to hell, but it won't be because she's unkind to animals.'

16

Colonel Cavanagh earned his name honestly. He fought in the Great War and had the medals, scars and restless nights to prove it. While he had a great love of country, he had a deep-rooted distrust of the politicians who ran it. He inherited this dichotomy from his father, the first Cavanagh to set his Irish arse down on American soil.

Ronan MaCardell Cavanagh was twenty years old the day he boarded the boat to America clinging to nothing but the family Bible. He put great faith in the holy book, particularly the Book of Psalms, where his father had meticulously written the family's secret whiskey recipe along the border like a prayer. Potatoes were rotting in the ground and the starving Irish were flocking to the new country. Ronan had no doubt they would be thirsty when they got there.

The Cavanaghs had been making whiskey for as far back as there was fire to distill it. It was not so much the clan's trade as their calling. Ronan started licking barrels the day he started crawling and by sixteen had the discriminating tongue of a master distiller. Water is to a whiskey maker what oil is to a Texan. There can be no color or mineral taste to taint the spirits. Ronan stepped off the boat at Ellis Island in search of perfect spring water. Over and over he was told, 'Tennessee is the place you're looking for.

Springs so pure and clear you can barely see the water gush from the ground. Hold a cup under a Tennessee spring and you won't know she's full till the water wets your lips.'

When Ronan crossed the Tennessee state line, he had no doubt they were right. Everywhere he turned there was water. Three great rivers crossed the state. The Tennessee River dipped briefly into Alabama, thought better of it, and turned right back. Creeks carved hollows into the Highland Rim and water wept from the hillsides. The state was floating on its most valuable resource.

It was not so much a problem for Ronan to find the right spring as to decide which one to go with. He nearly settled in a holler in the eastern side of the state, but the women were hard to look at and the men had an ugly streak as well. It was in the cool hills outside of Nashville that he found what he was looking for. A spring flowed from the mouth of a cave, water so pure it was like ice-cold air. He dipped his enamel-coated cup into the crystal clear water, raised it and touched it to his lips. A faraway look came into his eyes. He was back home in the green hills of Cork County.

Ronan imported his father's whiskey for three years while his own barrels aged. And business was good. He was making a wagon run to Memphis the day Union soldiers took Nashville. He arrived home just in time to watch a Yankee lieutenant lay a flaming torch to his house. The only thing Ronan managed to save was his Bible. He was trying to beat the fire out with his shirt when two soldiers grabbed him from behind.

The war was young and the lieutenant in charge was still full of himself. He gave Ronan a choice. 'Join the Union army,' he thundered, 'or join Jesus.'

Ronan was not particularly eager to meet his Maker, but Cavanaghs have a contrary nature. Tell them to do one thing and they're sure to do the other.

'I'll sooner see you in hell!' Ronan declared, spitting in the lieutenant's face.

A couple of blue coats tied him to a tree in the front yard and took turns explaining the etiquette of war one punch at a time. After rummaging through his few possessions and chasing his chickens around the yard, Lieutenant O'Malley and his band rode off with everything they could haul, including a wagon full of two-year old Cavanagh whiskey still in the barrels.

The young private left behind to shoot Ronan took his sweet time loading the gun. The boy looked like a broom standing on end, only slightly less steady. After he'd fumbled the lead ball twice, Ronan decided to pass the time with a little conversation.

'New to the army?' he called from the tree, spitting a bloody tooth from his mouth.

'New to the continent,' the boy admitted, as he combed the grass for his ammunition on his hands and knees.

'So they're recruitin' the Irish fresh off the boat now, are they?'

'Recruitin' would be one word for it,' the boy

said, finding the ball and climbing to his feet.

'And what be the name of the man who would be a killin' me?'

'Edan MaCardell, sir,' the boy mumbled, the powder cork clenched between his teeth.

'It wouldn't be the same MaCardells of Cork County, now, would it?'

'One and the same,' Edan said, shaking as much powder on the ground as in the gun he was trying to load.

'Why, my mother was a MaCardell from Cork.'

Edan looked up wide-eyed from his musket. 'No.'

'As sure I'm tied to this tree, she would be.'

'No,' Edan said, homesick to the core but doubting every bit of it.

'Don't be takin' my word for it.' Ronan nudged the Bible at his feet toward the boy. 'She's right there, she is.'

Edan leaned over the smoldering book. It was an Irish Bible all right. He could sense the melancholy. Lifting the charred cover with his bayonet, he carefully turned the fragile scorched pages until he found the family tree. Running the tip of his finger under the script, his lips mouthed the names. Suddenly, he looked up at Ronan, tears in his eyes.

'Cousin!' he cried, throwing his arms around Ronan and the tree.

That day Ronan and Edan pledged allegiance to the Confederacy. Exactly what they were fighting for was somewhat gray to them, but then war is never black and white until it has aged a bit. By the time the Confederacy surrendered at

Appomattox, Ronan, through the process of elimination, had been promoted to a Captain, and Edan could load a rifle with his eyes closed while dancing an Irish jig.

Ronan returned to Five Points and the business of making whiskey. Edan, being family, went with him. Besides being a master whiskey maker, Ronan was a master businessman. He expected the best, but prepared for the worst. While war raged, the two hundred barrels of sour mash he had hidden in the cave in Steamer Holler quietly aged. When he and Edan tapped one of the barrels and took a sip, a faraway look came into their eyes.

'She's the best I ever tasted,' Edan said, humbled as men are in the presence of greatness.

Solemnly, Ronan poured a shot of whiskey into the spring and a shot on the ground.

'For all the Cavanaghs that came before me,' he said, holding his glass up, 'all the Cavanaghs to come, and for all us poor sons-a-bitches in between.'

The sun shone for a solid week after that day, not a cloud in the sky. God's nod of admiration from one creator to another.

While the South struggled through reconstruction, Ronan and Edan did their part to ease the pain. It was almost two years after the war when a Yankee stepped off the train in Five Points. He was wearing a dandy's suit and wasn't quite so full of himself, but Ronan and Edan recognized the bastard immediately.

'Never expected to lay eyes on the likes of you again,' Ronan said.

The Yankee lieutenant, who had ordered Ronan shot and made Edan the intended instrument of his demise, bit the end off a cigar and spit it on the ground.

'Never doubted I'd lay eyes on you again,' O'Malley told him, striking a match. 'I'd seen this shanty Irishman shoot.'

Slipping a Colt revolver from its holster, Edan deftly shot the flame off the match O'Malley was holding.

'I see you've been practicing,' O'Malley said, rubbing the remains of his fingertips together.

'And precisely why am I a layin' eyes on you?' Ronan asked skeptically.

'Business,' O'Malley said.

Apparently, during his pillage of the South, O'Malley discovered his true calling — procurement and distribution. He was now, he explained, a distributor.

'A distributor of what?'

'That,' O'Malley said, pointing his cigar at them, 'is where you boys come in.'

It seemed that the wagonload of whiskey O'Malley had 'confiscated' from Ronan for the great Union cause had mysteriously ended up in a couple of Chicago entertainment establishments.

'Let's just say,' O'Malley told them, 'the windy city is eager for more.'

'How much more?' Ronan asked.

'How much you got?'

Naturally, Ronan had some trepidation about doing business with the man who had given orders to shoot him.

'Why should I be doin' business with the man who tried to send me to the grave?'

'It was war,' O'Malley shrugged. 'Nothing personal, mind ya.'

'You can't be arguin' with that,' Edan said to his cousin.

Robert E. Lee surrendered at the Appomattox courthouse in 1865, but true peace was made the day three glasses of sour mash whiskey clinked together to toast a business partnership. The only way to truly defeat an enemy is to make him your partner.

Along with the story, the businesses were passed from father to son. Cavanagh Whiskey was distributed by O'Malley Distributors and both families made more money than they knew what to do with.

Ronan and Edan died within days of each other and were buried near the mouth of Cavanagh cave. O'Malley helped lower them both into the grave.

Once a year, Ronan's only son and heir, Colonel Corbett Cavanagh, broke the wax seal on a bottle of his best. He poured a shot into the spring and a shot on his father's and Edan's graves.

'For all the Cavanaghs that came before me,' the Colonel would say, holding his glass in the air, 'for all the Cavanaghs to come, and for all us poor sons-a-bitches in between.'

Then he would take a sip and a faraway look would come into his eyes. The Colonel felt great comfort knowing someday his sons would pour a shot on his grave. He would have it no other way.

17

The day Tennessee prohibition became law, the price of whiskey went up over 500 per cent — when you could find it — and the Cavanaghs went from very rich to very richer. The Colonel ran his illegal bootlegging business just as he had run his legal one, six days a week, fifty-two weeks a year. On Sunday, the distillery rested, except for the men standing guard and the yeast fermenting in the mash. It was the Lord's Day. The Blue Law had absolutely nothing to do with it.

Workers left their cars at LaRue's Landing and took the ferry across the river where they were transported the rest of the way by covered truck. The whistle blew at seven in the morning and seven in the evening. While one shift sauntered in, the other shift sauntered out.

Anyone who wasn't supposed to be there knew better than to drop by unexpected. Just in case, the Colonel hired men to patrol the woods with high-powered rifles. It was a job the LaRue boys were bred for. Knowing a LaRue was wandering the hills looking for something challenging to shoot put the fear of God into trespassers and revenuers.

The LaRues were a dark feral people of few words and even fewer baths. They traced their roots back to a French trapper named Quenelle LaRue who fell in with a band of Cherokee who'd wandered off the Trail of Tears. The LaRues that followed were a mixed breed, possessing remnants of French, Indian and an occasional escaped slave, plus what some believed was a hint of wolf. 'Them French,' the locals said, 'will warm up to anything with a heartbeat.'

By the time a LaRue could walk, he could shoot a dove with one hand while passing the jug with the other. Being people of little imagination but great instinct, they kept to things they knew — hunting, drinking and procreating. LaRue's Landing was nearly five miles out of town. Five miles was a long way to go for a wife, and LaRue men were not much for traveling — the result being that somewhere along the line, the clan split. Every other fall, Miss Mabel Hilliard looked down at her first-grade roll book and found the names Quenelle LaRue and LaRue Quenelle, dark brooding cousins, inseparable and indistinguishable right down to their head lice.

Every so often a LaRue girl, wanting to improve her lot in life, would clean herself up on a Saturday night and walk into Five Points. She'd sit on the stone wall that surrounded St Jerome's cemetery in a thin cotton dress two sizes too small, knees wide and dirty feet kicking.

Devin Cavanagh, the Colonel's youngest boy, knew better than to fool with a LaRue. But he was twenty years old and the spring air was warm and sweet with honeysuckle, and it made him even wilder than usual. He was on his way home from dropping off payoff money at the courthouse when he spotted the feral-looking girl sitting on the rock wall. He looked both ways to make sure no one was watching. But he couldn't keep his eyes off her long. She had skin the color of maple syrup, a thick black braid down her back and wet brown eyes that haunted a man.

'What's your name?' Devin asked.

'Sess-a-lee.'

She said it like something wild calling in the night and it cut right through him. 'You want an ice-cream cone?' he asked, his voice husky.

Sessalee hopped off the wall and took his hand.

Gladys Green raised her eyebrows when she saw the Colonel's youngest boy walk through the door of the General Store holding hands with a LaRue. She glanced back over her shoulder at Sessalee as she dug a scoop of ice cream and plopped it on the cone.

'Your daddy know about this?' she asked, her eyes still on Sessalee as she handed Devin the cone.

Devin held up a dollar bill. Plucking it from his fingers, Gladys tucked it into her bra and twisted her lips like a lock.

Sessalee ate her ice-cream as Devin drove them down to the river. He could barely keep the car on the road for watching her lick that dripping cone. When she'd swallowed the last bite and sucked her fingers clean, Sessalee climbed over the front seat into the back. Her cotton dress slipped down her thigh as she tick-tocked her brown knees back and forth. Her mouth was still cold when Devin kissed her.

After that, every Saturday night Sessalee was waiting for Devin on the wall. Her being a LaRue, Devin couldn't be seen in public with her. If that bothered Sessalee, she never said it. But then, she never said much of anything. What it cost him in ice-cream, Devin figured he more than saved in gasoline by not having to pick her up or drive her home.

'What makes you smell so good?' he asked, his face buried in her neck.

'Jes skin 'n' rain water,' she said.

'God almighty,' Devin whispered.

She left him so lightheaded he had to lean against the car fender to buckle his belt. But making love to a LaRue was a dangerous business. Devin honestly had no idea Sessalee was only fifteen years old until he woke up in the middle of the night with the barrel of a Winchester shotgun pressed between his eyes.

Devin took one look at Sessalee's people standing around his bed in the ghostly moonlight and knew he was about to be gutted and skinned alive. Her brothers stared down at him with the same emotionless black eyes as the animals whose skins they nailed to the trees to mark their boundaries.

'Let me see 'im,' a woman's voice ordered from the door.

The brothers parted and the mother took her place by the bed. A LaRue woman went one of two ways. Either she had a dark mysterious way that haunted a man, or she was flat-out scary. Sessalee's mama loomed over him, carved wooden crucifix swinging from her neck and her dark face grim as the reaper, and Devin's blood ran cold. His heart hammered and he was breathing through his mouth. Underneath the smell of wood smoke and fried bacon on Sadie LaRue, Devin caught the slightest hint of rainwater.

'This you'ens house?'

'It was my granddaddy's place,' Devin said hoarsely, back pressed against the headboard and quilt pulled up to his chin. He had no doubt Sadie LaRue knew this. Everyone in those parts knew it was the little house Ronan Cavanagh lived in before he built the big house down the road. Everyone knew who Devin was. And everyone knew who his daddy was.

'Where's yer granddaddy, boy?'

'Dead and buried, ma'am.'

Which was a good thing. If Ronan had known his grandson was making hanky-panky with a LaRue, it would have killed him.

Sadie stared down at him and her cold eyes cut right to his core.

'Yer a cocky one, ain't ya? But yer honest, I'll give ya that.'

Sadie threw the quilt back and Devin threw his hands over his privates. She stared solemnly at what was still hanging out.

'He'll do,' she said.

The boys stood guard in the bedroom while Devin jerked his pants on. One brother held his shotgun on Devin while LeRoy LaRue cleaned his bowie knife on his pant leg. LeRoy worked for the Colonel, but Devin knew that would not help him under the circumstances. Blood was thicker than whiskey.

Devin took quick looks at each brother, sizing up the situation. His first thought was to take them all on. He never shied from a fight. More times than not, he was the instigator. But a part of Devin knew he deserved the beating he was about to get. The other part just hoped to hang onto his testicles. He was still shoving his foot into a boot when they pushed him out the door and down the hall with the butts of their shotguns.

LaRues don't need much light. A single bulb burned yellow in the living room. Expecting a thrashing, Devin was confused when he saw a preacher of sorts standing in front of the fireplace gripping a tattered Bible. His skin was pockmarked and sallow, his teeth stained yellow as kernels of corn, and bits of thick brown chew dripped down his stubbled chin. The preacher's black wool suit smelled like embalming fluid and his fingernails were so filthy it looked as if he'd just dug his way out of the grave. Along with being judge and jury of LaRue's Landing, the preacher married 'em and buried 'em.

Sessalee stood in front of the preacher, barefooted and holding a handful of yellow lady slippers she'd picked in the woods. The boys shoved Devin into his place beside their sister and the least LaRue boy laid an old whisk broom on the floor between them. Devin took a quick glimpse at Sessalee and was shocked at how slight she was. She barely came up to his shoulder. But then he had not spent that much time with her in an upright position.

The preacher rested his hand on top of the Bible and the LaRues bowed their black heads.

'Lord, a man's born a sinner and lest he finds Jesus is eternally damned to the fiery lake of Hell. A-men.'

'A-men,' the LaRues echoed.

The preacher looked hard at Sessalee. 'Sessalee LaRue, you gonna cook, clean, care for and, God willin', give this boy some babies?'

Sessalee's nod was so slight, Devin wasn't sure he saw her head move.

The preacher turned his eyes on Devin.

'Boy, you gonna do right by this here child?'

At this question, Devin's mind finally caught up to what was happening. In a LaRue's mind, when a man gave a girl ice cream and she gave him sugar, they were betrothed. It was not so much a moral issue as a matter of fair trade.

Devin's jaw dropped. He looked from the preacher to Sadie LaRue in disbelief. Then he looked at Sessalee. Even under the circumstances, his heart caught as it always did at the sight of her. The truth was, he had thought of nothing else but Sessalee LaRue since the first night he saw her sitting on the wall. He ached for her during the week, living only for the moment when her warm bare legs wrapped around his waist and her small hands guided his mouth to hers. But the Cavanaghs are a contrary clan. Tell a Cavanagh to do one thing and he was sure to do the other, even if that something was something he wanted to do.

Clenching his teeth, Devin stood firm.

Sadie LaRue solemnly nodded to her eldest. LeRoy jabbed his shotgun under Devin's chin and slowly forced his head up into a nod.

'I pronounce you man and wife!' the preacher thundered. 'What the good Lord has joined together, let no man put asunder! Amen.'

'A-men,' the LaRues echoed.

Sessalee stepped over the broom. And the next thing Devin knew, he was married.

While LeRoy and his brothers ransacked the house for supplies and the preacher searched the cabinets for moonshine, Sadie went through Devin's grandmother's trunk. She emerged from the front bedroom with a stack of hats on her head, a pile of dresses draped over her arm and all the jewelry she could wear. Putting two fingers to her lips she whistled. The boys came running from all directions, the least LaRue grabbing the broom on his way out.

The boys waited on the porch as Sadie took a last look at her only daughter. It had been Sadie's plan that Sessalee would someday take her place at Devil's Eye. She did her best to implant in Sessalee the sense of duty that had been planted in her. But it was not in Sessalee's nature to follow in her mother's footsteps. Devin assumed the rancor in the old woman's eyes was for losing her only daughter. In fact, Sadie was mourning her own loss.

Sadie gave Sessalee a stern nod from the doorway then the LaRue clan disappeared into the night like a pack of wolves.

Devin and Sessalee were left all alone in the house.

They stood in awkward silence for a time. Sessalee looked up at Devin, then cut her eyes toward the front bedroom. She was so sweet and willing, it made his throat hurt. There was no telling how many times he'd longed to have her in his house, to take her in his bed slow and easy instead of the backseat of his daddy's car, her long dark hair spilling over the feather pillow and her olive skin against the cool white sheets.

Tearing his eyes away from her, he grabbed his truck keys off the mantel. He pulled the front door open so hard it slammed back against the wall, driving the knob into the plaster. When she heard the tires spinning gravel down the road, Sessalee closed the door.

Her brothers had piled her things in the corner of the living room. Lifting the wooden crate, she carried it into the kitchen and carefully unpacked the gifts the women had given her to start her marriage. She set the coffee can with a burn plant growing in it on the window sill. Carefully unfolding the damp newspaper, she lifted the slips of mint, lemon balm, horehound, and dill her mama had dug from her own garden, placing them in a dishpan and sprinkling water on them until she could put them in the ground. With some reservation, she stored the bowl of sourdough starter in the Frigidaire. No one down at the Landing had an electric ice box and she worried some about it. If she killed the starter, it was sure to be bad luck. She put the jar of brandied fruit on the counter and, standing on a chair, slid the Maxwell House coffee can above the stove. Buried in the bottom was a roll of five one dollar bills her mama had given her for emergencies. 'Ever' wife needs a coffee can,' her mama had told her firmly.

Carrying the heavy double wedding ring quilt the women had pieced for her to the bedroom, she spread it over the bed. She hung her two dresses in the closet and laid her brush and comb next to Devin's comb on the dresser. Then she lifted her rag doll from the crate. She ran her finger over the tightly stitched mouth and button eyes and gently straightened the red yarn hair. Closing her eyes, she pressed the doll against her face and smelled it. Her mama had stuffed it with rosemary to make her dreams sweet at night. Lifting the mattress off the bed, she carefully hid the doll safely underneath. Sessalee didn't want her new husband to think he'd done married himself a child.

★ ★ ★

News traveled fast in Five Points. The next morning the Colonel knew all about his youngest son's shotgun wedding.

'Rumor has it you're a married man now.'

Devin stood in front of the Colonel's desk, his eyes at the floor. Bourne leaned against the wall behind the Colonel, arms crossed, toothpick in his mouth and grinning like the devil. Devin cut his big brother a hateful look and Bourne grinned even wider.

'Well?' the Colonel demanded.

Devin dropped out of the womb looking for an argument. When he was a boy, they called him the tooth fairy because he knocked out most of the baby teeth in town. He had a hairpin temper and a body coiled tight as a copperhead. He'd never met the man whose face he did not occasionally want to feel his fist against. There was only one man he feared. Devin was afraid of the Colonel. He wasn't afraid he couldn't whip his father. He was afraid he couldn't please him. His fears were justified.

There was a problem between father and son. When the Colonel was Devin's age he was married, Bourne was on the way, and he was already running the family business. Meanwhile, Devin was still biting his fingernails. But their friction went far deeper than Devin's lack of maturity. The Colonel felt a visceral wariness toward Devin. When he looked into Bourne's eyes, he saw his equal. When he looked into Devin's eyes, Devin looked away. Devin's spine bowed when he was around the Colonel, his shoulders slumped and his head hung like a whipped dog. The Colonel had done everything he could to give the boy a backbone. But if there was any Cavanagh in his youngest boy, the Colonel had never seen it. He loved his son, but the sight of him rubbed him raw.

'Boy, when I ask you a question, you answer me like a man! You hear me?'

'Yes, sir,' Devin mumbled.

'Now,' the Colonel asked, leaning forward and lacing his fingers on top of his desk, 'is she in the family way?'

Devin shifted uncomfortably.

'Well?' the Colonel demanded.

'I don't rightly know, sir.'

'You don't rightly know. Well, do you wrongly know?'

'She doesn't talk much, sir.'

'Holy Mother of God!'

The Colonel threw himself back in his chair and glared at Devin. If the boy didn't look just like him, he'd swear his wife had fornicated with a feeble.

'Well, if she is in the family way,' the Colonel roared, 'would it be the Cavanagh family way she was in?'

Forehead furled, Devin chewed on this. Was any man ever absolutely sure a child was his? Who knows what goes on with a woman when his back is turned? Sessalee LaRue had crawled into the backseat of his car for an ice-cream cone. How many other ice-cream cones had there been before him?

'Jesus Christ!' The Colonel hammed his fist on the desk. 'Say something, boy, even if it's wrong!'

'Yes, sir.'

'Yes, sir, what?'

Devin knew the Colonel was giving him a way out. All he had to do was say the right thing and he'd be a free man again. Sessalee LaRue would be out of his life for ever.

'Yes, sir.' Devin's eyes slowly turned up to meet the Colonel's. 'If she's in the family way, it would be the Cavanagh family.'

And Devin said it in a way that guaranteed he'd hurt any man who suggested otherwise.

It was the first sign of grit the Colonel had ever seen in his son and it took him by surprise.

184

He stared hard at Devin to see if this was a flicker of real courage or just a passing fluke. Under the Colonel's gaze, Devin folded and his eyes dropped to the floor.

The Colonel threw his hands up in disgust.

'Get out of my sight!'

* * *

Bourne was already leaning against Devin's truck by the time he got there, arms crossed and toothpick hanging on his lip. Devin had hightailed it out of the house as fast as he could after his trial with the Colonel, but Bourne still beat him. That had always been the way with them. No matter how hard Devin tried, Bourne always got there first.

While Devin fidgeted with his keys, his big brother stared past him at the Tennessee Walking Horses grazing on the hill, tails flicking and shiny coats dulled with a dusting of spring pollen. Bourne was ten years older than Devin, but it wasn't age or size that gave him the advantage. Everything came easy to Bourne — women, money and the deference of men. Bourne glided through life as though greased while Devin fought Lady Luck with both fists raised. Open the door for him and he'd climb through the window. Devin was contrary to the bone and this topped the reasons why he and the Colonel were at odds. But Bourne knew how to handle Devin. To guide his little brother in the right direction, nudge him toward the left.

Arms crossed, Bourne studied Devin. Not a

185

scratch or bruise on him. Bourne knew nothing and nobody could have forced his little brother down the aisle without a fight — unless that was the direction Devin was already headed.

'Can't imagine why a man would get married,' Bourne finally said.

'Yeah,' Devin huffed, 'and that's why you'll die alone in your bed.'

Bourne considered pointing out that the loneliest men they knew were married, but he was not the kind to rub salt in a man's wounds unless he had been the one who inflicted them. He knew what was eating at Devin. LaRue women were well known to be loose women, and Devin was not one to settle for hand-me-downs.

'Still,' Bourne continued with his thought, 'if a man had to settle down with just one woman, he'd be wise to settle on a woman with experience.'

Devin stared at his keys. 'And why is that?'

'Nothing holds a man's attention like a woman with mystery in her eyes.'

There was a hint of longing in Bourne's voice. Devin cut his eyes up.

'Besides,' Bourne shrugged, 'always figured the man who wanted a woman with no experience was a coward, afraid he couldn't hold up to the man who came before him.'

Devin rolled his eyes at his big brother. 'Easy for you to say, being as you're the *experience* half the men in the county have to live up to.'

It took a few seconds for Devin's brain to catch up to his mouth. He stared at Bourne and his eyebrows knitted. Why else would Bourne be giving him this speech, if he hadn't gotten to Sessalee first?

Letting out a holler, Devin flew into Bourne fists whirling. Twenty pounds and a lifetime of wrestling with his little brother gave Bourne the advantage. Sidestepping, he shoved Devin against the side of the truck. Grabbing him around the chest from behind, he lifted his little brother off the ground.

'What in the hell's the matter with you?' Bourne demanded, as Devin squirmed and kicked in the air.

'You and Sessalee are what's the matter!'

Bourne gave Devin a sharp jerk as if to straighten him out. 'Boy, you twist the facts like a damn lawyer! I've never even laid eyes on your little wife.'

'How do you know she's little?' Devin hissed through gritted teeth.

'What full-grown woman would want a Bantam rooster like you?'

Devin's elbow shot into Bourne's stomach like the kick of a mule. Breath knocked out of him, Bourne stumbled back. Shoulder down, Devin plowed into him at a full run. They hit the ground rolling, Devin's fists flying.

The blast of a shotgun made them both look up.

'I won't have Cavanaghs rolling in the dirt!' the Colonel roared from the front porch. 'You want to kill each other? Stand up and fight like men!'

Breathless and bloody, the two brothers stumbled to a stand.

187

'One of these days that temper of yours is going to cost you,' Bourne warned, spitting blood on the ground. 'You're a married man now. Grow up!'

Shoving Bourne aside, Devin climbed into his truck and threw it into gear.

'Thanks for the advice, big brother!' he shouted, glaring at Bourne wild-eyed and crazy mad. 'Then what should I do — fuck her sister?'

★ ★ ★

Sessalee spent her wedding night wrapped in her wedding quilt on the front porch swing, waiting for Devin to come home. When she heard his truck roaring down the road, she pulled the quilt tight and braced herself. The truck skidded to a stop in front of the house, gravel flying. Slamming the door as hard as he could, he stormed past her into the house without a word. He'd spent his honeymoon night tossing, turning and kicking in his truck. He'd parked at the river but it hadn't cooled him off a bit. He was mad at the Colonel, mad at the world and particularly mad at himself. And he traced it all back to Sessalee. Standing in the middle of the living room, jaw set and fists clenched, he swung around to confront her. He'd worked on what he had to say all night. He was going to tell Sessalee how it was — that he didn't appreciate being forced into anything, particularly marriage. And that they might be married until the day he died, but he would never forget what she did to him. And never forgive her. Never.

He opened his mouth to start his speech, but the sight of her, standing in the doorway wrapped in her quilt, made him lose his train of thought. Tearing his eyes away from her, he noticed something about the room was unfamiliar. Frowning, he looked around. The newspapers had been folded, his books put back on the shelf, and the floor swept and mopped. There were no piles of clothes on the floor or stacks of dirty dishes on the coffee table.

Like a flea-bitten dog whose bed had been washed, Devin couldn't decide how he felt about the change.

'What's that smell?' he asked, as though it were an accusation.

He followed her into the kitchen. It was warm from the wood stove and steamy from the pot of beans simmering there. She'd scrubbed the floor on her hands and knees, just about worn the enamel off the old sink and used boiled vinegar to get the grease glaze off the cupboard. Devin could not believe the cupboard was painted white. All his life he'd thought it was tobacco-spit yellow.

'Why is there salt on the chopping block?' he asked, lifting his chin at the layer of wet salt crusting on the pecan block.

' 'Show ya clean it.'

'Why?'

Sessalee stared at him as unreadable as a cat. She had no idea why you put salt on the chopping block. It had never occurred to her to wonder. Why things were done the way they were done had never been a driving concern for LaRues.

'You don't just do something because that's the way it's always been done,' Devin told her. 'You look for a better way of doing it.'

His eyes continued to roam, finally landing on the cayenne pepper plant growing in a rusty coffee can on the window sill. Sessalee had always been a quick study. She knew exactly why there was a pepper plant on the sill and jumped to tell him.

'Pepper's fer the beans,' she said, lifting the lid on the pot for him to see.

His grandmother had kept a pepper plant on the sill. Probably half the women in Five Points did. But Devin was looking for something to be mad at. He couldn't find anything else, so the damn pepper would have to do.

'I don't like dirt in my kitchen.'

He didn't seem to mind it caked on the floors, in his sheets and under his fingernails, but Sessalee held her tongue.

It was not so much the pepper plant as the principle that made his hands draw into fists again. It was his house. His kitchen. She was taking over like chickweed. He was fixing to pitch the damn coffee can out the door when the platter of fried chicken caught his eye. Crispy, brown and still warm from the skillet.

Devin had no recollection of hanging his coat on the back of the chair and sliding onto the seat. He reached for a piece and she glanced at his hands.

'They're clean enough,' he said gruffly. When

she turned her back to him, he wiped them on his shirt.

Grabbing a piece of fried chicken, he took a bite. The bones seemed petite for a fryer.

'What is this?' he asked, chewing.

'Rabbit.'

Devin stared at the remains of the tiny breast in his hand.

'Where's the buckshot?'

'Trapped it.'

His eyebrows lifted.

'How did you get it so tender?'

'Soaked it in buttermilk.'

He wondered when she'd found time to trap a rabbit, dress it, and walk to town to buy buttermilk to soak it in. He wondered how she knew he liked sorghum on his cornbread. He wondered how she knew he liked his tea sweet as syrup. While she was standing at the stove stirring the beans so they wouldn't stick, he got a good look at her. It was the first time he had seen her in broad daylight. She was a tiny little thing. Her dress hung off her shoulder and her shoes slipped off her heels when she walked. Her thick black braid hung down her back like a rope and her face was scrubbed until the skin shone. She looked like a little girl dressed up in her mama's clothes. When she stood next to him to spoon mashed potatoes onto his plate, he caught the scent of her skin. She smelled like rainwater.

'Good cornbread,' he said.

Cutting another wedge, she lifted it from the skillet, buttered it, and set it on his plate.

He stole quick glimpses at her stomach as she

191

stood next to him, but the faded cotton dress was so loose he couldn't tell much. And that got him to thinking. He wondered how many other men she'd fried rabbit for, how many other men's cornbread she'd buttered. He wondered if they'd been better men than he was. And the food hung in his throat. Scraping his chair back from the table, he grabbed his coat. She shadowed after him as he stormed through the house and out the front door. Standing on the porch, she leaned against the rail until she couldn't hear his engine any more. Rubbing her arms, she slowly walked back to the warm kitchen.

Sessalee stood at the table looking down at his plate. He hadn't touched her white beans. She walked all the way to her mama's to get the salt pork to season them. Sorted the dry beans on the table, soaked them all night and watched them simmer all morning. Added water twice to make sure they didn't cook dry.

Taking Devin's plate outside, Sessalee slung her honeymoon meal into the yard for the dog.

★ ★ ★

It was almost dark when Sessalee heard Devin pull up in the drive. Strapped down in the truck bed was a barrel from the distillery, the wood still green and metal bands shiny. Dropping the tailgate, Devin jumped up into the bed. Tilting the barrel with a grunt, he rolled it to the edge and dropped it as gently as he could to the soft ground. Hopping down, he and Sessalee rolled the barrel to the edge of the back porch. Breaking the gutter downspout at the seam, he aimed it down into the barrel.

'To catch rainwater for your hair.' He shrugged to assure her it meant nothing.

'Is it brand new?' Sessalee asked, as though she couldn't believe there was such a thing.

She ran her hand along the metal rim as if the barrel was the finest thing she had ever seen. Then she looked up at Devin, eyes shining, as though he'd done something grand. The look squeezed his chest. He ached to do something else, anything, to keep that look in her eyes.

'First thing anybody ever give me weren't hand-me-down,' she said.

They were standing so close he could have rested his chin on the top of her head. She turned her face up to his. It was so soft and willing. He knew he could kiss her if he wanted. He could kiss her till it hurt. She had never once denied him anything. His mouth was so close to hers he could taste it. And for a second, he forgot why he was mad at her.

Anger is an addiction that must be fed. Devin thought about the feel of that cold hard shotgun under his chin. He thought about what everyone in town must be saying about him behind his back. He thought about the first night he saw her and how easy she'd been.

But as he looked down at her, he could not block the feel of her skin and how warm and wet she always was. It took all he had to back away. It felt as if his skin was peeling away from hers. As he climbed into his truck, he looked back at her, dress sliding off her shoulder as if the slightest breeze would blow it away. He waited for her to beg him to stay. When she didn't, it made the whole reason for his leaving seem foolish. But he'd made a commitment, and he was sticking to it. Reaching under the seat, he grabbed a bottle of whiskey, pulled the cork out and threw it back. Then he stomped the gas pedal to the floor board and fishtailed across the lawn.

★ ★ ★

Devin woke up the next morning when the truck door swung open and he fell out onto the wet grass. Flinching and moaning, he threw his hand up to block the blinding sunlight. His teeth ached and his tongue was so thick it didn't fit in his mouth. It even hurt to blink.

'I take it you're trying to please your new bride by not sleeping with her.' Writhing on the grass, Devin squinted up. Bourne loomed over him, the sun behind his head like a halo of fire. Propping himself up on an elbow, he looked around to get his bearings. Tennessee Walking Horses grazed around the truck and the house he'd been born in rose out of the morning fog like a three-tiered white columned wedding cake. He'd been blind drunk, but his truck had found its way home like a homing pigeon. When his gaze landed on the Colonel glaring down at him, Devin closed his eyes and groaned.

'Another five feet,' Bourne said, taking a sip of coffee, 'and we'd be fishing your dead body out of the river right now.'

Pushing himself up onto his hands and knees, Devin peered over the edge of the bluff to the river several hundred feet below. The perspective made his head swim. Shoulders jerking, he gagged like a cat trying to spit up a fur ball. Bourne and the Colonel stepped back just in time to save their shoes. When his heaves turned dry, they each grabbed Devin under an arm and lifted him to a wobbly stand.

'Should have drowned this puppy when I had the chance,' the Colonel grumbled, as they dragged his youngest boy toward the house.

★ ★ ★

The Colonel lifted the percolator off the stove with a scorched quilt potholder and poured a neat shot of scalding coffee into his morning whiskey. The pot had been simmering since 4:30 that morning and the coffee had boiled down to a stiff viscosity. The Colonel liked his coffee the way he liked his women. If it didn't get the heart racing, what was the point?

The Colonel could not remember a time when men did not look to him for direction. As if to speed his authority along, his hair turned silver while he was still a young man. Now, nearing fifty, it was completely white, but his body was still as strong and vigorous as his sons. And so were his appetites.

Colonel Corbett Cavanagh was a rare breed. He was a man's man who loved women. He loved to watch a woman walk across a room, sit in a chair and brush her hair at her dressing mirror. He could stare indefinitely at the curve of a woman's neck and grow drunk from the smell of her skin. A woman's deep throaty laugh lit a fire in his soul. The Colonel loved women. He simply had never found one he particularly liked.

The Colonel had married twice. His first wife, the mother of both sons, died of natural causes. His second wife died from an answered prayer. Every day he was legally bound to the shrew, the Colonel prayed the Lord would put her out of his misery. Granted, he was not an easy man to live with. But everyone in Five Points knew the second Mrs Cavanagh had married the Colonel under false pretenses. She'd bagged him by baiting the field.

Jean Louise Carter hailed from Birmingham and was the widow of an Alabama litigator. If that wasn't warning enough, she was the aunt of Crazy June Bug Wallace. Jean Louise had been widowed less than a month when she spotted the Colonel during a visit to Five Points. After a thorough enquiry into his financial liquidity, she decided to extend her stay.

No woman ever appeared more enamored with a man. She hung on the Colonel's every word, lit his cigars for him and kept a closer eye on his glass than a bartender. Jean Louise, who likened a stroll in the rose garden to a safari, took up hunting and fishing. She swooned when the Colonel helped her with her coat and all but humped his leg when he kissed her hand.

The Colonel thought he'd found true love. His dogs knew better.

Animals sense what humans are too civilized

to see. The Colonel's redbone hound, Ulysses, named for the Greek not the Yankee, did everything but send up smoke signals to warn him. When Jean Louise walked into the room, he barked. When she reached her hand out to pet him, he growled, tucked his tail and ran. When she tried to win him over with beef bones, he wolfed them down, but with great reservation.

Jean Louise caught the Colonel at a vulnerable time and he was blind to all the warnings. He had a business to run, a house to keep and two small boys to rear on his own. Furthermore, he had deprived himself of a woman's affection since his wife died. A man starts to hallucinate when his John Thomas is left too long in solitary confinement. Before the Colonel knew what was happening, John Thomas had proposed.

Jean Louise showed her true colors right out of the gate. Her first week as the second Mrs Cavanagh, she substituted the Colonel's morning shot of whiskey with a bowl of stewed prunes.

The marriage went downhill from there.

The Colonel simply could not get a handle on his new wife. She didn't want him out of her sight, but she couldn't stand the sight of him. She complained when he came home late, but had a hissy fit when he came home early. She didn't like the way he dressed, but refused to look at him naked. There was no pleasing her and absolutely no effort on her part to please him. In fact, she seemed to thrive on the opposite. The Colonel couldn't understand why on earth she'd married him.

In reality, it's simple biology. When a man bags a woman he doesn't plan to keep, he throws her back. When a woman lands a man she has no taste for, she drags him home, bats him around until he's too weak to fight back, then grooms herself while she waits for him to die.

Little by little, Jean Louise took away the Colonel's every pleasure. She set forth the edict that there would be no hunting on Sundays or Christian holidays, a family tradition since the first Cavanagh ate meat. 'And no smoking in the house!' she ordered, as she carried his humidor to the porch. 'It isn't good for the boys.' The Colonel failed to see how smoking in the house could adversely affect the boys, seeing as how she'd quarantined Bourne and Devin to the yard.

The final straw came when the Colonel caught her beating his beloved Ulysses out the door with a broom.

'A house is no place for filthy dogs!' she told the Colonel fiercely.

He totally agreed and was on the verge of handing the rabid bitch her suitcase when the telegram came. The Colonel had been called back to serve his country.

Europe was at war and America was about to be. Bourne was fourteen years old at the time, Devin four. The Colonel hated leaving them with the shrew, but it was better than leaving them alone. His sons, he had no doubt, would survive. But he had serious concerns for his hounds. A dog needs humanity, something the second Mrs Cavanagh was sorely missing.

Blasting cannons and exploding grenades seemed like peace and quiet after marriage. Even his wife's letters were more caustic than gas warfare. Page after page of the inconvenience and hardship his being shot at was causing her. His fingers blistered just tearing open the envelope. The only reason he suffered through her carping was for news of his sons, of which she wrote little.

He was watching the Germans drive the Allies back in Marne when his aide handed him the telegram.

SHE'S DEAD. STOP. CHOKED ON A PRUNE. STOP. HAD PIT BRONZED. STOP. BOURNE.

The Colonel passed out cigars.

'But Colonel!' his aide declared, mortified, 'she was your wife!'

'Son,' the Colonel said, slapping the boy on the back, 'when a bitch bites because she's afraid, you win her with gentleness. When she bites out of meanness, you put her down. The good Lord just saved me the trouble.'

The Colonel carried the bronzed pit in his pocket to remind him of the misery of marriage. He had lived with two women. It nearly killed him losing his first wife. And it nearly killed him living with the second. He would not marry again.

Retrieving his cigar stub from the window ledge above the sink, he pulled open the door on the wood stove, touched a twist of newspaper to the fire and held it under the stub. Ulysses lay curled by the stove, guarding the box of sleeping pups while their mother took a morning run. Puffing, the Colonel tossed the torch into the firebox. He patted the dog's head as he latched the stove door. His housekeeper had been after him to get a modern gas stove, but the Colonel stood firm. You would never convince him that a biscuit baked in a gas oven tasted as good as one baked in a hickory-fired wood stove. Furthermore, only a fool would buy gas when he had fifteen hundred acres of oak and hickory trees surrounding the house.

Any evidence that a female had once occupied the Cavanagh house had long been removed. Muddy boots and grit had sanded the oak floors down to raw wood and the smell of whiskey, tobacco smoke and saddle soap permeated the plaster walls to the yellow poplar studs. Gun cases lined the hall and fishing vests hung on pegs beside the kitchen door. More often than not there was something dead on the butcher block waiting to be cleaned — doves, a wild turkey, a string of bass. The Colonel and Bourne seldom came home empty-handed. A mat of dog hair covered the rugs and drifts of their red silk rolled like tumbleweed with the slightest breeze. The Colonel's redbone hounds lounged wherever they pleased, sprawled on his late wife's cherished Chippendale sofa or curled in the middle of the unmade beds. It was a bachelor's lair and any man who entered felt his testosterone rise.

From time to time the housekeeper tried to

impose a bit of femininity. The Colonel would rest his arm on a useless crocheted doily or discover a cheese smothered casserole on the kitchen table. Lifting the lid, his lip would curl and his stomach would recoil. The Colonel was a meat and potatoes man. He saw no need for foods to be intermingled. 'Looks like something that's already been eaten,' he'd grumble, then sling it off the back porch for the chickens. He wasn't about to let his dogs eat the slop.

Reaching down into the wooden crate next to the stove, the Colonel pushed his hand around the litter of fat red pups. One shied away, one cowered in the corner, and one bit his finger out of pure meanness, drawing blood. He marked that one in his mind. One pup ran up to his hand, licking it, yapping and jumping up and down for attention. The Colonel pushed it aside.

All the while, one pup sat apart from the others, watching. The Colonel held the back of his hand in front of her nose. She neither backed away nor licked it, but simply took in his scent. Slowly, the Colonel ran his hand over her head and down the small solid body. One finger under her chin, he lifted her tiny head and searched the bright eyes for the rare quality he most prized. You can tell a lot about a man by the way he treats his dog. Some keep a bitch pinned until he's ready to hunt. Some whip her into submission. Some prefer blind obedience over intelligence. The qualities the Colonel treasured most were 'heart and try'. Gently lifting the pup out of the box, he tucked her inside his coat next to his heart.

Coffee in one hand and cigar clamped in the corner of his mouth, the Colonel went outside.

Easing himself into a rocker, the Colonel soothed the pup. Then he leaned back and studied his sons. Bourne had a shotgun broken open and was inspecting the barrel. Devin leaned over the rail, hands wrapped around a mug of coffee, staring off the porch at the valley below. They were deadly handsome boys. The Colonel would give them that. Devin had a thread of tragedy woven into his fiber that reeled women in. His mother had died while he was still nursing. The housekeeper put him on the bottle, but Devin still had a mouth that looked like it was yearning for a tit. No matter what age the woman, young or old, her eyes always went to his mouth.

There was nothing vulnerable about Bourne. If there had been he would have reached under his skin and torn it out. Bourne was as fearless as Devin was pensive. While the Colonel would never say it out loud, it was what made them perfect partners. They balanced each other perfectly.

The Colonel stared at his two sons and felt his life swell.

'Rise like Lions after slumber,' his voice rumbled deep. 'In unvanquishable number — Shake your chains to earth like dew, which in sleep had fallen on you . . .'

The Colonel quoted Shelley with an elegant Southern lilt that echoed their Irish roots. Bourne and Devin looked up at their father as though he were speaking in tongues. They glanced at each other, then went back to their own thoughts. Sighing, the Colonel kissed the pup on the top of her head.

It was not his sons' fault they were without poetry. The Colonel had been through war and survived it. His dance with death turned him into a philosophical man. And the philosophy that he had come to believe in was the survival of the fittest. He had not allowed any weakness in his sons. As a result, they had neither the time nor the inclination for poetry or philosophical debate. They were men of instinct, survivors. While they were, the Colonel had made sure, more fit for the new century than he, it made him no less lonely. He loved his sons. He would kill for them. He would die for them. But they were about as much company for a father's soul as the callus on the bottom of his foot.

The Colonel longed for intellectual discourse, to spend the day in verbal battle with an equal. Someone to keep the mind sharp as the body dulled. Someone to stoke the dying fire of his life. And while he was wishing, he wouldn't mind a grandchild either. 'He wants to be a lawyer,' Bourne said, nodding toward his little brother.

Devin choked on his coffee.

'What?' the Colonel thundered.

'You heard me,' Bourne said, going back to polishing the barrel of his Remington.

'How did you know?' Devin sputtered and coughed.

'Saw all those law books in your house,' Bourne shrugged. 'Figured you weren't studying to be a priest.'

The Colonel gritted his teeth so tight he nearly bit his cigar in two. What else could the boy possibly do to pain him? The only thing he had ever wanted was for his sons to carry on the family legacy.

'I think he might have a gift for it,' Bourne said.

'He's the one who wants to be a damn lawyer!' the Colonel roared. 'Let him plead his own case.'

Devin looked desperately at his big brother. Bourne shrugged to let him know he was on his own.

'One day the country's going to come to its senses,' Devin started, staring at his boots.

'Boy, look me in the eyes when you talk to me!'

Devin's blue eyes rose up to meet his father's.

'The politicians are going to have to admit that it costs more to police alcohol than to tax it. When that happens, we'll have to go legal. They won't let just anyone make liquor. We're going to need a lawyer to fight the lawyers. And I figure I'm the one suited for the job.'

The Colonel thoughtfully exhaled cigar smoke as he petted the pup.

'A man willing to argue both sides of the coin is only interested in the coin,' he said, as if moving a chess piece into check.

'The only way to defeat an enemy is to make him your partner,' Devin said firmly.

The Colonel stared at him so long Devin cut his eyes toward Bourne.

'I want to meet this new wife of yours,' the Colonel finally said.

Bourne grinned. He was fairly certain Devin's heart had stopped.

Taking his cigar stub out of his mouth, the Colonel studied it, then flicked it over the porch rail into the wet grass.

'Go get me another cigar,' he ordered, shooing Devin off the porch with his hand like a fly.

Sliding off the banister, Devin glared at Bourne on his way into the house.

'When did you plan to tell me he'd grown a backbone?' the Colonel asked, when Devin was out of hearing range.

'Figured it was something you'd want to see for yourself,' Bourne said, running the flannel cloth smoothly down the barrel of his rifle.

★　★　★

Devin fidgeted like a cat as he and Sessalee waited outside the Colonel's library door. He looked her up and down time and again. She could tell he wasn't pleased with what he saw. Sessalee looked down at herself. She was clean, no buttons missing. She could not figure what his problem was.

When the Colonel finally opened the door, Sessalee thought Devin was going to come out of his skin. Stepping aside, the Colonel motioned with his head for her to come in and closed the door in Devin's face when he tried to follow.

The Colonel nodded to the chair. Sessalee sat, back straight and small hands folded in her lap. She was a tiny little thing, even for a LaRue, with no expression to give her away. Her eyes were fixed on him, but the Colonel had no doubt she knew every exit in the room.

He dragged his chair close to hers so that their knees almost touched. Most women would have shrunk back. Sessalee stayed her ground.

'Cigar smoke bother you?' he asked, while striking the match.

He took her silence to mean, no.

'How did you meet my son?' he asked, rolling his cigar in the flame.

Of course, he knew the story. The whole town knew. Devin had picked up his new bride at the rock wall.

'Seen him in the woods.'

The Colonel's eyes cut to hers over the flame.

'In the woods?'

'He wuz huntin'.'

'Where in the woods?'

'Down in Steamer Holler.'

'When was this?'

'Winter 'fore last.'

Shaking out the match, the Colonel tossed it into the fireplace.

'You saw Devin in the woods, but he didn't see you.'

'Fog was real thick. Swirled when you walked through it.'

The Colonel leaned back in his chair and drummed his fingers on the arm.

'You followed him.'

'He's right clumsy,' Sessalee said, as though this might be news to the Colonel. 'Slippin' and trippin'. Figured he needed lookin' after. Pressed myself up against the tree like moss. Followed him all that mornin', so close I coulda almost reached out and touched him. He never knew.'

The question answered, Sessalee grew quiet.

'Then what happened?' the Colonel encouraged.

'He spotted a buck, ten-pointer proud as Paul. Wind was right. That buck just stood there pretty as you please. I coulda had it gutted and skinned by the time he pulled his rifle to his shoulder. Clean a shot as a man could have. He had the buck right in his sight. Finger on the trigger. But he just stood there starin' for the longest time. Then he dropped that rifle to his leg, like that deer weren't really what he was huntin' fer.'

Sessalee looked at the Colonel to see if he understood.

'And so you tracked him.'

'Followed him to his granddaddy's place. Watched him make coffee through the kitchen windduh. He likes it real stiff. Watched him sit on the porch and read. Lord, he loves his books. When his truck was gone, I'd slip inside and pick through his things. His clothes smelled real good. I put 'um back just like I found 'um.'

Sessalee offered no apology. It was the way things were done where she was from.

'How long did you watch him?'

'Till spring.'

By then, the Colonel had no doubt, Sessalee knew his son better than Devin knew himself. There was only one thing left for her to find out. Would Devin want her the way she wanted him.

'You knew Devin would be driving by the rock

wall,' the Colonel said quietly.

'Regular as the sun settin',' Sessalee said.

★ ★ ★

Devin was hunched in a chair outside the library door chewing his thumbnail to the quick when the Colonel walked out holding Sessalee on his arm.

'Go get your things,' the Colonel ordered. 'You're moving back here.'

'What?' Devin demanded in disbelief.

'While you're in law school, you'll be gone half the time. My daughter-in-law has no business being alone in those woods.'

'Hell!' Devin huffed. 'She can take care of herself better in those woods than I can!'

Devin might as well have been howling at the moon. The Colonel was already taking Sessalee on a grand tour of her new home, although the Colonel suspected she already knew the place better than he.

18

LeRoy LaRue leaned against his rusty truck squinting into the sun as Pearl Wilde stepped off the ferry at LaRue's Landing. He'd been told to pick her up and bring her back to the distillery. He had not been told to make her trip pleasant. For men born with nothing, opportunity lies in the loopholes.

Hand on hip, Pearl looked LeRoy over. Boys had turned into men in her absence, their soft mouths hardened and the shine in their eyes dulled.

'You Sadie LaRue's boy?' she asked.

LeRoy didn't deny it, so she knew it was so. Admission was not part of the LaRue culture.

The weather had taken an unexpected cold snap for March. The wind blowing off the river cut through LeRoy's ragged flannel shirt. Elbows gone and pockets torn nearly off, the chewed cuffs draped past his raw knuckles. His pants hung on his slim hips and the muddy hem dragged the ground. What LaRues lack in stature, they more than make up for in mettle.

'Gonna halfa tie a blindfold on ya,' he said, reaching for a bandanna in his back pocket.

As he walked toward her with the dirty bandanna, Pearl slipped a white silk scarf from around her neck and held it out for him. Taking the scarf, he slid it over her eyes.

'Usually, I'm the one tying a man in knots,'

she said, as he jerked it tight.

Her tease was wasted on LeRoy. Holding her roughly by the elbow, he shoved her up into the passenger seat of the truck. Tying the door closed with a piece of rope, he climbed into the driver's side. Grinding the starter, he pumped the gas pedal and the smell of oily exhaust filled the truck. Shifting into gear, LeRoy took off.

He drove around in lazy circles for a while to get her fully disoriented, then turned sharply off the road. The truck went bumping down a steep incline. Bouncing from side to side, Pearl gripped the dash. Shifting down, LeRoy guided the truck into rushing water. Even blindfolded, Pearl knew where she was.

'Yellow Creek is awful high to be driving across this time of year,' she said, but there was no concern in her voice.

Hanging her arm out the window, she let the tips of her fingers drag the spray. The cold triggered a memory and the past flooded over her. It was a white hot summer day. She and Kat had been skinny-dipping in Yellow Creek. They had climbed up the bluff to the diving spot, but Pearl, as always, had hesitated.

'You going to jump?' Kat chided. 'Or you going to stand there forever?'

Then laughing, Kat ran to the edge and jumped without ever looking down.

'Come on in!' Kat called up to her, motioning from the creek. 'The water's fine!'

But Pearl could never bring herself to jump. She'd watched her mother dive head first too many times. Pearl had to ease herself into things slowly.

LeRoy watched Pearl's face soften with the memory. Her cheeks were flushed and she was shivering. But a quiet had come over her as if her heart had found its rhythm. He could sense that for all her fancy clothes and fancy ways, the farther they moved from town, the closer Pearl Wilde came to home.

The truck spun up the muddy bank, water sloshing from the bed until the bald tires caught and pulled them back onto the road. They bumped and wound through the woods for some time until, suddenly, Pearl felt the truck veer sharply off the road. Her hand went to the dash as the truck bumped and jerked to a stop. She heard LeRoy switch the key off and the motor sputtered to a stop. Then there was nothing but the quiet of the woods. Her heart hammered as she sensed LeRoy pulling off his shirt. One hand reached to pull off her blindfold, while the other curled into a claw. She was fully prepared to scratch his eyes out when she felt the flannel shirt fall over her feet.

'She's cold as a witch's teet,' LeRoy said, as he tucked his shirt around her freezing feet.

Pearl turned her face away to the window. Kindness was the only thing she never saw coming.

LeRoy started the truck again and they drove until the air turned sour. Pearl knew they were close. Bootleggers raise pigs to cover the smell of the sour mash and it took a hell of lot of hogs to mask the Colonel's operation. It was feeding time and Pearl could hear the squealing.

'Feed the spent mash to the pigs. Feed the pigs to us,' LeRoy volunteered, as he turned into the yard. 'Them hogs have a smile on their face right up till the end.'

Shifting the truck to a stop, he went around to open the door for Pearl. Holding her arm, he helped her down and untied her blindfold. Pearl shielded her eyes until they adjusted to the sunlight. White steam rose from the distillery, hiding the Colonel's operation under a cloud of fog. The size and elaborateness of the clandestine operation never ceased to amaze the rare visitor. Half a dozen neat cedar-sided buildings were tucked in the holler, along with a small sawmill to cut wood for the barrels. A creek separated the mill from the charcoal rickyard. A waterwheel generated electricity. It reminded Pearl of a small village she'd passed through in Germany, or maybe it was Austria.

A gang of lanky men, arms crossed and cheeks full of chew, stood staring. It was not that often a woman came to the distillery, especially a woman like Pearl.

Reaching down into the floorboard of the truck, Pearl picked up LeRoy's shirt and shook it out. The men watched in curious silence as she held it up for LeRoy LaRue as if he were some kind of gentleman. A decent woman would never associate with a LaRue. Pearl had found enormous freedom in her ruined reputation.

Solemnly, LeRoy slipped his arms into the ragged sleeves and stood perfectly still as Pearl buttoned what few buttons there were. The men in the yard watched in envious fascination as Pearl Wilde, in her pearl necklace and long white fur coat, made a fuss over a LaRue.

'There,' she said, smoothing the front of the flannel shirt and straightening the ragged collar.

Normally, the men's minds would have gone straight to the gutter, but under the circumstances they felt it best not to let their thoughts wander too far for fear they might miss something. They would have been perfectly content to spend the rest of the day gawking. But one of them spotted Bourne Cavanagh in his office window and immediately alerted the others with a loud cough. Hands stuffed into their pockets, they sauntered back to work. Bourne was the last man on earth they wanted to rub the wrong way, and not just because he handed out their paychecks.

Bourne's office was little more than a rough sawn shack. He didn't have that much paperwork to attend to. It had a window, a desk, two chairs and a braided rug with a trap door underneath. The door dropped to a dug-out tunnel that resurfaced 200-feet from the distillery near the creek. Devin thought Bourne was crazy for digging it.

'The only way a revenuer is going to find this place is if he falls from the sky,' he'd said.

But the Colonel understood perfectly. Bourne had been caught with his pants down once. He would not be caught again.

Pearl took her time walking across the yard. Bourne was not the only man who could not take his eyes off her.

She climbed the steps to Bourne's office slow and deliberate. At his door, she grabbed the handle, then rocked back. She could feel him through the wood, pressing against her real as flesh. Her body readied — lips parting, nipples drawing, womb watering. Three years and ten thousand miles, and she still couldn't stop it. It made her so mad she hissed. She shook it off like a dog slinging water and forced her thoughts to turn. She had replayed that moment in her mind so many times it scratched and hung — Bourne looking back over his broad bare shoulder at her, 'Please, darlin', give me just one more minute.' Face frosted, Pearl turned the knob.

The second she stepped through the threshold, Bourne was on her. Kicking the door closed, he pinned her against it, his hand on her throat. His heart was thundering through his chest and his mouth was so close she could taste the whiskey on his hot ragged breath.

'Where you been, Pearl?' he asked quietly.

'Around.'

'Funny thing. You forgot to say goodbye.'

'As I recall,' she said, cutting her eyes to his, 'you said it for the both of us.'

Pulling his fist back, Bourne drove it into the door beside her face so hard it cracked the wood. Pearl didn't flinch, but the men loitering in the yard jumped a foot off the ground.

He loomed over her, knuckles bleeding and breathing like a racehorse. He was torn between slapping the shit out of her and taking her then and there. But then it had always been all or nothing between them. Pearl operated at full throttle. She didn't need foreplay in any form or fashion. As rough as Bourne could give it, Pearl could take it. He'd never found another one like her and God knows he'd tried. Grabbing fistfuls of her fur coat, he shoved her hard against the wall. Pearl smiled.

Jaw locked, Bourne walked around his desk, jerked the chair back, considered throwing it against the wall, then slammed his body into it. Straightening her coat, Pearl smoothed her hair, and poured herself into the chair across from his. She lit a cigarette, then crossed her legs, leaned back and stared at him. He had no idea what she was thinking. Pearl had always held her cards close. The only time he'd ever been certain she wasn't bluffing was when he was thrusting his way home inside her and she was begging him not to stop.

Slipping a piece of stationery from her purse, she slid it halfway across the desk.

'I'll need this to start. After that, put us on a weekly delivery.'

Bourne's eyes hung on hers and he felt the heat start to rise in him. Pearl could do more to a man with her eyes than most women could do with her entire body.

'What kind of deal can you cut me?' she asked.

He pounded his fist on the desk and a box of shotgun shells jumped and slammed back down.

'Give me a twenty per cent discount and I'll pay on delivery,' she said calmly.

He pounded his fist again and the shells scattered onto the floor like a string of broken pearls. Slapping his hand on her shopping list, he dragged it across the desk.

'Fifteen,' he said, studying her list.

Pearl smiled ever so slightly.

'Fifteen it is.'

He knew she would have settled for ten. He knew he'd been easy on her. He knew it wouldn't happen again.

'I can sell you three-year-old whiskey and save you,' he said, glancing up at her over the paper. 'No one will ever know the difference.'

'The men I'm serving will know the difference.'

The muscle in his jaw tightened so slightly no one else in the world would have caught it but Pearl. Every man has his 'tell'. Either a woman can read it or not.

'And I'm going to need twenty bottles of French champagne,' Pearl added.

'French?'

'If you can't handle it — '

'I didn't say I couldn't get it. It's just going to take some time.'

'I need it by the first of next month.'

Bourne didn't nod but he didn't shake his head either. 'We deliver on Tuesdays.'

'Make it Monday. It's the girls' day off. Devin still handling the money?'

Bourne didn't say no, so she knew he was.

'Well,' Pearl said, tapping her cigarette out in the ashtray on his desk, 'if we're through here . . . '

She was standing up to leave when Bourne opened a drawer, pulled out a bottle and set it firmly on the desk. At the sight of the whiskey,

216

Pearl's breath held for barely a second. It was so slight a mistake, no one else in the world would have caught it but Bourne.

'You know the rules, Pearl,' he said, unscrewing the top. 'Never sell whiskey to a man who won't drink it.' Filling two shot glasses, he slid hers across the desk. 'Or a woman, as the case may be.'

Staring at the glass, Pearl considered her options and saw she had none. Slowly, she lowered herself back into the chair.

'To the pleasure of business,' Bourne said, clinking his glass against hers.

'And the business of pleasure,' she replied, causing his drink to hang momentarily in the air.

Throwing the shot back, Bourne slammed the empty glass on the desk. Then he leaned back in his chair and waited.

Among Pearl's infinite assets was the fact that she was the cheapest drunk he had ever met. You could run the cork under her nose and she'd start dancing on the table. Bourne liked that in a girl.

Pearl lifted the glass and stared at it. She finally managed to bring it to her lips, closed her eyes and threw it back. She held her breath as she drank, winced as she swallowed, and shivered as the liquid fire burned its way down. When it hit the spot, a smoky sigh passed through her parted lips and a faraway look came into her eyes.

'Dressed up mighty fancy for a trip to the holler,' Bourne said.

'You don't like it?'

Truthfully, he preferred her barefoot, bare-faced, cotton dress pulled up above her knees and wading in the creek.

'I wouldn't kick you out of bed.'

'You're doing it in a bed now?' Pearl said, dry as salt.

Bourne refilled their drinks.

Clinking glasses, they threw them back simultaneously. This time, Pearl closed her eyes and swallowed smooth and slow. The only time a man could truly get a good look at Pearl was when her eyes were closed. Bourne took his time, lingering here and there. The years had been good to her, but then he'd always preferred his liquor and his women well aged.

It is important to be the first thing a woman sees after her second shot of whiskey. At that point even a jackass starts to look good. Pearl slowly opened her eyes into Bourne's and a watery blur came over her.

'Bourne Cavanagh,' she slurred softly, leaning across the desk, 'you're still as mean as a snake.'

'As I recall, you used to like that in a man.'

Pearl ran her tongue over her lips like a cat licking cream as he filled their glasses a third time. Pearl never did anything drunk she wouldn't do sober. She just did it better. Let her go past a good buzz and you never knew what direction she'd spin off in. Knowing the exact point to cut her off was more art than science.

'This is the last one,' Pearl said, the 's' running away from her.

'Is it?' he asked quietly.

He watched over his glass as she poured the drink down.

'You have to admit,' he said, 'we had some good times.'

Pearl didn't agree, but she didn't disagree either.

Bourne pinned her with his eyes and Pearl sat perfectly still. It was a look that would have disarmed her in her previous life. But to his surprise, Pearl looked back on equal terms. The corner of his mouth slowly curled up and his eyes shone.

'You've changed,' he said, voice husky.

Pearl gave him a look that left no doubt. She had indeed changed and in ways he could only dream of. It ran down him like a scald. Pushing herself to a stand, she weaved unsteadily across the room in her high heels like a lanky colt learning to walk.

'Don't bother to get up,' she said on her way out the door.

At that moment, Bourne couldn't have if he'd wanted to.

★ ★ ★

Pearl was pulling on her gloves when she heard her name.

'Hello, Colonel,' she said, without looking up.

The Colonel leaned against the porch rail of Bourne's office clipping the tip off a cigar. Tucking the cigar between his lips, he reached into his pocket for a match. Pearl already had her silver lighter open and lit. Cupping his hand over hers, he rolled the cigar in the flame. With his eyes down, she was free to take him in. Before she left Five Points, she had not appreciated how rare men like the Colonel were. He was the big dog. There was no contest. When the cigar was lit, she slipped it from his lips, took a draw, then put it back where she'd found it.

'Tell me, Colonel,' she said, on the exhale, 'why didn't you and me ever get together instead of that piece of shit son of yours?'

The Colonel laughed like the devil and thirty years melted away. She could play the Colonel, but he knew he was being played. That was a great relief for Pearl because she couldn't stop playing even if she wanted to.

The Colonel held out his arm and she took it. They stepped off the porch and headed across the distillery yard as if out for a Sunday stroll.

There is no harbor like being on the arm of a strong man. Pearl leaned against the Colonel's sleeve and breathed in the smell of dark fired tobacco, wool and shaving soap.

'What's your mother up to these days?' the Colonel asked.

At the mention of Lorna, the Colonel felt Pearl stiffen ever so slightly. It says a lot about the bloodline of a family that a daughter on the verge of opening a whorehouse should be embarrassed by her mother.

'We haven't heard from her in a while,' Pearl said. 'But wherever Mama is, you can be sure she's up to something.'

The Colonel smiled at the possibilities. Five Points had been downright dull since Lorna

Wilde ran off with Annabelle Boyd's fiancé.

The breeze shifted and the smell of fermenting mash drifted their way. Pearl buried her face in the Colonel's sleeve, but he turned his face into it and breathed deep.

'They call fermentation the noble rot,' he told her.

'I've met my share of fermenting nobles,' Pearl replied, eyes gleaming mischief.

'I have no doubt,' the Colonel chuckled, squeezing her arm warmly. There were few things he enjoyed more than a sassy woman.

Every eye was on them as they strolled across the yard. Chest out, the Colonel walked proud as they'd ever seen him.

'I suppose you've heard about my little business venture,' Pearl said after a while.

The Colonel looked down at her. Her eyes were flinty, but her cheeks burned like a guilty child's. Of course he'd heard. And he knew exactly what she was up to. Bourne had hurt her. Now Pearl was going to hurt him back. They were like two children trying to see who could stomp the other's toes the hardest.

'You should have stayed and fought for him,' the Colonel said sternly.

'He should have come after me.'

'Now, Pearl, you knew that was never going to happen.'

Pearl cut her eyes away from his. She'd spent three years looking back over her shoulder.

'Pearl, you need to ask yourself something. Do you want to get even — or do you want to get what you really want?'

221

He could see Pearl wrestle with this, but it wasn't in her to back down. Sometimes the trouble with having 'heart and try' was not knowing which should rule.

'A good word from you about my club would go a long way,' Pearl said. 'The men you don't know aren't worth knowing.'

The Colonel sighed long and hard. Sometimes you have to let a bitch bark up the wrong tree.

'Consider it done.'

LeRoy was waiting in the truck with the motor running. Pearl slipped her silk scarf out of her pocket and handed it to the Colonel. He was about to slip it over her eyes when he caught Pearl take a quick look back over her shoulder. When she turned back, her eyes dropped from his.

Tying her blindfold, he lifted her into the passenger's seat and closed the door. Pearl faced the Colonel with her blindfold on. He touched her cheek with the back of his hand and she nuzzled her face into it.

'You know what you're doing, Pearl?' he asked gently.

'Colonel, I always know what I'm doing. It's what I've done that I'm not so sure about.'

The Colonel threw back his head and laughed.

'Never look back, girl!' he said, slapping the fender for LeRoy to go. 'Never look back!'

★　★　★

Every evening Bourne walked the distillery from start to finish. The men working at each station stood quietly as he went through this daily ritual, contemplating and massaging each step of the process like beads on a rosary.

At the barrel shed he walked around a finished white oak barrel running his hand along the curved metal band. Taking a measuring tape off the wall, he measured the depth and diameter. A barrel had to hold fifty-five gallons and be level to stack steady.

'Inventory looks a little low,' Bourne said, surveying the shed.

'Had a man out this week,' the cooper answered.

'Which man?'

'Billy Lyle. Had to help his daddy take calves off to market.'

Bourne's eyes moved over the barrels waiting to be charred and the cooper could see him doing the math in his head.

'We'll have her caught up by Wednesday,' the cooper assured him.

Bourne nodded and the cooper felt the quiet contentment of having his work and his word respected by a man he respected right back.

At the rickyard, Bourne picked up a chunk of charcoal and ran it down the wall of the shed to check the burn. At the mill, he stood with his arms crossed and legs spread, solemnly watching grain fall from the hopper into the grinder. Raking the mound of finely ground corn with his fingers, he grabbed a fistful of meal and rubbed it between his palms.

'Any mold in this corn?' he asked, smelling the meal in his hand.

The mill man shook his head. 'No sir, Mr Bourne. She's sweet as it comes.'

At the mash tub, Bourne studied the thermometer to make sure the temperature was holding firm at 212 degrees. 'You check this thermometer lately?'

The mash man knew it wasn't a question. Taking a brand new thermometer out of the box, he dipped it in the mash. The two thermometers matched to the degree.

'Good,' Bourne said, patting him on the shoulder. 'This ain't fishing. We're not here to catch mistakes. We're here to make sure there ain't any to begin with.'

Bourne followed the liquor from the fermenting vat, where it earned the name sour mash whiskey, to the still house. While Bourne watched the alcohol quietly drip from the still, the still master watched him. He had known Bourne since he was a scuffed-kneed boy. And he'd bragged that he'd seen it in Bourne. 'Knew he'd follow in the Colonel's footsteps,' he'd said. 'Knew he'd be the one.' It can make a man uneasy working for the son of the owner. Just because a man inherits a business doesn't mean he has any business running it. Except for those who worried for the sake of worry, the men slept soundly knowing Bourne watched over the distillery and their livelihood.

The alcohol that passed through the still was then filtered through ten feet of packed sugar maple charcoal. This step, the charcoal filtering, is where Tennessee whiskey and Kentucky bourbon part ways, although the devout will swear they never had that much in common to begin with. Dipping a Mason jar into the filtered alcohol, Bourne held it up to the light studying the clarity and color. Smelling it, he took a sip.

'Hold a barrel of this run in the reserve,' he said.

'Yes, sir, Mr Bourne.'

★ ★ ★

After the alcohol passed through the charcoal filter, it was poured into charred barrels and sent to age. The aging barn was a two-mile hike from the distillery. If a man didn't know where he was headed, he would never get there. Bourne took his time making the pilgrimage. There are woods and there are woods, hallowed places in the hills where a man is so seldom seen, birds don't sing and insects hush. Dark as the womb, you doubt there's a sun in the sky, and a silence so deep you can hear God whisper in your ear. Bourne walked in silence, footsteps muffled on the rotting forest floor.

Most men, even his enemies, treated Bourne with deference. He knew few equals. When the Colonel died, he would know none at all. Bourne neither feared nor revered the Almighty. But he found quiet comfort in his company from time to time. He suspected the feeling was mutual.

Men had been known to walk right by the weathered gray barn tucked in the woods and never see it. As he neared it, Bourne cut a tender limb from a sassafras tree and waved the branch over his head. A LaRue stepped from behind a

225

tree, rifle resting on his shoulder, pants hanging on the bones. Bourne wasn't sure which cousin he was. It was impossible to tell them apart when you were standing right next to them, much less from a distance.

The Colonel was a firm believer in spreading risk. He did not keep all his barrels in one barn. No man knew the location of all the aging barns but a Cavanagh and the LaRue who guarded it. LaRues didn't talk amongst themselves, much less strangers. Bourne blinked and the cousin and his rifle disappeared. Blinked again and the cousin was right where he'd been, hadn't moved at all. Some thought it was their coloring, bark brown and fallen leaves, and some thought a LaRue could will himself to be gone from sight. Either way, Bourne pitied the man who tried to trespass.

It was cool and dark inside the barn and it smelled of earth floors, charred oak barrels and sour mash. Needlepoint rays of sunlight pierced through the cracks and knotholes in the boards, turning common dust into glitter. A quiet came over Bourne as he walked between the long dark rows of barrels, stacked floor to rafter and stretching for as far back as the eye could see. Every man has his cathedral and every man his day of reckoning. Bourne would be judged by the whiskey quietly aging around him, one way or another.

Sitting on a barrel, he pulled his knife out of his pocket. A man who didn't know any better would have laughed at the slim pearl-handled knife Bourne carried. Of course he wouldn't laugh long. Bourne could grab a man by the front of his shirt and lift his feet off the ground. On those rare occasions when his sky blue eyes turned cloudy, three grown men couldn't hold him back. Only a man like Bourne could get away with carrying a delicate pearl handled knife like the one he held in his hand.

Having whittled the leaves off the sassafras twig, he carefully stripped the paper thin bark off in single even ribbons. The twig was so young and tender he could have peeled it with his thumbnail, but that's not the way it's done. Sometimes it is the making, not the merchandise, that a man is really after.

Outsiders would have been surprised to see Bourne sitting quietly in the aging barn patiently whittling a sassafras toothpick, and even more surprised to learn about his nightly ritual. No one would believe Bourne Cavanagh had devotion in him. He had certainly never been faithful to anything else in his life. Ask Pearl Wilde. But there are men who go to work and there are men who are their work. Like his grandfather and his father, Bourne had the art of whiskey making in his blood. He loved the distillery and couldn't care less how other people saw it.

The difference between moonshine and whiskey is time. Moonshine drips from the still crystal clear and straight into the jug. Whiskey must mellow and age. The older it is, the more precious it becomes. Both make a man fall to his knees, but with whiskey the experience is far more reverent. Which a man prefers says more about the man than the spirit.

Every barrel of whiskey has its own way. No two are ever exactly the same. The grain can be picked from the same field, the sugar poured from the same bag, the maple for the charcoal cut from the same tree. Still, there will be subtle differences that distinguish each run, the depth of color, the degree of smoothness, the smoke absorbed from the charred barrel.

The first time Bourne laid eyes on Pearl Wilde, she went straight to his head like moonshine. After she left, he went through women like he was throwing back shots. He woke up in more strange beds than his own, thinking only of the next warm body he'd pin to the sheets. But none of them satisfied his thirst. Most women pass through a man undigested and unabsorbed. Bourne never understood what made Pearl different. He never tried. He just leaned back and let her intoxicate him.

As he ran the knife smoothly down the soft white wood, Bourne cocked his head and listened. A barrel 'breathes' as the whiskey ages — expanding in summer, contracting in winter, forcing the whiskey in and out of the wood and giving it color and flavor. As much as 30 per cent of the alcohol evaporates into the air by the time it is ready for the bottle. Distillers call this the 'angel's share'. It is a small sacrifice for the spirit that remains.

A woman is like whiskey. She evaporates a little over time, distilled by disappointments and grief. One can never predict if the angels will take the best of her or the worst. Only time will tell if the woman that remains will be bitter, dispirited, or aged to perfection.

Time stops at certain moments in life, making snapshots of the best and worst. Dreams and wishes fade to nothing. In the end a life is totaled and defined by a handful of memories that hang in the mind.

The first time the Colonel brought him to this barn, Bourne was wide-eyed and knee-high. The Colonel pressed his small ear against a barrel and whispered, 'Listen, son, and you'll hear the angels sigh.'

Pearl always sighed when he pleased her, body arching under his, head falling back, the breath rushing out of her like life itself.

Wiping the blade on his pants leg, Bourne thought of Pearl sitting across the desk from him, wrapped in white and gold, for sale to the highest bidder. Pearl had always been special. Now she had a depth and bite to her, dark smoky flavors he knew nothing about. Pearl had mystery in her eyes. It agitated him and it thrilled him.

Holding the pearl knife up, Bourne tilted the blade toward the light and read the inscription. 'To Bourne. Forever, Pearl.' He ran his finger across the words, then carefully folded the blade and slipped it back into his pocket.

Whatever made him think he could hold Pearl in reserve?

Sassafras toothpick in his mouth, Bourne stood for a moment, looking back over the long rows of barrels. The sun was going down and the light with it. Shadows fell across the stacks like eyes closing in sleep. Bourne looked down at the barrel he'd been sitting on, an eight-year-old reserve he had watched over since day one. Kneeling, he gently ran his hand over her. Closing his eyes, he pressed his ear against her belly and listened to the angels sigh.

19

Devin moved Sessalee into the big house on Thursday. She set up shop in the kitchen and immediately began practicing her trade. Growing up in a houseful of brothers, she knew all about the care and feeding of men. By Sunday night she had Bourne and the Colonel eating out of her hand, or any dish she slid in front of them.

Bourne found his boots polished and sitting by his bedroom door. The Colonel's coffee, stout just the way he liked it, was not only made but being poured as he walked into the kitchen in the morning. Their clothes were clean and ironed. The house was straight but in a livable way. Most important, the dogs loved her. The Colonel had to bribe Ulysses with beef jerky to get him to leave her kitchen for his walks.

As the Colonel finished off his third hot buttered biscuit with wild blackberry jam, he wondered how on earth they had ever managed without Sessalee. She was everything a man could want in a daughter-in-law. She sweetened his life like sugar in his coffee — as opposed to Devin who had always been a bitter pill to swallow.

'Sessalee,' the Colonel announced at breakfast, 'you are the child I always wanted.'

Having lost his appetite, Devin let his fork drop onto his plate.

The more tickled Bourne and the Colonel

were with Sessalee, the more sullen and contrary Devin grew. All his life, Devin had tried to compel some civility from his father and brother. 'Could you please not put your filthy smelly feet on the table while I'm trying to eat!' he'd yell. Prompting Bourne to wrestle him to the floor and stuff a dirty sock in his mouth. 'Would it be too much trouble to keep your damn muddy dogs off the couch?' Devin would holler at the Colonel, prompting the Colonel to grab him by the collar and send him flying off the porch.

Devin had tried logic, reason and force. But with little more than a mixing bowl and a spatula, Sessalee had Bourne and the Colonel trained and running the course. A sharp look at his muddy boots and Bourne backed out of her kitchen. An arch of the eyebrow and the Colonel slipped the chicken leg he was about to feed his dog back onto his plate. Sessalee said everything she needed to say with her dark eyes. It was a wonder God bothered putting lips on her.

But while Sessalee's mouth seemed strictly ornamental, Devin knew exactly what it was capable of. Whenever his eyes fixed on it, he could feel her soft moist lips making their way down his chest. But every time he started to forgive her, he felt the cold shotgun barrel jabbing him in the ribs and shoving him toward the unholy preacher from LaRue's landing. And Devin got mad all over again.

Once Bourne and the Colonel got a taste of her cooking, they didn't give a rat's ass about Devin's state of mind. Not that it had ever been that high on their priority list. Sessalee spoiled them rotten and they delighted in spoiling her back. Bourne, who had never committed a romantic act in his life, brought her flowers, apple blossoms he'd cut from the orchard, and bluebells from the creek by the distillery. The Colonel gave her his most prized possession. 'She's the pick of the litter,' he said, as Sessalee held the soft red pup to her face and rocked it like a baby. If Bourne and the Colonel had had their way, Sessalee would never have lifted anything heavier than a measuring cup or climbed higher than a step stool.

Meanwhile, every night, after he was sure the Colonel and Bourne were asleep in their beds, Devin stomped out to his truck and curled up in the front seat. He refused to sleep under the same roof with Sessalee, much less in the same bed. In the morning, if it had gotten chilly during the night, he'd wake up with an extra quilt over him, or, if it had started raining, the windows would be rolled up. Sessalee watched over Devin even when he didn't know she was watching. She served him first at every meal, gave him the best piece of meat and the largest slice of pie. But nothing she did would soften his heart. The harder Sessalee tried with Devin, the worse he treated her. Whether Devin was punishing her, or testing her, the Colonel could not be sure.

'This is a damn dishrag not a napkin!' Devin snarled, throwing it at her. 'Didn't they teach you anything in those hills?'

Bourne's chair scraped back and his hands drew into fists. But the Colonel stared him down. The Colonel could not abide a man who belittled a woman, especially his own son. But he knew this was a fight Sessalee would have to win on her own.

The tension in the kitchen weighed heavily on the Cavanagh men until the sound of metal scraping on stone drew their attention. Their heads swiveled to the butcher block. Sessalee smoothly slid the blade of a bowie knife up the oiled pumice stone, over and over, until it was as sharp as a razor. Slapping the trout Bourne had caught that morning on the block, she decapitated, gutted and filleted it so fast, the men barely saw her small hands move. Twirling the knife in her hand, she drove the blade straight down into the block. Bending over, she picked the dishrag off the floor.

As she wiped fish blood off her hands with the rag, she leaned next to Devin's ear.

'You needin' anything, darlin'?'

The Colonel smiled into his coffee cup.

20

Having graduated from the Vanderbilt School of Pillow Talk, Pearl Wilde knew a thing or two about commerce. For starters, if you want to open a business during a depression, you need clients who are not the least bit depressed.

The postmaster slowly flipped through the box of invitations Eddie McCowan had placed in front of him, carefully reading each envelope addressed in Pearl's perfect handwriting.

'It's going to take a while to stamp all these,' he said absently. 'Come back in an hour and I'll tell you how much the postage comes to.'

Eddie was barely out the door when the postmaster had Annabelle place the telephone call to the mayor's office.

'Hardin,' he said, his back to the window and hand over the phone, 'you better get over here.'

Mayor Hardin Wallace read each name on each envelope in somber silence. When he got to the back of the box, he started over.

'Pearl Wilde has some gall. I'll give her that,' the postmaster said. 'To think a state senator is going to come to a cathouse in Five Points. Lord, almighty.'

Holding an envelope up to the light, Hardin squinted to read the invitation. 'On the other hand . . . ' he said, gazing out the post office window, ' . . . if even one of these men shows up in town . . . '

Hardin called the emergency meeting of the city council for the usual time and the usual place. After sunset and behind closed doors.

'But where are we going to get the money?' Frank Merrill, the pharmacist, asked for the third time.

'I'm not saying we have to make Five Points look like Las Vegas,' Hardin said, as he refilled their glasses with eighty proof optimism. 'I'm just saying we need to look like a town a man should invest in.'

The councilmen glanced at each other over their glasses of Cavanagh whiskey. Hardin had pulled out the good stuff, so they knew he'd lost his mind.

'But where are we going to get the money?' Frank demanded yet again.

The Mayor waved away the men's concerns like a magician waving a wand over a silk top hat. Like all master politicians, Hardin knew how to make the details disappear.

★ ★ ★

The night Pearl opened her doors, car headlights glittered like a string of Christmas lights along River Road from the main highway to Five Points. No one had to stop to ask for directions. They just followed the starry tail lights in front of them. The Colonel had come through. He had got them there, now all Pearl had to do was find a way to keep them.

Entrance into the Five of Clubs was by invitation only. And Pearl was very picky about who she wooed. A rich man may want diversity in the women he rubs under the sheets, but he is very selective when it comes to rubbing elbows. A man had to lay down a small fortune for membership. In return, he received a twenty-four-karat gold-plated five of clubs playing card. No card. No entrance. Pearl put Eddie in charge of greeting guests and weeding out the party crashers at the front gate.

'It's a lot of responsibility for the boy.'

Maysie stood at Pearl's bedroom door, with her arms crossed.

'He's not guarding the crown jewels,' Pearl said, as she fastened the clasp on her bracelet at her dressing table.

When Eddie walked down the stairs in the tuxedo Pearl had bought him, it seemed inconceivable that he had ever worn anything else. Even Pearl's girls, who'd seen it all, grew quiet and sultry, as their eyes followed him across the room.

'Remember,' Pearl told him, as she pinned a white rose bud to his lapel, 'rich men prefer envy to deference.'

Eddie stared at her blankly. He had no idea what that meant.

'Forget it,' she said, giving him a push toward the door. 'Just pretend you're some movie star.'

Pearl and Maysie stood at the window watching Eddie walk down the drive. By the time he reached Woody waiting for him at the gate, his transformation was complete. His chin was high and there was a suave swagger in his walk. All that was Eddie had disappeared. Pearl smiled.

Eddie in a tuxedo was exactly the first impression she wanted to give.

'Are you sure he can handle it?' Maysie fretted.

If there was one thing Pearl had no doubt Eddie could handle, it was standing around and looking good.

Maysie stared out the window at her beautiful boy. The stray curl that she had so often brushed from his forehead now made him look daring and devilish. The perfect posture and manners she had drilled into him had evolved into effortless grace.

'I hardly know him,' Maysie said quietly.

Pearl suspected she never had.

Slipping away, Pearl left her alone at the window. Maysie watched Eddie straighten the cuffs of his shirt as though he'd done it a million times before. She could not believe how at ease he was in the shiny black shoes and silk cummerbund. More at ease than she'd ever seen him. How could she have missed what every one else had seen so clearly? Eddie was just passing through.

Leaning close, Maysie pressed her fingers against the window pane as if to touch him one last time.

★　★　★

The roadster pulled a little too fast into the drive as though fueled with testosterone. Woody and Eddie could smell the liquor when the driver rolled down his window.

'Good evening,' Eddie said, leaning down at the car window. 'May I see your invitation or membership card?'

As the young man held out his invitation, he turned his wrist ever so slightly so that Woody and Eddie could get a good look at his diamond cufflinks. The woman on the passenger's side rolled her eyes indifferently at Eddie. Then she looked again.

'My, my,' she said, running her tongue over her wet lipstick. 'Has anyone ever told you that you look just like Errol Flynn?'

'I was trying for John Barrymore,' Eddie said.

The woman laughed gaily. She had no idea he was serious.

'No,' she said, stretching over her annoyed date, 'you're definitely more the bad boy.'

'Errol Flynn has dark hair and a mustache,' her date chafed. 'This boy's blond and blue-eyed.'

'That's why you're *much* better-looking,' she purred at Eddie.

Good looks having trumped diamonds, the man stomped the gas. As the car sped through the gate, the woman leaned out the window and blew Eddie a kiss.

Woody stood puzzled by the scene. He was wearing a tuxedo too, but it wasn't having the same effect.

'What's the matter?' Eddie asked, looking down to see if his fly was open.

'What's with the fancy-man accent? You sound like a damn Yankee.'

Woody had known Eddie all his life. Eddie's

good looks had always been a given. What Woody had not realized until this moment was that beauty was currency, as good as gold. And Eddie had a potful.

'You look like a tow-headed woodpecker in that tuxedo,' Woody declared.

Grabbing him around the neck, Woody knocked on Eddie's head with his ball-peen knuckles until the pain brought tears to Eddie's eyes. Even then, he was beautiful.

The guests who didn't drive to Five Points arrived by private train car. Pearl paid Inky Mott fifty cents to pick them up at the station in his taxi, while Mayor Hardin slipped him a nickel extra to drive his passengers through town and around the square. Inky went around twice if they weren't paying attention the first time.

Native Five Pointers would not have recognized their own town square. The weathered plywood boards had been pried off the empty storefront windows and the displays cleaned and filled with merchandise as if business in town were booming. The hat shop, which had been closed for two years, now displayed the latest styles from June Bug Wallace's closet. Mr Mendelson, having lost the key, broke the lock off his old tobacco and newspaper stand, stocked it with big city newspapers and real Cuban cigars. He hired Bucky Darnell to man it. Bucky took right to the job, waving a paper and calling out the headline, just like he'd seen in the movies.

Dickie and the boys spent the week prior throwing buckets of hot soapy water on the sidewalks and scrubbing them with push brooms. They put up sawhorses to keep people from walking on them until they dried. The first rain the sidewalks foamed and bubbles floated into the air as if the town were taking a bubble bath.

Pots of red geraniums and petunias 'borrowed' from every widow's yard in town lined the sidewalk. The gas streetlights sparkled and the neon sign on the Roxy Theater glowed bright red. Frank Merrill's teenage daughter, a former Miss Houston County, stood at the ticket booth selling tickets to *Shanghai Express*. Thanks to a midnight run by the boys over to the Capitol Theater in Bingham, a life-size cardboard cutout of Marlene Dietrich stood outside the double doors. People took turns having their picture taken standing beside her.

Dickie Deason and a couple of boys played a little bluegrass on the courthouse lawn. They hadn't picked a tune together in a while, and even they were surprised at how good they sounded. City councilmen and their families, along with a few other coerced citizens, strolled along the sidewalks licking ice-cream cones, or sat on quilts on the courthouse lawn with picnic baskets. Gladys set up a couple of café tables outside the grocery along the sidewalk where people sipped free Royal Crown Colas, compliments of the city council. Five Points gave every impression of being a warm, hospitable and even prosperous town. And sometime during the night, the fact that it wasn't slipped the townspeople's minds. They started having as

241

good a time as they were pretending to have.

Normally on weeknights, the hourly trains passing through the Five Points switching station didn't have any passengers getting on or off, so the conductors didn't bother to stop. That night, they stopped on the hour. Inky ran a cab service back and forth to the club. He was surprised how many men brought female companions, beautiful women dressed to the nines in shimmering dresses and sparkling jewelry. But the real shocker was that some men even brought their wives. These women were the wildest of all, females so bottled up by their role in society they popped like champagne in the back of his taxi, bubbling and effervescing all over their husbands. Sometimes it was so intimate, Inky had to turn the radio up and the rear-view mirror down.

His last fare of the night was a lifeless couple, clearly affluent, and personal friends of the Colonel. The man wore his hat low and collar turned up, and the woman's face was hidden by a net, but Inky still recognized them from their pictures in the newspaper. He drove the state senator and his wife around the square twice. On the second round, Dickie and the boys broke into the 'When the Moon Comes Over the Mountain,' and the wife looked up.

'Oh, darling!' she exclaimed, rolling down the taxi window. 'It's our song!'

The senator rested his hand on Inky's shoulder, but Inky had already slowed the cab to a crawl. He watched amused as his wife swayed with the music. She was having such a good time he couldn't tear his eyes away.

'Oh, darling!' she said, turning to him. 'Isn't this the sweetest little town!'

The senator glanced past her out the window. 'Not bad,' he said absently. 'Not bad at all.'

★   ★   ★

Bourne sat on his usual stool at the counter in the grocery, hands wrapped around a coffee cup. He didn't seem to be the least bit interested in all the hullabaloo that was going on, but more than once Gladys caught him glancing up at the mirror.

'Sure you don't want a Royal Crown Cola?' she asked. 'Your tax money's paying for it.'

He tapped his coffee cup and she refilled it. Helping herself to a Royal Crown, she leaned against the counter on her elbows and let a shoe drop. Running her foot up and down her calf, she stared out the front window at all the expensive cars driving by. So far she'd spotted license plates from three states. She was banking on quite a few of those cars stopping for coffee and cigarettes on their way home.

'Looks like Pearl Wilde's out-wild-ed you,' Gladys said, as she turned up the bottle.

Bourne cut his eyes her way. Grinning, Gladys twirled the locket of her dead husband like the propeller on a Gipsy moth biplane. Bourne knew she was opening the door for a free grudge screw. All he had to do was say the word and she'd come on down for a landing.

'Appreciate it, Gladys,' Bourne said, sliding off

243

the stool and throwing an extra bill on the counter, 'but my heart wouldn't be in it.'

'Sure, honey,' she said, with a wink and a cluck of her tongue.

When the door closed behind him, Gladys's smile faded. Bourne's heart had never been her organ of choice.

★　★　★

With nothing more than word of mouth, the Five of Clubs was an overnight success. A man may not be a prophet in his own home town, but a woman can get a reputation without lifting a finger.

From the outside, no one would ever have suspected what went on inside the house on Dog Leg Hill. The elegant old house peeked coyly from behind magnolia trees like a geisha hiding her face behind a fan. During the day, gardeners quietly tended the grounds while maids in black uniforms with starched white aprons draped an endless sea of white bed linens, whipping and snapping, on the clothes lines.

But when the sun went down, the old house hiked her skirt up. A steady stream of headlights would begin again, winding up Dog Leg Hill and passing through Pearl's gate. The trill of laughter and jazz pierced the warm night air, drawing peeping Toms like cats to a dumpster. Bucky Darnell and his friends, hidden behind the hydrangea shrubs, pressed their young faces against the wrought-iron fence, their eyes fixed on the upstairs windows.

Years later, when the boys were old men, Bucky would tell the story of the night he saw one of Pearl's girls slowly slip an elbow length glove from her hand, one finger at a time. He would describe the dark red lipstick on her full lips, the black lace on her silk slip and the copper color of her hair. He would vividly recall the beauty mark at the corner of her mouth and the fragile gold chain falling between her creamy breasts.

What he would not remember was that the upstairs shades were always pulled at the house on Dog Leg Hill. Such is the secret of seduction. Reality has nothing to do with it.

21

Contrary to popular belief, Olivia Rudolph Hughes was not a foolish woman. She was merely a woman with too much time on her hands. A woman married to a man who is married to his work has all the symptoms of a mistress.

'Hello, Mrs Hughes.'

Olivia glanced at Hubert's secretary's nameplate as she pulled off her glove. The girl had been with Hubert since she graduated from secretarial school, but for the life of Olivia, she could never remember the young woman's name.

'Hello . . . Diane. Please let him know I'm here.'

The secretary smiled at Olivia as she dialed Hubert. While she spoke quietly into the phone, Olivia fussed with the contents of her pocketbook. She always felt the need to appear busy in front of women who worked, even women whose work she believed was inconsequential.

When the secretary glanced up at her over the receiver, a knot rose in Olivia. She knew what was coming. She had spent most of her life waiting for Hubert, waiting for him to notice her, waiting for him to propose, waiting for him to come home, waiting for him to come to bed . . .

'I'm so sorry, Mrs Hughes,' Diane said, resting the phone into the cradle. 'Mr Hughes said to tell you something has come up. He won't be able to have lunch with you today.'

Olivia's eyes cut to Hubert's closed office door, willing him to stick his head out. She did not expect him to pretend he was disappointed. Just give her the common courtesy of showing his face. But that would have struck Hubert as inefficient.

The secretary looked embarrassed, which embarrassed Olivia.

'Well, that's a relief,' Olivia said, in a tone meant to assure Diane that she had as little time for Hubert as he for her. 'I have so much to do today, I didn't know how on earth I was ever going to fit it all in!'

Diane opened her mouth to say goodbye, but Olivia had already turned crisply toward the door, giving a quick wave over her shoulder as though she simply did not have time for small talk. When the door closed behind her, Olivia stood in the hallway, heart pounding. She looked one way then the next before she allowed her face to burn. Nothing hurt her more than Hubert embarrassing her in public. It was one thing for him to ignore her in private; it was quite another for him to slight her in front of the help.

Olivia's life did not revolve around Hubert, it hovered. She hung suspended in ever-readiness for a call, a look, a kind word from him. She made herself ever available, filling her day with inconsequential appointments that could be easily changed or ignored should Hubert want her. She rushed from her morning appointment with her hairdresser, to her afternoon dinner at the country club, to her tennis lessons. There was bridge club on Tuesdays, book club on Wednesdays, and orchid society on Thursdays. When Olivia wasn't at a meeting, she was shopping for clothes to wear to her next meeting. Every second of Olivia's appointment book was neatly penciled in, in the hope that if she lived in constant motion, no one would notice that she had no destination.

Olivia had only one ambition in life. Hubert. He was her occupation and her preoccupation. Hubert, on the other hand, saw Olivia as a done deal. Even before their honeymoon, he had moved on to greater things.

Hubert's great passion was making money. Why, Olivia couldn't get a handle on. He had no desire for bigger boats or bigger houses. He still bought them. They just didn't mean anything to him. Olivia honestly believed Hubert would be perfectly content eating bologna and wearing second-hand suits if she did not take care of him. It wasn't money that motivated Hubert, but the strategy of making it. He accumulated wealth like a raccoon stockpiles bits of shiny tinfoil.

Hubert was like gravity to Olivia; she could see the effect but could not comprehend the physics. For years she tried to seduce him away from his work. She might as well have set her sights on making the sun revolve around the moon.

'Come to bed, darling,' she'd whisper in his ear.

'Yes. Yes,' he'd say to humor her, unwrapping

her arms from around his neck and pulling his head away from her kisses.

Then, without looking up from the reports he was studying, he'd pat Olivia as if he was patting the dog's head when it whined to go for a walk.

Olivia was not discouraged by this. It simply made her cling tighter.

She was sitting in the stall of the bathroom down the hall from Hubert's office, wondering what to do with herself for the rest of the afternoon, when she heard the two women walk in.

' . . . he dodged her for lunch again.'

Recognizing Hubert's secretary's voice, Olivia sat perfectly still, peeking through the crack in the stall door as Diane ran a cheap tube of dime store lipstick around her mouth in front of the mirror.

'He gives me a nickel every time I deflect her telephone calls.' Smacking her lips, she passed the tube to the other woman. 'I swear she must call ten times a day.'

'How pathetic,' the other woman said, as she ran the red wax around her stretched lips.

'The only way she's going to get Hubert Hughes's attention is if she starts spitting bearer bonds.'

'What are your chances?'

Diane shrugged. 'She owns half of everything. It would be a very expensive divorce.'

The other secretary twisted the tube closed and handed it back.

'A real woman can always get a man's attention,' she said, poking her bleached hair.

'Always,' Diane agreed, dropping the tube in her purse.

Bending over, Diane shook her firm young breasts high in her bra. When she stood up they protruded through her white cotton blouse like torpedoes.

Olivia could still hear them laughing as they walked down the hall.

She sat in the stall for a very long time after they left. Finally, swinging the door open, she walked to the mirror and took out her own lipstick. Very carefully applying it, Olivia considered her situation. She was married to a man who paid his secretary a nickel to deflect her calls. Hubert was getting quite a deal actually. She paid their butler far more to walk her dog.

Blotting her lips on a monogrammed Irish linen handkerchief, Olivia stared at her reflection. The lighting was too good in the white tiled bathroom. It cast a cold sterile clarity on the decision to be made.

Some women would have been hurt. Some would have been furious. They would have wept or raged at their husband. They would have mourned the inequity or set out to punish the betrayal. Some would have thrown his belongings in the front yard. Some would have filed for divorce. Some would have gone after his money and hit him where it really hurt.

Those women would never have what they really wanted in life.

★　★　★

When the grandfather clock, a Rudolph heirloom, began chiming the hour, Hubert looked up from his desk in his study and frowned over his glasses. It was nine o'clock in the evening and he had not had his supper. Picking up the bell, he rang until the maid came hurrying into his office.

'What happened to my supper?' he demanded.

'Mrs Hughes said not to fix any.' The maid stood pink-cheeked and winded in front of his desk, hands clasped in front of her. 'She looked a little peaked when she got home. I don't think she's feeling too well.'

Hubert frowned. Try as he might, he could not make the connection between his wife's peakedness and his supper.

'I see,' he said, even though he didn't. 'Well, bring me . . . '

Hubert was at a loss. He had no idea what he really wanted.

' . . . something.'

'Something?'

'To eat.'

'Yes, sir,' the maid said, backing out of the room.

Hubert tried to go back to work, but couldn't. He was not a man who put things on the back burner. The inconvenience and incompetence of the situation had completely destroyed his train of thought. A plan should immediately be put into place to prevent his ever going hungry again.

He found Olivia soaking in her bath, trailing her hand lazily through the sudsy water.

'I didn't have any supper,' he announced, standing in the bathroom doorway.

'Supper?' she said, as though she couldn't quite place the word.

He was about to launch into a tirade about how little he expected of her when Olivia looked up at him. And Hubert immediately knew. He saw in his wife's eyes what he had seen a hundred times before. It was the look of a client preparing to take her business elsewhere.

Hubert was first and foremost a capitalist. Nothing motivated him more than competition.

Reaching down, he grabbed Olivia by the arm and lifted her from the tub, soapy and dripping. Twisting his fingers in her wet hair, he pulled her head back. For an instant, she thought he was going to hit her. Instead, Hubert kissed her fiercely. It left her so lightheaded she could barely stand.

'Who is he?' Hubert demanded.

For twenty-six years, Olivia had longed for Hubert to kiss her this way. If she'd known all it took was his thinking she was having an affair, she would have started fooling around on their honeymoon.

'Do I know him?'

For over half her life Olivia had waited on and waited for Hubert. She had doted, adored, and catered to his every whim. She dressed to please him, made his interests her interests. She did things she never imagined a woman having to do to make a man notice her. The day she married Hubert, Olivia burned herself at the altar.

'How long have you been seeing him?' he

asked, his grip tightening on her arm.

Olivia had given herself to Hubert body, mind and soul. But it wasn't until she repossessed herself that he gave a damn.

'Do you love him?' he demanded.

Slipping free from him, she loosely wrapped a towel around her wet body.

'I haven't decided yet,' she said, as she floated out of the bathroom.

22

'You're telling me that a man pays a woman to give him a bath?' Addie Pewitt said skeptically.

Every day, news from the Five of Clubs flooded into the factory. And the girls could not get enough of it. Pearl's vulgar activities worked them into a heat. They gasped and shuddered and cried 'no!' until they were absolutely flushed and depleted. It is a fine line between indignation and titillation, and envy straddles the line like a two-dollar whore.

'There are eight bathtubs in that house,' Betty informed them, eyes wide. 'Eight! And that doesn't include Pearl's private bath.'

A quiet fell over the floor. Half of the girls didn't have indoor plumbing. They sponged off in the kitchen after the children were in bed. What must it be like to soak in one's own private tub, steam rising off the rose-scented water?

It came as quite a relief to learn that most of the things Pearl's girls did, all women were equipped to do. Who couldn't give a man a bath? Still, they had the nagging feeling that Pearl's girls had a trick or two up their sleeves that they weren't telling.

'That's it?' Luella squinted at Betty. 'They just scrub 'um down?'

'Hush!' Joy Lester hissed. 'You're inviting the Devil in!'

Joy's people had been known to handle a

snake or two. Even though most Meachums had moved out of the hills into town and infiltrated the holy rollers, the old beliefs still boiled and bubbled in their blood. Joy conjured Satan in every corner and could scare the bejeesus out of you when she set her mind to it.

But Kat Wilde did not scare easily.

'Satan knows better than to show up in a room full of women with scissors,' she joked, snipping the air with two fingers.

The girls laughed and Joy's eyes flashed. There was no joy in Joy and she could not tolerate it in others.

'Don't make light of the dark,' she warned.

'Luella's just curious,' Kat said, throwing a finished shirt on her pile.

'Curiosity killed the cat,' Joy said, as though willing it to be true.

When Buck heard Luella yell his name his first instinct was to make a run for it.

'Buck!' Luella yelled again. 'Buck, you hear me?'

He hesitated just long enough to let her know he wasn't at her beck and call.

'What?' he finally hollered back.

'Come in here!'

Cursing under his breath, Buck pushed himself off the couch. There were only two reasons Luella wanted him after dark anymore, either to tell him something was broke or to nag because he hadn't gotten around to fixing the last thing she told him was broke. Bracing himself for a ragging, he trudged down the hall. He groaned when he heard water running.

Another damn water leak. No man likes to plumb. If he were honest about it, even Roy Lester the plumber hated plumbing. Cursing under his breath, Buck shoved the bathroom door open.

Luella knelt by the bathtub stirring the steaming sudsy water with her hand, a bottle of Ivory dishwashing liquid on the floor beside her.

'Why are you washing dishes in the bath tub?'

'I'm not washing dishes!' Luella snapped irritably. 'I'm washing you!'

Buck rolled back on his heels. He just took a bath last Saturday. Lifting an arm, he sniffed. It was no worse than usual.

'Take your clothes off!' Luella ordered.

'How come?' he asked suspiciously.

'Just get in the damn tub,' she ordered, already exhausted by the whole ordeal.

Then it came to him. She'd heard about the eight bathtubs at Pearl's. Luella had a jealous streak as wide as the Tennessee River. He started to laugh at her and her bottle of Ivory dishwashing liquid. But then his eyes fixed on her hips as she leaned over the tub to turn down the water.

Buck undid his belt.

'Well, don't watch me!' he ordered, turning his back to her.

They'd been married for twelve years, had three children together, and he didn't want her to watch him drop his pants. Sighing, Luella threw her hand over her rolling eyes.

Clothes in a pile on the floor, Buck stepped into the tub, slowly inching his body into the scalding hot sudsy water. When she finally heard the bathwater settle down, Luella uncovered her eyes. Buck was hunkered in the tub with his knees pulled up to his chest. Lathering up a washcloth, Luella started scrubbing. As she scoured his back, she thought about all the things that needed doing. The basket of clothes that needed washing, the socks that needed darning, the shirts that needed ironing . . .

'Go easy there, woman!' Buck flinched. 'You're sanding my skin off!'

Blinking, Luella remembered where she was and what she was doing. She looked at Buck's back where she'd rubbed it red. Buck had a carpenter's body, lean and hard. She used to walk a mile out of her way to see him working with his shirt off. The sight of him standing in the sun, back glistening with sweat and tanned arms hard as stained ironwood, made her forget her religion. Once upon a time, the only thing Luella wanted in life was Buck Darnell. She had truly believed she would die if he did not marry her.

'How'd you get this scar?'

She ran her finger over the ragged white seam of flesh on his shoulder.

'Which one?' Buck stretched his head back over his shoulder. 'Oh, you remember. Got that one last fall building Tom's barn. Piece of tin roof slipped and nearly took my arm off.'

Luella did not remember. She remembered both boys had the measles and the baby was cutting teeth and crying all the time. She remembered money was so tight she picked chicken bones off their plates and boiled them to make soup. But she did not remember that her husband almost sliced his arm off.

Leaning down, she kissed the scar. Buck grew very still and quiet. Running her soapy fingers gently along his wet skin, she traced each muscle until it loosened. Slowly, Buck eased back in the tub. Eyes half open, he watched his wife bathe him.

★　★　★

The next evening Luella dragged home from the factory so tired she could barely think. Hanging her sweater on the peg by the door, she went to the kitchen to start dinner. She reached down into the kindling box as always and, as always, it was empty. Cursing, she reached for the handle on the firebox to empty the ashes, but the handle was gone. Frowning, she stepped back. There, where the old cast iron wood stove had set, was a gas range with knobs that said on and off.

'You like it?' Buck asked, leaning against the doorway of the kitchen.

She ran her finger over the knobs. The oven had a temperature control. She could bake or broil herself to death if she wanted to.

'It ain't new,' Buck said. 'Mendelson picked it up at a bankruptcy auction over in Lyle. Traded him some new cabinets for it.'

Turning, Luella gave Buck a look he had not seen in years. Taking his hand, she pulled him toward the bathroom. Buck made no effort to resist. Truthfully, he was feeling a little dirty.

★ ★ ★

One of the boys on the loading dock noticed first.

'Get a load of them lips,' he said, leaning over the rail to watch the women file into work.

In a sea of faded cotton drabness and gloomy faces, a pair of wet red lips bounced toward the factory. Luella Darnell was wearing lipstick. By the reaction of the men on the dock, you'd have thought that was all she was wearing.

'You look like a tramp,' Joy Lester said, as she punched her timecard into the clock.

Joy's words fell on deaf ears. Luella squinted transfixed at the blurred reflection of her red mouth on the shiny chrome metal on her sewing machine, and a secret smile formed on her face that made the girls raise their eyebrows at each other.

Arms crossed, Crockett glared down at Luella's shiny red lips from his office like a forest ranger spotting a tiny brush fire. He was on his way to stomp it out before it spread when he noticed the boy who picked up the finished shirts and ran them up to buttons. Normally, Crockett had to put a mirror under the kid's nose to see if he was breathing. Suddenly, the boy had more energy than he knew what to do with. Grabbing armloads of finished shirts beside each sewing machine, he tossed them into his cart and ran out the double doors. He managed to deliver them to the buttoning department and get back to the sewing room before the double doors stopped swinging. Then leaning against the wall

259

with his arms crossed, he stared at Luella until the finished piles were large enough to gather up again.

Despite the fact that Luella spent most of the morning staring at her own reflection, she was ahead of quota when the whistle blew for break. Since Kat rearranged her work station, Luella was spitting out shirts almost as fast as Kat.

Standing in the sun on the loading dock, Luella took a small mirror out of her pocket and carefully reapplied her lipstick. Arms crossed, Crockett's eyes cut from Luella to the men. Normally, they unloaded a rail car as if they were dragging a ball and chain. With Luella smacking her lipstick and Kat blowing smoke rings, the men flew through their work with muscles flexed.

At the end of the day, Crockett sat at his desk and studied the day's production. Looking up from the report, he seriously considered passing out a tube of lipstick with each of the girls' paychecks.

23

For most of the afternoon, the Colonel sat in Sessalee's kitchen studying on something. More than once, Sessalee looked up from her pie dough and found him watching her, his thumbs tapping together on his chest.

'You needin' something, Colonel?'

'Not at the moment, thank you, Sessalee.'

After his afternoon coffee and pie had settled, the Colonel lifted his hat off the rack and swung open the kitchen door.

'I'll be back for supper,' he told her. He gave a short whistle, Ulysses and the pups scrambled to their feet and swam around his legs like copper minnows.

The schoolhouse was a half a mile walk from the house and still on Cavanagh land. The Colonel's father had built the one-room frame school and the Colonel maintained it. The contents were left to Miss Mabel.

Miss Mabel set the chalk down when she spotted him in the doorway, and dusted her hands.

'Colonel.'

'Miss Mabel.'

Removing his hat, he strolled around the room feigning interest in the maps pinned to the walls and the week's spelling words she was printing on the blackboard when he came in. There were wooden pegs beside the door for those children who had coats, and a bench to pull on galoshes. A yellowed cardboard banner of the alphabet ran above the blackboard. A calendar and framed copy of the Constitution were mounted on the wall behind her desk. Miss Mabel believed in teaching the fundamentals. She stuck to laws that had been proven and would prove useful in life: reading, writing, arithmetic and love of country. She was lucky to keep a child eight years before they married, or worse. She had little time for theories or tomfoolery.

When the Colonel finished his tour of the room, Miss Mabel motioned for him to take her chair.

'To what do I owe the honor of this visit?'

The Colonel leaned back in the wooden chair and rested his hat on his knee.

'My youngest, Devin, has his mind set on being a lawyer.'

This was not news to Miss Mabel. A good teacher knows the direction her children are headed.

'Devin's a fighter,' Miss Mabel said. 'Better a courtroom than an alley.'

The Colonel nodded.

'You've heard I have a new daughter-in-law.'

'Sessalee LaRue.'

'Fine girl.'

Miss Mabel made no comment. Her definition of fine did not include picking up men at the rock wall and shotgun weddings.

'Sessalee has a sharp mind,' the Colonel went on.

'She learned what she had to learn, while I

262

had her,' Miss Mabel replied.

The Colonel drummed his fingers on her desk. 'A wife who doesn't keep up with her husband gets left behind.'

Miss Mabel made no comment. In her mind, every woman who married got left behind.

Standing, the Colonel walked to the small shelf of books under the window that served as the library.

'There's no poetry here,' he observed, running his finger over the spines.

'These children will have neither the time nor the need for poetry.'

The Colonel made no comment. In his mind, a woman without poetry had no passion. Sessalee carried the poetry of the hills in her, but Miss Mabel would never hear it.

He looked around the schoolroom. He had made a mistake. A man's plans often spoil when exposed to the air. He came looking for a way to arm Sessalee. But erudition was not the weapon she needed to hold her ground with Devin.

'Miss Mabel,' he said, putting on his hat, 'I'll let you get back to your work.'

She followed him to the door, confounded by his visit and even more so by his abrupt departure. His dogs danced in the yard eager to get going.

'Good day, Colonel,' she called from the doorway.

'Good day, Miss Mabel,' he called back, as he walked briskly toward Dog Leg Hill.

★ ★ ★

263

Devin was shooting the shit on the front porch at Green's general store while Sessalee grocery shopped when he noticed Inky Mott was not listening to a word he said. Inky's eyes were at half mast and his bony ribcage moved up and down with his breathing. He looked like a hungry coyote on the scent. Devin figured Gladys Greene must be up the ladder and turned to get an eyeful up her skirt. But it wasn't the widow Inky was drooling over. It was Sessalee.

To punish his wife, Devin had ignored her. In his ignorance, he had failed to notice the changes Sessalee had been undergoing of late. He was the only one.

'What are you looking at?' he snarled at Inky.

Stuffing his hands in his pockets, Inky gazed off the porch and started whistling.

As Devin loaded the groceries in the back of the truck, he took a good look at Sessalee. Her black braid that usually hung down her back was twisted up on her head exposing her slender neck and tiny teardrop pearl earrings hung from her soft earlobes.

'You're wearing your hair up,' he said.

She ran her small hand down the back of her bare neck.

'I don't want you cutting it,' he ordered, exercising his husbandly authority.

As the truck bumped along, he cut his eyes away from the road taking quick glimpses of her. She was still fresh as spring water but a hint of sophistication had surfaced. It was unsettling.

'Is that a new dress?'

She nodded.

'Where'd you get it?'

'Miss Pearl picked it out fer me.'

Devin's jaw clenched and his knuckles tightened on the steering wheel.

'What were you doing with Pearl?'

'The Colonel took me fer a visit.'

Devin's face flared.

'I don't want you wearing that dress shopping!' he ordered. 'It's too fancy!'

'This one's fer town,' she explained patiently, as it had been explained to her. 'My fancy one's hangin' in the closet.'

Sessalee sat placidly on the passenger's side, facing forward, her small hands resting in her lap. Devin's eyes jumped from the road to her. In the hierarchy of things a man observes when he studies a woman, hands rank only slightly above elbows. But it was not Sessalee's hands that actually caught Devin's attention. It was her wedding band. Truthfully, it had never occurred to him that she wore one. Furthermore, something about the ring struck him as a bit off. He leaned down to get a closer look then looked up at her in open-mouthed shock.

'It's a damn brass nut!' he blurted, as if she hadn't helped her brothers work on enough old truck motors and wringer washers to know a brass nut when she was wearing one.

He retraced all their stops that day tallying who had seen that his wife's wedding band was a three-quarter-inch tarnished brass nut. Humiliation stiffened him from head to toe.

'Take it off,' he ordered.

Jaw set, Sessalee shook her head. It was the first time she'd ever said 'no' to him, and it set him back.

'Give it to me!'

Truck swerving, he grabbed for her hand and she jerked it behind her back.

'It isn't a real wedding ring!' he yelled, slamming his fist on the steering wheel.

'Maybe not tuh you!' she yelled right back.

They glared at each other at a deadlock. LaRues were wiry, but they had a cast-iron disposition. He could see her mind was made up and there was absolutely nothing he could do about it.

Devin slammed on the brakes and the truck fishtailed in the middle of the road before skidding to a stop.

'Stubborn hillbilly!' he shouted, slamming the truck door.

Stomping to the front of the truck, he paced back and forth, pounding the hood with his fist and kicking the dirt. After a couple of more curses and throwing his cap on the ground, he settled down and accepted what had to be done.

Mendelson's pawn shop was the closest thing they had to a jewelry store in Five Points. Fingers laced and standing on tip-toe, Sessalee leaned over the glass case and studied the tray of hocked diamond rings. She finally pointed to one and Mendelson reached inside the case, plucked it from the tray and handed it to her.

Mendelson's heart was not in his work. He had inherited his father's trade but not his father's passion for making a living off the failures of others. Truthfully, he found most customers a sad interruption to his day. Nothing darkened his mood more than hearing the front door bell ring and being torn from a good book he was immersed in. Folks in town had labeled him antisocial. The truth was Mendelson was sentimental. He was moved by the great loves of Shakespeare and Tolstoy. He was especially moved by young love. But then, being the town pawnbroker, he hadn't seen that much old love.

Turning the ring this way and that, Sessalee studied every sparkling facet and handed it back. Bending over the tray, she pointed to another.

'Well?' Devin demanded impatiently, after she'd carefully considered every ring in the display case.

Sessalee shook her head.

'What the hell's wrong with them?'

Devin looked at the tray of diamond rings and couldn't see a dime's worth of difference. But Mendelson understood completely.

'Too much history,' Mendelson said with understanding.

'Sweet Jesus,' Devin grumbled.

Being the only Jew in the county, Mendelson's experience with Jesus had been anything but sweet. On the best of days he was treated like lox and bagels in a basket of fishes and loaves. Mendelson had lived in Five Points most of his life and only one man ever invited him to supper. That man's son stood before him now.

Disappearing through the curtain into the back room, Mendelson returned with a small velvet box.

'This ring has never been on another woman's

finger,' he assured Sessalee.

'How'd you come by it?' Devin asked.

'A man ordered it,' Mendelson shrugged, 'but he never had need for it.'

Lifting the lid, he tilted the box for Sessalee to see. 'Oh,' was all she said. Devin knew there would be no parting her from it.

'How much?'

Mendelson held up four fingers. Devin figured it was half what the ring was worth, but he didn't haggle. As the Colonel's son, he was accustomed to special treatment. He went out to the truck to get the whiskey, but hauled five cases to Mendelson's storeroom instead of four. As the Colonel's son, Devin also knew never to take advantage and never to insult a gift. When he got back, Sessalee had her small hand stretched out in front of her, her face dewy and dark eyes liquid. She had slipped the diamond on her finger along with the brass nut, but Devin had to admit it didn't look all that bad.

'Give my regards to your father, Devin,' Mendelson said.

Devin tipped his cap and led Sessalee out of the shop. She did not take her eyes off her hand all the way to the truck. Devin had to guide her by the elbow to keep her from walking into people and stepping off the curb. Lifting her into the passenger's side, he walked around the truck and climbed in beside her. Glancing over at her, he drummed his fingers impatiently on the steering wheel.

'You want an ice cream?' he finally asked.

Sessalee looked up at him and smiled.

24

Colonel Cavanagh had broken state and federal laws, led his sons down a path of crime and corruption, and contributed to the moral decay of many a man with hard liquor. Other than that, he was a rock-solid citizen and a gentleman.

Men were always surprised when they stood shoulder to shoulder with the Colonel. Height was not what kept a man in the Colonel's shadow. When he walked into a room, no matter who occupied the room or what title had been ceremoniously tacked onto their name, all ceded to the Colonel. Power gravitated to him like an apple falling from a tree. He deflected it the best he could. He was a leader who had no desire to lead. That kept him on peaceful terms with most politicians. He'd had his fill of herding men during the war. All he wanted at this point in his life was to walk his dogs, read his books and enjoy the occasional company of a woman.

Nothing attracts a woman more than God-given power. It is the ultimate aphrodisiac. And the Colonel was brimming with it. In a room of richer or better looking men, it was the Colonel women smiled at. But the Colonel believed in the dying art of chivalry. He did not fool with married women or fool single women into thinking he would marry them. Not once had he crept out the back door of another man's home or driven his car through a cornfield with another man's wife hiding on the floorboard. There had never been an unaccompanied woman in his home — except for his housekeeper, who would have to pay a mosquito to bite her.

The wives in Five Points assumed his declining their invitations meant his abstentions were universal. Women believe what they want to believe. Men who know what's good for them keep their mouths shut.

There are three things a red-blooded bachelor cannot or should not be expected to do without — food, shelter, and fornication. A man isn't damned for buying a house or sitting down to a plate lunch. The Colonel could see no reason why he should be damned for purchasing the last essential on the list. He simply wanted his machinery lubricated on a regular maintenance schedule by a woman who knew her way around his chassis. He saw no need to marry the mechanic.

And so, every Saturday night the Colonel made a visit to Miss May's brothel in Bingham. He would have gone twice a week if the trip had not taken longer than the trick. There were plenty of women in Five Points who offered to save him the trouble, but he graciously declined. The Colonel was a southern gentleman. He firmly believed a gentleman paid for services rendered. Furthermore, it had been his experience that the hidden costs of a charitable woman were just too damn high.

A visit to Miss May's kept him in a good humor for about three days. But by Wednesday morning he would wake up with a restless confliction. By Friday he'd bite your head off if you looked at him wrong.

Saturday afternoon he bathed and shaved. It was raining cats and dogs when he climbed into his Cadillac and headed for Bingham. As he passed his herd of cows, he slowed the car to a stop. Lick Creek had swollen beyond its bank and backed up into his lower pasture. The cows were lined up at the fence with no place to go. Any other day, he would have herded them to the upper pasture himself. But the Colonel was in a hurry. His pump was primed and ready.

Turning off the road, he headed to the main barn where he was most likely to find his foreman. Their paths crossed about halfway down the drive. The boys riding in the bed of the truck were soaked to the bone, shirts sticking to them and felt hats drooping around their faces. 'Just headin' that way,' the foreman called from his truck. 'Would have already moved the cows to the north pasture, but the bridge has washed out. Me and the boys had to drive over and pull Tom Merrill's Ford out of the river. We were just headin' back to put up the warning barricades.'

News that the bridge was out made the Colonel bite his cigar in two. It meant he would have to drive ten miles to Stewart's Landing and take the ferry across, which added an hour to the trip each way. He would barely have time to get to Miss May's before he'd have to turn right back around to catch the last ferry home. There are certain things a man does not like to rush. Furthermore, Lonnie Stewart, the ferryman, wasn't much of a businessman. He'd been known to drift a mile off course when his weekly delivery of moonshine arrived. The Colonel did not like being stranded on the wrong side of the river. It meant staying the night at Miss May's, which he never did. After a career of sleeping on army cots, the Colonel didn't like sleeping in a foreign bed, no matter how appealing the foreigner was.

Given the situation, he decided it was time to visit the Five of Clubs.

It came as quite a shock to the Colonel to find Eddie McCowan standing at the gate dressed in a tuxedo. The boy had finally found an occupation, holding a clipboard.

'Good evening, sir,' Eddie said, as though he'd never laid eyes on the Colonel in his life. 'May I see your membership card?'

'Membership card?'

Eddie pointed to the brass plaque on the gate.

FIVE OF CLUBS
PRIVATE
MEMBERS ONLY

Under normal circumstances, the Colonel would have eased out of his Cadillac and shown Eddie a whole new use for that clipboard. But it was getting late and he was getting fractious.

'Eddie McCowan, I have known you since you were a snot-nosed baby hanging on your mother's overalls!'

'Just doing my job, Colonel,' Eddie said, calm and professional.

Running his finger down the list of names on his clipboard, Eddie found the Colonel's and drew a crisp little check.

'Here we are, sir. You're listed under honorary memberships.'

This rubbed the Colonel raw. He did not like being an 'honorary' anything. He earned his way or paid cold cash. But cars were starting to line up behind him and he didn't like causing a scene either.

'Just open the damn gate!' he roared.

Eddie raised his hand motioning for Woody to swing the gate open.

'Have a good evening, sir.' Eddie gave a little salute as the Colonel drove past. 'We apologize for the delay.'

He was still in a huff as he gave the valet his keys. But as the Colonel climbed the front steps to Pearl's, he was struck with a heavy heart. In his own way, he was a faithful man. Except when he was stationed in France during the war, he had never once strayed outside Miss May's. He told himself he would do this, but only once. The minute the maid opened the front door, he knew it was a lie.

Men raised their glasses and beckoned the Colonel to join them as he passed through the front parlor. But he was not in the mood for social foreplay. The maid led him down the hall to the back parlor. 'Have a good evening, sir,' she said, as she pulled the door closed behind him. Spotting a girl standing at the bar with copper hair, lively eyes, and a saucy attitude he could taste from across the dimly lit room, he headed her way. He whispered in her ear and they reached a quick understanding.

Taking his arm, she guided him toward the back stairway. He was already nuzzling Sophie's neck on the landing when he heard humming. He tried to ignore it, but the familiarity of the song and his inability to name it got the better of him. Lifting his face out of Sophie's hair, he cocked an ear. It was an alluring hum, deep and smoky. Taking a step back, he ducked low and peered down into the warm yellow light of the kitchen. The woman humming was rolling pie dough with her back to him.

'Who is that?' he asked.

'Our cook.' Sophie's breath was warm on his ear as she slipped open the buttons on his shirt. 'Maysie McCowan.'

Maysie was dressed as usual, but the kitchen was so hot and humid from all the food boiling, frying and baking that she'd taken off her shirt. She was wearing one of Eddie's sleeveless t-shirts under her overalls, her bare arms dusted with flour and her hair in damp wisps around her face. It took a minute for the Colonel to believe it. Why, he had no idea the widow had such a tight little figure.

'Maysie McCowan,' he called down.

Brushing her hair back with her forearm, Maysie turned and looked up. Sophie hung on the Colonel's shoulder like a silk scarf, languidly twisting his graying chest hair into soft curls with her painted fingernail.

'Colonel,' Maysie said.

'What's that song you're singing?'

'Just an old hill song.'

'My mother used to sing it to me.'

'Did she now?'

He felt Maysie's eyes on his open shirt and his chest swelled like a sail. The corner of Maysie's mouth turned up in amusement and it irked him like a dare.

'Well, then . . . ' he said gruffly.

'Well, then . . . '

Maysie turned back to rolling her dough and the Colonel and Sophie continued up the stairs. But for the rest of the night the Colonel felt unusually restless and insatiable. Every time he thought he was finished with Sophie, the memory of Maysie McCowan smirking at him in that tight little tee-shirt stirred him up all over again. Even after he left Pearl's, that damn tune she was humming kept running over and over in his mind, haunting him as hill songs tend to do.

★ ★ ★

The Colonel was back at Pearl's every other night after that and it quickly took the bite out of the dog. The snarl smoothed from his face, his disposition mellowed and he had the energy and friskiness of a puppy. The housekeeper thought they should call the doctor.

'He's sick, I tell you,' she insisted, as she and Sessalee watched the Colonel dance and wrestle a bone from his prize bitch in the yard.

Sessalee simply smiled.

Like its patrons, the Five of Clubs' prudish façade concealed an enlightened interior. In the

275

front parlor, antique mahogany mantels displayed lithe art deco nudes. French champagne chilled in silver ice buckets alongside brown earthen jugs of moonshine served in Mason jars, but by far the drink of choice was Cavanagh Whiskey. An ebony-black piano player dressed in a white tux played an enamel white grand piano scattered with red rose petals. He could play any song called out to him, or hummed if the name had slipped the mind. If a man were in a more meditative mood, newspapers and the latest periodicals and journals lay fanned on the coffee tables in the library and leather bound books lined the shelves. One of Pearl's girls kept his glass full and cigar lit. In the dining room, a man could get pretty much anything he wanted to eat, any time of the day. In the rear parlor, he found whatever else he might be hungry for.

While highbrow décor flirted with lowbrow in the front of the house, it got down to business in the back. Heavy velvet curtains draped the windows from the ceiling to floor, and muted light from fringed Tiffany lamps kept one's activities safely in the dark. The scent of expensive cigars mingled with expensive perfume. And beauty beckoned.

The Five of Clubs aroused all of a man's senses and a few that had started to atrophy. Except for sleeping in his own bed, the Colonel could see no reason why a man should ever leave.

At Pearl's the Colonel smoked good cigars, talked a little business with the other men, listened to good music, and ate like a king. And from time to time, he made a trip upstairs.

'*They say that her beauty was music in mouth,*' he recited to Sophie on their way up the back stairs. '*Men that had seen her drank deep and were silent . . .* '

' *. . . And O she was the Sunday in every week . . .* ' The last line floated up to him lightly from the kitchen.

The Colonel's head shot down to the butcher block. Maysie McCowan did not look up as she pared an apple, the green peel winding in a single curling ribbon.

⋆ ⋆ ⋆

After a trip upstairs the Colonel was always famished. Maysie kept the buffet table stocked and fresh. There was a ceaseless supply of ham, fried chicken, tenderloin, smoked trout, and so on. But when the bread basket held yeast rolls instead of biscuits, the Colonel lost his desire for everything else. He had come to build his meal around Maysie's biscuits. What accompanied them made little difference.

'There's a table full of food in the next room,' Maysie said, drying a pan and hanging it above the butcher block.

'I was more in the mood for breakfast,' the Colonel said, as he took his coat off, draped it over a chair and made himself at home at the kitchen table.

Flipping the oven to 500 degrees, Maysie pulled out two iron skillets.

'Hope you don't mind if I smoke in your

kitchen,' he said, as he shook out the match.

He took her silence to mean that she didn't.

'How do you want those eggs?'

'Over easy.'

Maysie filled a pot with water under the faucet for the grits and set it on the stove to boil. Leaning back in the chair, the Colonel watched Maysie cook. A woman who knows her way around a kitchen is beautiful to behold. Country ham sizzled in the pan, coffee percolated in the pot, grits quietly thickened, and Maysie made biscuits.

Biscuits are the simplest of breads. Milk, flour, soda and butter. How a woman managed to mess them up, the Colonel could not imagine. But mess them up they did. Some women got in a hurry and baked them too hot, so that they burned on the top while the center was still dough. Some baked them too slowly, so they came out of the oven dry as crackers. Some women smothered them with fancy ingredients hoping to hide their inability to perfect the basic bread.

'What makes your biscuits so light, Maysie?'

'Heavy cream,' she said without hesitation.

Maysie was not the kind of woman who left an ingredient out of a recipe so that other women might fail. Humming, she rolled the soft white dough on the cutting board, fingers light on the pin, a dusting of white flour on her lean arms.

'I suppose you think I'm an immoral man.'

'Do you care what I think?'

'Can't say that I do,' the Colonel said, staring at the burning tip of his cigar.

'Then I'll tell you.' Cutting a biscuit with a tomato can, Maysie turned it in melted butter and placed it in the iron skillet. 'I like a man with a healthy appetite.'

The Colonel's eyes turned up from his cigar.

Pulling open the oven door, she bent low and slid the biscuits onto the middle rack. Most men steal looks at a woman like a thief. But the Colonel stared honestly. If the woman was offended, she could be sure he would not look again. He was still running his eyes over Maysie when she turned around. Her body became warm and pliable under his gaze. When his eyes reached hers, Maysie's were waiting.

A noise at the back door broke their gaze. Wiping her hands on her apron, Maysie went to open it. Ulysses trotted into the room and stood panting by a large mixing bowl on the floor as though he'd been there before.

'Hope you don't mind dogs in the kitchen,' she said, as she scraped steak scraps into the bowl.

She took the Colonel's silence to mean that he didn't.

★   ★   ★

Most nights, Pearl could be found at the poker table. Some players play the cards. Pearl played the players. She knew every move a man would make long before money hit the table. She knew when to stroke a man's ego and when to freeze him out in order to make him throw more

279

money down to impress her. Upstairs, down-stairs, the skills were not so different.

When the cards were hot, Pearl could double what the house brought in. When the cards were cold, she retreated to her private rooms. As madams go, Pearl believed a little mystery went a long way.

'How's business?' the Colonel asked.

'Making more money than I know what to do with,' Pearl said, flicking her lighter and holding it under his cigar.

The Colonel grinned from behind the smoke. It was well known that Pearl knew exactly what to do with money. Her opinion in money matters was as valued as any man's. She certainly didn't get that from her mother. Money ran through Lorna Wilde's fingers like water.

Life is like a poker game. Some players fold while holding a winning hand. Some win holding nothing but a pair of deuces. It isn't the hand you're dealt in life. It's the hands that hold the cards. Pearl Wilde was very good with her hands. And she had gotten that from her mother.

'I'm guessing you don't plan to be in this business long,' the Colonel said, as she poured him a drink.

'Already have a buyer.'

'Without you, he's just buying real estate.'

'It's a she. But then you already know that. I believe it was you who put the idea into Sophie's head.'

The Colonel grinned. 'Sophie has a very good head on her shoulders.'

'And very good shoulders,' Pearl said, pouring

herself onto the chaise across from him.

The Colonel studied the tip of his cigar and Pearl could tell he was finished with small talk and ready to get down to the real reason for his visit.

'So, what can I do for you, Colonel?'

★   ★   ★

At the end of the night, Maysie always brought Pearl a glass of ice cold milk to help her sleep. She usually found Pearl playing cards with herself at the round poker table. Bessie growled 'Follow the Deal on Down' on the phonograph as Pearl shuffled the deck.

Maysie watched Pearl deal six hands around the table, the cards sliding into place neat. Pearl liked to play six hands at a time to keep sharp.

'If you played life as well as you played poker . . . ' Maysie observed.

'Well,' Pearl said, turning her hand over and spreading a full house in front of her, 'we'll never know.'

Gathering the dirty glasses around the room, Maysie stacked them on a tray.

'The Colonel came to see me tonight,' Pearl said casually, as she raked in the cards and reshuffled.

'Did he now?'

'Seems he wants to spend the night with one of my girls.'

'The Colonel never spends the night,' Maysie said, emptying the ashtrays then polishing them clean with a rag.

281

'I told him it would cost him a hundred dollars.'

Maysie raised an eyebrow. One hundred dollars was a lot of money.

'I guess you nipped that notion in the bud.'

'He didn't bat an eye.'

'Must want something real special.'

'He does.' Pearl took a drink of the cold milk. 'He wants you.'

Maysie blurted out a laugh. When she realized Pearl was serious, she grew somber.

'Take all the time you need to decide,' Pearl said, parting the cards and shuffling.

'Yes,' Maysie answered without a moment's hesitation.

Pearl turned her eyes up to Maysie's.

'Yes, what?'

'Tell the Colonel, yes.'

Pearl studied Maysie's face to make sure she was sure.

'The house takes half,' Pearl said, as she dealt another round.

★   ★   ★

On the day of her appointment with the Colonel, the girls bathed and dressed Maysie. Cooing and preening, they rubbed her feet and elbows with lemon, buffed her nails and waxed her legs. Maysie stood perfectly still as they massaged almond oil into her skin and powdered parts of her she had long forgotten she had. While one brushed her hair into a soft twist, another did her make-up. 'Not too much,' Sophie ordered, looking over Maysie's shoulder in the dressing mirror. 'A rose doesn't need rouge.'

Pearl gave Maysie a powder blue silk dress to wear that matched her eyes and clung in all the right places. 'Just something I had hanging in the closet,' Pearl said, as Sophie snipped the price tag off the back.

When the girls were finished, they turned Maysie around to face the mirror. The room grew quiet as Maysie turned her head from side to side and telescoped in and out from her reflection. Sophie passed her a hand mirror and Maysie held it up to somberly review her rear view. Maysie had to do the math to figure her age. She could not believe she was almost forty-five years old. She didn't feel any different than when she was twenty.

'The old dog may have a few gray hairs,' Maysie concluded, handing Sophie the mirror, 'but she still hunts.'

Inky Mott leaned against the cab waiting for Maysie with his arms crossed. He thought the Colonel had lost his mind paying one hundred dollars for the widow. But when he caught sight of Maysie coming through the front door, he pulled his hat off. He had no idea she had such a tight little body.

'Why, Miss Maysie . . . you look . . . '

It was all Inky managed to say, but the way he said it was enough.

To protect Maysie's reputation, the Colonel thought it best they spend the night in Nashville. And so he paid Inky Mott a pretty penny to drive her all the way to the Hermitage Hotel. And to keep his mouth shut.

'It's a mighty luxurious hotel,' Inky said, as he opened the cab door for her. 'Had to set the Colonel back a pretty penny.'

Maysie had only been inside one hotel in her life. It was nothing like this one. The Hermitage doorman was wearing a black satin top hat and white button gloves and bowed his head slightly as she passed. As she walked across the marble-floored lobby, she stared wide-eyed at the exotic potted fronds, shiny brass sconces and tasseled velvet furniture with lion claw feet and wondered what in the hell the Colonel was up to. She didn't need impressing. For a hundred dollars, he could have had her at the Feed and Seed.

'Colonel,' she said, when he opened the door.

'Miss Maysie,' he replied, taking her bag.

While she took a look around the suite, he took a look at Maysie. Truthfully, he preferred her in the little T-shirt and overalls, but he wouldn't kick her out of the hotel bed.

'I thought we'd have a little dinner and then — '

'If it's all the same to you, Colonel,' she said, turning to face him, 'I'd just as soon we get right down to business.'

This was not what he had planned, but he quickly made the necessary adjustments.

The Colonel had worried that, when push came to shove, Maysie would be timid. He had no patience with timid dogs or timid women. Truthfully, he found them annoying. But as Maysie unbuckled his belt, pushed his pants

284

down to his ankles and shoved him onto the bed, it was suddenly he who suffered from shrinking courage.

Standing at the foot of the bed, Maysie took her own sweet time running her eyes over him.

'Colonel,' she finally said, 'you are a fine specimen of a man.'

Maysie's hands had milked cows and kneaded bread dough. She had pulled birthing calves from the womb and tossed hay bales. With a touch light as sunshine, she had rubbed clove oil on Eddie's swollen teething gums and crocheted lace with thread fine as angel hair. A man's body was hardly a challenge for her. As her fingers moved over him like hot breath, the Colonel hoarsely whispered, 'Sweet Jesus,' and his courage was restored.

'Colonel,' Maysie said, as she pulled the pins from her hair, 'I'm going to do things to you no woman has ever done.'

Maysie hadn't done them either, but then she had always cooked from scratch.

The rest of the night was like the blur of battle for the Colonel. After the sheets had settled, he had no idea which side had won. When Maysie finally retreated to her side of the bed, he lay flat on his back staring up at the chandelier.

'Frankly, madame,' he said, 'I feel a bit used.'

'Colonel,' Maysie sighed with utter satisfaction, 'you were used when I got you.'

★ ★ ★

As is the way of men, the Colonel immediately fell into a sleep deep as death. He awakened shortly before daylight, stretched, scratched and remembered where he was. Maysie had caught him off guard the night before. Now, he was ready for her. He turned and reached for her, but her side of the bed was cold. Sitting up, he switched on the lamp on the nightstand. Maysie's bag was gone. And so was she.

Furious, the Colonel threw back the covers. The agreement had been for all night. He jerked the telephone from the cradle to give Pearl a lecture on business ethics, when he noticed the envelope on the nightstand leaning against the lamp. Tearing the seal, he yanked out the note.

THANK YOU, COLONEL,
FOR A LOVELY EVENING.
MOST SINCERELY,
MAYSIE MCCOWAN

Folded inside the note was a hundred dollar bill.

★　★　★

It was barely light when Inky parked the car beside the stone wall at St Jerome's church.

'Wait here,' Maysie told him, leaning in the cab window. 'I won't be long.'

A fog lay over the graveyard. Dewy cobwebs marked the graves of those forgotten, and the silvery paths of snails and slugs painted the stones. When she swung the iron gate open, a covey of mourning doves took flight into the morning. She walked straight across the grounds. She didn't care whose grave she stepped on.

Some women marry for love, some for money. Maysie had married Morris McCowan because he asked her. Everyone thought Morris was a catch. And in her younger days, Maysie put all her faith in what other people thought. Morris was twenty years older and had never married. He'd lived with his mother until she died and owned his tobacco farm free and clear. What more could a plain-faced old maid of twenty-five like Maysie hope for?

'You'll be an old man's darling,' her mother whispered, as she gave Maysie a push toward Morris after church.

While they courted, Morris made no effort to hold her hand. 'He respects you,' her mother said firmly. The need to breed was surging through Maysie. By the time she finally took her wedding vows, she was so fired up, the touch of her own fingers on her lips made her shiver. But when Morris lifted her veil and grazed her cheek with his thin tight lips, Maysie knew. There wasn't enough starch in the man to make a collar stand up.

For their drive to the mountains, Maysie wore a new dress, a pale blue organdy with matching buttons and lace around the throat and sleeves. Morris took one look at her and his face grew dark.

'Woman, cover yourself!'

It was August. The air blowing through the open windows of the car was like heat blasting from a furnace. The dress and Maysie's hope wilted like lettuce. But she kept her sweater buttoned to the chin.

Their honeymoon night Morris made her kneel by the bed while he read the Bible. As they lay side by side, Maysie reached for his hand.

'A man doesn't like a fast woman,' he said, pulling his hand away from hers as though she had forgotten to wash it.

From Maysie's point of view, she'd taken it slow all her life. She'd saved herself like a Christmas gift, and by God, she was ready to be unwrapped.

The second night when she tried to touch him, Morris turned his back to her.

'Am I doing something wrong?' she whispered in the dark.

Morris lay perfectly still, pretending to be asleep. But she could tell by his breathing he could hear her.

'Please,' she whispered, slipping her hand inside his pajama top.

Morris swung around and slapped her so hard she tasted blood.

'No man likes a woman who acts like a whore!'

The words hurt far worse than his hand. They cut so deep, a part of Maysie died.

It rained every day of her honeymoon. Fog rose like pale smoke on the mountains and the streams churned white water. Maysie watched it all through the hotel window. When she suggested they go for a walk, Morris's silence suggested she had no say in the matter.

He spent the day stretched on the bed, reading the newspaper and napping. He saw no need to waste money at the restaurant. They ate food she'd brought in a picnic basket. He had her bring his plate of fried chicken and deviled eggs to him in bed. It was good practice for being an old man's darling.

'I think I'll go buy a postcard in the lobby,' she said, reaching for her purse.

'It isn't appropriate for a wife to walk around alone,' Morris told her firmly.

'Why did you marry me?'

'Just be grateful. I could have married better.'

Slowly, Maysie sat back down.

Morris had lived too long with his mother. Her apron strings were still tied tight. He expected Maysie to slip into his mama's shoes, to wait on him, to care for him. But his mother's shoes would always be too big to fill. Nothing Maysie did would ever be good enough. And the one thing she could give him, he pushed away. Morris was sickened by a woman's love. His mother had seen to that. Even in death, the old woman would not let him go.

While Morris snored in the other room, Maysie sat on the edge of the bathtub and the cold reality of her situation began to sink in. Maysie, the woman who insisted on tasting an apple before she bought a bushel, the woman who refused to order a dress from the Sears, Roebuck catalog because she couldn't try it on first, the woman who had never bought a pair of shoes without walking around the store twice to make sure they didn't pinch, that same woman had vowed to spend the rest of her life sleeping with a man she had never so much as kissed.

Gripping the sides of the commode, Maysie threw up.

The last night of her honeymoon, Maysie made Morris a tonic.

'What's this?' he asked, sniffing the cup.

'To ward off the influenza,' she said.

Being a man who warded off just about everything, he drained the cup. Maysie had made up her mind. If she could not have a husband, she would at least have a baby. She found the sleeping powder in his shaving kit. It only took a few minutes before he started to sway. When his eyes rolled back, Maysie sat down on the bed next to him. Morris immediately scooted away from her, but not as far as usual. Maysie put another tonic in his hand and guided it to his slack mouth. When Morris finally passed the point of refusal, Maysie took matters into her own hands. She was a farm girl and she knew things — not one of which worked on Morris.

When he finally passed out, Maysie curled double on the floor. 'Please, God,' she cried, fingers laced so tight her knuckles were white, 'don't let this be my life.'

It was still dark when she awakened with her wet face on the floor. The bathroom door was ajar casting a dingy yellow light on her situation. She could see Morris's bare feet through the crack. They were hideous feet, white as a belly-up fish, the nails gourd-yellow and curled. Crawling to the door, she quietly pushed it open a little wider. Morris stood at the sink. He was naked and playing his instrument like a slide trombone. 'Jesus. Jesus,' he muttered through gritted teeth, as his hand jerked up and down.

Granted, a man who has spent fifty years taking matters into his own hands would naturally have trouble relinquishing control. But the least he could have done was share. He was building to a crescendo when he caught sight of Maysie in the mirror. Wide-eyed and mortified, he stumbled away from her.

Truth be told, it was entirely his fault. If his hand had been free, he could have easily caught himself. Tripping backward into the tub his head hit the faucet so hard the fixture broke away from the wall. They have excellent water pressure at the foot of the mountains. Warm water gushed from the broken faucet, spraying into the room like a fire hose. While Maysie spit water and tried to pry his fingers loose from his still perfectly erect appendage, Morris stared up at her in the steam, mouth gaping and glassy-eyed. Finally freeing his hand, Maysie stepped out of her underpants, lifted her cotton nightgown and climbed on.

When water started flooding the room below, the hotel manager broke into the honeymooner's room. He found Morris dead in the bathroom and Maysie sitting on the bed bawling her eyes out. He thought she was grieving the loss of her new husband. In fact, she was crying with relief. Her prayer had been answered. She didn't know whether to give thanks or ask forgiveness.

Mrs Maysie McCowan returned home from her honeymoon widowed and pregnant. After the funeral, she scrubbed the make-up off her face, packed her dresses in a trunk and buried her desires alive. She put on an old pair of Morris's overalls, laced up a pair of his boots, and tucked her hair under a John Deere tractor cap. She leased out his five-hundred-acre farm and tobacco allotment, rented the big house and moved into one of his small tenant houses in town. That would have been enough income for a normal woman to live on. It was more than enough for Maysie.

At first people thought she was crazy with grief. Eventually, they just thought she was crazy. After a while, she started getting on their nerves. Mankind is rarely kind to women who stray. Womankind is vicious. No one threw Maysie a baby shower when Eddie was born. When she came down with the flu while tending her new baby, no one stopped by to check on them. Having abandoned societal mores, Maysie found herself abandoned by society.

She drank coffee alone at her kitchen table. And after a while she preferred it that way. Never again would she care what other people thought. Never again would she trust anything but her own intuition. Independence was a lonely place to live, but once she'd been there a while, she could never go back.

Maysie stared down at Morris's grave. For some women a flesh-and-blood man doesn't pose near the threat as that of a memory. She hangs like a broken record, playing the same verse over and over, unable to go forward, unable to go back. It had been nearly twenty years since they lowered Morris's body into the grave. But the cut he'd made inside her still bled.

Lifting her arms like wings, Maysie took a slow turn in her high heels and low-cut powder blue silk dress. She wanted Morris to get a good, long look at her. Kneeling, she slowly ran her hands over his arched marker, feeling smug satisfaction at his inability to escape. She leaned close, pressing her cheek against the cold gray granite as if whispering in Morris's ear.

'How do you like your fast woman now, you son of a bitch?'

25

'Try again.'

Hubert Hughes stood at his office window looking down at the river below.

'I've tried to reach her all morning,' his secretary insisted. 'Your maid swears she has no idea where Mrs Hughes went.'

When Olivia suddenly stopped calling the office a dozen times a day, Diane knew the Hughes marriage was in trouble. She immediately escalated her efforts to snag Hubert. Short of painting red nipples on the tips of her bra and hanging silk stockings on his lamp, she had tried everything to stage a friendly takeover. But for the first time in his life, Hubert's mind was only on Olivia.

'Did you try that psychic of hers?' He snapped his fingers to sharpen his memory. 'Lady Laetitia. Did you call Lady Laetitia?'

'Yes,' Diane said, the 's' hissing like a snake.

'Well?'

'I asked if she'd seen Mrs Hughes.'

'And?'

'She said 'not in the flesh'.'

Hubert had always been a haughty man. Why Olivia adored him was a mystery, even to Hubert. But she had worshipped him and he had grown not only to expect it but to depend on it. For her to suddenly withdraw her pandering and affection without any warning was unforgivable.

Not knowing where the devil Olivia was or who she was with had totally distracted him. He could not concentrate. He could not focus. Hubert, who ran a business empire with absolute certainty, could not decide what he wanted for lunch. He stared at the menu, at a loss. The men at his club lifted their eyebrows and threw knowing looks at each other. Hubert Hughes, once a titan among titans, was losing his edge.

Olivia's adoration had always annoyed Hubert. He not only didn't appreciate it, he mocked her for it. Hubert Hughes believed he was a self-made man. He never considered that Olivia's faith in him fueled his faith in himself.

Lowering into his chair, Hubert dropped his head into his hands to think. Diane's eyes fixed on his gray, thinning crown. Her crush on Hubert chilled. Without his conceit, he was just another fading, middle-aged man.

'Have you tried your lawyer?' Diane suggested.

Hubert looked up. 'Lawson?'

'If Mrs Hughes is divorcing you, he'll know.'

'Divorce?' The word hung in the air.

Grabbing his coat, Hubert stormed out of his office.

Diane stared after him and smiled. Olivia had paid her a week's salary to keep Hubert off her trail. The irony did not elude Diane. She suspected it hadn't eluded Olivia either.

Having the office to herself, Diane dropped into Hubert's leather chair and swiveled around to look out the window at the Nashville skyline.

She had worked for Hubert for five years and where had it gotten her? Stealing a rich husband was hard work and such a long shot. She was going to give some serious thought to making the damn money herself.

26

Every day, Mason swung his roadster into the owner's parking place during Kat's ten o'clock break. The boys on the loading dock could set their watches by him. Of course, he had no intention of doing any real work. He would sit at his desk for a couple of hours with his feet propped up pretending to study the production reports, while in reality studying Kat working at her sewing machine.

But then one day, Mason accidentally read the production numbers.

'Are these right?' he asked Crockett dubiously.

'No,' Crockett said, taking them from him. 'Those are a week old.'

He handed Mason the current report. Swiveling around to his desk, Mason crunched the numbers in the adding machine and fell back in his chair. He couldn't believe it. The shirt factory had a profit margin higher than any other Hughes company. Granted, it was still pocket change. But with a little attention and loving care . . .

After a couple of days of study, Mason started thinking about adding a second shift. It was absurd to let the machines sit idle sixteen hours a day. The manpower was available. Hell, two thirds of Five Points was available. All he needed was another good contract. After getting the second shift up and running, he'd find enough business to start a third.

And just like that, he was hooked.

Mason Hughes did not make being rich look easy. He was the first to arrive at the factory in the morning and the last to leave at night. Sometimes, he didn't go home at all. Crockett arrived at work in the morning to find Mason still hunched over his desk, tie loose, sleeves rolled up and poring over the numbers.

Little by little the town began to notice. When Gladys arrived at the general store in the morning, Mason would already be leaning against the porch rail, waiting for her to throw on the coffee pot. On Saturdays, his roadster was usually in the owner's spot in the factory parking lot. And on Wednesday nights after church the light in his office window still glowed.

Mason's long hours and hard work sent a wave of panic through the men of Five Points. After a lifetime of telling themselves that wealth was the luck of the draw, they feared their bluff was about to be called. 'You can be sure Mason Hughes doesn't sit around all day spitting chew and taking snorts out of the jug!' their wives took to saying. 'If Mason Hughes can work six days a week, surely you can find enough work for one!' The men retaliated as best as they could. 'I'd work my ass off too if I was rich!' they'd huff. They had made a career of making excuses. And they had grown to love their lack of work. They stared somberly, if not soberly, up at Mason's office light burning into the night and knew all that energy and enterprise could only lead to no good. The men sensed their life of leisure slipping away.

As Mason walked to and from the factory to the general store, he passed by the train station and noted the number of boxcars passing through town, where they were headed and what they were hauling. Standing at the river, he'd smoke a cigarette and calculate the square footage of the empty warehouses and count the barges headed toward Bingham. On the way back to the factory, he'd add it all together and ideas would storm into his head like music. Kat Wilde still smoldered in the back of his mind, even though she no longer saw any evidence of it.

As Lawson Mitchell had predicted, Mason and Mrs LaRue struck a bickering truce. Mason conveniently forgot all about ordering Lawson to fire her and begrudgingly grew dependent on the old woman. Mrs LaRue took care of Devil's Eye as if it belonged to her. And she took care of Mason's every need leaving him free to devote all his energies to the factory. Much to his amazement, she was also surprisingly insightful when it came to business. She knew all about the factories and stores that had closed in Five Points, what had caused their failure, and how many men had lost their jobs. Mason even took to running his ideas by Mrs LaRue.

'What you need is a military contract,' she said, when during supper he told her his plans to start a second shift. 'Uniforms, that's what you need.'

It was so obvious Mason was embarrassed he

hadn't thought of it.

'I can see yer mama in ya,' she decided, head tilted as she studied him.

Mason huffed as he spread the dishcloth on his lap.

'I'm *nothing* like Olivia.'

'It's the only part of ya worth keepin',' she told him flatly.

Any appreciation Mason had for Mrs LaRue's business sense was always cancelled out by her annoying observations into his character.

'You should talk to the Colonel.'

'The Colonel?'

'Colonel Cavanagh,' she said, filling his coffee cup with the sludge that would keep him working through the night. 'The men the Colonel don't know ain't worth knowing.'

Mason doubted anyone in Five Points would have the connections his father had, but he wanted to do this on his own, without Hubert. Besides, there was something about Mrs LaRue that made him listen. She was surprisingly intuitive about the shirt factory. Often she saw where Mason was headed in his thinking and got there before he did. It was almost as if she'd been bred for business. He filed Colonel Cavanagh's name in the back of his mind.

It is the way of wealthy men to give and the way of poor people to think they should. When Annabelle Boyd told Mason she needed money to fix the pipe organ at St Jerome's, Mason wrote out the check. It felt surprisingly good. And so, when the mayor mentioned the courthouse could use painting, Mason wrote out another.

The town thought better of him for it. The boys shot the shit with him at the general store, Gladys ran a tab for him, and Bucky Darnell kept his car washed and waxed for a dime.

And just like that, he was hooked.

Mason thrived. In no time at all, he could barely remember his life before moving to Five Points. When he did think back, it seemed a vague, boring blur. He had nothing to show for his days as a carefree playboy. But in Five Points, every minute could be measured. In Nashville, Mason was and always would be Hubert Hughes's son. In Five Points, he could feel himself taking hold.

And so, when he looked up from his desk at Devil's Eye and saw his mother's limousine coming up the tree-lined drive, his world reeled.

'What are you doing here?' he demanded, as he watched Olivia's driver unload a mountain of suitcases from the trunk of the car.

'I've left your father,' Olivia declared, as she ascended the front porch steps.

'But what does that have to do with me?' he asked bewildered.

'Darling, you'll never know I'm here!'

She patted his cheek with her glove as she passed, followed by her driver weighted down with luggage, her maid balancing a stack of hatboxes, a yapping Pomeranian, and a psychic.

Sadie greeted the invaders as if she'd been expecting them. She ordered the driver and maid to carry the luggage and hatboxes upstairs, and with a single clap of her hands had Olivia's dust rag of a dog obedient and sitting at attention.

Lady Laetitia was the last to drift into the house. She swept by Mason, then suddenly stopped in the middle of the foyer, tilting her silk turban.

'This house is ... how you say ... oc-cu-pied?'

Mason glared at her in annoyed bewilderment.

'Delicious!' Lady Laetitia declared, as she floated up the stairs to her room.

★ ★ ★

The only way Mason could escape being sucked into the flurry of chaos that always surrounded his mother was to make a run for it. Grabbing his car keys, he drove straight to the factory. When he swung the car into his parking spot, he was surprised to see Kat Wilde standing on the loading dock.

'I left my lunchbox,' she explained, as Mason unlocked the side door.

A forgotten lunchbox was no small slip at the factory. In the night janitor's book, it was one of the seven deadly sins, along with tobacco spit on the sidewalk, cigarette butts in the planters and missing the urinal in the men's room. Charlie was a fastidious man who did not tolerate anything that created more work for him. A forgotten lunchbox meant mice. Mice meant setting mousetraps. Mousetraps meant disposing of the stiff little corpses. And you couldn't just throw them into the trash. They attracted larger vermin, rats, cats and possums. A forgotten lunchbox was a nasty business from start to finish. Charlie had discovered if he eliminated the source of the problem, he eliminated the problem. In his own way, he was before his time in quality assurance.

Black metal lunchboxes lined the shelves in his janitor's room in the basement. If an employee wanted hers back, it would cost her a nickel. Most of the girls went to carrying paper sacks, which could last a couple of weeks if they didn't get wet.

'Evening, Charlie,' Mason said, as they passed. Charlie did not look up from his mop.

'You forgot to shut the lights off again last night,' Charlie scolded gruffly, as he slopped the heavy wet mop back and forth.

'Thank you, Charlie. I'll make myself a note.'

'It's not easy changing those bulbs,' Charlie grumbled on. 'Have to haul the twelve foot ladder up the stairs. And new bulbs cost a pretty penny.'

Kat had no doubt the old troll was trying to figure out a way to take the lights down from the ceiling and ferret them away in the basement.

Light bulbs started Mason thinking about how dim the workstations were, which started him wondering if better lighting would speed up production. Lost in thought, he walked so fast Kat had to jog to keep up with him.

As she hurried along beside him, Kat's face grew hotter and hotter. Only a few weeks ago, Mason had been totally infatuated with her. Now, as far as she could tell, she didn't exist. Granted, she'd told him he didn't have a chance with her. But she'd never lost a man's lust so quickly. And it irked the devil out of her.

Kat thanked her lucky stars she hadn't taken that ride with Mason Hughes. She could not stand a man who lacked conviction, even if that conviction was getting her into the back seat of his car.

But as she was throwing him a hateful look, she realized Luella was right. With his hair uncombed, sleeves rolled up and a determined look on his face, Mason Hughes made a girl's heart jump. It takes fortitude to hate a handsome man. You have to focus on the flaws. At that precise moment, Kat couldn't find any, and so felt obligated to go over him with a fine-tooth comb.

'How did you get the scar?' she asked, as her eyes ran over him.

'Football,' he said, absently touching his cheek.

'You look too small to play football.'

'I am.'

'Then why did you play?'

'To prove I wasn't too small.'

Kat had never been drawn to men whose battlefield had goalposts. She couldn't fathom what was accomplished by fighting over a ball. Sweat and heavy breathing, Kat believed, should be saved for more meaningful contact.

'I don't like football,' she told him.

'Truthfully,' Mason admitted, 'neither do I.'

He held the swinging door to the sewing-machine room for her and Kat walked straight to her workstation. Grabbing her lunchbox, she hurried back toward the door. In her urgency to get away from him, the lunchbox flew out of her hands. The crash startled Mason out of his trance. He looked down at Kat raking everything back into the box and blurted the first thing that came to mind.

'How's your dog?'

'Alive and well,' she said, as she climbed to her feet. 'How's your ghost?'

'We haven't heard any rattling whiskey bottles in a couple of days. Apparently, Uncle Cyril has a short attention span.'

'Apparently,' Kat said dryly, on her way out the door, 'it runs in the family.'

★ ★ ★

After Kat left, Mason had trouble concentrating. He sat at his desk and tried to focus, but his mind kept drifting. Giving up, he grabbed his coat. He remembered to turn the lights off on his way out the door.

Mason was rounding the square when he spotted Bourne's truck at the general store. He parked the roadster out front and went inside.

'Mind if I join you?' Mason asked, sliding onto a stool at the counter.

Bourne sat at the counter fingering a small pearl handled knife. His laid-back manner was deceiving. While he seemed to be casually gazing into his coffee while Gladys filled Mason's cup, the truth was his focus was on the mirror across from the counter. It was no coincidence that he could see the whole town square in the mirror's reflection. Bourne always kept one eye on his

305

back. Mason's focus, on the other hand, was always on what lay ahead.

'You wouldn't happen to know a Colonel Cavanagh, would you?' Mason asked, taking a sip of coffee.

'My father.'

Mason had assumed as much.

'My housekeeper seems to think your father and I should meet.'

'And why is that?'

Mason told Bourne his plans of going after an army contract for the shirt factory and Bourne could see where he was headed. The men the Colonel didn't know weren't worth knowing.

'You can catch him at Pearl's most nights,' Bourne said.

Mason was not a sensitive man. You could be dead on the sidewalk and he wouldn't notice unless he had to step over you. But he sensed a shift in Bourne's mood when Pearl's name came up.

'If Pearl Wilde is anything like her sister, she must be hell on wheels.'

'Pearl and Kat are as different as whiskey and moonshine,' Bourne said sourly into his cup, 'but equally addictive.'

The familiarity with which Bourne said this sent Mason's back up. Mason had asked Bourne if he and Kat were familiar. Maybe he hadn't asked the real question.

'Did you and Kat ever . . . '

'It's a small town,' Bourne said, turning the pearl knife end on end on the countertop.

Mason flared like a match struck against

sandpaper. He didn't stop to see how illogical it was to be jealous of a woman he had no claim on, much less of her past. Fumbling a dollar bill out of his pocket, he threw it on the counter. He was pushing to a stand when Bourne grabbed his arm. Mason was going to hear about it sooner than later. He might as well hear it straight from the jackass's mouth.

'Pearl Wilde and I were . . . ' Bourne's jaw twisted, as though loosening for the truth to come out, ' . . . well, you might say we were engaged at the time.'

Slowly, Mason lowered himself back onto the stool.

Bourne's eyes cut to Gladys who was pretending to dust cans on the ladder. He shook his head. It wasn't like the whole town didn't already know the story.

'We'd been on a run to Jackson all night. We started hitting the bottle around Centerville and by Dickson, I was too drunk to drive home. The boys dropped me off at Wilde Lane.'

Mason quietly watched Bourne's face in the mirror. He was still furious, but he was even more curious.

'The day was a scorcher. Even the breeze was hot. Pearl wasn't inside the house. So I figured she was cooling off at the springhouse.'

Bourne flipped open the pearl-handled knife and ran his thumb lightly along the blade until Mason felt sure he was going to lay the skin wide open.

'I remember going into that springhouse . . . and I remember crawling out. But for the life of me, I don't remember a thing that happened in between.' Frowning, he strained to remember then shook his head. 'Maybe we did. Maybe we didn't. Either way, it didn't mean a thing to me. But it sure as hell flew all over Pearl.'

'Pearl caught you in the act?'

'Or not in the act,' Bourne cut him short.

Mason let this sink in.

'You're saying you didn't want to sleep with Kat?'

'Now, I never said that,' Bourne corrected quickly. 'Any man who tells you he doesn't want to jump in the sheets with Kat Wilde is either a sweet thing or a flat-out liar.'

Mason couldn't argue with that.

'Would you jump in the sheets with her now?' Mason asked, staring him straight in the eyes.

'I haven't touched her since that day.'

'That's not what I asked.'

Mason had learned his lesson. You had to be specific with Cavanagh men.

'I don't trespass on another man's property,' Bourne swore.

The two men sat quietly at the counter.

'Tell me something,' Bourne said after a while. 'If you do get Kat, what are you going to do with her?'

Mason stared into his coffee and said nothing.

★   ★   ★

'Sadie, tell me all the latest gossip.'

Olivia poured two glasses of milk as Sadie rested at the kitchen table. Olivia spent her childhood summers at Devil's Eye when Sadie's mother was the housekeeper. She and Sadie played together as girls, cutting paper dolls out of Sears, Roebuck catalogs in the attic on rainy days and swimming at the creek. The easiness between them remained.

'Well, we have a new house of ill repute in town.'

Olivia nodded as she slid the spatula under a warm teacake, lifting it off the pan and onto the blue willow platter. Of course she'd heard of the Five of Clubs. Every woman in her circle had.

'And yer boy's done turned into the Saint of Five Points,' Sadie said, dunking a teacake into her milk.

'Mason?'

'Tossin' money ever' which way. Givin' money to the mayor to fix up the courthouse . . . money to the church fer the organ . . . money to Miss Mabel fer school books . . . '

'My Mason?' Olivia blurted a laugh. 'Whatever for?'

'Tryin' to impress Kat Wilde would be my guess,' Sadie said, chewing.

'And is he impressing her?'

'Saints ain't what turns a Wilde woman's head.'

'Well,' Olivia said wryly, 'I have that much in common with Miss Kat Wilde.'

27

Everything about Olivia Hughes reeked old money. The way she sat in a chair. The way she held her cup. She had a relaxed poise that only comes from generations of financial liquidity. The comings and goings of fashion did not concern her in the least. The clothes in her closet never went out of style. Olivia's life was one of quality and refinement. She had no need to flaunt her pedigree. She could trace her family tree back to the seed.

And so it would have shocked most people to see how perfectly at home she was sitting in a whorehouse drinking tea with a madam and one of her girls. It was a testament to Olivia's good breeding that she felt absolutely no need to establish her superiority. She was so securely perched on the top rung of society that she had nothing to gain by looking down at others.

'I suppose you wonder why I'm here,' she began.

Taking a sip of tea, Olivia rested the cup on the saucer.

'The first time I saw Hubert, he took my breath away. Every woman in the room had her eyes on him. Not because he was the most handsome man — which he was — but because he was the most enterprising. You could feel it from across the room. There was no doubt that

Hubert Hughes would make something of himself.'

Olivia smiled into her cup like a woman who had spotted a good investment and made a killing on it.

'When Hubert asked me to marry him, it wasn't for love.'

Olivia saw no need to elaborate. Pearl and Sophie understood perfectly. Love is the legal tender of the poor.

'We've been married for twenty-six years now. And every time I look at him my heart still races. Hubert is the first thing I think of when I open my eyes in the morning. He is the last thing I think of when I close them at night.'

Olivia spoke matter-of-factly, as though describing the symptoms of her disease to her physician. Pearl and Sophie listened with professional objectivity.

'I am in love with Hubert. But he is not in love with me. And he never has been.'

Olivia had received the best and most expensive education available to a young woman of means. She had studied Latin, Plato and read all the classics. She could play Chopin on the piano, jump a horse and dance any ballroom dance. But for a woman whose primary goal in life was a happy marriage with a man like Hubert, she had been cast into the world ill prepared. Olivia knew how to set a table, but had absolutely no idea how to thrill a man. As had been recently brought to her attention, a misplaced fork did not carry nearly the consequences of an unfulfilled husband.

311

Tilting her head, Olivia carefully considered what she was about to say.

'I'm not here for me. It's not about what I'm missing. It's what Hubert is missing. I feel as though throughout our marriage . . . as though I have deprived him. I feel as though I owe him.'

Another woman might have been embarrassed by this admission. Olivia was determined. She had no intention of letting Hubert take his business elsewhere without a fight. And she would do whatever it took.

In Olivia's world, when you wanted something done right you engaged the services of a professional. When she wanted a luncheon to go smoothly, she hired a caterer. When she wanted to learn tennis, she hired her club tennis pro. It seemed perfectly logical to her that if a woman wanted to learn how to thrill her husband, she should do the same.

'I want to know things . . . to be able to do things . . . I want you to teach me everything,' Olivia said. 'I want to take Hubert's breath away. And I couldn't care less how much it is going to cost.'

Having explained the situation, Olivia folded her hands in her lap and waited for Pearl to consider her request.

Lighting a cigarette, Pearl fell back on the couch. Her eyes moved critically over Olivia as if interviewing a new girl. Olivia had the equipment and could be taught how to use it. But just because you have ten fingers and a piano doesn't mean you can play the blues.

'A woman can do everything a man wants, or

thinks he wants,' Pearl said at last, 'but still not be what he desires.'

Olivia nodded. She understood the terms. Pearl's services did not come with a guarantee.

'Well, then.' Tapping out her cigarette, Pearl excused herself and left the two women alone.

Everything about Sophie reeked sensuality. The way she sat languidly on the couch. The way she fondled her cup. Her rust red hair draped over one eye like a curtain. Her ripe lips pouted. She crossed her long white legs like silk ribbons on a box from Tiffany's waiting to be opened. With every breath, her firm breasts rose and her eyes half closed, as if air was a drug that kept her in a perpetual state of arousal. She had the relaxed poise that came from knowing she possessed a power and knew exactly how to use it. Sophie could make a man fall on his hands and knees and beg like a dog, and pay for the right to do it.

'How do you like your tea?' Sophie asked.

Olivia blinked at her blankly. Try as she might, she could not make the connection between tea and apprenticing in the oldest profession in the world.

'It's delicious,' she answered hesitantly. 'I've never tasted anything quite like it.'

'It has a dash of pepper.'

'Really?'

Olivia looked down into her cup. She could not imagine putting pepper in tea.

'It is the unexpected that turns the ordinary into the extraordinary,' Sophie said, as she lifted the delicate china teapot to refill Olivia's cup.

As she poured, her eyes turned up to meet Olivia's. And the look Sophie gave her made Olivia suck in her breath.

'Oh, my,' she whispered, with a little imperceptible shiver.

And with that, Olivia's lessons began.

★　★　★

It was dark outside when Olivia finally walked down the backstairs at Pearl's. She was passing through the parlor when she heard a familiar voice.

'Lawson?' she said.

Lawson Mitchell looked up from the red velvet divan, surprised — then mortified.

'Olivia? Good Lord!' He jerked his hand from the thigh of the woman he was fondling and his eyes darted to see who else might have caught him in the act. And then he did a double-take on Olivia.

She looked much the same as the last time he had seen her and much the same as the night he planned to ask her to marry him, civilized and impeccably dressed. But something was different. He couldn't quite put his finger on it.

'What in the world are you doing here?' he demanded.

Olivia laughed a deep lusty laugh that lacked all gentility. It struck him as more barmaid than belle of the cotillion ball. Lawson was simultaneously aghast and titillated.

Olivia looked at Lawson the way a woman looks at a former love, with both familiarity and wonder. If she had married Lawson, he would have adored her. He would have surprised her with gifts, clung to her every breath, and trembled when she kissed him. He would have eagerly gone wherever she wanted to go, done whatever she wanted to do. If Olivia had married Lawson, she would have gained another lapdog.

'I won't tell Hubert,' Lawson quickly swore, naturally assuming she would reciprocate the favor.

'Oh . . . ' Olivia's smile was inscrutable as she pulled on a glove, 'please do.'

★ ★ ★

When Eddie whispered in her ear that a potential new member was waiting to see her, Pearl excused herself from the poker table and made her way to her private parlor. Walking into the room, she stopped short.

'Miss Wilde,' Mason said, standing. 'My name is — '

'I know who you are.'

Pearl stared at him, devoured him actually. She'd only seen him that day at Kat's from a distance. Up close, she could see there was more to Mason Hughes than a good name and breeding. A carefully managed dark streak ran through him that would trump other men's assets. Chances were he would never have to use it. Its presence alone would keep most men in check. And most women in waiting. Pearl's eyes moved over Mason so intimately he combed his fingers through his hair and laughed, but not because he was nervous.

Pearl pulled the sliding doors closed behind her.

'What can I do for you, Mr Hughes?'

After doing some checking, Mason had discovered that Colonel Cavanagh did indeed have connections, as did many of the members of the Five of Clubs. Robber barons wheeled and dealed alongside governors, state legislators, and US congressmen. European tobacco buyers, who couldn't speak a word of English, when asked what they would most like to see during their stay in the south, would say in impeccable English, 'Five of Clubs.' With all the business that was conducted inside the house on Dog Leg Hill, it was a wonder President Roosevelt hadn't claimed it as part of his New Deal.

As Pearl fixed him a drink, he compared her to Kat. Pearl was as different from Kat as whiskey from moonshine, as Bourne had said. But Mason could see how a man could develop a taste for both.

'I understand membership is by referral or invitation only.' Mason reached inside his coat and pulled out his wallet. 'I can provide you with whatever references you need.'

'That won't be necessary.' Pearl slipped the wallet out of his hand as she handed him his drink. 'For you, Mr Hughes, membership is on the house.'

A hint of a smile rose on Pearl's face as she slid the wallet intimately back inside his breast pocket.

28

Hubert knew the minute he asked Lawson Mitchell about Olivia that he was holding something back.

'Olivia hasn't called you?' he asked again.

'As I said,' Lawson answered, as he poured Hubert a drink from the liquor cabinet in his office, 'Olivia has not called me.'

'Then have you seen her?'

'We bumped into each other quite by accident.'

'By accident?'

'Entirely.'

Hubert held Lawson's eyes and Lawson laughed nervously. Hubert punched him in the face.

'Are you seeing my wife?' Hubert demanded, his hand pulled back ready to hit him again.

'For God's sake, Hubert!'

Lawson held both hands over his nose, reeling from the pain. Blood gushed through his fingers and splashed onto his starched white shirt.

'Are you sleeping with Olivia?'

'Have you lost your mind?'

'Are you?' Hubert roared.

'I saw her at the Five of Clubs!'

Pulling a handkerchief out of his coat, Lawson held it tentatively to his nostrils to dam the bleeding. 'She told me to tell you I saw her there.'

Lawson paused to make sure he had Hubert's full attention. Twenty-six years ago Hubert stole Olivia from him. Lawson had taken it like a gentleman. For twenty-six years he wished he hadn't.

'She was coming down the back stairs.'

The devastated look on Hubert's face was far more satisfying than any punch Lawson could have thrown.

29

After Devin bought Sessalee a real wedding ring at Mendelson's pawn shop, the Colonel sensed a change in the marriage. Apparently, it had finally occurred to Devin that denying Sessalee husbandly affection was punishing him far more than her. He was still mad as a hatter about the shotgun wedding, still sulked and seethed around the house, and refused to look Sessalee in the eye. But now they were going at it like rabbits.

'You look like hell,' Bourne said, to his little brother.

Devin didn't have the energy to argue with him. After a week of Sessalee riding him hard and draining him dry, he didn't have enough spit in his mouth to swallow.

Bourne and Devin stood guard while LeRoy LaRue and a couple of his brooding cousins unloaded boxes of liquor off the back of a truck and hauled them into the Five of Clubs. Pearl's weekly order had gotten so big Bourne was afraid of being hijacked. He worried a little less now that Devin and the LaRues were family. While everyone else in town clucked that Bourne's little brother had married a LaRue to keep his snake charmed, Bourne immediately grasped the business implication. Once Devin was a lawyer he would handle any legal problems, while his new in-laws would handle

319

any problems outside the law. Steal from a LaRue and you'd end up scalped, skinned and nailed to a tree.

When the LaRues finished unloading the boxes, Maysie herded them all into the dining room.

'Eat some of that breakfast the girls are letting go to waste,' she ordered, waving her hand at the buttermilk biscuits, scrambled eggs, grits and hash browns.

Pearl's girls lounged around the table in sleepy repose, their hair like seaweed under water and their smudged eyes glazed and dreamy. Yawning, stretching, and wiggling their painted toes, they stared vacantly at the morning. Maysie shoved Devin into a chair in the midst of them and he blended in just fine. LeRoy took the chair across from his new brother-in-law to keep an eye on him. It was unnecessary. If Pearl offered to pay for her weekly order in trade, Devin would have had to take a rain check.

The LaRue cousins did not have to be encouraged to eat. They quickly grabbed empty seats as if playing musical chairs. The girls' diaphanous chiffon dressing gowns draping off their creamy white shoulders left nothing to the imagination, which was fortunate as the cousins had none. The LaRue boys stared like hungry wolves until Maysie set a platter of country ham in front of them and their priorities immediately shifted.

'Keep them in line,' Bourne said to Maysie.

Crossing her arms, she took up watch at the head of the table.

Bourne followed the sound of Bessie singing on the phonograph through the empty house. Pearl's parlor door was open. As he walked across the room a photograph on the mantel drew him. Lifting it, he stared at Lorna Wilde, the mother hellcat. Kat and Pearl looked just like their mother, black hair, blue eyes, bodies meant for sin. But they couldn't hold a candle to the smoldering original. It was a wonder Lorna's photograph didn't singe his fingers.

Pearl's bedroom door was ajar. Bourne pushed it open without knocking.

'Your money is on the dresser,' Pearl said without looking up.

Leg hiked up on a stool, she slipped a silk stocking over her arched foot and rolled it up her calf. Bourne's eyes lingered before he scanned the room. The bed was unmade. The sheets tossed. But only one pillow had been slept on.

'Were you able to get more champagne?' she asked, glancing back at him over her shoulder.

'Four cases.'

Dropping into a chair, Bourne leaned back and slipped a sassafras toothpick in his mouth.

'I didn't say you could sit.'

'I didn't ask.'

Pearl's expression remained frozen. Throwing open her dressing gown she hooked the stocking to her garter. His eyes traveled up her thigh to her hip. He couldn't help but grin. She wasn't wearing underwear. It was nice to know some things never changed.

'Normally, I make a man pay for this,' she

said, pulling her robe closed and cinching it tight.

'Oh, you always made a man pay,' Bourne said, rolling the toothpick from one side of his mouth to the other. 'You just dealt in different currency back then.'

The silver brush came hurling toward him, hitting the wall an inch from his ducked head. Pearl always had a strong pitching arm for a girl.

'Too bad you lost your sense of humor, Pearl. It was always your best feature.'

Bourne always knew how to press Pearl's buttons. Blinded by three years of pent-up hurt, humiliation and fury, she came at him, a leaded-crystal perfume bottle raised above her head and dressing gown flying. He grabbed her wrist as it was coming down and twisted it until she cried. Teeth clenched, he tore the sash away, shoved the gown open and ran his free hand up. She was so wet a man could drown. Holding her, wriggling and fighting, with one hand, he jerked his belt loose with the other. She slapped him once with her left hand and all it did was fuel the flame. The second slap sliced a gash down his face nearly to the bone.

'Shit, woman!' he shouted, shoving her away from him onto the bed.

Bourne touched his face then looked at the blood on his finger. Then he looked at Pearl. It is a fine line between love and hate. At that moment, he was seeing double. He swept the money off the dresser on his way out the door and only looked back to see what had sliced his face open. Then he looked again.

Pearl was wearing her engagement ring.

★ ★ ★

'You're not going to have a face left if you keep messing with her,' Maysie said, tilting his head back to clean the fresh gash.

'Just tell me about the ring,' Bourne said quietly.

'She always wears it to bed,' Maysie told him, as she doused the wound with iodine. 'Even when she's working.'

30

Devin pretended to be asleep when he heard Sessalee slip out of bed. He lay perfectly still as she padded barefoot across the floor in her flannel nightgown and wrapped her quilt around her. When she glanced back at him from the bedroom door, he closed his eyes and steadied his breath.

He waited until he heard the creak at the bottom of the stairs, then pulled on his pants and set out after her. Sessalee flew through the trees like an owl. Normally, Devin couldn't walk across a mowed lawn at high noon without tripping. But he was determined to follow Sessalee without her knowing. Feeling from tree to tree, he quietly traced her steps, biting his tongue until it bled every time a limb slashed him in the face or a briar dug into his leg. When he realized where she was headed, the pain bent him double. He had no doubt what she was up to. Devin had accepted there had been other men before him, but he couldn't live with this.

He leaned flat against the wall on the front porch of his grandfather's house, eyes pinched shut to hold the tears back. When the kerosene light glowed in the bedroom, he kicked the door open. Sessalee nearly jumped out of her skin.

'You followed me here without me knowin'?'

Throwing open the wardrobe doors, he ripped

the clothes from the hangers as he searched the inside.

'Why, I never even heared ya!'

Sessalee seemed far more shocked by his improved tracking skills than getting caught.

'Where is he?' Devin dropped to the floor and started running his arm under the bed.

'He who?'

'The dead man you're meeting?'

Sessalee stared at him stunned.

'There ain't no other man, Devin.'

'Then why did you sneak off in the middle of the night?'

Sessalee seamed her mouth shut and drew back against the wall. He had no doubt she was hiding something from him. Pushing himself to a stand, he towered over her, fists bunched and mouth twisted. Sessalee turned her face up at his and her eyes stroked him like a warm hand, kind and loving. But jealousy had blinded Devin and he hardened his heart to her.

Slowly, his breath steadied and his face became an expressionless waxy mask.

'I don't believe you,' he whispered with lethal calm. 'I don't believe any of it.'

Some men hit with their fists. Devin was far more dangerous. He could cut Sessalee in places no man would ever see, so deep her soul would slowly bleed out of her. She'd seen those women. Women men had gutted like a deer, with their dead vacant eyes and all the hope gouged out of them.

'You would have fucked anyone and anything to get out of that dirt floor dog's den you called home,' he said quietly.

If only Sessalee had said something, he might have stopped there. But Devin could not see her bleeding and so he went in for the kill.

'Who taught you to fuck, Sessalee? Who? Was it your brother? Did he teach you how to trap a husband the way he taught you to trap a rabbit?'

Sessalee's body swayed ever so slightly, as though the bones that supported her had been crushed. He was about to go on, but he caught sight of something she was hiding behind her. Grabbing her arm he twisted it around. As he wrenched what she was holding from her fingers, he heard the fabric tear. Opening his hand, he stared down at a rag doll with red yarn hair and mismatched button eyes, the rosemary fill spilling through his fingers.

Falling to the floor, Sessalee crawled on her hands and knees carefully gathering the rosemary into her nightgown. Devin stared down at her, his arms hanging lifeless as though the strings that controlled him had been cut.

'I'll fix it, Sessalee,' he tried to say, but the words choked him.

All the cruel things he'd said and done to her came rushing at him. He squeezed his eyes shut to keep them out, but they burned through his eyelids like a brand.

'I swear Sessalee, I'll fix it.'

Slowly, Sessalee turned her face up. He could have handled hurt or hate in her eyes. But what he saw knocked the breath out of him. Her eyes were vacant. She had no feelings in her for him, no feelings at all.

326

Slipping her wedding ring from her finger, Sessalee pressed it into his palm.

'Yer free tuh go. Ya always were.'

A cold washed over Devin so intense he went numb. He was sinking in black water. He couldn't breathe. He couldn't fight. He had never done anything to earn her love, and so had no idea how to earn it back. His legs gave and he dropped to his knees in front of her. His lips parted, but no words came. He knew what he had done. He knew no words could undo it.

The most powerful prayer is the one you cannot find words for. Devin hung his head and his eyes closed. Sessalee stared at him for the longest time. She searched for some sign that his remorse was true. But you cannot tell by looking which man will repent and which will repeat. Ultimately, forgiveness is a leap of faith, and the odds are fifty-fifty you'll be crippled by the fall.

What came to her was a single moment. Devin was standing in the woods with that trophy deer in his sight, one eye closed, finger squeezing the trigger. Clear a shot as a man could pray for. Then he let the rifle fall. Devin would never take what he didn't need and he didn't need the admiration of any man but one.

'Just tell me what I have to do, Sessalee. Just tell me.'

Inside this boy was a man worth loving. But it would take a woman to show him the way out.

'Forgive me,' Sessalee said.

He was crying now, shoulders shaking, face wet as a squalling child. He could barely see as he took her small hand and pushed the ring back on. He held her hands so tight their fingers fused.

'Don't you ever go wandering around in the dark without me again!' he blustered, wiping his face on his sleeve. 'You hear me?'

Some women would have made a man pay for what he'd done.

'Never again,' Sessalee promised.

Devin pulled her to him and gave her a fierce hug. When he started to pull away, Sessalee held him a little longer.

'Let's go home,' he said hoarsely into her hair.

She turned the wick down on the kerosene lantern and threw them into pitch black. Devin took one step, tripped on the footboard of the bed and crashed into the edge of the door.

Taking his hand, Sessalee led them home.

★ ★ ★

Sessalee waited until Devin's breathing was deep and sound. Leaning up on her elbow, she studied the man in her bed in the moonlight. It was the only time she could. He was a wonder. Leaning close she smelled him, the bittersweet scent of his ears, the salty smell of his neck. She traced him lightly with her fingers, his cheekbone, his mouth, the sandpaper stubble on his chin. Her fingertips moved down the silky hair on his chest, his flat stomach and below. Lifting his hand, she pressed her mouth against his palm. He barely flinched.

Sessalee did not question why she loved this man. Some things simply are.

'I love you more than life,' she whispered into his ear, seeding his dreams.

In his sleep he pulled her close, tucking her tight against his side. She nestled into him, resting her head on his chest, listening to his heart beat. Then closing her eyes Sessalee thanked God for this single moment.

31

At the first of every month, Crockett picked up the wooden suggestion box in the lobby, carried it up to his office and promptly dumped the contents into his large gray-green metal trash can.

'What's that?' Mason asked, hesitating as he passed Crockett's door.

'Suggestion box.'

'We have a suggestion box? Whatever for?'

'Beats the hell out of me,' Crockett said, slapping the last slip into the trash can.

Mason continued toward his own office until curiosity got the better of him.

Crockett was a man of infinite interests, none of which his wife allowed inside her house. His office was where he really lived, a place Mrs Crockett had never been invited. Shadow boxes of flint Indian arrowheads covered the walls and cloudy green and amber medicine bottles lined the window sill. Union cannonballs he'd dredged from the river rolled on the floor, boxes of brass Civil War uniform buttons were shoved under the couch and a stuffed bobcat snarled from the top of the wooden filing cabinet. Crockett's work was not the love of his life. But as long as he got the job done, Mason didn't care where Crockett's heart lay.

Dragging the garbage can between his knees, Mason pulled out a suggestion.

'Install radios at the work stations,' he read aloud.

Crockett huffed into his stained coffee mug. 'All we need is something else to take their minds off their jobs. Between the gossip, hurt feelings and their monthlies, it's like herding three-legged cats as it is.'

They shared a chuckle and Mason picked up another.

'Mothers should be allowed to bring their babies to work. That way they can breastfeed on their breaks.'

The two men were howling so hard the girls' heads turned up from their sewing toward the office window. They'd never actually seen Crockett laugh and it was oddly disturbing. Unbuttoning his cuffs, Mason rolled up his sleeve, and dove his arm down into the trash can for more.

'Give a bonus for going over quota.'

Mason looked up from the suggestion slip. Crockett was still wiping tears from his eyes.

'What happens when a girl exceeds quota now?'

'Usually, she kicks her feet up and stares at the ceiling,' Crockett said, feet kicked up on his desk and staring at the ceiling.

Mason looked thoughtfully at the slip before setting it on the corner of Crockett's desk. Reaching his arm down into the can, he pulled out another form. On the sheet was a carefully drawn flow chart of the factory. There was a detailed drawing of the train at the loading dock and the three floors of the factory, with arrows

331

pointing to each step of production. Bolts of material were unloaded on the dock then carried to the first floor where the fabric was rolled out and the shirt pattern sketched with chalk and then cut. The unassembled pieces were transported to the second floor on the freight elevator via pushcart for assembly. The assembled shirts were then carried up to the third floor for the buttons to be sewn on. From there, the shirts were hauled back to the first floor for pressing, folding, packaging and crating.

The suggestion was simple. 'Move buttoners to a workstation next to the sewing machines on the second floor.'

Mason studied the chart carefully. The advantages were obvious. The assembled shirts could move via conveyor belt from the seamstresses straight to the buttoners without runners having to transport them up to the third floor, only to turn around and haul them down to pressing.

Mason glanced down at the assembly floor through Crockett's window. There was more than enough room to make the change.

'Why are the buttoners on the third floor?' Mason asked, studying the diagram.

Crockett gave this some thought and shrugged.

'Been doing it that way for as long as I've been here.'

Truthfully, Mason hadn't given any thought to the factory's third floor, and for good reason. It didn't have one. It was actually the attic. The freight elevator stopped at the second floor.

'Whose idea was it to have a suggestion box?'

Mason asked, as he and Crockett climbed the dark stairs.

'Mrs Hughes's.'

Mason stopped short and looked back over his shoulder.

'Mrs Hughes? My mother?'

If there was another owner named Mrs Hughes, Crockett had not made her acquaintance.

'My mother comes here?' Mason asked incredulously.

'From time to time.'

'Whatever for?'

'Beats the hell out of me,' Crockett shrugged.

When one owner doesn't have a clue what the other owner is up to, it's best to stay neutral.

As he looked down at Crockett, Mason wondered how the runners could possibly drag the carts of shirts up the steep, narrow stairway.

'Have to haul them an armload at a time,' Crockett told him.

At the top of the stairs, Mason ducked under a support beam and scanned the cavernous attic. Diffused light filtered through small dormer windows. Stacks of old time-cards and boxes of ledgers formed a wall for as far back as the eye could see. Pigeons cooed in the distance. Even with the windows open, the attic was airless and smelled of mice.

The buttoners worked at a long wooden table with large spools of thread, boxes of buttons and pincushions neatly arranged down the middle. Backs bent over their work, the women sewed silently. When they heard Mason's footsteps on the plank floors, they looked up wide-eyed and startled.

'Ladies, I'm — '

'We know who you are, Mr Hughes.'

The spokeswoman for the group looked too old to be alive, much less still working on the line. Her fingers had held a needle so long the index bone had bowed and her thumb had conformed to the shape of the thimble. She gave a short sharp nod to the others. They bowed their heads and went back to work, thimbles and needles going up and down as if strumming a dulcimer.

'A suggestion has been made that we — '

' . . . move buttons to the second floor,' the woman finished his sentence.

Shirts made at the Rudolph & Hughes factory had sixteen four-hole freshwater pearl buttons, seven down the front, two on the button-down collar, two on each cuff, and a spare inside the hem. Each button was sewn on one at a time by hand. A blind man could see the buttoners were a bottleneck in the production.

Flipping through the forms in his hand, Mason found the suggestion he'd spotted earlier. 'Modernize the plant with button machines.'

Mason didn't know how to ask the next question without looking like a fool.

'You're wondering why we're way up here in the attic,' the old woman said, pushing the needle into the button and pulling it through from underneath. 'We used to be on the second floor. They moved us here while they installed the hoist in the ceiling to move the bolts of material from the loading dock to the cutters. They never got around to moving us back.'

'When was that?'

'When'd they move us up here, Mae?'

'It was the year Mr Cyril died.'

'That was over twenty years ago,' Mason frowned.

'Twenty years.' She shook her head.

Biting the thread, she fished another button out of the box in front of her.

'Your uncle died of a broken heart, you know,' she said, lining the button up with the buttonhole. 'After Fidela passed, he just lost the will to live.'

'Fidela?'

Mason was sure his uncle had never married.

'Fidela's granddaughter is the one keeps putting all those suggestions in the box.' She nodded toward the paper in his hand as her needle went steadily up and down. 'How long you reckon she's been putting them in the box, Mae?'

'Going on four years now,' Mae said.

'Right ironic, Fidela's kin working here.'

Mae nodded.

Mason shuffled through the suggestions he'd culled from the trash. None of them were signed, but the handwriting was the same. On each sheet under reasons why the company should implement the recommendation was boldly written, 'To improve efficiency.'

'What was Fidela's last name?' Mason asked quietly.

'Married four times, but always kept her first

335

husband's name. It suited her. Didn't it, Mae?'

'She was a wild one,' Mae agreed.

'Wilde,' the old woman said. 'Fidela Wilde.'

★　★　★

Mason spent half the night going over Kat's suggestions. The only thing he could find wrong with them was that he hadn't thought of them himself.

He wondered if this was what Kat was working on that afternoon he was at her cabin. He thought of her standing by the creek, hair blowing and shirt tied at the waist. The same old heat for Kat ran through him. Then it abruptly cooled. When a man discovers he's attracted to a woman's brain as well as her body, it complicates matters severely.

★　★　★

'Kat Wilde!' Crockett called down from the rail.

Kat looked up from her sewing machine.

'Mr Hughes wants to see you in his office!'

An anxious twitter ran through the girls like hens in a henhouse when one is being pulled flapping and squawking from the flock. It was their nature to assume the worst. No woman called to the boss's office had ever returned. They glanced sideways at Kat, simultaneously ashamed and relieved that it was she being sent to the chopping block and not them.

Kat pulled the rag off her head as she climbed the stairs. She looked back down at Luella.

Luella gave her the 'I told you so' shake of her head. Kat had not only rejected Mason Hughes, she'd been insulting about it. Luella knew — all the women knew — it was just a matter of time.

'Come in,' Mason said, when she knocked.

He was sitting at his desk studying some papers, a long spiral of adding-machine paper curling to the floor. Kat tilted her head and read enough to figure out that he was studying the profit and loss report.

'I'm going to implement your suggestion and move the buttoners back to the second floor,' Mason said, looking up at her.

Nothing humbles an overeducated man more than being trumped by natural talent. Kat had a gut instinct for business, but, as she stood in front of his desk, Mason focused slightly higher on her anatomy.

'Why?'

'To improve efficiency,' he said dryly.

Mason held up her stack of suggestions. Slowly, she took them.

'Work up the payback on your other suggestions and I'll consider them too.'

Kat crossed her arms tightly. She had no idea what a payback was, much less how to figure it.

'You know damn well I don't know how to do that.'

'Somehow, Miss Wilde,' Mason said coolly, his attention returning to his work, 'I think you'll figure it out.'

★   ★   ★

Kat went first to Miss Mabel for help. But when she asked the old maid school teacher how to figure 'payback', Miss Mabel lifted her whiskered chin and informed Kat that she hadn't a clue.

And so Kat turned to the town expert on paybacks.

'A payback in business is the same as a payback in life,' Bourne explained. 'It's all about getting even.'

They met at the general store for her lesson. Kat had a legal pad and pencil and leaned intensely toward him over the table.

'Figuring it is simple. You just got to ask yourself, is the payoff worth the price?'

Bourne looked at the window and nodded toward the train station.

'Say a man takes the train to Nashville every day to work but wants to buy a car instead. He can't just figure the cost of the car versus the cost of his train tickets. He has to take into consideration the price of gasoline, oil and wear and tear on the tires. How much is his time worth? Is it faster by train or by car? Will there be a loss of opportunity if he works on the train, but can't in his car?'

Kat nodded as she wrote it all down.

'What are you trying to figure payback on?' he asked.

'A button machine at the factory. They have one at the coat factory in Bingham. They can spit out a coat faster than you can snap your fingers.'

Bourne took his toothpick out of his mouth.

'You know if the factory gets a button

338

machine, women are going to be let go.'

Kat did not look up from her pad. She knew exactly which women would lose their jobs. She could see their faces.

'Be sure to figure in that some folks will want to get even.' Bourne slipped the toothpick back into his mouth. 'A payback in business is just like a payback in life. Figuring it is simple. It's the execution that gets complicated.'

32

Joy Lester was the kind of woman who hated first and then built a case for it. 'Judge not lest ye be judged' was a scripture she tended to gloss over.

'What happened to your neck?' Bud asked, flinching at the bloody red line across Roy's throat.

'Joy moved the clothes line during the night,' Roy croaked, plucking a clothes pin from his shirt. 'Bitch just about decapitated me.'

Since Joy set her sights on becoming a widow, Roy looked like a road kill. His face was still black and blue from where she'd dropped the hammer on him from her bedroom window. He managed to dodge the hammer, but in the process stepped on a hoe that flew up and slammed him straight on. He hobbled like an old man from stepping on the tacks she tossed through the window onto his chicken-coop floor, the hair on the crown of his head had been singed off when she soaked his kindling in lighter fluid, and he'd wrenched his back climbing out of his overturned truck after she loosened the bolts under his hubcap and a rear wheel fell off.

If Joy had put as much effort into loving Roy as hating him, no telling the man he might have been. Instead, his life had become a mine field. Joy had drained the brake fluid from his tractor, frayed the wires on his soldering gun and sprinkled ground glass on his chewing tobacco. Never knowing where she would strike next, Roy had turned skittish. He flinched, ducked and ticked like a spastic chicken. When a car backfired, Roy's eyes rolled back and he dove for the floor.

The boys were starting to worry about him.

'Maybe you should move into my back room for a while,' Bud said, nodding toward the storeroom.

Roy shook his head as much as his back brace would allow.

'I was born in that house and I'll die in that house!' he rasped.

The boys would have bet on it, if they could have found anyone dumb enough to bet against it.

33

Kat continued to run a shirt through her sewing machine while the other girls spilled out the double doors and hurried toward the time clock.

'You coming?' Luella asked, latching her lunchbox. 'Or have you decided to live here?'

'Go on,' Kat waved her on. 'I'm going to get a head start on tomorrow.'

Normally, Luella would have been suspicious. But it was Wednesday night and she had to feed the boys before church.

'See you tomorrow,' she called from the doors.

When Kat was finally alone, she opened her lunchbox and pulled out the roll of papers.

Mason's office was the workplace of a man with only one thing on his mind. The top of his desk was covered with cotton cloth samples, defective shirts to be examined and boxes of various styles of buttons. Stacks of reports lined the window sill blocking the view of the river below. But then, Mason never took time to look out.

Standing in front of the desk, Kat handed him the roll of papers.

Smoothing them flat on his desk, Mason went over her numbers. He sat perfectly still, fingers laced, chin resting on his thumbs. Only his eyes moved as they burned down the page.

'Where did you get your labor costs?' he asked, without looking up.

'Crockett gave them to me.'

'And where did you get your cost for the machine?'

'I called the company that makes them.'

'They just gave you a price over the phone?' he said doubtfully.

'I told the secretary what I was doing. She pulled the quote the salesman had given you.'

Mason stared at her without expression, then his head bowed back down.

'Your return on investment is slightly better than what I came up with,' he finally said.

Falling back in his chair, he looked at her.

'Yours is right. I didn't calculate lost production when buttoners are sick.'

Somehow, the victory carried a sense of loss. Mason's cockiness had waned. And she missed it.

'Good work,' he said.

With this she was dismissed. Mason's head dropped back to the papers on his desk. He was already lost in thought when he heard the lock on his office door clicking into place. He looked up as Kat pulled the Venetian blinds on the window closed.

For men, desire is a straightforward proposition. If they like what they see, they go for it. If they don't like what they see, they've been known to close their eyes and still go for it. But for women, desire is a moving target. Half the time, they don't even know what they're aiming at.

'This doesn't mean a thing,' Kat said, as she walked toward his desk. 'You understand that, don't you?'

In Kat's mind, Mason Hughes was an arrogant, spoiled, vain, rich boy. For weeks he had ignored her, dismissed her, then set her up for failure. Kat had never wanted a man more in her life.

By the time she came around the desk, his pump was primed. She undid his belt and was sliding his pants down when he reached to kiss her.

'Don't try to participate here,' she ordered, shoving him down in the chair. 'You'll just mess things up.'

Lifting her skirt, she straddled him on the chair. The accusation that he'd been trying to get into Kat Wilde's panties was baseless. Kat wasn't wearing any. Licking her fingers, she wet herself. Licking the other hand, she wet him. As she slowly lowered herself down onto him, Mason held her eyes. When she was half seated, she sucked in a breath. This was one sport he wasn't too small to play. The surprised look on her face made Mason thrust deeper. Her cry was sharp and he quickly pulled back.

'Am I hurting you?' he whispered.

His tenderness embarrassed them both. Holding her breath, she seated herself on him fully.

'Am I hurting you?'

In fact, she was killing him.

Hands on the arms of the chair, she rode him slow and smooth to let it build. When she saw the urgency in his face, she held him back. 'Not yet,' she ordered. 'I'm not through with you.' He gripped the seat of the chair until the wood or his knuckles cracked, he wasn't sure which. He dared not take his eyes off her. She was eating him like rock candy.

When she knew she couldn't stop herself, she set him free. 'Now!' she shouted. 'Now!'

Grabbing her hips he drove into her. Like lightning before thunder, her body arched before the scream. Her cry echoed through the empty factory as he shot into her, a million blazing comets thrusting deep. The room rolled, his eyes went back and time stood still.

Normally after lovemaking, Mason was the one who hit the floor running. But he'd barely caught his breath when he realized Kat was climbing off him. He reached for her, but his hand grabbed air. 'Wait,' he tried to say, but his throat was dry and she was already out the door. Mason slumped boneless in the chair, knees sprawled, pants around his ankles, his well pumped dry. The word 'efficiency' came to mind.

★   ★   ★

Kat sat on the front porch of her cabin watching lightning bugs blink in the pitch black. The creek flowed below and the sound of owls, frogs and katydids clashed like a symphony tuning up. Satan was stretched on the swing beside her, his big scarred head heavy on her lap. Kat absently scratched his chewed ears as she thought of Mason Hughes.

People were wrong about Kat Wilde. She might go through men like jelly beans, but she was nothing like her mother. Her mother had seen to that.

Lorna Wilde could not sleep in an empty bed. And so she'd settled for the easy pickings. Unintentionally, Lorna had set the perfect example of what Kat did not want. Even if neither of them knew it.

Kat thought of Mason sitting at his desk studying her numbers. He was a smartass, but she liked that in a man. And he was so sharp she would have to run to keep up.

All Lorna needed from a man was a warm body. Kat wanted a greater return on her investment.

Mason stood at the window in his office, hands in his pockets and staring down at the lights on a tugboat passing on the river. He absently noted the cargo, the number of barges and guessed its destination as he thought of Kat Wilde.

People were wrong about Mason Hughes. He was all about making money, but he was nothing like his father. Hubert had seen to that.

Hubert Hughes had wanted a proper wife. And so he'd settled for a woman who did not excite or challenge him. Unintentionally, Hubert had set the perfect example of what Mason did not want. Even if neither of them knew it.

Mason thought of Kat's suggestions and drawings so carefully rendered. She was crude, but he liked that in a woman. And she was so creative and clever he would have to run to keep up.

All Hubert needed from a woman was a

mother for his son. Mason wanted a greater return on his investment.

Mason was everything Kat wanted to be. Kat was everything Mason was missing. Together they would make one hell of a pair.

Then, of course, there was the sex.

34

The boys sat in their usual seats at the hardware store, legs stretched straight, hands wrapped around their RC bottles and staring at the pot-bellied stove. It was too warm for a fire, but they stared at the cold stove anyway. It had been a while since they had congregated and there was an awkwardness in the air. Roy fidgeted in his chair, shifting and wiggling. Finally, he jerked the cushion out from under him and flung it across the room. Things had changed and he could not get comfortable with it.

Rumor that the shirt factory was starting a second shift had made folks optimistic. The store was too busy for Bud to sit with them for long anymore. The bell on the front door jangled steadily. It was mostly dollar and dime, but it was enough business to put Dickie on full-time. Business had picked up so much at the general store, Inky had to get Woody to drive the cab during the day. Buck hardly ever came around anymore. It wasn't just carpentry work that was keeping him busy. He and Luella were now fused at the hip — or some other part of their anatomy. Why any man would prefer the company of his wife over his friends was a mystery to Roy.

'Pearl Wilde took some pictures of me,' Eddie finally broke the silence.

'What for?' Woody asked.

'She sent them off to a man she knows.'

'What kind of pictures?'

'Just pictures,' Eddie shrugged.

'Were you wearing the tuxedo?'

It was more an accusation than a question.

Eddie didn't say he wasn't so Woody knew he was. It was one thing to fall into good luck. It was another to conspire.

'He wants me to come to Hollywood and try out for a movie he's making.'

The boys grew quiet. Buck turned up his RC and Dickie tossed back a handful of peanuts. No one was surprised. Somehow they always knew Eddie was just passing through. It was as if the stork dropped him in the wrong town to begin with.

'It's just a bit part,' Eddie mumbled, eyes on the floor, 'a walk-on.'

It probably would have helped if they'd known what a walk-on was.

'What'd your mama have to say about it?' Woody asked.

'She told me not to forget where I came from,' Eddie said.

The boys knew his leaving was a done deal. Maysie had finally cut the cord.

'When you going?' Woody asked.

'Next train out.'

Woody's eyes cut to the clock on the wall.

'You need any money?' Inky asked.

Eddie shook his head. 'Mendelson gave me a real good deal on the gold pocket watch mama gave me, even with the inscription.'

Bud had no doubt it was more of a donation.

Their goodbyes were short and gruff, a lift of the chin, a quick wave from the chair. Bud slipped a twenty in his pocket as he patted him on the back, told him to make them all proud, then went to help a customer. Woody sat with his arms crossed tight staring at his boots.

On his way out the door, Eddie dropped an IOU in the can for old times' sake. They knew he would never be back to pay it.

35

Cracking the newspaper open, Hubert leaned back in his chair. For the first time in his married life, his study was peaceful. No yapping dog . . . no yapping wife. His supper had been served precisely on time, his humidor was stocked, the ice bucket filled. All his needs had been met and his world was in order. The servants were amazed at how easily he had adapted since Mrs Hughes left him. There was no hint he'd noticed she was gone.

When Olivia's hideous grandfather clock began chiming the hour, Hubert glanced up over his glasses at the time. Then his eyes fell to a silver-framed photograph of Olivia on his desk — smiling, eager, annoying as hell. Calmly opening the bottom drawer, he pulled out his revolver. Taking careful aim, he fired until the gun clicked empty. Gunpowder smoke choked the air. Shattered glass, splintered wood and brass clock guts splattered across the room as the crippled pendulum swung spasmodically.

After a moment of silence, he could hear the German gears grinding and scraping.

Reloading, Hubert shot it again.

★ ★ ★

'What can I get you?' Gladys asked, climbing down from her ladder.

351

'Coffee.'

'Coffee it is,' she said, going for the pot.

Hubert did not remember driving to Five Points. He was so furious at Olivia for wasting a day of his time he was still silently cursing her as he climbed onto the stool at the General Store.

He wasn't sure why he was there or what he was going to do now that he was. Olivia had been gone two weeks. And he had not missed her. In fact, he enjoyed the solitude. The household staff filled her domestic void without disruption. And as far as sex was concerned, well, he'd had better.

Olivia's lovemaking had the ambiance of a pep rally. There was a lot of bouncing and aerobatics, but after the screams had died, the game was never really played. They'd been married twenty-five years and she didn't have a clue how to seduce him. In her efforts to please Hubert, Olivia neglected pleasing herself. What she never understood, or was unwilling to chance, was that it was a woman's pleasure that pleased Hubert. Nothing aroused him more or provided greater release, than having a woman warm and desperate beneath him breathlessly begging, 'Don't stop! Please. Don't stop!' Hubert's pleasure was being the source of pleasure. He was not a giver. He liked the control. He liked the power. If that was selfish, so what?

Hubert's carnal thoughts drifted over the counter and penetrated the receptive widow Green's. Her hips instinctively disengaged. She smiled provocatively as she filled his cup, her widow's eyes glowing green as 'go'. But Hubert, annoyed at femalekind as a whole, dismissed her with a stoic stare.

'What brings you to Five Points?' the man sitting at the end of the counter asked.

'I have a stray wife,' Hubert grumbled into his coffee cup.

'I hear strays can be right difficult to round up.'

'So I'm learning.'

The two men traded cigars and whiskey then grew quiet, comfortable with the company if not their own thoughts. For men, it is the silence that binds.

'I married my wife to keep another man from having her,' Hubert huffed with bitter sarcasm.

'And how did that turn out?'

'Apparently, not that well.'

Hubert did not need Olivia. He had never needed her. Without her, he would have been just as successful. And it would not be difficult to replace her. The world was full of willing women. He glanced at Gladys. She was already looking back. In some ways, his life would be easier.

'This is excellent whiskey,' Hubert said, taking a sip. 'I'd be interested in buying some.'

'That can be arranged. I'm well acquainted with the man who makes it.'

Taking a puff on his cigar, the Colonel stared thoughtfully at the burning tip.

'So when did you figure out you loved her?'

Hubert did not miss Olivia. What he missed

353

was the man he was when he was with her. Without her, his edges were too sharp, his criticisms too caustic. Without Olivia, Hubert could barely stand himself.

'Right around the time she left me.'

36

Hoochie Booth, whose blurry-eyed, hungover face had not darkened St Jerome's red doors for fifty-one Sundays prior, solemnly trudged up the stone steps for Easter service. Hoochie belonged to that ecumenical order of men who prefer their religion condensed and à la carte. For them, Christianity is the church of choice. The theory being that for three hundred and sixty-four days a year a man can raise holy hell — and on Easter Sunday get his ticket punched for heaven.

Stumbling into the dark sanctuary, Hoochie hugged the marble baptismal font until the room stopped spinning. Musty hymnals, sweaty pews, his own stale breath, and the nauseating sweetness of Easter lilies made his stomach roll. Dipping his fingers into the font, he splashed a little holy water on his face.

Founded by wealthy Scotch-Irish plantation owners, St Jerome's once had the highest spire in Five Points. But after the Civil War, their aspirations dropped dramatically. They lowered the roof and used the hand-formed brick from the slave balcony to build the attached parsonage. It brought the lofty little church down to size. Now the herringbone rafters hung low over the parishioners like the picked-clean ribcage of a corpse.

Licking his parched lips, Hoochie rationalized that enough effort had been made to get his slate wiped clean for the year. He was making the sign of the cross as he planned his getaway when a breeze brushed his stubbled cheek, lightly turning his attention toward the altar. The eternal flame flickered in the red globe and a single ray of sunlight pierced through the azure eyes of the stained-glass Savior pointing the way. Hoochie's bloodshot eyes popped open, his clouded vision cleared and he was struck cold sober.

There, luminescent as angels in flowing white satin, kneeled Pearl Wilde and all her girls, their silky heads bowed and supple hands folded at their breasts. A couple of the angels were chewing gum.

Hoochie thought it was a miracle. The rest of the congregation was less impressed.

It was as if Pearl and her girls had the plague. No one sat next to them. No one sat anywhere near. With the exception of her few loyal followers — Maysie, Inky, Woody, Roy, Buck, Luella and their boys — no one even sat on Pearl's side of the church. Bud walked through the doors, heard the cock crow, and quietly backed right out.

The pews on the right side of the church yawned empty while those on the left groaned under the weight. Even though many in the room were directly or indirectly beholden to Pearl for the Easter clothes on their backs, they stacked themselves on the left side of the sanctuary, scrunched so tightly together their thighs overlapped like sardines in a tin. Buck, being a carpenter, fixed his eyes on the creaking rafters. He figured if one more parishioner sided against Pearl the old church would tilt on its stone foundation. Joy Lester glared at Roy from the choir, mouth seamless and her face as blazing red as the eternal globe. If looks could kill, hers would have nailed Roy to the cross.

The saints looked down on them from the stained glass windows and the sanctuary was as silent as the tomb. While the choir nervously awaited their cue, Annabelle Boyd sat posture perfect at the organ, lips pursed, arms crossed, and refusing to play. The priest, a stanch believer in consensus, wrung his hands and paced, waiting for some kind of sign.

And so, when the double doors behind them swung open, every head turned. There, standing in the doorway, was Kat Wilde. The women couldn't help but notice that Kat was wearing the same Easter dress she'd worn for two years running.

Kat looked from the angry crowd to Pearl and her girls and immediately ascertained the situation. She'd always been quick that way. The parishioners' heads swung smugly from Kat to Pearl. They had no doubt which side Kat would take. And so it came as quite a shock to all concerned when Kat walked down the center aisle, made the sign of the cross, and kneeled beside Pearl.

'Hello, Pearl,' Kat said, fingers laced and staring straight at the lily-covered altar.

Pearl looked at her beautiful little sister in that golden Easter morning light and before she could stop it a wave of affection washed over her.

Memories reduced to blurs of emotion, those tiny pearls of the past buried so deep she could not gouge them out, made her bypass all reason. She wondered if the sister she once loved still lingered somewhere inside the enemy kneeling beside her. And Pearl's cold heart began to melt.

But then the fleck of the Devil's mirror floating in Pearl's eye shifted. The vision of Kat lying beneath Bourne — legs spread, naked and writhing — crystallized, and Pearl's heart turned back to ice.

'Look what the cat dragged in,' Pearl said, swiping the words across Kat's face like a paw.

But Pearl's tone didn't faze Kat. Her eyes were shining, her skin glowed and she gripped the pew as though to anchor herself. Kat looked at Pearl and her bright face betrayed the secret she seemed desperate to tell. It had been three years but Pearl could still read her little sister like a book. Kat was in love.

Guilty as charged, Kat's cheeks flushed and a small laugh fizzled from her like champagne effervescing. It was true. She was in love. So much in love, she floated euphoric in the hallowed air. Love is like a baptism. All that has passed before is washed away and forgotten. Kat radiated joy and reeked good will. It was all Pearl could do to keep from slapping her. Kat beat her to the punch.

'Pearl,' Kat whispered breathless and bright-eyed, 'I'm sorry.'

You could have heard a penny drop in the collection plate. Every parishioner was riveted on the Wilde women.

Meanwhile, Pearl simply stared at her sister in disbelief. Did Kat honestly think it could be that easy? That all she had to do was ask forgiveness and her slate would be wiped clean?

'Pearl,' Kat urged, 'I would forgive you.'

With that, Pearl frosted.

'Well, of course you would. You'd forget why you were mad fifteen minutes after it happened.'

Those who know us best know best how to hurt us.

'You've never been faithful to anything,' Pearl said. 'Hell, you'd cheat on yourself if you could find a way to do it.'

Kat's eyes narrowed and a low growl came out of her.

'Why you holier-than-thou whore . . . '

'Don't play the whore card with me, you little slut!' Pearl said, hissing the 's' like a cotton-mouth.

Chins tucked and backs arched, their fingers curled into claws. They were about to scratch each others eyes out when a familiar voice boomed in the church air.

'Christ almighty! If Jesus hadn't risen, he'd roll over in his grave!'

Every head whipped toward the door.

'Mama?' Kat and Pearl sang in harmonious astonishment.

Looming in the doorway was Lorna Wilde. Even with her face half hidden under a swooping black hat, they could see that the fatale in her femme had not faded. Lorna scanned the sanctuary with fire in her eyes. No man was Lorna Wilde's judge, and she wasn't about to let anyone judge her daughters. Wherever her attention fell, cheeks burned scarlet and eyes dropped. Many a man had feasted at Lorna's table and if their wives found out, they could be sure it would be their last supper. Chin high and shoulders back, Lorna proceeded down the center aisle, arching an eyebrow over each pew of sheepish parishioners until their condescension withered.

Pausing at Mayor Hardin Wallace's pew, Lorna leaned down and whispered something in his ear. Hardin's face went white and his political future passed before his eyes. Finally setting into the pew in front of Kat and Pearl, Lorna opened her prayer book and crossed her million dollar legs.

Until that moment, no one had noticed the man tailing behind her. But when Lorna's new husband sat down beside her, every jaw dropped.

Of all the things women found to whisper about behind Lorna Wilde's back, her deadly handsome lovers topped the list. 'He may be a liar, a thief and a worm,' they'd say, 'but he sure is easy on the eyes.' And so Lorna's new husband came as quite a shock. Black hair covered the tops of his hands, crawled down the sides of his dark simian face and grew like Johnson grass from his starched white collar. Underneath his tailored suit one imagined that hair was sprouting everywhere on his hulking body. His widely spaced teeth were the color of corn and his smashed nose forced him to breathe through his mouth in a wet rasp. There was no doubt in anyone's mind he must be richer than Midas.

With her new husband settled beside her, Lorna turned and gave the Mayor a sharp stare. Some men are born to lead and some leaders are born to be blackmailed. Hardin sprang from his pew like a jack-in-the box. Hymnal held high, he began singing the opening song like a canary. Slowly, the others shuffled to their feet, staggering in off-beat and out of tune. Unable to take any more, Annabelle was forced to accompany on the pipe organ.

It being Easter, the church service lasted an eternity. When the priest finally said, 'Go in peace and serve the Lord,' Kat and Pearl, forgetting their feud, flew out the double doors to their mother.

'We were married last week.'

Lorna smiled at her new husband across the churchyard. He was already being courted by the mayor and several of the city councilmen.

'Roscoe isn't much to look at, but he's a crazy little monkey in the bedroom.'

'But what happened to your last husband?' Kat insisted.

'Ancient history,' Lorna said, with a wave of her diamond-studded hand.

Usually, the parishioners rushed home to dinner after church. But that day, they stayed for the show. The Wilde women cast a spell on the churchyard. As the mayor yammered away, Roscoe stared across the yard at his wife with lascivious pride. One would assume the three women were sisters. But of the three, it was Lorna most fixed on. A few laugh lines and a few gray hairs simply added to her allure. Underneath the tailored suit, expensive jewelry and billowing sail of an Italian hat, Lorna Wilde was still a siren. And that's exactly why Roscoe married her.

'But what are you doing here?' Pearl demanded.

'We're going to live here!' Lorna announced ecstatically, throwing her hands up into the air as if bursting out of a cake — which was how she met her third husband. 'Roscoe's into canvas. You know . . . tents. He got a huge contract from the army and I convinced him to open a new factory here in Five Points. Believe me, you do not want to live north of the Mason Dixon Line after Labor Day. It's cold as a witch's tit.'

Lorna gave a little shiver and her own mammaries shook like Jell-O.

Kat and Pearl were as seduced by their mother as the rest of the crowd. It was easy to see why no man had ever been able to resist her. For all her faults, a person came alive just by standing next to her.

'Good Lord.' Lorna squinted toward the sidewalk. 'Is that Annabelle Boyd? Why, she looks like the African pygmies got a hold of her.'

Lorna's old nemesis glared darkly at her over the wrought-iron fence, her pinched mouth puckered shut as if it had been stitched.

'Look and learn, girls,' Lorna said knowingly, as she pulled on a glove. 'Nothing wrinkles the face like holding a grudge.'

At that Lorna rolled an accusing look toward Pearl.

'You stole Annabelle's fiancè, Mama,' Pearl defended.

'Hell, I was so drunk I didn't know what I was doing,' Lorna insisted, shrugging off the incident as if it had been completely out of her control. It wasn't her fault if she was designed to keep other women on their toes. 'Besides, Annabelle should thank me for it. The man was a baboon.'

Pearl and Kat's eyes drifted across the courtyard to Roscoe. They weren't sure if he was picking his teeth with a palm cross or eating it. Lorna naturally assumed the disconcerted looks on their faces were for her.

'Girls,' she said somberly, taking their hands to brace them, 'this time it's for good. I took his name.'

Kat and Pearl stared at her speechless. Wilde women never took their husbands' names. It was a matter of principle and paperwork.

'Oh, babies,' Lorna said, squeezing their hands, 'he's smart as a whip and he worships me. And when you reach my . . . *stage* in life, it feels good being up on a pedestal.'

Lorna smiled provocatively across the court-yard at Roscoe.

'Especially when the pedestal is twenty-four-karat gold.'

Roscoe smiled back at his wife and the sisters got a glimpse of what their mother saw in her new husband. Roscoe was a coarse brute, but in the best sense of the word. He had a low center of gravity. No matter how hard Lorna tried, and no doubt she would give it her best, she would never be able to knock Roscoe off balance or push him around. Lorna had met her match.

Turning sharply, she faced her daughters.

'Now,' she said firmly, 'Roscoe and I are moving back to town and I want us to be a family, a real family, with Sunday dinners together and . . . whatever the hell real families do. This feud has gone on long enough. I want you girls to make up and move on.'

Kat looked at Pearl hopefully.

'Forgive and you'll be forgiven, Pearl,' Lorna said.

Slowly, Pearl opened her arms and Kat fell into them — like a rabbit jumping into the pot.

37

Maysie McCowan returned to an empty house after Easter service. Eddie was gone. She stood at her kitchen sink staring out the window at the blue-black crow perched on her clothes line, claws curled tightly around the wire, feathers ruffled and head drawn low. The crow's bead-black eyes stared back at her unblinking. Change or death was in the air. For Maysie it was one and the same.

Rinsing her water glass under the tap, she turned it upside down on the sink next to Eddie's glass. She didn't have it in her to put his away. They had sat side by side since he took his first drink from anything other than her breast.

Maysie had never considered any occupation other than motherhood. Truthfully, it was the only reason she married. She had devoted herself body, mind and soul to the job. It never occurred to her that her life's work would leave her feeling used up, empty, and alone.

She gave twenty years of her life to Eddie and he left so fast when he kissed her goodbye his lips missed her cheek. A son's independence might be the sign of a mother's job well done, but Maysie simply felt irrelevant.

The tap on the screen door startled her. Swinging around, she held her breath that Eddie had come home. He'd changed his mind and his leaving had all been a silly mistake. The visitor standing on her back porch startled her even more. Tucking the stray strands of hair back under the pins, she glanced down at her overalls and sighed.

'What can I do for you, Colonel?' Maysie asked through the screen door.

'I wanted to return this.'

Maysie stared at the one-hundred dollar bill he held in his hand.

'Keep it,' she said, crossing her arms tightly. 'You earned it.'

Actually, the Colonel had hoped she would earn it this time. But he sensed now was not the best time to make the proposition.

'I was about to fry a chicken,' she said, pushing the screen door open.

'Actually,' the Colonel said as he passed, 'I was more in the mood for breakfast.'

He patted his leg and Ulysses padded in behind him. Circling a spot by the stove, the dog curled on the floor, resting his head on his paw. The Colonel draped his coat over the back of a chair and made himself at home at her kitchen table. He pulled out a cigar and Maysie slid an ashtray in front of him. Shaking out the match, he leaned back and took a slow look around. You can tell a lot about a woman from her kitchen. Maysie's was clean and sparse. There was a path worn in the floor between the stove and the sink. No useless doodads hung on her walls. No frilly quilted potholders or ornamental cast iron trivets. Everything in Maysie's kitchen was useful and used.

He lifted a marked book from the table and read the spine.

'You're reading Joyce.'

'Trying to wade through it,' she said, as she filled a pot with water under the faucet for the grits.

'Never attempted it,' he said, licking a finger to turn the page.

'Wish you would. Then you could explain it to me.'

His hand hung in the air. It was a simple request, perhaps the least ever asked of him by a woman, yet it warmed him in the pit of his stomach. Poetry had passed over the heads of both his wives like clouds. He had never been aroused by a woman with his eyes closed. And he had never aroused a woman with as little as his mind. The Colonel felt curiously intrigued by the challenge.

Setting the pot on the stove, she opened the cupboard and pulled out the lard can that she stored her flour in. She measured two cups with her hand, made a hollow in the mound with her fist, and filled it with heavy cream.

'My youngest boy is headed to law school this fall and has decided to take his bride with him.'

'Think they'll make it?' she asked, one hand turning the bowl as the other worked the dough.

'It won't be Sessalee's fault if they don't. She'll always find her way.' Leaning his head back, he exhaled to the ceiling. 'Wouldn't mind keeping the daughter-in-law and throwing away the son.'

Maysie felt her face soften. She knew the

Colonel would cut the heart out of any man who tried to hurt his sons. He was a man who protected the things he loved, one way or another. She knew because she had seen the scars. Some women would have been appalled by the violence he had done and was capable of. Maysie found it strangely comforting. She had fended for herself all her life and was fiercely proud of it. But with the Colonel sitting at her table, the tightly wound coil inside her eased.

'It's going to be lonely in the old house.'

Maysie nodded as she shook flour on the biscuit board.

'I guess you heard my boy's headed to California.'

'Eddie will do just fine. He has your grit.'

The Colonel said it in a way that left no doubt. And a ragged cry freed itself from inside Maysie. She rested her flour-dusted hands flat on the table and bowed her head over the bowl. Eddie's leaving had left her so raw and so afraid for him. But Eddie did have her grit. And knowing he carried this small part of her with him would sustain her somehow. She took a deep breath to steady herself. Then standing straight, she turned her dough out onto the table. As she dusted the rolling pin, her eyes met the Colonel's. For some women sadness quenches passion. For some it is the other way around. He saw affection and desire in her wet eyes. Wrapping his hand around the brass pit in his pocket, he squeezed until it hurt.

'Maysie, I will never marry you.'

Maysie's hand hesitated, suspended above the

bowl. Then she returned to rolling out her dough as though nothing had changed.

Is a woman nothing more than a fertile plot of dirt where a man plants himself to grow? Maysie had given herself to two men. It had just about leached the life out of her. And what did she have to show for it? She had no intention of letting another man sink his roots into her. Still, it was one thing to choose not to marry and quite another to have a man tell her it wasn't an option.

'You rejecting marriage as a whole, Colonel, or just me in particular?'

'You know the answer to that.'

Maysie's eyes stayed fixed on the bread board. 'Colonel, do you love me?'

He stared at the burning tip of his cigar. The truth was, when he told Pearl he wanted Maysie, he had no idea what he wanted from her.

'I believe I do.'

'How long you plan on loving me, Colonel?'

The Colonel looked up at Maysie in her overalls and tight little tee shirt. Most men would have promised forever. But most men make promises they cannot or do not plan to keep.

'Maysie, I will love you for as long as you are a woman worth loving.'

Most women would have drop-kicked him off the back porch. But most women did not have Maysie's grit.

'Then, Colonel, you'll love me till the day you die.'

And Maysie said it in a way that left no doubt.

369

38

Jaw set and knuckles white on the steering wheel, Hubert Hughes raced up the tree-lined drive toward Devil's Eye. Suddenly frowning, he leaned toward the windshield. Up ahead, Olivia was strolling across the hay field, her fingers combing the high fescue. Hubert couldn't believe his eyes. His wife hated nature. If Olivia had her way, they would have upholstered their front lawn.

The weather had taken a nasty turn. Black clouds churned and boiled to the west. Indifferent to the brewing storm, Olivia drifted dreamily across the field. When thunder grumbled in the distance, she looked up at the threatening sky and laughed defiantly. After her lessons with Sophie, Olivia felt capable of taking on the heavens.

Hubert ground the car to a stop in the middle of the road. Rain was already splattering on the windshield. Cursing, he climbed out of the car and slammed the door. Before he could open the umbrella, the sky cracked open. Olivia made no attempt to run for cover. In fact, she was walking into the storm. By the time he slogged across the field to her, she was drenched to the bone.

'Are you drunk?' he shouted over the rain, trying to hold the wind-whipped umbrella over her as best he could.

A flash of lightning in the distance made him flinch. Hubert had built his life on logic and calculated risk-taking. He could not think of anything more idiotic than standing in the middle of an open field holding a metal rod over his head during an electric storm.

Meanwhile, Olivia was twirling in the field like a ballerina.

'Don't think I don't know what you've been up to,' he yelled at her. 'What the hell were you doing at the Five of Clubs?'

Slowly, a salacious smile rose on Olivia's face. And Hubert knew. He knew she could tell him everything that happened at Pearl's, every delicious detail, every erotic element, but there was now a secret part of his wife that he would never possess. It irked the devil out of him. But he had to admit, he was just a little excited by it.

Slipping free from Hubert, Olivia ran farther into the field. Face uplifted, she stretched out her arms and took a slow turn. Her silk dress dissolved from her breasts down to her legs, and her hair turned liquid and ran down her throat. Dropping her head back, she slowly licked the rain as it ran over her lips. Turning, she gave Hubert a look that shot through him like lightning.

He could not take his eyes off Olivia as she undid the tie on her dress. He had no doubt, if another man had been standing in the field, she would have been equally as willing. This did not disturb him in the least. If anything, just the contrary. Hubert understood the

371

mercurial nature of opportunity. In fact, he thrived on it.

Olivia's eyes closed as her hand ran down her wet slick skin. Her own touch made her shiver. Hubert was moving too slow; she would start without him. In her mind, their marriage had been twenty-six years of foreplay. The storm didn't hold a candle to the energy she had bottled up inside her. She wanted to strip away all convention and decorum. She wanted to toss and lick and roll and bite. She wanted to use every trick she'd learned at Pearl's and improvise a few of her own. She did not want to make love to Hubert. She wanted to take him like a wild mindless animal, but she couldn't quite say the word.

Hubert stared at his wife writhing, oozing and half-naked in the rain.

'Have you lost your mind?' he said flatly, grabbing her arm and dragging her toward the car. 'Lawson Mitchell's uncle was struck dead by lightning on the golf course. The seventeenth hole.'

As if to confirm this fact, a jagged bolt suddenly ripped across the sky so close they could smell the electricity. Instinctively, Hubert threw his body over Olivia, holding her head tight against his chest. With a deafening explosion, the lightning drove into an old oak tree in the middle of the field. The thick trunk split like kindling and burst into flames.

Olivia turned her wet face up to Hubert and he held it in his hands. It had been a very long time since he looked at her as a woman. Perhaps, he never had. When his mouth met hers, his heart hammered.

Another flash of lightning streaked the sky. As the thunder rumbled, Olivia and Hubert ran for their lives across the field, holding hands and laughing like children.

39

Roy Lester sat snug and dry in his chicken coop after Easter church service. He had a fresh wad of chew in his mouth — from a brand new pouch he had not let out of his sight — and was reading the Friday newspaper by the light of his little window. He was perusing the obituaries when he heard the scrape at his door. Pushing up from his rocker, he tried the door. It was jammed tight. Swinging open his little window, he stuck his head out and squinted into the rain. A crowbar had been wedged through the door handle. Joy, still in her Easter dress, was shaking a kerosene can around his chicken coop, splashing the oily fuel on the walls.

'Joy, honey,' he called cautiously from the window, 'watcha doin' out there?'

Joy glanced over at Annabelle Boyd's house. The windows were dark and the curtains pulled. Annabelle had gone to her sister's in Bingham for Easter dinner. There would be no witnesses to what Joy was about to do.

Gray mist rose in the hills. A storm was headed their way. A jagged streak of lightning ripped across the sky and touched down near Devil's Eye. Crouching under the eave of the tin roof, Joy counted the seconds between lightning and thunder, waiting for the storm to move overhead. All the while Roy chattered incessantly from the window, trying to reason with her.

'Joy, honey, is this about me poisoning your chickens? Hell, I'll buy you a whole new flock! Why, I'll build you a henhouse bigger than the house. I swear. Joy, darlin', think about what your doin' here.'

When the storm was almost on top of them, Joy slid the tin open. Over and over she struck the match, but the damp air kept snuffing it out. Eventually, it got the better of Roy.

'Lord almighty, woman!' he yelled. 'Get one off the bottom where it's dry!'

For the first time in their marriage, Joy did what Roy told her to do. Digging to the bottom of the tin, she pulled out a dry match and struck it against the side. It caught immediately.

'What'd I tell ya,' Roy huffed smugly.

Joy held the match to a twist of newspaper and it burst into a blazing torch. Roy's eyes popped open. Looking at him to make sure he was watching, Joy touched the torch to the kerosene that was dripping down the walls. The coop went up like a tinderbox.

As the flames licked up the walls, Joy calmly pulled on her Jesus Saves oven mitt. As soon as the fire died down, she would recover the red hot crowbar from the embers, eliminating all evidence. They would find the jug of moonshine she'd tucked under his bed along with Roy's charred body and put two together. 'Roy was passed out drunk when lightning struck the coop,' the sheriff would console her. 'He never knew what hit him.' Drunkenness had been the death of many a husband.

The storm was working itself into a fury.

Thunder boomed and lightning flashed in the black clouds. Huffing and puffing, Roy managed to squeeze one shoulder out the little window, but then wedged. The coop was burning so hot, there was hardly any smoke. Stepping up onto the chopping stump, Joy lifted the skirt of her Easter dress. And as the thunder drummed, Joy danced a little jig while singing at the top of her lungs, '*A frog went a courtin', he did ride . . .* '

Roy wiggled and squirmed until he finally fell back into the burning coop. Unable to wrench his body through the window or kick the door down, he searched frantically around the small room for something to save him. Grabbing his wash pitcher, he doused his quilt. Dropping to his knees on the floor, he pulled the wet quilt over his head. Surrounded by four walls of fire, he was baking like a biscuit in a wood oven. Roy knew his time was up.

By some folk's standards, Roy didn't have much to show for his years on this earth. Men who work with their hands are seldom celebrated. But Roy hadn't been a bad man. He'd taken a snort from time to time, but he wasn't a drunk. He'd borrowed on a permanent basis, but never stole. Exaggerated, but never lied. He never once betrayed Joy. He thought about it on a regular basis. But he never followed through. Still, under the circumstances, Roy feared that wasn't quite enough.

'God, forgive every thing that needs forgivin',' he prayed fitfully under the hot steaming quilt. 'And forgive Joy. It ain't her fault. She's a Meachum.'

376

As the words left his trembling lips, a wind rose so fierce the tin roof shook and rattled as if it was trying to fly away. The sky cracked wide open overhead and white light seared through Roy's little window, blinding him through the quilt. Squeezing his eyes shut, Roy threw his hands over his ears and curled into a tight ball. His eyes felt seared to the sockets and he thought his eardrums would burst and bleed. He'd never been so afraid in his life.

Suddenly, it was quiet and the air turned unnaturally still. Roy was too weak from fear to move. When he felt a cool breeze over him, he nearly cried with relief. He'd died and gone to Heaven. Cautiously, he raised his head out from under what was left of the steaming, scorched quilt. His first thought was that it had never occurred to him that Heaven would have clothes lines. Then he realized he was kneeling in an open air pavilion. Blazing debris dropped all around him and his charred black rocker creaked back and forth in the breeze. The walls of the chicken coop had gone up in a flash. All that remained was the burned and buckled tin roof overhead, the red paint melted and bubbling. The four corner posts glowed red hot and sizzled in the rain. Roy thanked God that Buck Darnell had framed the coop with steel train rails.

Pushing himself to a stand, Roy gingerly touched himself to see if anything was missing. He looked like a boiled crawdaddy, every hair singed off his body and his skin blood red, but he was still breathing.

Across the yard, Roy caught sight of the charred chopping stump. Lightning had hit it dead center. A smoking mound hissed and spit in the rain beside it. Slowly, he staggered over to it. Leaning down, he immediately jumped back with a scream. Joy's black incinerated corpse gaped up at him, the flesh seared to the bone. Even the gold in her teeth had melted. Tears in his eyes, Roy reached down and gently picked up all that remained of Joy, her Jesus Saves oven mitt.

40

'To see the future, you crack the egg. To see the past, you shake the bones.'

Lady Laetitia shook the bones and let them fall.

After Hubert passed out, drained and satisfied in the bedroom upstairs, Olivia and her psychic set out to rid Devil's Eye of the spirit of Cyril Rudolph. They burned more candles, fanned more incense and chanted more chants than priests at a High Mass. All of this just seemed to piss Cyril off. Even with the new furnace on high and the fireplaces roaring, frost sparkled on the inside of the windows. The study was so cold Olivia could see her breath.

Sadie tucked herself deep and small into the couch, her hand gripping her wooden cross. It was not good to call the dead. Especially the dead Lady Laetitia was calling.

Candlelight flickered off the dark portrait of Cyril Rudolph. Except for the crackling fire, the house was still. The King James Bible resting on Cyril's lap in the portrait lay on the table between them, the cracked leather cover peeling from the spine. The book lay open to the family tree, the names etched in fine black cursive down the page. Cyril's branch stopped with Cyril. No wife. No children.

Olivia placed one hand on the Bible and held the other palm up.

'Blood calls blood,' the spiritualist said, running the silver knife through the candle flame. Grabbing Olivia's hand, she pulled it to her.

Olivia turned her head away as the Lady sliced her finger deep. Opening her eyes, she stared at dark oozing blood. Then she touched each yellowed-ivory bone with her bloody finger.

'Guard our souls from the spirits of hell,' Lady whispered, licking the knife clean.

It is always easier to look back than forward. The dead have much to say. Pulling her wrap around her, Lady Laetitia leaned low over the table, her bloodshot eyes fixed on the bloody bones.

She saw a woman running toward the river, flower petals scattering behind her. She saw Cyril Rudolph standing in the churchyard, young and strong, eyes clear and blue. The seasons changed around him, spring, summer, fall, winter . . . but still he waited. His blonde hair grew to his shoulders and faded to white. His handsome face drew and shriveled. His clothes rotted on his wasting body. Cyril withered into an old man, hate burning him like paper.

When the Lady had seen enough, she leaned back on the couch. Her eyes fixed on Sadie. And Sadie knew the island woman knew the truth.

'It is your story to tell,' the Lady said quietly.

Somehow, Olivia was not surprised. Sadie's mother had cared for her old uncle. After she died, Sadie took up where she left off, feeding Cyril, bathing him, tending him until the day he died. Sadie watched over Devil's Eye as if it were her own. Olivia believed it was out of loyalty, or respect, or even love.

'Please, Sadie.' She rested her hand on Sadie's arm. 'It's all right.'

The candle flickered on Sadie's dark face. She stared into the flame as if searching for the story she was so reluctant to tell. The story she had never told anyone, not even her own daughter. A ragged sigh escaped from her as if a door had creaked open setting her breath free. She knew the story as if she'd lived it.

'It all started with Fidela Wilde,' Sadie said quietly. 'Fidela, she was a beauty. Every man wanted her. But she weren't jest lovely to look at. Fidela had the life in her. Lord, she brought light into the darkest room. She'd flounce those skirts and bat those eyes. And the men, they'd sit when she said 'sit'. And they'd come when she said 'come'. The fire in her drew Mr Cyril like a moth to a flame.

'Mr Cyril, he had to have her. And what Mr Cyril set out to get, he got. He was rich and Fidela was poor and she agreed to marry him. A woman makes a livin' off a man one way or a'nuther.

'They say Mr Cyril was a right decent man 'fore he fell fer Fidela. It was the wild in her that got his blood boilin'. And it was the wild in her that drove him mad. Knowin' she'd marry him didn't put his mind to ease. He still feared he'd lose her. And so he set out to clip her wings. They say he watched her like a hawk, jealous of every man who came near her. She weren't 'lowed to go no place without him. She weren't 'lowed to ever be alone.

'But the tighter he squeezed, the wilder she fought. Until finally, at her own weddin', Fidela, she jest up and flew away. After she left him, Mr Cyril, he went crazy. He sat in this here room starin' at that fire all night long, didn't eat, didn't sleep. Couldn't get him to bathe or even change his clothes.

'Then one night he had one of his slave girls brought to him. He'd seen her in the field. She was light skinned and only a child, no more than fourteen. The other slaves, they had tuh drag her mama away and lock her in the root cellar. You could hear her screams all over this house, but nobody was listenin'.

'Mr Cyril, he dressed that child in Fidela's dresses and he dabbed her with Fidela's perfume. He told her from then on, her name was Fidela. Then he had his way with her. Tender at first. Kind. But she could not take away his hunger for Fidela Wilde. And it turned him rough and mean. He chained her legs so she couldn't run and whipped her till she bled fer not being the one he wanted.'

The flame on the candle flickered for no discernible reason.

'Mr Cyril, he grew old fast, weak as water, and died slow and painful. He was pleadin' fer forgiveness right till the end.'

Sadie's dark face turned up to the portrait and a strange gleam Olivia had never seen before came into her eyes.

382

'You could hear his screams all over this house. But nobody was listenin'.'

★ ★ ★

Sadie waited until the lights in Olivia and the Lady's bedrooms went out and the house was quiet. The small door fit into the study wall like paneling. If a person didn't know what to look for, they would never see it. Taking the old key from inside the fireplace, she slipped it into the lock. Cool, damp earthy air sighed out of the dark doorway. Holding the kerosene lantern above her head, she carefully climbed down the narrow wooden steps. She made her way through the dusty shelves of Mason jars, rolls of rotting wool rugs and forgotten furniture to a small metal door in the farthest corner. Sweeping the cobwebs away with her hand, she pulled the rusty wrought iron handle.

The dank stagnant air smelled like the grave. The walls glistened and wept. A hemp bed, the rope rotted away, was shoved into the corner. A rough sawn table with a single chair and a tarnished black candle holder sat in the middle. Ivy covered the small barred window, concealing it from the outside. Even at noon the room was dark as blindness.

Setting the lantern on the old table, Sadie searched the back wall, running her fingers over the rough handmade bricks until she felt the braid of hair that had been pulled from Cyril's brush and pressed into the mortar. Then she whispered the words, repeated so many times,

383

they passed from her like breath.

'Never forget. Never forgive.'

Sadie never questioned why she hated a dead man who had never lifted a finger or even his voice to her. Some things simply are.

'Come to me,' she whispered, stroking the soft blonde hair. 'Come to me, as she came to you. Come to me.'

She sensed she was no longer alone in the room. She could feel his yearning. Hand gripping her cross, she slowly turned. Cyril Rudolph stood before her, pale as smoke, his rasping breath reeking of decay. Evil filled the room, cold and solid. But it did not emanate from the spirit of Cyril Rudolph.

Cyril was never locked in this living grave, buried alive in total darkness for months at a time. He was never chained to a bed or whipped till he bled. Cyril was never any man's slave. But the Black Fidela had seen to it that Cyril's spirit would forever be bound within the walls of Devil's Eye. And she had seen to it that her descendants would carry on her revenge.

Sadie took care of Devil's Eye as if it were her own, because rightfully it should have been. But that wasn't why she hated Cyril Rudolph. She could barely walk the first time her grandmother brought her down to this dark place and pressed hate into her like the braid she'd pressed into the mortar.

Cyril's bony hand reached for his granddaughter and his watery blue eyes pleaded. Forgiveness would free them both. But hate owned Sadie, body and soul. In cursing Cyril, the Black Fidela had cursed her own. Now, like Cyril, Sadie could never leave Devil's Eye even if she wanted to.

'Never rest! Never sleep!' Sadie hissed, her face twisted and her black eyes gleaming mad with hate. 'Suffer! Suffer till the end of days!'

Cyril's rotting mouth gaped and a hollow desperate scream rushed out of him. It rose like steam up the cellar stairs and echoed through the halls of Devil's Eye. But no one was listening.

41

Bourne was unloading cases of whiskey from the back of his truck trying to beat the electric storm, when he saw the car fishtailing up the drive.

'It's Pearl!' Sophie yelled urgently out the window.

'What about her?'

'She needs you!'

Bourne didn't ask any questions. He just jumped into his truck and floored the pedal all the way to Pearl's.

He was out of his truck before it rolled to a stop in front of the house. Being Easter, the Five of Clubs was empty. All the windows were dark except for one.

Bourne took the front steps two at a time up to the porch. The front door was cracked open and he immediately knew something was not right. Running through the foyer to Pearl's parlor, he shoved the door open and came to a dead stop.

There in the warm flickering glow of candles was Pearl, wearing nothing but an iridescent string of pearls — and Mason Hughes.

Slowly, Pearl looked back at Bourne over her pale bare shoulder, her face blurred with whiskey and desire.

'Please, darlin',' she said, eyes gleaming vindictively, 'give me just one more minute.'

Bourne stood for the longest time in the doorway. Then strolling casually across the room, he poured himself a drink and took a seat in front of them.

'Pearl, honey,' he said, leaning back, 'take all the time you need.'

About this time the front door slammed shut.

'Pearl?' Kat's voice echoed from the foyer.

Pearl had invited Kat to a reconciliation supper. She had neglected to mention what she was serving.

Kat cautiously pushed the parlor door open and peeked inside. She saw Bourne sitting in the chair. Then she saw Pearl. Then she saw Mason spread-eagled underneath Pearl. Kat immediately ascertained the situation. She had always been quick that way.

Storming across the room, she grabbed Pearl under the arms, dragged her off Mason and slung her sprawling onto the rug.

'What did you do to him?' Kat demanded, as she lifted Mason's head and pried an eye open. 'Drug him?'

That's what she would have done. It was far faster and more efficient than seduction. Kat looked down at Mason, hair messed, shirt open and reeking of whiskey.

'Kat,' he slurred, thick-tongued and grinning up at her, 'you missed cocktails.'

'You idiot,' she said, letting his head drop.

Slowly, Kat cut her narrowed eyes to Pearl.

'OK, Pearl,' she seethed, 'you've had your revenge. But I swear, you come near him again and I'll put you on my sewing machine and sew that little bear trap of yours up tight!'

Bourne chuckled into his glass.

'What are you laughing at?' Pearl yelled, as she grabbed her robe and jerked it on. 'You started this little pissing contest the day you screwed Kat!'

'It wasn't Kat.'

Pearl, Kat and Bourne turned in unison. They stared blankly at Mason slumped on the couch.

'It wasn't Kat in the spring house,' Mason slurred, as he fumbled to button his pants.

'Of course it was, you idiot,' Pearl blazed.

Mason shook his head dizzily from side to side.

'I had Crockett pull the time-cards at the factory. Kat was punched in all day on Black Friday. Believe me, Crockett would have noticed if she'd been . . . ' The word escaped his inebriated brain. ' . . . gone.'

Pearl's head swiveled to Bourne. He was just as shocked by this as she was. Then she looked to Kat.

'But you were wearing my shoes . . . ' Pearl stuttered.

The sisters' eyes locked. Slowly, a look of realization came over Pearl's face.

'Don't be mad at mama, Pearl,' Kat said. 'She doesn't remember a thing.'

Kat had kept the truth from her all this time. Kindness was the only thing Pearl never saw coming.

'How could you let me believe it was you?' Pearl asked.

'How *could* you believe it was me?'

'Because it would have been if you'd gotten there first,' Pearl retorted.

'Don't flatter yourself, Pearl,' Kat huffed at her. 'If I'd wanted Bourne Cavanagh, I would have snatched him up long before he put that ring on your finger.'

Draping Mason's arm over her shoulder, Kat hoisted him off the couch.

'Where are we going?' Mason asked, as they headed toward the door.

'I'm taking you home,' she said decisively. 'I've decided to keep you.'

They were halfway out the door when Pearl called to her.

'Kat . . . '

Shifting Mason's dead weight on her shoulder, Kat kept walking. But at the doorway, she hesitated. Exasperated, she rolled her eyes back at Pearl.

'Isn't it fortunate,' she said dryly, 'that I can only stay mad for about fifteen minutes?'

When they were alone, Pearl slowly turned to Bourne.

'Mama?' she roared, slapping the side of his head. 'What in the hell were you thinking?'

The one and only thing Bourne was sure of about that day in the springhouse was that thinking played absolutely no part in it. But he sensed Pearl was not in the mood for a lecture on the nature of man. And so, Bourne did what every man does when backed into a corner of his own making — blame the woman.

'If you loved me,' he shouted, jabbing his finger in her furious face, 'you would have done

389

exactly what Kat just did!'

'If you loved me you would have come after me!' she screamed back, fists balled.

'Hell, Pearl! Catching me with another woman wasn't the reason you left Five Points! It was the excuse you'd been looking for. If I'd gone after you, you would have spent the rest of your life wondering what was down the road you didn't take!'

The truth stunned Pearl. Bourne knew her better than she knew herself. If she'd never left Five Points, she would have withered and died. And she would have resented the man who kept her from going. Pearl had to know what was out there. Now, she'd seen the world and she'd seen all she wanted to see. Some of it, she wished she hadn't. But she had no regrets or apologies. Whatever life she lived from here on out would be the life she chose — not a life she had settled for.

'Bourne, if I hadn't gone down that road you would have been bored with me before the honeymoon started.'

Bourne couldn't deny it. The truth was his eye started wandering long before she caught him in the act.

'So, now what?' she asked.

For the past three years Bourne had run through women like a hound through tall grass. He had no regrets or apologies. He had to know what was out there. Now he knew for certain that the only woman he wanted was standing right in front of him.

'I say we get married.'

Pearl looked as if he'd slapped her in the face. Dropping onto the couch, she simply stared at him in stunned disbelief. Was he out of his mind? After everything that had happened did he honestly think it could be that easy? That all they had to do was kiss and make up and everything would be forgiven and forgotten. Did he really believe their slate could be wiped clean?

Bourne knew forgiveness would free them both, but he was not the kind of man to beg. He waited for an answer and when she didn't have one, he pushed out of the chair. He didn't bother to say goodbye. She'd said it for the both of them.

Pearl flinched when the front door slammed. She heard Bourne's truck grind into gear. She watched his tail lights disappear down the drive through the window. And she was alone. She sat quietly in the empty parlor. The candles had all but burned away, wax dripping down the holders and puddling in soft warm mounds on the mantel. She felt equally spent. Revenge had taken up so much of her for so long. Now, she felt as hollow as an empty barrel. She had been around the world and ended up right where she had started.

She sighed and the dying candle on the coffee table flickered. Her eyes fixed on the flame and for some unknown reason a single moment came to her. She was climbing into a limousine in Chicago when she heard her name being called. Her breath had caught and she'd spun around. But the man calling her name was Frank Merrill, the pharmacist. And her heart sank like a stone.

Pearl had spent three years looking back over her shoulder, and the man she had been looking for had just walked out her front door.

Folks on Dog Leg Hill had their heads bowed and were saying evening grace as Pearl Wilde ran past their dining-room windows, white feathered high-heeled mules slapping on her feet and filmy chiffon robe flapping wide open in the breeze. Even the dogs were too stunned to bark. They simply sat on their haunches with their tongues hanging out and watched her fly by in the moonlight. Bourne actually caught sight of her in his rearview mirror as she passed through the gate, but he decided a run would do the bitch good.

★ ★ ★

At the first of the month a postcard arrived at the Five Points post office. On the front was a glossy photograph of mossy green hills and lichen-laced rocks. It might have been Steamer Holler if not for the Atlantic Ocean foaming white against the misty cliffs. Miss Mabel turned the postcard over and ran her finger longingly over the postmark of Cork County, Ireland, then read the message.

Dear Kat,
  I finally made the jump. Come on in. The water's fine.
                    Mrs Pearl Cavanagh

We do hope that you have enjoyed reading this large print book.

Did you know that all of our titles are available for purchase?

We publish a wide range of high quality large print books including:
**Romances, Mysteries, Classics
General Fiction
Non Fiction and Westerns**

Special interest titles available in large print are:
**The Little Oxford Dictionary
Music Book
Song Book
Hymn Book
Service Book**

Also available from us courtesy of Oxford University Press:
**Young Readers' Dictionary
(large print edition)
Young Readers' Thesaurus
(large print edition)**

For further information or a free brochure, please contact us at:
**Ulverscroft Large Print Books Ltd.,
The Green, Bradgate Road, Anstey,
Leicester, LE7 7FU, England.
Tel:** (00 44) 0116 236 4325
Fax: (00 44) 0116 234 0205

Other titles published by
The House of Ulverscroft:

LIES AND LOYALTIES

Rachel Billington

One March morning in London, MP Leo Barr is told that his brother, Charlie, is dead after hanging himself from a chestnut tree in the grounds of a mental hospital. His family reacts in different ways. Charlie's mother, Imogen, can't pretend that life is still worth living — Charlie was her favourite. Leo and his lawyer brother Roland continue to fight over Charlie. The fourth brother Ron, a Catholic priest, must break the news to Charlie's wife, presently in HMP Holloway. Now, the conflict builds among members of this complex family. Who really loves whom? And Charlie? He follows no rules, not even about dying and it becomes clear that his tragedy is only part of a web of mystery and deceit that connects them all.

THE FAMILY TREE

Barbara Delinsky

Dana Clarke has it all — a husband, Hugh, whom she adores, a beautiful home and a baby on the way. But, when her daughter, Lizzie, is born, what should be the happiest day of her life turns out to be the moment that her world falls apart. As a family is divided by bitter mistrust, all their beliefs in each other, in their family background, are challenged. Will the birth of their first child destroy their marriage or can they overcome the repercussions of a secret told years ago?

TAKE A LOOK AT ME NOW

Anita Notaro

There are defining moments in our lives. When time stands still and our lives change forever. For Lily Ormond, that moment came when she answered the late night knock on the door to discover that her sister Alison had been drowned. Losing her only sibling was devastating, but becoming a mother overnight to Ali's three-year-old son Charlie, and discovering that her identical twin had been leading a secret life was almost Lily's undoing . . . And so begins a journey linked with four men who'd been part of a life she never knew existed. A journey that forces Lily to come to terms with a father who'd never really cared for her, a child who needs her too much and a sister who wasn't what she seemed . . .

TELL IT TO THE SKIES

Erica James

Venice has been Lydia's home for many years. Living there has given her a sense of peace and fulfilment. But one day, in a heart-stopping moment, the glimpse of a young man's face in the crowd threatens to change everything: long banished memories of a dreadful secret come flooding back . . . As a child Lydia and her sister were sent to live with their grandparents. There in a cruel, loveless world Lydia grew up fast. She learned to keep secrets and to trust sparingly. And through it all she was shadowed by guilt and grief. Now, twenty-eight years later, Lydia is persuaded to leave behind the safe new life she has created and return to England to face the past. And maybe her future . . .

RUN

Ann Patchett

It is just after Christmas, and the New England weather has worsened. Doyle has dragged his reluctant sons to a speech by Jesse Jackson, despairing at their indifference to politics. The two boys, both adopted, are close in age, but in character they couldn't be more different: Teddy, warm and affectionate, believes his calling is in the Catholic Church. The older by a year, more serious by nature, Tip is happiest alone in his lab, labelling and categorising fish specimens. When they are involved in a violent accident on the icy road, the family is forced to confront certain truths: about how the death of Bernadette, Doyle's wife, has affected the family, and about the anonymous figure, never discussed, who is the boys' real mother.